LETHAL JUSTICE

A gripping cross-genre thriller

Crime/police procedural with a supernatural twist

Book One
DCI Matthew Holt and The Dra

Jay Jones

Copyright © Jay Jones, 2025

The right of Jay Jones to be identified as the author of this work has been asserted in accordance with the Copyright, Designs and Patents Act 1988.

All rights reserved.

Without limiting the rights under copyright reserved above, no part of this publication may be reproduced, published, printed, stored or introduced into a retrieval system, or transmitted in any form or by any means (electronic, mechanical, photocopying, faxing, recording, scanning or otherwise) without the prior permission of the copyright owner, nor be otherwise circulated in any form of binding or cover other than that in which it is published and without a similar condition including this condition being imposed on the subsequent purchaser.

It is illegal to copy this book, post it to a website, or distribute it by any means without permission.

This novel is a work of fiction. Names, characters, businesses, organisations, places, events and incidents are the product of the author's imagination or are used fictitiously. Any resemblance to actual persons, living or dead, events or locales is purely coincidental, and no identification with actual persons (living or deceased), places, buildings, and products is intended or should be inferred.

1st edition 2025

ISBN: 978-1-7384433-2-1 eBook

ISBN: 978-1-7384433-3-8 Paperback

www.jayjonesbooks.com

For George

And to my first readers & critiques
Rajan, Gavin and Aviv
A big thank you.

1

Durgapur, India

Deepak

She screamed.

Deepak Verma shot upright, his pounding pulse as loud as the shriek shattering the silence. He fumbled for the bedside lamp switch.

4.45 bloody a.m.!

'No, no, no—' wailed his wife beside him.

Oh, God! Not again! He reached across and shook her shoulder, gently at first, then harder as she continued to writhe and moan, unable to escape the grip of her nightmare.

'Wake up, Jyoti, come on.'

Shake. Shake. No response.

She was elsewhere, trapped in a world to which he had no access.

He sat her up and reared back as her flailing fist connected with his jaw.

Eyes wide open, she howled, her cries the echoes of a soul sundered.

Deepak picked up the insulated stainless-steel jug from her bedside table, unscrewed the cap and upturned a litre of ice-cold water over her, jumping back in time to avoid the splash. Jyoti gasped, awareness returning to focus her eyes.

'You were screaming and shouting. I couldn't wake you. You awake now?'

Jyoti hunched over, buried her face in her hands and rocked back and forth. With a wary eye on her hands, Deepak rubbed his jaw and perched on the bed.

'Was it the same nightmare? It's okay. It's only a dream.'

'Not this time,' he thought she whispered through chattering teeth.

Jyoti shivered, whether from the icy water drenching her torso or from the remnants of her nightmare, he couldn't tell.

Deepak dragged the sheet off the bottom of their bed, triple wrapped it around her and held her close, feeling her tremors through the layers of cotton. He almost jerked away when Jyoti laid her cold, soaking wet head on his shoulder, but forced himself to stay still.

'You're freezing! You need to change those wet clothes.'

But lost in her memories, Jyoti was impervious to the cold.

***

4,236 miles away in a park in Southampton, England, their son, Suraj, lay in the icy rain beneath the dark mantle of a midnight sky. Rivulets of his blood scurried across the grass and gravel to sink deep into the soggy, but still thirsty, earth.

LETHAL JUSTICE

***

And somewhere in the realm of the unknown, far beyond human imaginings, where substance and reality end, an entity stirs. The weight of the woman's dread, of grief, sharp and sudden, pulses through the dark void, to touch the old, forgotten being's consciousness.

2

Tails swishing, the two German Shepherds whined and strained at their leashes, causing a minor jam at the front door as their laughing owners tried to get out.

The icy drizzle eased to a mist as the foursome crossed into Southampton City's Holburn Park, leaving behind the glow of the streetlamps. Fur prickling with static from the storm-charged air, the dogs sniffed the wind, paws flexing into the sponge-soft grass. Released from their leads, they bolted, looping out and back, marking territory, returning to their owners only to dart away again.

Deeper into the park, Annie, the older dog, froze. Head raised, her hackles flared, and a low snarl rumbled deep in her throat. Ears twitching, Rufus, the younger dog, tensed and sniffed the air.

The scent hit them. They recognised it instantly.

Muscles taut, bodies trembling, they surged forward before their owners could react.

'Rufus! Annie! Come back!' Walter McCabe's voice cut through the night.

But the dogs were gone. Their barks turned to high-pitched howls.

'Something's wrong. Stay here!' Walter called to his wife as he flicked on his torch and sprinted after them.

'Annie!' Julia shouted, running after him.

Her voice cracking with urgency and desperation reached the dog faster than her commands. Annie yipped, turned back, and raced toward her mistress.

But the younger dog, Rufus, ran on, unable to resist the scent hauling at his instincts. He crouched low, snarled and circled something.

A mound. A shape. No, shapes.

Rufus jerked up his head, distracted by a movement. Figures running in the mist-shrouded distance.

'No, Rufus—stop!' Walter's voice, closer now.

Generations of obedience battled with the dog's reflex to chase, to hunt.

'Rufus, come! Heel!'

The dog hesitated, then slunk back to his master. Walter knelt, clipped on his lead, and held him tight.

Together, man and dog watched the fleeing shapes vanish into the distant darkness.

Julia arrived with Annie. Rain streamed down, heavy, unrelenting. A jagged bolt of lightning split the sky.

They saw the bodies.

Three of them. Huddled together on the path. Still. Unmoving.

Walter raised his torch. The dark pool spreading beneath glistened in the torchlight.

Julia screamed.

3

Holt

Detective Chief Inspector Matthew Holt rolled to a halt on the main road behind the blue flashing lights of vans and cars near the entrance to Southampton City's Holburn Park. Blue and white tape stretched around the park's perimeter, manned by uniformed police with crime scene officers scurrying to and from their vans. Luckily, there were no signs yet of any curious spectators. Although the rain had now eased to an annoying drizzle, the earlier storm and heavy rains seemed to have kept them at bay.

He held out his warrant card to the uniformed officer manning the gate, who entered the details along with the time into the form on his clipboard.

'Through there, sir,' he pointed down a dimly lit path.

Holt pulled up the collar of his raincoat and brushed the droplets off his eyes and hair. As usual, he'd left his umbrella behind in the car.

'Morning, sir.' Detective Sergeant Rowena Williams, who was waiting for him outside the pop-up tent erected to preserve the crime scene, handed him a kit of protective clothing.

Despite the baggy white disposable coveralls, its hood shielding her hair from the drizzle, Rowena still looked elegant and alert, but her voice was strained.

'Sorry you had to come out tonight,' said Holt. 'You OK?'

Rowena shook her head. 'It's bad, sir. Really bad.'

Holt nodded but said nothing. Rowena was a seasoned officer and had seen more than her share of victims. 'Who's in there?' he asked, tipping his chin towards the tent.

'Chris Cummings and the CSI, sir.'

'That's good. I'm sure Chris will speed up pathology and forensics so we can get a head start on our investigation.'

'I'm not so sure.' Rowena grimaced. 'They aren't a happy bunch in there. The deluge before they erected the tent made a right mess of the evidence. Especially out here in the open.'

Holt scanned his surroundings. Despite the streetlights and lampposts along the pathways, stretches of Holburn Park were in total darkness, their obscurity intensified by the massive oak, cedar, and ash trees that were the pride of the park.

'It's almost 1.30 a.m. and pointless searching for evidence now. Have the PCs extend the cordon to cover all of this area of Holburn Park and begin fingertip searches at first light. Have them post more uniforms on guard. They're not to let anyone in. We don't want spectators and especially not the media trampling all over our crime scene.' Holt zipped up the coveralls and stopped Rowena as she turned to follow his instructions.

'Where's the couple who discovered the bodies?'

'I took their statements and sent them home with a PC, sir. I've also asked him to collect their clothes and shoes for trace evidence. They live just beyond the park. They'd been waiting out in the storm with their dogs after calling emergency services and were freezing.'

'Do they normally walk their dogs this late, especially with the weather forecast predicting a storm?'

'I asked them that, and they said no, they're never out this late. But it seems they'd just returned from visiting their daughter in Birmingham, and with the dogs being cooped up in the car all day, they thought they'd give them a quick run in the park. The dogs must've heard something, because they took off and then, well, then they found them.' Rowena gestured helplessly at the tent.

'We can go talk to them as soon as I've had a look in there. Meanwhile, check them out and verify their movements. Get Ian to check their car against the motorway ANPRs and local CCTVs. Make sure we have the daughter's details too.'

'Sir, you can't think they'd—.' Rowena glanced at her boss's raised eyebrow and nodded, a wry smile twisting her lips. 'Of course, you do. Suspect everyone. I'll tell Ian.'

'Good. Give me five minutes inside. I don't suppose Chris will allow me any longer than that.'

Holt pulled the hood over his head, donned the mask, stooped and entered the tent, treading on the stepping plates laid out by the CSIs. He spotted his friend, the tall, lanky Dr Chris Cummings, kneeling alongside three other white overall-clad and hooded figures.

The chief pathologist looked up.

'Hey Matt. I was expecting you.' He signalled to his colleagues, and they stood up to give Holt a clear view of the victims.

'Oh, Jesus!'

Even Rowena's briefing during his drive here from his home near Winchester had not prepared him for the stark display under the intense glare of the floodlights.

They look so young... He had seen nothing this bad since the motorway road traffic accident five years ago. Mangled bodies inside a minibus. He'd saved one victim then, kept up an unrelenting sequence of CPR and rescue breaths until the paramedics arrived.

Holt swallowed and locked his knees, fighting the impulse to crouch beside the three young men and breathe life back into them.

'God, Chris, that's... Were they alive when the paramedics got here?'

'No, Matt. There was nothing they could do.'

That crash had been an accident. But this?

Holt turned to the chief pathologist. 'How did they die? What can you tell me, Chris?'

'Not much at this stage, I'm afraid. These two victims—' with a sigh, Cummings pointed to the two young men, one lying face up in a small puddle with the other draped across his torso. 'They were stabbed. This lad in the stomach and that poor man multiple times in the back.' He turned to the third victim. 'The only obvious injury to this lad was the cut across his throat. I can't tell you anymore until I've examined them properly.'

Holt nodded.

'They're drenched,' said Cummings, 'and the rain's messed up the evidence. Incidentally, we found no weapons nearby.'

'We'll get searches started at first light. You here much longer?'

'No, we're done for now. We'll be moving them out soon. I expect you want the autopsies done fast?'

'Yes, absolutely. Prioritize it, please.'

'Well, then I'll need to bring in additional help, so tell your boss to expect requisition forms from us.'

'Thanks Chris. I'll check in with you later.'

Holt ducked out of the tent and found Rowena waiting for him. She held out three evidence bags. 'The paramedics found

IDs on them, sir. Their names are Suraj Verma, Ravi Verma and Arun Kapoor. All three are, er, were, students at the Faculty of Medicine at St. John's campus.'

'The names sound Indian. What do we have here? A racist attack? I'd better warn the superintendent – this place will soon be crawling with media.' Holt sighed.

'There's nothing we can do here now. Let's go see what our witnesses have to say.'

4

Holt

'Yes, ma'am. Of course, ma'am—' Superintendent Howard Simpson held the phone away from his ear. The panicky crackle of the Assistant Chief Constable's voice and the thud as she slammed the phone down reached Holt.

With shoulders slumped and bushy eyebrows creased in a frown, the Superintendent replaced his handset and turned to Holt.

The man's bulk filled the room. But the giant was a gentle one. Quick to reprimand blunders, but quicker to praise the deserving, his scathing reprimands took place in the privacy of his office, but the praises were often in the open, within hearing of colleagues. Loved by those who reported to him, his superiors considered him a dinosaur. But results counted, and much to their chagrin, the Super consistently delivered them.

'That was the ACC. And guess what? She's not happy. What the hell's going on? Those students – please tell me it's not a racist attack. We haven't had one in a long time, and never this bad. I want to keep it that way.'

'Just because the three victims are ethnically Indian doesn't necessarily mean it was a racist attack, sir. But unfortunately, that'll be the media's first conclusion. I've seen the bodies; it was vicious, and there were no obvious signs of struggle. I don't think the victims were expecting trouble.'

The Superintendent groaned. 'Why here? Why now? This will hit the international media.'

He paused and stared at Holt. 'Matt, for now you are the SIO. There's some discussion about it upstairs but let me worry about that. Just find the bastards who did this, and quickly. I want them under lock and key. Both the Chief and I are already bombarded. I have upgraded it to Category A+ homicide. God knows we'll need the increase in budget for staff and more resources. We'll need to increase presence and patrols, especially around the parks to address residents' concerns about safety. What a nightmare! Oh, and we have a codename. Operation Storm. Bloody good name, I thought. Just hope it doesn't end up wreaking havoc on us. Who's informing the lads' families?'

'It's a problem, sir, as none of the victims' parents are in England right now. I understand that they're on holiday in India for a family get-together, so I contacted our High Commission in New Delhi. They're sending someone to notify them, and I expect the family will rush back. And I've nominated DC David Plummer as the FLO.'

DC Plummer, trained as a Family Liaison Officer to work with the families of victims of crime and to provide liaison between them and the police, was from a mixed ethnic background, and Holt knew the young detective constable's familiarity with Indian culture and customs would be helpful.

'Good choice.' The superintendent knuckled his eyes. 'Oh, Christ, what a mess. No one's to release any names to the press until the families have been informed.'

'Of course. Everyone on the team already knows, and we'll keep it very contained here. I've also warned the paramedics who attended the victims, but we should still be prepared for leaks.'

The Superintendent groaned. 'What about the witnesses who called it in?'

'We may have struck lucky there. The couple, Walter and Julia McCabe, were out walking their two dogs when they found the bodies. They don't recognise the victims – said they looked like any of the scores of other university students we see around town. The McCabes rarely walk in that part of the park as it's badly lit, but something got their dogs spooked. They ran off and wouldn't return, so Walter McCabe went after them and found them circling the bodies. He called emergency services and waited for them to arrive. McCabe claims he saw four figures running out of the north exit, but they were too far away to make out any details.'

'Strange they'd walk their dogs so late.'

'Yes, I thought so too. But they've checked out. We've motorways cameras showing them on the M40 and 42 as well as on the A34 last night. And for once, the CCTV on their street was working and showed them arriving at 11.20 p.m. and, a bit later, walking towards the park with their dogs at 11.48 p.m.'

'That's a lucky break.'

'He's a good witness, too. Very credible. Although he's in his mid-70s, his eyesight's good. He said the figures he saw moved like the young do – fast, agile. He's also certain he caught a flash of something on the back of one of their jackets. Like the glow on a high-vis coat. Karl has already been in contact with Traffic and the Council's CCTV team and is chasing it up.'

'That's excellent. I'd like to have them in custody before this turns into a media circus. Go and—'

The Superintendent growled as the classic trilling ringtone interrupted him. He glared at the phone, but the caller's name on the small screen grabbed his full attention.

Probably the ACC again, or maybe it's the Chief Constable, thought Holt. It could even be someone higher up the food chain. With a mumbled, 'Excuse me, sir,' he left his boss to deal with the fallout from the multiple murders and hurried towards his own smaller office across the floor.

Detective Inspector Karl Stringer, his second in command, paced outside the door. Waving Karl to one of the deep blue chairs cramping his office, Holt walked around his cluttered desk and lowered himself into the high-backed swivel chair.

He pushed files and papers to one side. *So much for a paperless office,* he thought. The open slats of the vertical blinds revealed a lightening sky, with a strip of daylight breaking across the horizon.

DS Rowena Williams joined them, carrying two large mugs, and handed one to Holt.

'Thank you, just what I need,' he said, inhaling the strong black coffee.

'The Super's classifying this as an A+ homicide, codenamed Operation Storm,' he told the two senior members of his team. 'The memo will be out soon. All leave's cancelled with immediate effect. Unless we catch an early break, it's going to be twenty-four-seven. Sorry, Karl,' he addressed the dishevelled DI, who looked like he'd dressed in a hurry.

'No, that's OK, sir. I understand. I was expecting it anyway. My wife understands, too. I'll ask her to get her mum down to help; they both will love that.'

With two children already in their teens, two dogs and a cat, Karl Stringer and his wife now also had a two-month-old baby

– a surprise addition to their family, and the normally laid-back 46-year-old DI looked frayed around the edges.

'Good.' He turned to Rowena, who, despite having been up all night, looked immaculate in her blue tailored suit, her red-streaked, frizzy hair tamed into a tight bun at the nape.

'Sorry about your tour next week, Rena.'

Off duty, the detective sergeant was a drummer in a rock band with her husband, a bass guitarist.

'Can't be helped,' she shrugged. 'I've already told Aiden. It's a shame as we have some good bookings, but he'll get someone to substitute for me.'

'When this is over, get us all tickets to one of your concerts. We'd love to watch you bash those drums again. I got myself a brilliant pair of earplugs.'

Rowena laughed. 'Will do, sir, with pleasure.'

'Any news from forensics or pathology?'

'The chief pathologist's office confirmed they'll prioritize these autopsies, but toxicology and other results will still take a couple of weeks. He knows you want his preliminary observations and asked you to go see him at five this afternoon,' said Karl.

'And the Labs are also pulling out all stops, giving us priority slots to process the victims' clothes and crime scene samples. But it'll still take time. Two of the victims had their mobile phones on them, but one's still missing. All three had IDs, wallets, some cash, their credit and bank cards on them, so it doesn't look like robbery was the motive,' added Rowena.

'Maybe they didn't have time, or the dogs scared them off before they could take anything. What about the missing phone?'

'Still searching for it, sir. We've tried tracing it, but it appears to be switched off. Cell site shows it was last used in the park. Unless the killers took it, it should still be there. We should have better luck when the sun's up.'

'Whose phone was it?' asked Rowena, fingers poised over her laptop keyboard to add the information to her notes.

'Ravi Verma's,' replied Karl. 'We've asked the search team to let us know as soon as they find it. Tech guys are monitoring all incoming and outgoing calls on that number.'

Holt nodded. 'Right! Let's see what we've so far.'

'They are setting up the big major incident room for us, but for now, I've set up a board and screen.' Rowena pointed to the far end of the open office, where a large screen, table, and projector stood prepped and ready for use.

'Good, let's go.' Holt glanced at his watch. Almost 6.00 a.m. Which made it 11.30 a.m. in India. By now, someone from the British High Commission would have delivered the news to the victims' parents and crushed their world to smithereens.

5

Durgapur, India

Deepak

Deepak Verma studied the lab reports on his desk and traced a finger across certain points on the X-ray, myelography and CAT scans clipped to a lightboard behind him as he dictated his diagnosis and recommendations for his secretary to type up.

Voile curtains shaded his study from the blazing sun, but the air conditioning kept the temperature ten degrees cooler than the 33 deg. C outside. It would steadily get hotter over the next three months, with the temperature climbing to 48 deg. C in this part of India.

Unable to concentrate, he switched off the dictaphone and combed his fingers through his full white beard. The worry lurking in the background crashed through to the forefront of his thoughts.

Although Jyoti was out shopping now, he'd come down to breakfast only to find her in the box room prostrated before the idols and images of the many Hindu gods to whom she turned for solace. His gaze had landed on the centrepiece, a six-inch obsidian statuette of the Goddess Kali, whose etched eyes seemed to seek him out.

The small idol represented the black goddess in her 'benign' form, in that her face was serene, her lips softened in a smile. But each of her four hands held an implement of war, of pain and torture. One had a sword, one a trident; the third, a noose; the last, a skull-cup.

Deepak had turned away with a shudder.

He leaned back in his chair, removed his glasses and pinched the bridge of his nose.

What do I do about Jyoti? Her nightmares are getting worse. It's the third time this week. She can't go on like this...

But despite pleading with her, Jyoti refused to tell him the details of her nightmares, merely revealing that it concerned their only son, Suraj. She believed her vision predicted something terrible would happen to him, but despite months of sleepless nights, she rejected any suggestion of professional help.

Deepak understood her reluctance to speak – it stemmed from her belief that saying the words aloud or describing her nightmare would somehow make it come true.

Superstitious nonsense, he grouched. But that didn't allay his wife's fears or transmute her beliefs. So, Jyoti spent more and more time praying, visiting temples and performing every suggested ritual in the hope, nay, belief, that her prayers and sacrifices would ward off the evil in her nightmares.

LETHAL JUSTICE

The crunch of tires and the soft revs of a familiar car engine alerted him to Jyoti's arrival. He straightened up and waited for her to call out to him as she usually did. His smile faded when he heard nothing. Frowning, he pushed back his chair and stepped out into the hallway. Outside, their nonplussed driver held the passenger door open while Jyoti remained inside, still as a statue, staring straight ahead.

What on earth is she doing?

Deepak strode out of the front door and stopped mid-descent on the wide steps when a sleek black Jaguar pulled into their drive.

'It's from the British High Commission, *saab*,' said their driver, who'd recognised the car.

'British High Commission? Why're they here?'

Perplexed, Deepak turned to his wife, but she sat motionless, gazing into emptiness. With a chill in his stomach and a pounding heart, he watched the two sombre-faced officials from the High Commission approach.

'Mr Verma, we're so sorry...' said the Deputy High Commissioner.

More words followed, words that shattered not just his world, but also those of his brother and their best friend.

6

The sledgehammer of the humans' emotions slams into the entity's consciousness, impossible to ignore.

An unfathomable force, without shape or form, the entity neither breathes nor lives. Yet, it is alive, but not in any sense mortals understand.

A creator and destroyer, the entity hovers on the fringes of human awareness. Omnipresent yet elusive, it inhabits a realm beyond human perception. Present when this planet was conceived, it will watch as Earth breathes its dying last.

*The first people called it the **Dra**, which, in their limited vocabulary, meant many things – the all-powerful, the other, the unseen, protector... It also meant 'lookout – danger.' With the Dra's help, they evaded the monsters roaming the earth, but because of its help, the clan became extinct.*

The ancient ones who came after called it the Azkareth, meaning First Flame in their tongue. It kept them warm, then burnt them to cinders. Over the ages, others named it The Sleeper, The Answerer, The Nameless, Olodumare, Ginnungagap, Para Brahma, Chukwu...

Named or not, it existed. And if it chose to, it answered, or was just as likely to ignore, any and all names.

And it wore many faces, some radiant, others monstrous.

Now humans paint it into corners, trap it in names, creeds and idols. God, devil, saviour, destroyer... each faction claims theirs to be the only true version, each intolerant of divergence.

True faith and belief, once the Dra's lifeblood, are scarce now. Faith rotted in men's hands and became a transaction. Belief warped into currency, traded for comfort or control.

Perhaps the Dra is a manifestation of hope and desperation. Hope, flickering like dying embers, clings to human dreams.

But desperation? Thick, bitter and bold, desperation with its innumerable arms of supplication, trickles into the dormant entity's consciousness like wisps of fog.

Once, the Dra strode strong and proud amongst humankind. It was respected then. Feared. Occasionally, even loved.

Now, it is gone in their forgetting. But not entirely.

Perhaps it will take only one true call for the forgotten being to return.

7

Holt

Detectives, their uniformed counterparts, technical and other support staff trooped into the major incident room already crammed with staff assigned or hastily scrambled from other departments or locations and diverted to Operation Storm. True to their word, the superintendent and his bosses had channelled the resources he'd asked for. As the SIO, Holt would lead the operations and direct the investigation, liaising with the core members of his team, who would then assign tasks to other detectives, technical and support staff, and feed reports back to him.

This—the first of the two daily briefings for the entire team working on Operation Storm—was an opportunity to update everyone, review progress, exchange ideas, and determine the next course of action. DS Rowena Williams and DI Karl Stringer joined him at one end of the room, where gigantic monitors dominated a wall alongside maps, whiteboards, and pin boards.

'Morning. For those I haven't met yet, I'm DCI Matthew Holt, the SIO for this investigation. With me are DI Karl

Stringer, my Deputy SIO, and DS Rowena Williams. They will be your prime liaison and contact, along with DC David Plummer, our FLO. DC Ian Shepherd will be the primary liaison for the HOLMES team. He and DC Salim Khan will provide IT and technical support. The codename for this investigation is Operation Storm. As you're aware, three medical students were fatally attacked in Holburn Park. Two of them still had their phones. The third is missing. From their text messages, it appears they were returning home from a birthday party. Local residents, Walter and Julia McCabe, who were out walking their two dogs, found them and called emergency services. Despite the paramedics arriving within six minutes, it was too late, and they were declared dead at 00:20 hours.'

'This case will attract significant media attention, both domestically and globally. I want to be absolutely clear – no one speaks to the press. I repeat, no one. And the ban applies to posting anything on social media, blogs or chat rooms. Everything goes through the PR department. It's "no comment" to all questions from the media. No exemptions and no excuses. Is that clear?'

Heads nodded as Holt's gaze raked each person in the room. Satisfied they'd got his message, he continued, 'because of the victims' ethnic origins, the media's first conclusion would be that this is a racist attack. We'll prioritize and investigate that angle, but we cannot ignore other motives. And there's no dearth of them – drugs, rivalry between students, gambling debts, girlfriends, boyfriends, cultural conflicts or it could be a professional hit or even just wanton killing.'

Holt paused and assessed the assembled group, gratified they were listening, many taking notes. 'Although the investigation is still in its early stages, we've got some key information. Walter McCabe, our witness, reported seeing four figures fleeing the north exit, but was too far away to make out any details. However, he said they moved fast and thought they were young. He also claims he caught a flash of a fluorescent pattern on the back of one of their jackets. They may or may not be the killers, but we need to find them. DI Stringer has already started the ball rolling with Traffic and the Council's CCTV teams. DS Williams will now brief you on the victims.'

Rowena connected the projector to her laptop and tapped the keyboard to beam photos of the three victims taken at the mortuary onto the large projector screen. Alongside each was a copy of his student ID images. Her voice devoid of expression, she clicked the mouse to zoom in on the first set of photos and recited from her notes.

'This is Ravi Verma. Twenty-three, born in Weybridge, Surrey. His phone's missing.'

The two images differed dramatically. In life, Ravi had been a round-faced youth, with a prominent nose, high brows, unruly curly black hair, laughing brown eyes, and a cheeky smile. In death, with the vitality and the twinkle in his eyes missing, he appeared to be wearing a death mask.

Rowena cleared her throat and clicked on the second set of photos.

'Next, we have Arun Kapoor. Twenty-three, born in Basingstoke, Hampshire.'

They studied the images of the handsome, hazel-eyed young man. With his high cheekbones, slim, straight features, and thick, soft brown hair, Arun would have attracted admiring gazes from most women and many men. His ID photo showed an unsmiling man with a wary expression in his eyes. Aloof. Holt sensed a man always on guard, one who watched the world from behind layers of barricades. In death, he was relaxed, almost smiling, with no further reason to shelter within his self-erected fortress.

Rowena clicked on the photos of the third victim. 'And this is Suraj Verma. Twenty-two, also born in Weybridge, Surrey.'

'The two Vermas, are they brothers?' asked Karl.

'First cousins. Their fathers are brothers, and Arun Kapoor is their childhood friend.'

Except for the trimmed hair and slimmer face, Suraj's mortuary photo was almost identical to that of Ravi. The difference between them was more evident in their ID photos. Suraj looked calm, with a slight crease on his forehead, eyes staring into the camera with a sombre gaze. A man who viewed the world seriously, thought Holt. Someone who listened a lot more than he spoke.

'All three were fourth-year medical students at St. John's Campus, Southampton,' continued Rowena.

'Am I right in thinking that Suraj is engaged to Arun's sister?' asked Holt.

'Yes, sir. We found her photo in Suraj's wallet and loads more on his phone.'

Rowena clicked the mouse, and the image of a beautiful young woman who bore a strong resemblance to her brother, Arun, lit up the screen. The girl looked happy, with a wide smile, large hazel eyes and dark hair springing back from her wide forehead.

Holt sighed, shook his head.

'The victims' home address, a three-bed semi on Carson Road, is secure and declared a crime scene,' continued Rowena.

'Good. Get forensics in there. Let's make sure the address is not involved. Drugs could be an obvious motive. Get the drug squad and their sniffer dogs in to check it out. Collect all laptops, tablets, and anything else that's relevant and start speaking to the neighbours,' Holt told Rowena before turning to the room. 'As a priority, find out where they were before they went to the park and speak to everyone at that party. I also want D2Ds on all houses and businesses near Holburn Park and check out all private security camera footage in the area. We'll need to talk to the victims' friends, tutors, and staff at the hospital where they're training.'

7.30 a.m. and their list of tasks was growing exponentially. 'That's it for now, everyone. DI Stringer and DS Williams will organize the investigation teams and assign tasks. We'll regroup at 6 this evening, and I want everyone here again then. By then, we should have a lot more information. And remember my warning about speaking to the press or chatter on social media. Thank you.'

***

Back in his office, Holt slipped behind the desk. Unlike the superintendent's office, which was adorned with framed photos, trophies and accolades, Holt's office was still as impersonal as the day he moved in. The walls featured nothing but large maps. His desk likewise held nothing personal, gave no insight into the man. He recognised that the room's stark impersonality itself was a revelation, but he simply couldn't be bothered.

Whose photos would I have anyway? he wondered. He had no wife—not now, not since Alicia—no kids or pets. As quickly as it had come, he shut out the thought of his ex-wife. *Not going there again...*

A picture of his uncle John and Susan, his real family, at their farm? That'd be a good choice. He could pretend they were his parents; he'd wished often enough that they were. Or a picture of the watermill and its conversion. But that would invite comments and questions he had no wish to answer. Besides, this was his workplace, so he kept it impersonal with no external distractions.

He gazed at the images of the three young victims on the computer screen. Their lives cut short, their dreams unfulfilled and their potential unrealised. From the witness, Walter McCabe's statement, the suspects were young too.

Was this racially motivated, or are we fixating on it because of their ethnicity? Holt wondered. *And if it was racist, was it indiscriminate and opportunistic, or were they targeted? Ian found nothing on the web – no one claiming 'credit' or brandishing the usual slogans.*

DC Ian Sheppherd, the pale, bespectacled, quiet, thirty-one-year-old with a permanent worried frown, was the team's IT wiz, and if there was anything to find, Holt was certain Ian would've found it by now.

A knock on his door disrupted his train of thought. 'Come in,' he called and waved Karl and Rowena in.

'We've assigned PCs to do the door-to-doors, CCTV checks and to interview the victims' friends and tutors,' said Karl. 'Salim Khan and Larry Ives are leading on the racist angle and DC Ian Shepherd's trawling through social media and chat rooms again to see what's out there.'

'Good. Anything from the park CCTV yet, Karl?'

'The night duty operator at the Council said that neither the lights nor the cameras in the immediate vicinity of the crime scene is working. The one at the north exit only takes still photos. He's had a look and said the camera captured a couple of images of four hooded figures but shows them outside the gates. The quality's rubbish. I'll ask our guys to work on them.'

'Okay. Anything from traffic?'

'We have a list of all vehicles in the park's vicinity between 11.00 p.m. and 1.00 a.m. and are working through them. But nothing so far, sir.'

'Anything from their mobile phones?'

'They last contacted one another to determine each other's whereabouts. It seems they were going to a birthday party for someone called Emily, but there's no surname listed. She appears to be a friend of a friend. We'll get her details later this morning, sir,' said Rowena.

'Get our tech and data analysts working on the victims' digital presence and footprints. I want their complete background and histories, who their friends are, who didn't like them, where they were, who they talked to. I want to know them better than they knew themselves.'

Holt looked at their worried faces. 'This'll be big, and the Chief wants it cleared fast before it turns into a media nightmare, but we have some good leads.'

The detectives nodded. 'Sir, I'm meeting with Prof. Gordon Moore this afternoon,' said Karl as he and Rowena prepared to leave Holt's office. 'He's the Dean of the Faculty of Medicine and is also the boys' emergency contact after their parents. Apparently, he's an old family friend and knows them well.'

'That's great. I'll go with you,' said Holt. 'I'd like to learn more about the victims and their families,' he added in response to the surprise on Karl's face.

Of all the cases to land on my desk, this one's a live grenade, thought Holt.

8

Lily

Lily Webster reached over and bashed the button on the top of her alarm clock to turn it off. That was her third snooze; this time, she had to get up. Eyes still shut, she swung her feet to the floor and snatched a few more seconds of sleep before snapping upright.

She stretched and padded barefoot to the window. The storm last night had cleared the air, and sunlight streamed through glass that could do with a clean, especially on the outside. Yet another chore to add to her endless list, but she had other priorities. Meanwhile, she still had an hour of 'me' time before the twins woke up.

She rubbed eyes gritty from lack of sleep and headed to the bathroom for a shower. Last night's storm had kept her awake, and she'd slipped into her girls' bedroom to check on them, but the five-year-old twins did not even stir. They lay close together, faces turned towards each other, their hair spread across their pillows like chestnut brown honey. Storms never bothered them, whereas it had doomed her to a wakeful night.

Showered and dressed for work, Lily set about laying the table for her daughters' breakfast.

With a colleague off sick, work was hectic, and she would need to log in this evening again after putting the girls to bed to clear some of the backlog. But yesterday had been interesting.

The surrounds of Winchester were not her usual patch, but replacing her indisposed fellow buildings inspector to check the structural modifications to the old watermill had led to her meeting its owner.

The Planning Application, submitted by an architect's firm, only listed the owner's name – Matthew Holt, and his address was a farm located just a few miles outside the cathedral city of Winchester and right next door to the watermill she had visited which he was converting to a house. She'd checked, but the forms contained no further information about him.

Lily munched on a piece of toast and smiled at the memory of her first sight of him.

Standing at the top of the drive, grey from head to toe, she had mistaken him for a life-sized statue. Her heart lurched, and she'd nearly crashed her car when the statue moved. On closer inspection, the grey in Matthew Holt's hair and face turned out to be fine plaster and stone dust. His deep, well-modulated voice was a surprise too, as was the steady, watchful gaze of his slate-grey eyes.

'Call me Matt,' he'd said.

The project was fascinating, and when renovated, the once-derelict watermill would make a unique and beautiful home. She'd especially loved the large entrance hallway with its cavernous, vaulted ceiling. Like a child, she'd twirled around the middle of the empty room, tilted her neck far back, and called 'hello, hello,' up into the void above, laughing aloud as her voice echoed and bounced amongst the rafters.

'Sorry, I couldn't resist that. I love buildings when they are at this stage of construction. They remind me of cathedrals,' she'd said before switching to professional mode and marching forward to carry out the inspections. She reddened, remembering the intensity of his gaze.

Lily had been aware of Matt's interest in her – of course she had. He'd even made it a point to mention he'd moved there after his divorce and that he lived in a cottage on his uncle's farm next door.

And for her part, the flutter in her stomach and consciousness of his presence confirmed her attraction to him.

But she'd been a fool. The invisible, instinctive, and involuntary barrier she raised on realising her own interest in him had him retreating just as fast.

That was really lame! I've scared him away. The next move, if any, was up to her. But she already dreaded the outcome and feared this too would mirror past disappointments, either fizzling before it began or ending after a few dates upon their meeting her twins.

You won't know till you try, protested her rebellious heart. *Maybe all isn't lost,* she thought, remembering that he'd stayed to watch until her car had turned the corner.

Her phone buzzed with a reminder. 7.00 a.m. Time to wake the girls up.

An hour later, holding her daughters by the hand, Lily led them to her car. Chatting to them despite their lack of response, she paid no attention to the car parked opposite.

Nor did she glance at the driver, who aimed his phone camera in her direction.

9

Holt

Relieved to escape the roomful of very senior and very stressed people, Holt headed down the stairs to the major incident room, but the weight of his responsibilities replaced his relief. They'd spent most of the two hours upstairs discussing media strategy, for no one underestimated the impending international press attention.

'Nothing gets to the media without us knowing about it first,' Assistant Chief Constable Angela Larson's pebble-black eyes roved the room. 'And everything goes through the press office. No impromptu interviews, not even if they catch you out on the street. God knows there's enough of them waiting to do just that.'

She turned to the Head of PR. 'Anita—'

'The PR incident room's already set up,' said Anita Chowdhury, an astute media strategist, well-respected for her calm, unflappable demeanour and her extensive experience dealing with the press. 'We'll deal with all media enquiries and information that's sure to flood in from official police releases and stories originating from sources over which we have no control. And there'll be plenty of those.' She smiled at Holt and Superintendent Simpson. 'If it's OK with you, sir, I'll continue to attend DCI Holt's briefings. That was a great one this morning, and it gave me enough to feed the press. I'll liaise with you directly, Matt, and do my best to keep the media off your backs.'

They nodded their thanks. The ACC picked up the lead again, her normally pleasant countenance stern and her husky voice grave. 'DCI Holt, we're formally confirming you as the SIO. Tell us what you need, and we'll make sure you get it.'

Holt murmured a 'thank you,' his face revealing none of his doubts and fears nor his worry that they'd bring in a Senior Investigating Officer with experience of handling a major crime like this.

ACC Larson fixed Holt with an unblinking stare. 'Currently, we're uncertain if this is a hate crime, a mugging gone awry, an escalated student dispute, a cultural or revenge killing, or if it's drug related. And until we do, the media will assume whichever attracts the most attention. The university and students are already up in arms, as are the residents, and there'll be protest gatherings and marches.'

Holt almost wished they had brought in an external SIO, so all this burden would be someone else's responsibility. He'd never dealt with a case this big or complex. Neither had most of the people in the room, and their confidence in him was both reassuring and bloody nerve-wracking. The weight of the entire operation rested on his shoulders. Every error would now be his fault, and he'd be the magnet for all the crap.

The ACC's mouth twitched at the crease of worry on Holt's forehead. 'But we—,' she indicated the PR team, the Chief Superintendent seated beside her in full uniform, and Superintendent Simpson, '—we'll handle all that. You focus on solving the case. And remember, we expect you to inform us immediately of any developments.'

His mouth was dry as he walked out of the meeting, conscious of the eyes on his back.

The decor of the murder squad's office and the major incident rooms on the fifth floor mirrored the floors above and below. Holt had once walked up to the sixth floor and pushed the door to the corner office of a startled finance manager before realising his error.

Some called it a soulless space, but Holt liked its clean straight lines, comfort and access to modern equipment. It looked more like an upmarket corporate office than a police station. In fact, the entire building did. Unlike its predecessor's classical architecture, the present Solent Constabulary Headquarters and Southampton City Police Station, occupied a modern iconic limestone building with a curved glass-fronted façade.

The major incident room reverberated with the clack of fingers tapping on keyboards and people on phones. Focussed on their tasks, no one looked up as Holt pulled a dark blue chair up to a white-topped, chrome-legged desk to face the wallboards.

Little information on there now, but soon, detectives' notes would fill those boards. What was conspicuous by its absence, were suspects, even the most tenuous ones.

Three medical students walking home from an evening out, stabbed to death for no apparent reason. This police nightmare was a bonanza for the press.

He turned at the muffled clicks of hurried footsteps.

'Sir,' said DS Rowena Williams, 'our tech experts have gone through the victim, Arun Kapoor's phone records. He and another student – Justin Brennen, seem to have had a relationship, which ended recently. And Justin's been bombarding him with calls and text messages since then. A *lot* of calls and messages. Nearly 200 of them in the last six weeks! I'd call that stalking. He could be our killer.'

'Who is Justin Brennen? What are the messages about?'

Rowena scrolled through her laptop for data cloned from the victim's phone.

'Justin Brennen, twenty-two, third-year Graphics Arts student at the Winchester campus at Southampton Uni. No form, not even a parking ticket. He made eighty-six unanswered calls, most lasting between ten and twenty seconds, enough to leave a voicemail message. Then there are a hundred and twelve text messages. Most are quite short, saying, "Please call me" or "I'm thinking of you," and several longer ones. Here's one saying, "I love you, and I know you feel the same way about me. Please talk to me. I need to hear your voice."'

Holt grinned, watching Rowena's face grow pink as she read out the messages.

'Those aren't threatening.'

'Ah, here's a more recent one where he sounds aggressive.' Rowena continued, '"What kind of coward are you? Can't you even face me? Look me in the eye – tell me you don't care for me. I'll come to your house and tell your friends about us. Please just call me."'

'That's not exactly violent. Do any of the messages threaten physical harm? Implied or otherwise?'

'No, not really, sir,' said Rowena. 'One message says, "You are killing me" and "I die every day I see you and don't get to touch you." But there's nothing about killing Arun or anyone else.' She glanced up at Holt and persisted, reluctant to let their only possible suspect go. 'Perhaps he was too savvy to put threats in writing; we may strike lucky with his voicemail messages, but it will take time to retrieve those. However, the sheer number of calls and messages is serious harassment.'

'Did our victim, Arun, complain?'

'No, not to us. There's nothing on our records, but I'll check with the Uni. Arun may have complained to them.'

'Maybe he killed Arun in a rage,' said Rowena.

'What? Killed all three of them? All by himself? Or are you suggesting he hired a gang of killers to do the deed?' Holt's laughter turned to a frown. 'Now that's a possibility—'

'Shall we arrest him?'

Holt glanced at his watch. Almost noon. It was borderline, and Brennen was a person of interest. But arrest? Was he just a lovesick young man or a dangerous stalker turned murderer?

'Mr Brennen is definitely a suspect, and we have sufficient grounds to bring him in for questioning under caution. Take a couple of PCs with you and arrest him if you need to. Get a search warrant for his flat, too. Seize his clothes, shoes and all electronic gadgets. Talk to his flatmates. Get Tech to check his computers and social media and get full transcripts of those voicemail messages.'

'How brilliant would it be if Justin Brennen turned out to be our killer, or at least one of them?' said Rowena.

10

Holt

'Bloody brilliant, it's raining again.' DI Karl Stringer eyed the distance from the car to the Dean's office building as they pulled into the visitors' car park at Southampton University's St. John's campus.

'A fast jog will get you there without getting too wet,' grinned Holt. Karl's aversion to exercise was legendary, yet he passed every annual fitness test.

Karl smiled and pulled out a small foldable umbrella from his raincoat pocket. 'I won't get wet at all, sir.'

Holt laughed, turned up the collar of his raincoat and jogged into the building.

He'd meant what he said to his team that morning – *I want to know the victims better than they knew themselves*. *Who* they truly were would lead to *why* they were killed, and to their killer's identity. Not always, of course, but most times.

Hence this meeting with Prof. Gordon Moore, the Dean at the Faculty of Medicine and an old friend of the victims' families.

At the desk marked 'Reception,' the detectives introduced themselves to a smartly dressed woman in her late forties, her eyes red-rimmed and puffy.

'The Dean's expecting you,' she said, leading them into a room behind her.

The dean's office was not large, but the big window gave it an airy feel. The man looked a wreck, his eyes swollen and bloodshot. Fatigue stooped his frame and etched deep creases on his face.

'Thank you for seeing us, sir. We appreciate how difficult this is for you,' said Holt, settling into one of the tub chairs around a low centre table.

'We're trying to gather as much background information as possible on Suraj, Ravi, and Arun, so anything you can tell us about them would be most helpful.'

'All three are... were undergraduates, now in their fourth year. Ravi Verma and Arun Kapoor joined us when they completed A-levels at St. Vincent's, that public school in Winchester?'

Holt nodded. He knew it well. It was his alma mater, where he boarded during the school term while his parents were overseas.

'Their A-level scores were well above our requirements, and all three impressed their assessors in their interviews. Suraj Verma was an international student intake; although he was born in England and has a British passport, his family moved to India about three years ago, where he completed his A-level equivalent. His grades were off the charts, and he sailed through all the entry exams.'

The Dean sighed. 'I've known Deepak Verma—that's Suraj's father—for over 25 years. We were both at Guy's Hospital. He's a well-known neurosurgeon. Worked for years as a consultant in London before moving back to India. It was a sad loss for us. Besides being brilliant in his field, he's one of the nicest people you could ever hope to meet.'

The dean's mouth twisted in a grim smile. 'Suraj could have gone to any university in the world, but he came here. Partly because of my friendship with his father, but mainly to be with his cousin Ravi and their friend Arun. Their parents thought Southampton would be a safe place for them.'

'What about the other two young men? How is it you know them, Dean?'

'I've known their fathers from when we were all students. Prem Verma, that is Deepak's younger brother, was also studying medicine, two years behind us. He is now a consultant cardio-surgeon at the Hampshire County Hospital. And his best friend, Roopesh Kapoor, was doing engineering at Imperial College London. The four of us used to get together often. Over the years, we've attended each other's graduations, weddings, funerals and celebrated the births of our children. Even after Deepak moved to India, my wife and I still get together with Prem, Roopesh and their families at least twice a year.'

'We understand Suraj is engaged to one of the—,' Karl paused mid-sentence. *They were people before they became victims,* he reminded himself. '—engaged to Arun's sister,' he amended.

'Yes, Suraj and Anjali got engaged last October. My family and I attended their engagement party.' The dean gave a short laugh. 'Apparently, when Anjali was about ten, she decided she'd marry Suraj. Then last summer, she confronted him, demanded if he loved her and when he stammered "*Yes*", she said, "*Good, I'm going to tell my parents, and we are going to get engaged.*" The poor lad didn't know what hit him. At the engagement party, he just stood grinning like all his

Christmases, or Diwalis in his case, and birthdays had arrived at once.'

'Did they set a date for the wedding? Don't—er, didn't the boys have several more years before they could practise?'

'The wedding date was open-ended, and yes, they had five more years to complete before they could start working, as a GP, for example. To specialize would be another three to five years or even longer, and I know all three wanted to.'

'That's an exceptionally long engagement. What was the rush?'

'Anjali told me she didn't want Suraj getting ideas, especially with all the pretty nurses around!'

'Did he? Get ideas about the nurses, I mean?' asked Karl.

'Absolutely not! I doubt he ever looked at or thought of any other girl in his entire life. I can't imagine how Anjali is going to cope. It's good that she's staying on in India with her mother.'

'What about the other two? Any girlfriends, lovers?'

'Not that I'm aware of. No one steady, anyway.'

'What about enemies, anyone they didn't get on with? Anyone with a grudge against them?'

The dean shook his head. 'They were popular and got along with everyone. Ravi is, er, was the most outgoing of the three. He made friends easily. But with so much coursework, they simply wouldn't have the time to mess around. Plus, they need to put in several hours at the hospital. It's exhausting work. I don't recall it being so tough in my student days.'

'How is the family coping?' asked Holt.

The dean blinked hard. 'Talking to them was the hardest thing I've ever had to do. The parents are flying in overnight and will be here tomorrow morning. They asked to meet you, Detective Chief Inspector. They also want to see their sons, which I understand your Family Liaison Officer has arranged with the coroner's office and the mortuary.'

'Yes, of course. We'll have them picked up at the airport to get past the media. I understand that Ravi's parents live just outside Winchester and Arun's parents in Basingstoke. Will they be staying in their homes?'

'No, they're worried about the paparazzi and will stay at the Titanic Hotel. The management has arranged additional security for them.'

'That's a wise decision,' said Holt.

The press would also dog the dean and his staff, like they were doing with the senior police ranks, as well as Holt and his team. Sneaking out, using unmarked cars, avoiding public places, brushing past media hounds, keeping faces expressionless and staying tight-lipped were already the norm.

On their way out, Linda, the dean's P.A., stopped the detectives.

'I've compiled a list of their tutors, lectures, study and work schedules. Also, the names of some of their immediate circle of friends.' She handed Holt a plastic folder containing several pages of tabulated data.

'Thank you!' Surprised but delighted, Holt accepted the folder. She'd saved them hours of work.

'If you need more information, please let me know.'

Karl said, 'They were at a birthday party earlier yesterday evening for someone called Emily Dickson. Her name appears on Arun Kapoor and Suraj Verma's phones.'

'Emily Dickson...' Linda searched her memory. 'I don't believe we have an Emily Dickson at this faculty. They could've met her outside the university. These parties happen spontaneously, friend of a friend, sort of thing. Hang on. I'll check the Student Registry. She may be on another faculty. The three lads have... had different rotas at the hospital, so it's rare for them to have time off together.' She searched the database as she spoke. 'Ah, found her.'

A minute later, Linda pulled a sheet of paper off the printer. 'Here's some basic information about Emily Dickson. She's a third-year student at the Faculty of Law and Business.'

Linda waved off their thanks. 'Please, just find whoever did this.'

Holt scrolled through his messages as they walked to the car. The rain had eased off, and the sky clung to a vestige of daylight.

'Message from the Super. The victims' parents have asked to meet with us at 9.00 a.m. tomorrow morning.'

'Oh God, that's going to be so tough.'

Holt sighed as he drove out of the campus. 'It'll be nothing compared to their visit to the mortuary to identify their sons.'

11

Rowena

Accompanied by two police officers, Rowena mounted the stairs to the first-floor flat Justin Brennan shared with three other students. She banged on the door, which, to her surprise, opened within seconds by a harassed-looking young man in his early twenties.

'Oh, I—I thought you were—' he stammered, his expression changing from relief to shock as his eyes focussed on the uniformed officers behind her.

'Is Justin Brennen in?' asked Rowena, moving squarely into the doorframe should the man decide to close the door. But he stepped back, opened it wider, and swivelled his neck to the room behind. Taking that as an invitation to enter, the three officers marched into the room set up as an open-plan living-dining room.

Rowena had assumed the wail she'd heard outside came from the TV, but the mandatory big screen mounted on the pale grey wall was blank, and silence now filled the room.

Her gaze swung to the two ashen faces staring at her from a large sofa, where a good-looking man lay curled up with his head on a young lady's lap. For a moment, Rowena wondered whether they had interrupted an intimate act, but then she realised everyone was fully clothed and tears ravaged the young man's face.

'Justin Brennan?' she asked.

The man sat up, but the young lady beside him kept her arm around his shoulders even as her eyes narrowed, and mouth tightened.

Justin dashed the back of his hand across his face and nodded.

'What's this about?' asked his friend.

No, not his lover. Maybe a good friend, certainly a protective one, Rowena evaluated the girl who was no older than the man she was mothering.

'Justin,' said Rowena, ignoring the girl's question, 'we'd like to bring you to the Station for questioning. You can either come voluntarily, or we can arrest you.'

'Why? What's he done?' The girl shifted to position herself in front of Justin. 'Can't you see how upset he is? You can't take him away.'

'Why're you arresting him? He's done nothing. Doesn't he need a lawyer or someone to go with him?' asked the other man, moving to stand beside Justin.

Rowena sighed. 'Look, I haven't arrested him yet.' She emphasised the word "yet". 'We need to question Justin at the Station and, as I said, he can come with us voluntarily or I can arrest him now. Come on, Justin, get up,' said Rowena. On cue, the two burly officers moved in closer.

'Mandy, maybe it's best he goes with them.' The young man who'd opened the door to them laid a hand on the girl's shoulder, while Justin gazed up at the officers in bewilderment as they stood him up.

'Justin, are you willing to come with us for an interview under caution?'

'Yes,' whispered Justin.

'We'll call his parents and his lawyer,' said the girl, making it sound like a threat.

'Yes, please do,' said Rowena. 'Justin, you are entitled to legal representation while we question you, and if you don't have a lawyer, we'll arrange one for you. OK?'

Justin nodded.

Rowena couldn't help feeling sorry for the young man drooping between the two PCs.

But, she thought, *criminals come in many guises. Some even wear the face of angels.*

12

Lily

I'll dig through my coursework on renovations of old waterside buildings and put together some practical tips and drop it off at the watermill, thought Lily on her way to collect her daughters from school. *A list of reliable suppliers for his construction materials might help him too.* She smiled. Since morning, she'd been racking her brains for a valid reason to revisit the watermill near Winchester, where with a bit of luck, she might run into Mr Matthew Holt again.

The twins were ready and waiting when she went into their classroom at the Bluebell Grove Special Needs Primary School. As always, they ignored their teacher's cheerful goodbye and accompanied their mother to the car.

With roadworks blocking off a couple of streets, the journey home took longer than usual. Lily glanced in the rearview mirror at her daughters, who sat holding hands, staring out of the window but saying nothing either to each other or to her.

In the thickening evening traffic, Lily's attention was on avoiding pedestrians as she manoeuvred through the narrow gaps between cars. The sole occupant of the black Toyota Prius tucked between two cars drew in a sharp breath as she passed within touching distance.

A minute later, the vehicle turned and headed off in a different direction. The driver didn't need to follow Lily. He knew where she lived and where she'd be going next.

***

'Phew, that journey wasn't much fun, was it?' said Lily, unlocking her front door and ushering the twins inside. 'You'd think they'd know better than to start the roadworks just as schools finish instead of in the middle of the day. But we're back home. Let's go upstairs and get you changed.'

She deposited the girls' school bags into their playroom, a cheerful space with flower and animal patterned wallpaper, before going to their bedroom to help them out of their uniform and into matching tracksuits.

'Come along. I'll get you a snack, and then we can go to the park.'

The children sat at the dining table, staring at their plates of chicken sandwiches and bowls of fruit while she tucked paper napkins into the necklines of their T-shirts. She placed another on their laps – eating fruit could be a messy business – and chatted to them about her day. With their attention focused on getting the food into their mouths, the girls showed no sign that they were even listening to Lily.

Identical in everything else except for their colouring, the five-year-old twins were slender and tall for their age, with delicate, perfect features. They shared the same burnished brown hair with strands of sun-kissed gold and amber-coloured eyes framed by thick, long dark lashes.

Just like David, their father. Who doesn't even know he is a father...

Like their father, Cara was dusky, her skin a soft, dark bronze, while Mia took after Lily – peaches and the palest cream.

They were heart-wrenchingly beautiful. Exquisite. But they viewed the world through eyes that revealed nothing. After a quick glance at friends and strangers alike, those extraordinary irises darted away in a flash of gold. And they never said a word. Hadn't uttered a single decipherable word since their birth. Sounds, yes. Cries, certainly. But no laughter. No giggles. Not even a smile.

The girls understood everything, reacted to nothing. No, that wasn't quite right. They reacted selectively, depending on whether or not they chose to follow instructions.

None of the many specialists, consultants and psychologists who'd examined the twins over the years had agreed on a firm diagnosis. Some mooted they could be on the autism spectrum – *'whatever the hell that means,'* Lily had thought – while others suspected Social (Pragmatic) Communication Disorder or selective mutism. As far as she was concerned, giving it a name changed nothing, and none offered a solution other than to advise her to 'keep encouraging them.' But they had done her one huge favour by recognising their neurodivergence and that they had special needs, which helped them secure a place in the highly rated Bluebell Grove Special Needs Primary School.

Despite their lack of response, Lily chatted to them almost continuously about mundane things. About her day, hopes, dreams, things they saw, heard, experienced. She read to them, drew for them, played with them, or rather played with their toys while they sat and watched. Her life was a series of long monologues, interspersed with three-person dialogues—all delivered by her alone.

But sometimes, it got to her – the loneliness, the stress and the sheer weariness tore her apart.

With a shiver, she shook off her melancholy and, with a bright smile, tidied away the remnants of their meal.

Twenty minutes later, dressed in padded and hooded jackets against the damp chilly March afternoon, the trio walked the half mile to the park, where the twins headed straight to the roundabout. Lily suspected they liked it best because they could be close together. They also liked the seesaw provided they could both sit together at one end while Lily, or occasionally other children, took the seat opposite.

'Hi Janet,' she called out to the woman seated on a park bench. Grinning, Janet, her friend, or rather, 'park buddy' as their friendship began and ended at the park, removed her backpack from the bench to make room for Lily.

Becky, Janet's five-and-a-half-year-old daughter, ran to join the twins on the roundabout. Despite the lack of response from the twins, Becky appeared to enjoy playing with them, chatting away almost as if they were responding to her.

'.... I got a new dress for my dolly! No, not the big one. The little one. It's so sparkly. I wanted to bring it, but Mummy said no. It would get dirty or lost...'

Lily smiled and joined Janet on the bench.

Eyes on the children, they chatted and took no notice of the man litter-picking nearby, dressed in a bright lime-green high-visibility jacket with the Council's logo on the back.

***

F rom beneath his peaked cap, the man's eyes slid to Lily, in annoyance and in relief. Annoyance because she was minutes later than he'd expected and relief that she'd turned up at the playground just as he'd predicted.

He gnawed his lip, wondering if he could get closer without being noticed, but prudence tempered his impulse.

No, he decided. *Best not to draw attention.*

13

Holt

'That was a good briefing, Matt. You covered a lot in an hour. I like how everyone kept their reports concise,' said Superintendent Simpson.

'Detailed notes, concise reports. The guv's been drumming that into us these past four years,' said Karl, jerking his head at Holt.

After the evening briefing for the entire Operation Storm team, DCI Matt Holt, DI Karl Stringer and DS Rowena Williams congregated in the Superintendent's office.

The Super said, 'Did I hear it right? Was this waste of human lives to do with drugs?'

'We aren't sure, sir,' said Holt. 'When DC David Plummer talked to their housekeeper, she mentioned—'

'Hang on! Did you say housekeeper? Those students had a housekeeper?'

Holt nodded. 'Their families are well off. Apparently, when the mothers saw the mess, they insisted someone come in twice a week to clean, do their laundry and cook for them. Mrs Harrison's been looking after them for four years now. She thinks the world of them, calls them "her boys". When David pushed her about drugs, she admitted seeing a couple of joints in Ravi's room last year and threatened to tell his parents. He promised he wouldn't do it again. Mrs Harrison said they all denied ever using hard drugs, and she's found nothing since.'

'Only a couple of joints?'

'Yes, sir,' said Rowena, 'but maybe they were dealing in drugs and were killed for encroaching on someone's patch or stealing from their suppliers.'

'The drugs squad checked their home and found no trace of any narcotics, no cash or burner phones. They also said they've never come across our victims' names or address,' added Holt. 'But they'll dig deeper and let us know.'

'What about drugs from the hospital? They interned there, didn't they?'

'No one has reported anything missing. They seem popular, and everyone likes them there.'

'What about this suspect, Justin Brennen?'

'He was in a right state. We had to call a doctor in who gave him a sedative and we took him back home. He's in no condition to be interviewed tonight, but we're hoping he'll be calm enough tomorrow,' said Holt.

'Hmm. Anything else I should know?'

'We interviewed Emily Dickson at her house, where the victims were last seen. All three plus ten other students were at Emily's house on the Thursday evening to celebrate her birthday. God! Was that only yesterday? Apparently, Emily knew one of our victims, Arun Kapoor, and invited him. He asked whether he could bring his friends. That's how she met Suraj and Ravi. Witnesses said that Emily and Ravi spent most of the evening flirting with each other.'

Rowena consulted her notes. 'The party started at 7 p.m. The three victims got there at about 8. Everyone brought their own drinks. Emily and her housemates provided the food. Our three victims left first as they were on the 6 a.m. shift the next morning at the hospital. They left together a little after 11.15 p.m. Emily said everyone else stayed on and no one left before half past midnight. We have a list of all the housemates and their guests, and their alibis check out.'

'So those lads were just walking home after a party when someone attacked them?'

'It would seem so, sir. But they could've planned to meet their assailants at the park, although there's nothing on their phones to confirm this.'

'Maybe they used burner phones,' suggested the Superintendent.

'If they did, we've found none. It wasn't on them or their home, nor in their campus lockers. But we'll keep looking,' said Rowena.

'Hmm. What else?'

'Holburn Park's north exit CCTV images are with IT, and they're trying to enhance it,' said Karl. 'Nothing so far from forensics or TAC Ops on bin and drain searches around the park yet. Council and Highways are helping with their CCTVs, and we've also recovered footage from most of the private cameras in the area, but it'll take time to go through them.'

'I've spoken to the Chief Pathologist. They'll start the autopsies after the victims' parents have been in. Chris knows how urgent this is, so he's brought in two more pathologists and additional help. He's planning to carry out the three autopsies simultaneously but warned that it won't be cheap. Said he's already sent you the requisition, sir,' said Holt.

'Yes, and I almost had a stroke. That plus forensics will make a serious dent in the budget. But it's got to be done. Anyway, I've signed it off.'

'Chris Cummings gave me his preliminary from the visual examination of the bodies. He's convinced there were three or more weapons involved. Knives of some sort. And at least three killers. He stressed that's unofficial, but with Chris's experience, I'd say he'd be spot on. It ties in with what our key witness claims to have seen.' Holt groaned and stretched his back. 'That about sums it up. I'm making this lot go home soon. They've been up since midnight,' he added.

After the team bid their bosses goodnight and left, the Superintendent turned to Holt. 'Sorry about your day off, Matt. Did you get any work done on your watermill?'

Holt's thoughts skidded to his long-term off-duty project.

What a difference a day makes, he thought. Yesterday—his day off—had been good. Damn good, in fact. He'd spent it working on his project of converting the once-derelict watermill into his new home, but the highlight of the day had been his serendipitous meeting with Lily Webster, the Council's attractive Buildings Inspector sent to check the structural modifications to the watermill. Yesterday, for the first time in years, he'd envisaged a life that was more than just work.

Yesterday.

Yet, meeting the lovely Lily Webster seemed to have happened a lifetime ago.

And now, this—

The crack of the Super's fingers snapping just inches from his face jerked him back to the present.

'Sorry, sir.' Holt smiled sheepishly. 'I sanded down four limestone walls, and my back and shoulders are still killing me. It looks good, but I still need to seal them.'

'Well, wrap up this case quickly and I might let you have a day off.' The Super's grin faded. 'Matt, you too have been up since midnight. You should rest, too. Are you going back to the farm?'

'No, I'll be staying in my flat in Ocean Village,' said Holt.

'Well, go on and get some rest. This could go on for weeks. Save your energy for the long run.'

'I will, sir,' said Holt. 'You should go home too, otherwise Mrs Simpson will forget what you look like.'

'Oh, no fear of that, lad. I'm unforgettable.' The Super's booming laugh followed him out.

14

Holt

'Sir, they're here.'

Holt shut his laptop and turned to DC David Plummer. The family liaison officer sported dark circles beneath his eyes, and his shoulders drooped.

'Thank you for picking them up at the airport, Dave. Can't have been easy for you. How're you holding up?'

'I'm OK, sir.' Plummer straightened up. 'Really, sir, I'm fine,' he added at the concern on his boss's face.

'Are all the parents here?'

'All three fathers but only one of the mum's here. They're in meeting room 4.'

'How are they?'

'Not good, sir. They are calm and in control of their emotions, but it's like a dam about to burst.'

'Rowena,' called Holt, stepping out of his office. 'Join us, please.'

LETHAL JUSTICE

The three men rose as the detectives entered the room, but the woman remained seated, her pale-knuckled hands clasped in her lap.

Holt introduced himself and Rowena, murmuring, 'We are so sorry...' as he shook their hands and heard their hoarse, flat, dull replies, 'Thank you.'

He almost jerked his hand out of the woman's clasp. Her hand was ice cold, but her alert dark eyes blazed into his, assessing, judging.

All four visitors had the same dull grey undertone to their skin and signs of fatigue etched deep into their faces; their eyes were red-rimmed with a million shed and unshed tears and lack of sleep.

'I'm Deepak Verma and this is my wife, Jyoti.' The oldest man laid a hand lightly on the icy-handed woman's shoulder.

Suraj's father, guessed Holt. Despite the man's full white beard, the resemblance between father and son was striking, and if his student ID photo was anything to go by, Suraj also seemed to have inherited his parent's solemnity.

'We're Su—Suraj's parents.' Deepak stumbled over his son's name, drew in a deep breath, and cleared his throat before turning to his companions.

'This is my brother, Prem. Ravi's father.'

Holt studied the brothers. From the background information his team had put together, he knew both men were surgeons, Deepak specialising in neurology and Prem in cardiology.

Except for the two-year difference in their ages, the brothers strongly resembled each other. Same balding heads fringed with salt and pepper hair, bushy eyebrows, glasses over prominent noses and strong jawlines. In contrast to Deepak's full white beard and moustache, the younger brother, Prem, sported a grey-threaded goatee.

But the creases and expression lines etched on their faces over a lifetime marked the difference between them.

The frown lines grooving permanent furrows on Deepak's forehead spoke of a man with a serious outlook, a reticent introvert, whereas the clear brow, and crinkles in the corners of his eyes and mouth on his younger brother showed Ravi's father to be quick with a smile and a far more cheerful attitude to life. Under normal circumstances, that is.

Now, however, Prem responded with a dazed stare. Holt suspected self-medication.

'—and this is our friend, Roopesh Kapoor. Arun's father.' Deepak laid a hand on the third man's shoulder. Holt could only wonder at the effort it took Deepak to remain so calm, to keep his voice so steady.

Roopesh Kapoor, the third victim's father, was taller, slimmer and distinguished looking, with clean-shaven, aquiline features, a full head of wavy hair clipped short and brushed back from his broad forehead. He was a successful entrepreneur and a handsome man by any standard.

'Sadly, their wives weren't well enough to join us. Anjali, Roopesh's daughter, also stayed behind in India,' continued Deepak. 'And thank you for arranging our pickup at Heathrow Airport.'

'The media somehow got wind of your travel details, and we knew they were out there waiting for you,' said Rowena.

Deepak nodded. 'They were at our homes in Durgapur, too. We had to get extra security guards. They were also at New Delhi Airport, but the staff and Delhi police were very helpful. We understand from our friends here that they are at Prem and Roopesh's homes, too, which is why we're staying at the Titanic Hotel.'

The three men exchanged a glance before Deepak leaned forward.

'Chief Inspector, is it possible this is a mistake? That they are not *our* sons? A mistake in their identities, perhaps?'

The desperation in Deepak's voice wrenched Holt's heart as four hope-filled faces turned to him. The victims' parents already knew there'd been no mistake, but that didn't stop them from yearning, wishing that this was an error of identity.

'I am truly sorry. We found their student IDs on them, and we've also matched their fingerprints with those in their house.'

The four visitors shrank back as hope collapsed and despair barged in.

'Please, Detective Chief Inspector, may we go see them now?' Jyoti, the icy-handed woman, stood up, catching everyone off guard.

'Of course. DC Plummer and DS Williams will accompany you.'

'Then, we'd like to return here, if we may. I'm sure you have many questions for us. I would like to speak to you too, please.'

None of the startled surprise showed on Holt's face. Framed as a courteous request, it left little room for denial. Although her husband looked wary, none of them seemed surprised. They calmly awaited his response.

'Certainly, Mrs Verma. Please take your time and return when you are ready.'

He felt like a ten-year-old again, summoned before his headteacher for a misdemeanour he couldn't recall.

15

Holt

With the preliminaries and introductions completed, the interview under caution was well underway when Holt entered the remote viewing room.

Justin Brennen had been too distraught to interview yesterday but seemed much calmer now despite the tears streaming down his cheeks. The young man with his long blond hair tied in a ponytail sat beside his counsel facing DI Karl Stringer and DS Rowena Williams.

Karl lifted his gaze to the camera in the interview room and gave a hopeless shrug. Of course, Justin might have been a superb actor, but Holt's instincts said otherwise.

'Well, so what? Arun never complained, did he?' Justin asked his interviewers.

Karl leaned forward. 'You realize that could be interpreted as stalking?'

'I was not stalking him!' said Justin. 'I... I, er, I love him...' he mumbled. 'And I know he felt the same! I just wanted him to accept it.'

The two detectives glanced at each other.

'That seems unlikely,' said Karl. 'Arun didn't respond to any of your calls or messages.'

'He did in the beginning, after we first met.'

'Oh? When was that?'

'Back in October, soon after the term started. We both attended a seminar at Winchester Campus and got talking afterwards when a bunch of us stayed behind.'

'You've been seeing each other, then?'

'Not exactly seeing each other. We met only a few times for drinks and dinners. We went to the cinema once.'

All true so far. A download of the victim's text messages confirmed an arrangement between him and Justin to meet at the local cinema back in December, and a subsequent message from Justin saying how much he had enjoyed their 'date'. In response to Justin's much more ardent missive, Arun's reply was a simple 'me too'.

'What happened then? Did you two break up?' asked Rowena, her tone soft, inviting confidence.

'There was nothing to break up. Arun said his family would never accept it. He said it would destroy his mum knowing her son was gay. They wanted him to marry and give them several grandchildren. Arun said that even if he couldn't do that, he would not shame them. Shame. That was the word he used.' Justin sounded very bitter about it.

'Did he ask you to stop phoning and texting him?'

'No, he did not! He only said that he wouldn't... he couldn't see me again. That it was impossible for us. But he never asked me to stop trying to talk to him or text him.'

Upset again, he said, 'If Arun didn't want me to call or text him anymore, he only had to ask me to stop, and I would have.'

'Would you?'

'Yes! He asked me not to meet him again, and I didn't. But I was trying, hoping to get him to change his mind.'

'When was the last time you met?'

'Seven weeks ago, when we had dinner together. He said then that he couldn't see me again.'

'Because he was straight?' asked Karl.

'No! Of course not! It was because of his family. I said we could pretend to be just friends around them. But he said it wasn't enough; that it'd hurt too much.' He paused, took a quick swipe at his eyes with the sleeve of his jumper.

'Why do you keep asking me all these questions? You can't suspect me of... of... of hurting Arun. I wouldn't, I couldn't!'

'We need to understand why you would call Arun 86 times and send him 112 messages in just the last six weeks. We think you didn't like being spurned. No one does. Did you kill Arun because he rejected you? Or did you have him killed, and his friends were simply in the wrong place at the wrong time?' asked Karl.

Justin's jaw dropped, and he gasped for air. His counsel patted his back and glared at the detectives. Karl paused the interview, announced a ten-minute break, and stepped out of the room with Rowena.

'Can't see how it's him, sir,' said Karl, voicing his thoughts.

The search of Justin's flat had yielded nothing, and his flatmates confirmed he'd been in all evening, working in his room, and couldn't have left the flat unseen. His laptop showed he'd logged into the university network at 11.15 p.m. and uploaded his assignment at 11.50 p.m., so he couldn't have been in the park killing anyone. His bank account showed no unusual activity or evidence of his student loan being used for anything other than to cover his tuition fees, boarding and lodging, leaving little for any extraneous expenditure.

'I agree. This isn't getting us anywhere. Release him under investigation. We may need to speak to him again.'

Well, what did you expect with your luck? thought Holt. It hadn't been that promising a line of inquiry anyway, but at least he now knew a lot more about one victim, and it also gave him an insight into the family dynamics.

16

Holt

'The victims' parents are back, sir,' said one of the many unfamiliar faces seconded to assist with the investigation. 'They are in conference room 4. Uniform found the missing phone – the one belonging to Ravi Verma. It'd been caught in the branches of a tree. The battery had come loose, so it wasn't sending or receiving any signal. It's with forensics now.'

Holt thanked her and made his way to the meeting room. Hand on the doorknob, he steeled himself to meet the bereaved. They sat in a semicircle at one end of the oblong table beside the two detectives. His gaze lingered on his officers, both of whom were pale and looked drained, their eyes haunted.

Should I have gone to the mortuary instead? he reproached himself. But no, it had to be done. Dealing with trauma was part of their job. *But perhaps this'd been too much?*

Holt acknowledged his detectives with a sympathetic nod before shifting his gaze to the visitors, each hunched in a chair, staring blankly ahead.

As before, the men started to rise to their feet, but Holt stayed them with raised palms.

'No, please. Do sit down.' He pulled up a chair and sat down beside them.

The oldest man, whom he recognised as Deepak Verma, said, 'Thank you for arranging the visit to the m-m-mortuary and for allowing David and Rowena to accompany us. That was very k-kind of you,' he stammered, his voice wobbling with a gamut of emotions.

Holt leaned forward and said, 'I'm so very sorry.'

He waited while Deepak attempted to push back the recent agonising memories to the dark recesses of his mind. Hollow-eyed, with dried blood crusting cracked lips, only sheer willpower held him together. But his bloodshot, dark eyes were still alert.

Beside him, his wife was a granite statue, her face pale and expressionless, but the brown eyes were as watchful as her husband's.

'DCI Holt, how did this happen? How did our sons end up dead?' asked Deepak. His hands floundered for an instant as if reaching for his missing son, before he fisted them on his knees.

'They were attacked on their way back home after a party and discovered by a couple walking their dogs in the park. The ambulance arrived within six minutes, but there was nothing anyone could do.'

'Did anyone see who attacked them?' asked Roopesh. Arun's father stooped in despair, his tall frame shrinking within his tailored suit. Holt flinched when he met the hazel eyes, filled with all the pain his companions concealed.

'No. The attackers had fled the scene, probably when they heard the dogs. It was dark, and the dog owners were too far away to identify them.'

'The media says that it was a racist attack. Was it?'

'With the student population, we have a very diverse mix in Southampton. However, the number of hate crimes here, including racially motivated crimes, is no higher than the national average. But we haven't eliminated racism as a possibility.'

None of the visitors looked impressed. They knew all about prejudice, often unconscious and unintended. They'd lived and worked in England for most of their adult lives, and although each had built a successful career, they had done so despite the bigotries, big and small, intended or not, which they encountered in both their professional and private lives.

'Was this a random attack? A mugging gone wrong?'

'We're considering all possibilities. We're also considering whether someone targeted them specifically. Can you think why anyone would wish to harm your sons? Have you received any threats? Would anyone use your sons to get to you?'

Stunned silence met his questions. The men looked puzzled.

'Mr Kapoor, you're a successful entrepreneur. Would any of your rivals do this?'

'My rivals? No one is capable of this! I am a metallurgist. I manufacture and sell special instruments, technical products for a small niche market. They're the best in the world, and I run a profitable business, but it's dull. There's nothing about my products or my business that'd excite anyone. So far, no one has shown any interest in buying me out.'

'Would you? Sell, I mean, if a buyer came forward?'

Roopesh considered the idea. 'No. No, I wouldn't.'

Holt turned to the Vermas.

Deepak shook his head. 'My brother and I are a threat to no one. We're good at our jobs, but although we haven't been able to save everyone we treat, we've always informed them and their families of the risks. Sometimes, there's just nothing we can do, but no one has suffered under our care.'

Holt was aware of the brothers' reputation. They were among the best in their chosen fields in a worldwide arena.

'How about a more personal motive? A grudge or revenge, maybe? Did you or your sons cross anyone? Can you think of someone who may wish them harm?'

The brothers exchanged glances. Prem, the younger brother, now seemed more shocked than dazed. Holt figured the sedative's effects were fading.

After a long, bewildered pause, Deepak said, 'We cannot think what we or our boys did to deserve this.'

'What about demands for money?'

'None other than the usual requests from charities and the occasional sob stories. We've received no threats, calls, notes, or anything like that.'

'Besides,' added Roopesh, 'if they wanted money, they would've got it. We'd have given them whatever they wanted rather than risk our sons' lives.'

Deepak nodded. 'We'd have traded anything and everything for them. Even our lives.' Conviction lay behind the simple words.

'Thank you. We need to explore all angles, you understand.' Holt turned to Roopesh. 'Mr Kapoor, I know this will be difficult for her, but I'd like to speak to your daughter, Anjali. I understand she is... was engaged to Suraj. She may be able to tell us about their lives here. If you prefer, I can arrange for either someone from the British High Commission or the New Delhi police to visit her.'

'That won't be necessary. We understand, and my daughter will, too. She's strong; my girl's very strong. When would you like to speak to her? We can arrange it through a video link.'

'Thank you.' Holt glanced at his watch. Almost 1 p.m. now, so it'd be around 6.30 p.m. in India. 'Could we call her in an hour's time? We need to talk to her alone.'

'Yes, I understand. I'll call her now and ask her to be ready. She can speak to you from her room.' Mobile phone in hand, he stepped outside to make the call.

'And now, Chief Inspector,' said Deepak. 'My wife has something to say to you.'

17

Holt

The lift shuddered to a halt at basement level two at St. John's Hospital, and the doors squealed open. The smell of bleach, methylated spirits tinged with putrefaction and human waste assaulted Holt as he stepped into a small hallway.

Dr Chris Cummings, still in his green scrubs, met him at the door to the big, stark white, high-ceilinged room that resembled an operating theatre.

Holt wondered why people thought a mortuary was quiet. The machines droned, the extractor fans whirred, and the air conditioners hissed, making the area anything but quiet. And occasionally, as Cummings had once told him over drinks at a pub, there was 'the fart symphony of the dead.'

The chief pathologist looked exhausted and sweat beaded on his forehead despite the cool temperature.

'Hey Matt! Come on in. We've finished the autopsies, attended by six of your brave souls.'

The tall, thin medical examiner with a shaved head, high cheekbones and straight, sharp angular features reminded Holt of a stork. All angles, gawky, jerky movements until he picked up a scalpel. Then, he became a ballet dancer – grace in every sweep of his hand, fluidity in every flick of his wrist, every cut as smooth as silk.

As promised, Cummings had brought in extra help to carry out the postmortem examinations witnessed by Holt's detectives. Two corpses lay beneath their grey-green shrouds while a locum pathologist and his assistant finished the Y-shaped suture on the third body.

'Shall I give you a summary before we get around to writing it up formally?' asked Cummings.

'Yes please, Chris. My detectives have submitted their reports, but I'd like your take on this.' Holt waved a hand and cast a despairing glance at the three bodies on the waist high stainless steel tables surrounded by various drain tubes, rinsing hoses, weighing scales, directional lighting, audio and video equipment, and the inevitable trays of cutting tools still bearing the bloodstains and gore from the recent autopsies.

'Sure, that's not a problem. Your team did really well; it can't have been easy for them. I've not seen anything so bad since that bus crash five years ago. At least then we knew why. But this – this is awful.' Cummings shook his head. 'And that storm destroyed all trace evidence and any possibility of recovering any of the perpetrators' DNA. I barely had to wash the bodies – the rain took care of that, too. Forensics got nothing from the scene either, which doesn't surprise me. They're going through the lads' clothes, but I doubt they'll find anything useful. Anyway, here's what we have...'

Cummings fell silent for a long moment, contemplating his 'patients', as he called them, though none would ever recover. All he could do for them was provide some answers.

With a sigh, he began. 'Three males, all of Indian origin. IDs confirmed by their parents.' He led Holt to the first steel table.

'First victim – Suraj Verma. In good health, with fair muscle tone, but not an athlete. Age twenty-two according to his documented ID. Stabbed twice in the abdomen by someone directly in front of him. Twice! This was a vicious attack. Quick upward thrusts, most likely a switchblade with a four-inch blade. It pierced deep both times. One punctured a kidney, but the other was fatal. It penetrated the abdominal aorta. He died in minutes. Painfully, too.'

He walked a few paces to the second table. 'This is Arun Kapoor. Same ethnicity, age twenty-three.' He studied the young man. 'He must have been a very good-looking lad. I'd say he was kneeling or crouching when it happened. We found the first victim's blood on his hands and jacket. He probably knelt to staunch the bleeding, presenting a perfect target. Stabbed four times in the back and side. Two of his wounds came from the same blade used on the other victims. I've sent tissue and blood samples for analysis and, if I am correct, I expect them to show their DNAs. There's a third wound from a different blade, longer and wider than the others. It went through the left lung, right into the heart. That's what caused his death.'

He sighed and moved on to the third victim. 'Ravi Verma, slightly overweight, but healthy. Strong resemblance to the first victim. Brother or cousin?'

'Cousin,' said Holt.

Cummings nodded and continued. 'Twenty-three years old. Throat cut from left to right. So, a right-handed assailant, standing behind him, at least as tall, maybe taller. The weapon was a short-bladed knife, but not a normal kitchen one; I am thinking something like a Stanley knife, thin blade but sharp. He'd have bled out and died quickly. Within two minutes, I'd say.'

He continued, 'They were not expecting the attack; there're no defence wounds on any of them. It happened fast.

Were they at a party just before? They had snacks and cheap alcohol, though not in excessive quantities, in their stomachs. Digestion had barely begun, so they died soon after leaving the party. And before you ask, I'm waiting on toxicology, but initial tests don't show any drugs in their system.'

'What, none?'

'Nope. Not even a joint.'

'More than one attacker?'

'Definitely!' said Cummings. 'Different forces and at least three different blades, unless, of course, one perpetrator had a knife in each hand. There's also a small puncture on the second victim – Arun Kapoor. It barely penetrated the skin. So, there was possibly a fourth attacker. It's difficult to be certain, but I believe it's more likely there were three or more attackers.'

'How do you think it went down?' asked Holt.

'You are asking me to speculate. It won't be in my report, you understand. But if it helps, this is what I think happened...

'First, Suraj, I'll use their names if you don't mind. Suraj, our first victim, is stabbed in the abdomen. His attacker pulls the knife out and, wham, thrusts it back in. Suraj clasps his stomach, folds over and collapses, curling into a foetal position.

'Arun, that's victim number two, kneels over him, takes off his jacket, rolls it into a ball and presses it to Suraj's stomach. They stab him in the back as he kneels over his friend.

'Ravi, our third victim, is attacked either at the same time or immediately after. I understand he was dialling 999 when his attacker slashed his throat. His killer then kicked his feet away. There's evidence he fell and hit his head hard on the ground.'

Cummings accompanied his recitation with actions. Under different circumstances, the ungainly choreography would have been funny, but Holt felt far from laughing.

'These lads had no time to put up a fight. Their priority seems to have been to help their fallen friend.' Cummings rubbed his eyes. 'This is pure conjecture, you understand, and I repeat, it won't be in the report. This is just my take on what could've happened to these poor souls. All three died within minutes of each other, so it's impossible to say who was attacked first. Even if he were attacked first, the poor lad Suraj lingered in pain, aware of what was going on.'

He turned to Holt. 'Sadly, his parents would know this, too.'

18

Holt

Half an hour to midnight, but Holt still paced back and forth before the evidence board, the events and discussions of the day crowding his brain, each elbowing for attention.

There was his video conversation with Roopesh's daughter, Anjali. Younger sister of victim number two – Arun Kapoor. The beautiful, happy young woman whose image was the wallpaper on her fiancé, Suraj's phone.

Her face ravaged by sorrow, Anjali had been dry-eyed and calm throughout their video interview. In control of herself, despite the harrowing events. She'd answered every question Holt and Rowena had asked. And volunteered nothing.

Rowena had put it down to the trauma, or a mild sedative, to take the edge off her pain. Holt wasn't so sure. That girl was hiding something. Knew or suspected something or someone. It could of course be totally unrelated to the murder.

And before that, the bizarre conversation in his office with Deepak's wife, Jyoti Verma.

'Detective Chief Inspector, I've been having these visions for the past six months. I thought they were just bad dreams, nightmares. I couldn't tell anyone. Speaking about it would've given it a voice. Caused it to come true.' She gave a short bark of laughter, bordering on hysteria, but immediately controlled herself. *'It made no difference. It all still happened...'*

Her dark, empty gaze latched onto Holt's. *'I came here hoping that it wasn't true, that it hadn't happened. Prayed that they weren't our sons. They were someone else. Some other mothers' sons.'* Her voice cracked, and she choked on a sob. *'What kind of person does that make me?'*

'It's only natural.'

But Jyoti ignored Holt's mumbled assurance. *'I made the boys promise me they would not walk through the park at night. They broke their word.'* Her voice crackled with genuine anger.

'Then, that night, the night they died – it didn't feel like a dream. I was there when our sons died. I tried to reach them; to stop it, but I couldn't move. I could only stand and watch and cry and scream. I saw him. My son's killer. He was beautiful, like one of Botticelli's angels, the boy with very blue eyes and short golden hair. I saw him stick a knife into Suraj's stomach. Twice. He smiled all the time. There were three others with him, but I couldn't see them clearly. I saw our boys fall; Suraj first, Arun next, and then Ravi. They stood and watched them die. Then two big dogs appeared out of the mist, and the killers ran away. I tried to stay there, to help them, but I found myself back in my bed.'

Jyoti had stopped with a gasp. Terror, sorrow and anger twisted her face – Holt's first glimpse of emotion. She'd ducked her head, picked up the glass tumbler and taken a big gulp of water. Eyes shut, she'd drawn in deep breaths while all expression drained from her visage. Composed once again, she had faced Holt and waited for his response.

Holt had turned his head to find her husband, Deepak, watching him, fingers raking his beard. An unconscious habit, Holt had guessed. Beside him, Prem and Roopesh, too, were staring at him with equally neutral expressions, all three awaiting his reaction.

Holt had quelled the blaze of flaring anger. Whatever else he had expected, it certainly wasn't this! *How could these qualified surgeons and this metallurgist, men of science, believe such mumbo jumbo?* He already had dozens of psychics, clairvoyants and mediums calling in with their visions, readings, predictions, and insights.

'Thank you for telling us. We'll make a note of that description.'

Holt hoped that neither his attitude nor his voice betrayed his feelings. What he needed were facts and evidence, not the visions of a grieving mother.

Now, as he paced the floor, Jyoti's calm voice reverberated in his skull. He stopped, returned to his office and noted his decision in the Policy File. Tomorrow, he'd instruct a technician to meet with Jyoti to put together an e-fit image of her son's killer. Even though they would not release it to the public, it might help with the case. However bizarre, he would be thorough, methodical.

After all, as Shakespeare said, *There are more things in heaven and earth, Horatio,*

Than are dreamt of in your philosophy.

Perhaps he was going down the same path as Hamlet.

19

Deepak

The three fathers sat in silence around the glass-topped centre table while their untouched meal congealed on the room service trolley. Jyoti had retired to her bedroom to lie staring at the ceiling.

The trauma of seeing their sons' bodies and subsequent meetings had left them exhausted and emotionally drained. From apathy and necessity, they spent the evening incarcerated in their apartment suite at the iconic Titanic Hotel. A necessity because the paparazzi and journalists were everywhere, waiting to pounce, hoping to capture a photo shot of the grieving parents to add to their sensational media submissions.

Following their return from the police station, Deepak, Jyoti, and Roopesh had met with their son's housekeeper. Poor Mrs Harrison had tried so hard to be brave but had broken down, and they had consoled her. Eventually, after thanking her for taking care of their sons, they had requested one of the accompanying PCs to take her home.

The shrill hotel phone shattered the deathly quiet. Roopesh Kapoor grabbed it off its cradle.

'Yes, of course. Please send him up. Thank you.' He turned to his companions. 'That was Reception saying Gordy is downstairs. He'll be up in a minute.'

Too weary to show their surprise, the Verma brothers nodded. They'd already spent the afternoon with their old friend, Prof. Gordon Moore, the dean, making polite conversation to hold off the images of the shrouded figures on the gurneys. But the memory of green sheets being lowered to reveal each of their son's faces remained stubbornly imprinted on their minds.

Roopesh opened the door to greet their visitor and frowned, seeing the four young people behind him. 'Is everything alright?'

The dean nodded. They piled into the room, red-eyed and sombre, and shook hands with their friends' fathers.

'The students have organised a vigil for the boys. Please, would you join us?'

***

Despite just six hours' sleep in the last forty-eight, Rowena had insisted on joining DC Plummer at the vigil. Anything was better than what her boss was doing – plodding through mounting paperwork, trawling through the reports flooding in or pacing the narrow space in front of the wallboards still bare of any useful evidence.

She arrived early and walked among the attendees, scrutinising each one before realising the futility of her action as the numbers grew and grew.

What had she expected? That the killers would return to the crime scene and be instantly recognisable? That their deed would somehow mark them? Make them stand out? Or that they would have an aura that she would instinctively perceive?

The killers may well be here, but she had no chance of finding them.

Rowena elbowed her way through the throng. She knew who she was looking for. *The killer with short blond hair, deep blue eyes and the face of a Botticelli angel*, Jyoti's voice whispered in her head.

Her phone buzzed an alert – the victims' parents had arrived.

***

Flanked by his brother Prem and Roopesh, Deepak Verma stared into the semi-darkness. Jyoti had remained behind at the hotel.

'Is this where—?' Deepak's voice quivered.

The dean shook his head. 'No, that's still a crime scene and is taped off. But it's close by.'

He led the three men into the park. Heads swivelling, they watched people flow in from all directions. Holburn Park was full. Over a thousand people – made up of local residents, busloads of students from other universities, activists of all kinds, mourners, spectators and the curious – cramped into the open area.

Rowena joined the dean and the students, who formed a tight cordon around the fathers and guided them towards the small clearing in the centre covered with flowers and cards.

Their shoulders wracking with sobs, the grief-stricken men huddled together. The crisp, chilly night sky was alight with the glow of candles placed at the makeshift memorial site and beams from mobile phone torches.

The bells of a nearby church pealed midnight when a young student stepped up to the centre and the haunting, melancholic sound of 'Amazing Grace' resonated into the cold silent night, while a thousand flames and lights swayed in time to the music echoing around the park.

Surrounded by his friends, Justin Brennen gazed at the starlit sky. He'd only met Arun a few times, but he would never forget the shy, serious hazel eyes or the feel of the clasp of his hand. Deep down, Justin knew there had never been any possibility of a future together. Yet he had dared to hope for a chance to fight for it at least.

Not far away, a pretty, petite, brown-eyed girl looked at the name and number on her mobile phone. Ravi – the boy with laughing dark eyes who had stayed with her throughout the evening of her birthday party, who had caused a flutter in her stomach and her heart to sing. Emily had laid a bouquet of white roses with a simple card – 'I will remember you forever' on the pile in the centre of the park. For a little while, she, too, had dared to dream.

Among the residents at the vigil were Walter and Julia McCabe, both still shaky from their recent experience. Walter held his sobbing wife and ignored the tears coursing down his cheeks.

Also among the crowd were Lily Webster with her twin daughters. Despite the lateness of the hour, Lily had gone into her children's room to find them sitting up in bed, alert and waiting for her. Not knowing how to explain, she simply said, 'we're going to the park to pray for three young men who died.' Donning warm clothes and jackets over their pyjamas, they held their mother's hand and joined their neighbours on their way to Holburn Park.

A choir of voices accompanied the lone singer in the last refrain, the wall of sound lifting the notes sky-high. *Surely no*

God can ignore this plea for grace, thought Rowena, wiping her face.

The poignant melody died away, to be replaced by a deep hush. With an effort, Deepak Verma stepped up to a microphone.

'Thank you all so very much,' his voice choked with emotion. He turned full circle, taking in the surrounding multitude. He cleared his throat and tried again. The silence carried his voice to the edges of the park.

'Thank you all for coming, for being here, for this tribute to our boys. Our sons loved this place and the many friends they made here. They had such high hopes and bright futures. They wanted only to help people. To do good. But their futures were stolen from them. No one deserves to die like they did, or so young. If anyone knows who did this and why, please, please contact the police. Please give them any information you may have. Soon, we will take our sons home with us, home to their mothers.' A sob caught in his throat. 'Thank you, everyone,' he managed. 'This means a lot to us. Thank you from the bottom of our hearts.'

Hands reached out to touch the men as they left.

20

The Watcher

Mesmerised, the naked man on the bed watched the flickering images unfolding in stark clarity and vibrant colours on the large television screen. His breath grew shallower and faster.

The camera panned to the wide eyes and gaping mouth of the pale female beneath the masked man on the screen. It paused for a moment on the arched neck, the trembling pulse, the arms struggling against her tormentor.

The artistic shots.

Her gasps and cries of pain spurred him on.

'Fuck, that's brilliant!'

Spent, he leaned over and pressed the stop key on his laptop. *That was bloody fantastic! I am an artist! Even I would pay me to watch that.*

That was Sarah Mitchell on the screen. Sarah Mitchell, who had vanished without a trace nearly eight months ago. The police and her family were still looking for her.

Yet here she was.

Captured and immortalised.

His forever.

These audio-visuals would suffice for now. But they lacked the touch, feel, and smell of the real thing.

Good thing I've already picked the cast for my next masterpiece.

He picked up his laptop, opened a folder, scrolled through the images, his finger slowing when it reached one. A tap to open it, a pinch-out to zoom it to the full screen.

The photograph of a slim blonde woman outside her house with her arms around her two daughters.

21

Deepak

Silence accompanied the three men after the vigil, joined them in the lift to the twelfth floor and trudged beside them in the corridor to their suite in the Titanic Hotel.

Deepak twisted the knob, and the door swung open. Darkness within.

Good, Jyoti must be asleep.

He switched on the lights, gasped aloud at the sight of his wife sitting upright in an armchair, her hands resting on her knees, watching them.

'That must've been so very hard,' she said. 'I am sorry I wasn't with you. How was it?'

'I can't describe it. It was... it was beautiful and heart-breaking.' Deepak choked back a sob. 'There were more than a thousand people there. So many came to say goodbye, some from afar, to pray for our sons. We weren't expecting that.'

Jyoti nodded and got up. 'I'm glad. I'm going to bed. No, Deep, you stay here. I'll be fine.'

The three men hovered uncertainly as she padded off into her bedroom.

'I need a drink.' Deepak strode to the well-stocked bar, held up a bottle of brandy. When the others nodded, he poured and handed out generous shots in cut-crystal glasses.

Drinks in hand, they sat in the suite's comfortable armchairs in a loose triangle, each within touching distance of the other, but miles apart in their thoughts. Except for the occasional clink of ice against the glass and the rustle of leather furniture, silence filled the room. Up here, not even the hum of traffic or hiss of the sea breeze penetrated the large, double-glazed windows.

An odd guttural sound disturbed the quiet. The men lifted their heads. Listened. They frowned at each other, glanced around the room.

What was that? Where was it coming from?

The noise repeated, grew louder, more urgent.

Deepak clanged his tumbler on the glass-topped table and sprang to his feet. Rushed towards his bedroom, followed by his brother and Roopesh. Pushed open the heavy door, holding it ajar with his shoulders as its fire safety mechanism fought to keep it shut.

Bed – empty. *Jyoti must be in the bathroom*, he thought.

The flickering light of a small LED *diya*-shaped lamp on the dressing table caught his attention.

Praying again. He searched for the small black idol that invariably accompanied his wife's adulations. *Where is it?*

Another step forward. He saw his wife then, on the thick, pale cream carpeted floor at the foot of their bed. Dressed in white cotton pyjamas with a red scarf around her neck, its ends trailing down the front of her nightshirt.

Why is she wearing a scarf to bed?

The familiar metallic, coppery tang hit his nostrils. He threw himself forward.

Jyoti sat with her legs outstretched, leaning against the base of the bed for support, her once white nightdress soaked in blood. A small idol of the Goddess Kali in her bloodied hands. The shiny black exquisitely carved obsidian statuette seemed to writhe in the lamplight.

'Oh God, Jyoti! What have you done?'

Deepak lunged forward to stem the flow of blood from her torn neck, but Jyoti grabbed his hand with surprising strength.

'No! Don't...' she pleaded.

Gasping in horror, Roopesh sank to his knees beside Deepak while Prem dashed to the bathroom and grabbed a bath towel. He squatted beside his brother and tried to press the towel to the haemorrhaging neck, but Jyoti stayed his hand, too.

'No, please don't,' she whispered, her voice weak and hoarse, every word a strain. 'I... I'm truly sorry. This—all my fault. I should've saved them! My visions – I knew this would happen. I should... should have made them come home! I... I let them die. Forgive me, please—'

'*Bhabhi*[1], please don't do this,' begged Prem. 'Please let me—'

He reached out again with the towel, but Jyoti reared away, rasped 'No!'

Deepak reached out and held his brother's wrist. 'No, Prem. Let her go. Let her suffering end.'

Jyoti reached for their right hands, pressed the small black statuette, hot and slick with her lifeblood, into their palms.

---

1. Elder brother's wife.

She was getting weaker by the second, but the dark eyes in her pale, bloodless face were insistent, full of awareness. 'Forgive me, *Devi ma!*'

She tightened their hands around the idol. 'Avenge them—'

Through their shock, despair and horror, they felt the heat of the idol. It was hot beyond the warmth of fresh blood covering it. For a moment, they were holding a live creature. Four slim arms bound them. The obsidian eyes scoured their souls.

'Promise me!' whispered Jyoti even as her breath rattled in her chest and fled her body with a hiss. Death's film clouded her eyes, extinguishing their light.

***

The call had been strong, very strong. The Dra has a shape now – a shape and form that the dying human gave it. It's a familiar form; one it has used before, a form now enshrined in mythology and worshipped as a deity.

The Dra ignores the men's despair and implorations – their pleas to undo the woman's fate. No, fate had already sealed her destiny. Her death is now a fact and a past. History.

Soon, it will once again play a part in the affairs of humankind. Soon the Dra will walk the earth again, sensing and feeling human emotions.

Soon, but just not yet.

22

Deepak

Deepak caught glimpses of his wife's prone body with its red, red neck through the wide-open door of the bedroom and the ever-shifting gaps between the shoulders and legs of the paramedics struggling to revive Jyoti.

As if she's still wearing a red scarf. No, I won't remember her like this...

He hunched forward in the armchair, eyes fixed on the blood-covered statue clutched in his fist and mind teetering on the edge of sanity.

26 years ago

The young man stood beside his bride. She, resplendent in a red and gold bridal saree, with part of the pallu—the decorated end of the 8-meter long silk fabric—draped over her head, the overhang shielding her face.

The pair put their bare right feet forward over the threshold of the groom's house. A ceremonious entry, symbolic of the start of their life as a couple.

LETHAL JUSTICE

One hundred and one diyas—oil lamps—and scented candles set the place ablaze with light. Flowers bedecked every surface; their perfume made headier by the scent of incense. The loud music, fireworks, bawdy jokes and pealing bells fell silent as the newlyweds entered their home, welcomed by the groom's mother.

The couple knelt, bowed low to touch the older woman's feet; she laid her hands over their heads, murmuring words and prayers of blessing. When they arose, the young man looked down at his mother, the flickering, twinkling lights reflected on her face, a contented smile on her lips while her eyes brimmed with tears. She cupped her hands around his face, drew his head down, kissed his forehead, and turned to his bride.

'Welcome, my beti[1]. You embody the goddesses Laxmi, Saraswati, and Parvati in this house. With their blessing, you will bring prosperity, wisdom, and strength to our family. I hope you will be happy here. I know you will make my son very happy. Give me your hands, my child.'

The older woman placed the obsidian figurine of the black goddess Kali into the bride's cupped palms and wrapped her hands around the younger woman's.

'This has been in our family for centuries, passed down from the oldest son to his oldest son through generations and always looked after by the lady of the house. The Goddess is now in your care, as she was in mine. Look after her, and she will protect and care for you and our family.'

While the groom stood shuffling his feet, his mother led the young bride to her special room – her pooja room, dedicated to the myriad gods where she started her mornings early with prayers and rituals, repeated at twilight.

---

1. Daughter.

When they returned, his mother signalled to the women of the bridal party. Giggling, they led the bride across the red rose petal strewn path to her bridal chamber. The men took the groom into another room, plied him with drinks and advice to boost his courage on his wedding night.

***

Deepak brought the statue closer, staring into its sightless eyes.

And she did, he raged. *She cared for you every single day, morning and evening. You were supposed to protect her. Protect our family. And what did you do? You took our son, and now you've taken her, too. Why? Why?*

His mind edged closer to the abyss, to the comfort of madness, and raised a foot to step over the edge into its welcoming depths.

A hand on his shoulder shook him. He looked up into his brother's ravaged face.

'The police are here. They want to talk to us,' said Prem.

But Deepak saw only the welcoming black void instead of the face he knew as well as his own. Every ounce of him propelled him forward into the dark, empty embrace. Then...

His eyes refocused. Police had now joined the paramedics in the room.

He looked for their friend Roopesh, saw him leaning against the wall, staring at his bloody hands.

Deepak nodded towards him. 'Look after him, Prem. I'll be OK.'

Afterwards, Deepak would swear the idol had reached out and pulled him back from that precipice.

For a moment, the eyes chiselled on the tough, black, glassy volcanic rock were alive and aware, as man and idol gazed at each other.

***

The Dra watches the man. That was interesting – that peep into his soul.

Its gaze locks on the obsidian idol clutched in the man's hand. It recognises the depiction of the goddess. Born in the age of myths and legends, when faith ruled over logic, mythology gave birth to this goddess, Kali, to combat the forces of evil.

The dead woman had believed in the idol's power. Believed, oh so strongly. Hers had been an implicit, unshakable faith, blind logic defying rationality.

Whereas the man – no, not so much. Not yet.

But he will. Soon. And then they'll meet again.

23

Holt

'Hi Chris. I wasn't expecting you, but I'm glad you are here,' said Holt recognising Dr Chris Cummings amongst the masked group wearing blue overalls and stooped over the supine body on the plush carpeted bedroom floor.

'I was at work anyway when I heard the names. Put two and two together and decided to take a look. Terrible, terrible thing.'

Cummings beckoned the identically clad Holt forward, pointed to Jyoti's throat, where a black gash grinned in the blood-painted neck.

'That seems to be the cause. I can't see anything else obvious, but I'll let you know after I get her on the table. And that looks like the weapon.'

A blood-covered scalpel lay on the carpet close to Jyoti's thigh.

'Brand new. The packaging was in that waste bin.'

'Was there a letter or a note?'

'We didn't find any. Maybe her husband has it?'

'Hmm, I'll ask. So, is it suicide, as they claim?' Holt jerked his head at the trio waiting in the living room with DS Rowena Williams and DC David Plummer.

Cummings raised startled eyes to Holt's. 'Why? Do you suspect otherwise?'

'I don't know. Two of them are surgeons, and they could make a murder look like a suicide.' Holt shook his head in frustration. 'Oh, I'm just being paranoid. This afternoon, she seemed to be coping remarkably well, accepting her son and his friends' deaths. If this is suicide, I should've seen the signs. I should've prevented this.'

Especially with my psychology degree and all those hours of workplace training, he thought bitterly.

'That's nonsense! You cannot take this on yourself. From what I see here, she knew exactly what she was doing. However, I'll keep your concerns in mind when I carry out the PM. I'll prioritize this one, too, and prod Valerie in forensics for you.'

'Thanks Chris. I'll see you later. Now I'd better go talk to them.'

***

With their hotel apartment taped off and declared a crime scene, the victims' fathers moved to a smaller two-room suite. Following Jyoti's death, Prem, the younger of the two Vermas, seemed to have relegated his own misery and stayed close to his older brother and their friend.

Holt could well understand why as he watched Deepak's trembling hands wrap around a mug of tea, even as tremors spasmed through his body. Their friend Roopesh's eyes were glazed; his will and strength tested to the limit.

'Can we hold the interviews elsewhere, Detective Chief Inspector?' Deepak had asked through chattering teeth. 'Even the police station would be preferable. I can't stay here knowing Jyoti is still up there.'

The three men assented to every request; even signed the consent forms for blood samples against the advice of their counsel, and much to the latter's consternation, submitted with quiet dignity to being fingerprinted, photographed, swabbed, and wordlessly donned the track suits and trainers provided in exchange for their clothes and shoes.

Each reacted differently to this latest tragedy.

Deepak appeared calm and emotionless but for the involuntary shudders that spasmed his body every so often. Each time Prem glanced at his brother, which he did frequently, his eyes flooded with tears, and he apologised every time he dashed them away. Roopesh sat stock-still staring at nothing, needing several seconds for every question to register and even longer to form a response, which he then delivered in a monotone.

Their stories matched: *Jyoti had taken herself off to bed while they sat in the lounge sipping brandy. They heard a strange noise but could not pinpoint it or its source. Then, realising the sound originated from Jyoti's room, the trio rushed into the bedroom – Deepak leading the way, with Roopesh and Prem following closely behind. They found her on the floor, bleeding. She died within seconds. No, she hadn't left a note, only said, 'I'm sorry'.*

'She blamed herself for our sons' deaths, DCI Holt,' said Deepak. 'Said she should have insisted they leave or at least transfer to another university in another city. She made them promise not to walk through the parks at night. Did they break their promise several times or just that once? But once was all it took. You cannot change fate, can you, Detective Chief Inspector?'

Questioned about the scalpel, Deepak said, 'Yes, it's one of mine, from a new batch I ordered a few weeks ago. Jyoti always does—did our packing. I didn't even realize she had brought it.'

'Mr Verma, I intended to ask your wife to help put together an e-fit of her vision of your son's killer. Maybe I could've prevented her death had I asked sooner.'

Shock on Rowena's face at his apparent indiscretion. A thoughtful look on Deepak's.

'You believed her then?'

Holt opted for honesty. 'No, not really. Even now, I don't. Not in the visions, but beyond premonitions, there could be a rational explanation. Last night, I decided it wouldn't hurt to ask Mrs Verma to help with an e-fit. It was mainly curiosity on my part. We couldn't use it as evidence, but perhaps it would have given her a reason to live. I'm sorry my decision was too late.'

Deepak sighed, his hand reaching for his beard. Aware of the unconscious action, he snapped his palm on the tabletop. 'You, Detective Chief Inspector, at least considered it. Which is more than I did. To me, it was all superstitious nonsense, and I repeatedly told my wife so. I had no patience with her visions. I wanted her to get help. Psychiatric help, but she would not listen.'

He hunched forward; hands clasped between his knees. 'I should have believed her or at least pretended to.'

He looked up at Holt and Rowena, shook his head. 'No, that wouldn't have worked. She knew me too well; she'd know I was lying. As for whether you could've prevented her death by telling her of your decision, DCI Holt, I very much doubt it. At best, you would've postponed it by a day or two. She was determined to die. I know that now.'

An absolution freely given, but one Holt did not believe he deserved.

'Mr Verma, what can you tell us about this?' Holt laid a clear plastic evidence bag on the table. As one, the three men reared back, their gaze glued to the blood-covered black statuette nestling inside.

'Mr Verma—' prompted Holt when the silence stretched out.

Deepak cleared his throat and raised wide, blood-shot eyes to Holt.

He's afraid of it. They all are, realised Holt, scanning the trio. He squinted at the exquisitely carved, four-armed idol, its surface marred by drying blood. When his gaze returned to Deepak's, the man had regained control of his emotions.

'That, Chief Inspector, is an image of the Hindu goddess Kali. Some call her the demon goddess. It belongs to my family, and my wife worships—worshipped it daily. Believed it would protect our family.' He barked a laugh. 'Some protector it turned out to be, eh?'

'Is her death related to this, Mr Verma? Is it some sort of religious ritual or sacrifice?' Holt's tone was harsh, unable to keep the anger from his voice. He hefted the evidence bag and brought it closer to the men.

'Careful with that, Mr Holt,' Deepak snapped, his hand raised to stay the DCI's. He straightened up in his chair, his face taut with tension. 'That statue is a priceless family heirloom, and it's over 400-years old. Although it looks strong, it's extremely fragile. It's carved from obsidian, which is essentially volcanic glass and is very brittle. I didn't realize my wife had brought it with her. It always remains at home when we travel. I'd like it returned as quickly as possible, please.'

Holt nodded and carefully replaced the bag on the table. 'My knowledge of the goddess Kali is solely from books, the internet and Hollywood depictions. I've read that some scholars claim she existed before the gods of Mesopotamia or the Egyptian pantheon. Could you tell me more about her?'

Deepak laughed, if the harsh sound he made could be called laughter. 'You know, I used to be terrified of it when I was a boy. One of our nannies said it comes alive at night and chases after naughty boys with a big sword. For months, I had nightmares that the goddess Kali was coming to cut off my head. I outgrew it, of course. As for the legend, I can only retell the stories told to me in my childhood—'

***

Millenniums ago, Hindu mythology birthed yet another goddess to add to their assembly of divine beings.

In the age of turmoil and struggle for power between gods and demons, a powerful demon named Raktabija terrorized the three worlds. The gods had granted him a boon that made him nearly invincible: each drop of his blood that touched the ground spawned a clone as powerful as himself.

Unable to defeat Raktabija, the gods turned to the warrior goddess Durga, who rode into battle on her mighty lion to strike down the countless clones. Yet, each time she reached Raktabija and wounded him, his spilled blood multiplied his army until the battlefield overflowed with monstrous foes.

Realising ordinary means would not defeat him, Durga summoned the darkest and most ferocious aspect of herself—Kali. She emerged from Durga's forehead in a burst of fire. Adorned with a garland of skulls, her skin was dark like the void, her eyes burned with untamed fury, and her long tongue flicked hungrily. An enormous tiger materialised beside her, growling and pacing impatiently.

Kali vaulted onto the tiger's back, and the pair leapt into battle with an ear-shattering roar. The two goddesses' multiple arms and powerful weapons slashed through the demon army until they reached Raktabija. Standing feet wide apart, arms akimbo, the arrogant demon laughed, knowing they couldn't wound him for fear of regenerating his army.

But the two goddesses had a strategy. With each slash of Durga's sword, Kali extended her tongue to catch every drop of his blood before it touched the earth.

With no more demons sprouting to defend him, Raktabija soon fell, ending his reign of terror. But Kali's had only just begun. Her fury unspent and intoxicated by bloodlust, she continued her rampage, slaying indiscriminately.

The gods, fearing she would annihilate the world, pleaded with her consort, Lord Shiva, the destroyer, to intervene. Unable or unwilling to restrain her, Shiva laid himself down in her path. When Kali stepped upon him, she stopped, shocked on realising whom she had trampled. In her shock, she bit her tongue in remorse.

***

'____ and that gesture is immortalised in many of Kali's images and statues,' said Deepak. 'But this one,' he pointed to the evidence bag, 'is Kali in her benign form, worshipped as the divine, loving, and benevolent mother. And to answer your question,' he continued, 'no, my wife's death was not a religious ritual or a sacrifice to this or any other god. Somehow she knew – she believed her visions warned her, yet she could do nothing.' He scoffed. 'But believe me, it wasn't for lack of trying. She wanted to take all three boys out of Southampton Uni. Insisted they should continue elsewhere. But none of us believed her. I thought she was mad and told her she needed help.'

He stopped and met Holt's gaze. 'No, DCI Holt. Her suicide was purely guilt. Guilt for not preventing our sons' deaths.'

24

Holt

While a quick shower in the Station's facilities eased the tight bands of tension headache, Holt's nausea from lack of sleep and excess of caffeine persisted. He needed a night's rest, but it wasn't on the menu.

Following a discussion with the Superintendent and the Head of Public Relations, the former grouching like a rudely awakened bear and convinced that all this was a personal vendetta against him and his beloved city, Holt called his core team to his office.

'I've just come from a meeting with the Super and Anita and while we won't be able to keep Jyoti—um, Mrs Verma's suicide out of the press, we've decided there'll be no mention of the obsidian idol or anything that adds the speculation of a cult or ritual sacrifice to the mix,' said Holt to the ashen-faced detectives staring at him in horror at the news of the previous night's events, their shoulders slumped in fatigue.

Their gaze dropped to the statuette sheathed in the transparent evidence pouch, to the serene face and the contradicting items in her four hands.

'That represents the Hindu goddess Kali,' said Holt. 'I can only imagine what the press will make of it and its connotations. We can thank the Indiana Jones movies for that. We don't need that kind of publicity on top of the hate crime and racial tension we're already dealing with,' Holt continued. 'So, this stays strictly between the four of us.'

'To be fair, sir,' said DI Karl Stringer, 'just because Jyoti Verma held this statue while dying does not mean it was a ritual sacrifice. It could be the equivalent of someone holding a Bible, a cross or a rosary. Symbolic, yes, but probably nothing more significant than that.'

'You're right, Karl. It could be purely symbolic, but we still need to consider whether there was any ritualistic element to Jyoti's death. All three men denied any religious significance to the suicide, but despite their professions and scientific backgrounds, it's clear they still retain their religious beliefs. Question is, just how strong are those beliefs and practices? But I'd like to investigate that discreetly.'

Holt turned to DC David Plummer. 'David, as their FLO, you have greater access to them than most and can gauge just how deep their religious practices go. Are you OK to take that on?'

The young DC squared his shoulders and nodded.

'Thank you,' said Holt. 'We'll support you. Just tell us what you need. We need to establish whether this was a suicide or a homicide.'

'You think—?'

'I don't know,' said Holt, frustration straining his voice. 'Not yet. But we have to consider the possibility, especially as her husband and brother-in-law—both of whom are surgeons—and their friend were all present at the crime scene. If it was suicide, for whatever reason, then there's little we can do. However, if those three men were involved or participated in Jyoti's death, then it's a different matter.

***

Shocked silence followed Holt's announcement of the news of Jyoti Verma's death at the team briefing.

'Did she show any sign of her intention to do that, sir?' asked one of the DCs.

'Of course not. We would've done something if we'd suspected.' Rowena interrupted Holt's intended response, her voice loud and sharp.

'Sergeant,' Holt reprimanded quietly. The stress was getting to her, getting to all of them.

'Sorry, sir.'

Holt rubbed his eyes and waved her to continue.

'I'm sorry,' Rowena said to the red-faced Detective Constable, her pitch several notches lower. 'It's been a long, harrowing night. You're right to ask. Her husband insists she meant to kill herself. She came fully prepared, secreted one of his scalpels in her luggage and did not call out until it was too late.'

Was that true? Did they get to Jyoti too late to save her? Two surgeons in the next room – could they really not have saved the woman?

Holt's mind skittered away from the possibility that Deepak had caused Jyoti's death. But he had to consider it. That was his job. Especially when it was someone he had grown to like and admire, even on such a brief acquaintance.

Like a viper slinking through the dense undergrowth, a thought, just as venomous, slithered into his mind.

Is this ritualistic? Did the three men slit Jyoti's throat as a religious sacrifice? Did they also orchestrate their sons' deaths? He drew a sharp breath. *That's pure evil. No one could do that!* But as he well knew, people did all that and more.

But what father would sacrifice his son? No God would ask that... Then he remembered the story from Genesis 22. God had indeed asked Abraham to sacrifice his only son Issac on Mt. Moriah. All to test his follower's faith. And apparently, Abraham did not even question or hesitate to obey the command because he feared his God and loved him more than he loved his own son. *Is that what this is about? A test of faith?*

'Sir?'

Holt looked up, refocused. 'The coroner has opened an inquest and ordered a post-mortem. Dr Cummings promised to prioritize the autopsy, and while we wait for the results, I'd like you to consider why any, or all of the three men may want her dead.'

Eyes widened at his bald statement.

'You don't think—? Sir, do you really believe they killed her?'

'Well, it looks like suicide, and God knows there's enough reason to explain her actions. Barely a few hours before her death, Jyoti—Mrs Verma—was at the mortuary identifying her only son's body. Although she appeared to be coping, I suspect she was in a very fragile state of mind. But we still cannot rule anything out. We treat this death like any other. Look for any extramarital relationships, money. Who profits from her demise? What insurance policies did she have? What was the couple's relationship like? Did Jyoti cause any problems for or among them?'

Glum nods.

'What about those visions Jyoti told us about, sir?' asked Rowena.

'What visions, Sarge?' asked DC Larry Ives. The big, paunchy 38-year-old's face mirrored the blank faces of the other detectives.

'Yesterday afternoon, Jyoti Verma told us she'd been having visions.' Holt curled his fingers into fists to stop them from making air quotes around the word visions. 'Nightmares about the three young men's deaths. Her family brushed them aside as superstition or paranoia. Yesterday, she described the crime scene and her son's wounds to us in uncanny detail. She didn't get that from the media reports. We've released nothing about the wounds to the press.'

'Visions, sir? We're not turning to psychics and mediums now, are we?' Larry's scathing tone earned him a glare from Holt and his colleagues.

'No, Larry. We'll wait for a week at least before we do that,' Holt snapped, then continued more normally.

'She also described her son's murderer. My initial reaction was the same as yours, Larry, but Jyoti's description intrigued me. I planned for a technician to work with her to put together an e-fit of the alleged killer.'

'Do you believe in all that, sir?' asked DI Karl Stringer.

'No, of course not. There could be a logical explanation. She may have met or seen this person before, even had some interaction she didn't remember. Or noticed something going on between him and her son or his friends. I thought an e-fit could help.'

'Sir,' interrupted Rowena. 'IT just sent the messages from the missing mobile phone. The one found in the tree.' She held up her open laptop.

'Good, get it up on screen.'

'The phone belongs... belonged to Ravi Verma. The last number dialled was incomplete. He tapped 99, reckon it must be to 999. Forensics think the attacker grabbed the phone before he finished dialling. They're checking for fingerprints and will let us know if they find any. This is his last text message. It's to his mum.'

Rowena fiddled with her laptop and soon the large wall monitor displayed the message, drafted just seconds before the attack.

The message on the large screen read:

'... *Ma, great party. heading home now. met luvly girl Emily. I REALLY like her. U wl luv her 2...*'

'Did Ravi send it?'

Rowena shook her head. 'No, he didn't get the chance.'

25

Holt

Day four of the investigation and bugger all to show for it. The multiple filaments of inquiry lines continued to branch, stretch and radiate, growing into Holt's most complex and showiest cobweb, yet not a single gnat adhered to any of its sticky strands.

A hate crime or racist attack seemed less and less likely. No amount of aggressive or subtle questioning, poking, prodding, or probing into those dark corners yielded any results. Certain organisations had even taken the trouble to deny responsibility. Which tied in with Holt's gut feeling. This was personal. Someone killed those medical students because of *who* they were, not *what* they represented.

The team continued to dig into the victims and their families' backgrounds, which so far had produced zilch. He now knew a lot about them, their finances, their comings and goings, but not why they or someone else would kill their sons.

Reports and notes continued pouring in as officers interviewed victims' friends, fellow students, tutors, lecturers and hospital staff. They had even interviewed the staff of the takeaways delivering pizzas and curries, which were the victims' staple diet, when they ran out of food cooked by their housekeeper.

Nada on bins and drains searches around the park. Ditto from door-to-doors. Nothing from forensics. The hours spent going through CCTV footage produced nothing but eyestrain, with several hours of recordings still to be viewed.

The family liaison officer, DC David Plummer, reported no untoward religious inclinations or practices by the three fathers, and the evidence board remained depressingly blank, except for two photos from a CCTV at the north exit of Holburn Park. The first showed the backs of four hooded figures; the second was a magnification of a jacket's logo.

Holt leaned in, squinted at the fluorescent logo. *Was that a skull? Looks like one.* The tech chaps had done their best, but the image was still too fuzzy to tell for sure.

Waiting for a break was the hardest part, especially with the Super breathing down his neck and the media hounding their footsteps.

'Sir,' said Karl, joining him. 'One of the Westlands estates PCSOs recognised that logo. She described it as a clever design. A silver skull sitting above an X made up of a bone and a lightning bolt. Inside the lightning bolt are the letters 'treem'. Combined with the X, they form the gang's mark 'Xtreem'. She'll ask around and get us some names soon.'

'Finally, something to get us started.'

***

By noon, Holt decided he had cleared enough email messages, signed off more requisitions than he could recall, and read all the reports he could stand. He stood up to go for a walk when knuckles rapped on his office door, and it opened to reveal DI Karl Stringer.

He sat back with a sigh. *This had better be good.*

'Sir,' said Karl, 'IDENT1 threw up a match on the partial fingerprint on Ravi Verma's phone. It belongs to one Duncan Hughes, eighteen-and-a-half-years-old. He lives on the Westlands Estates.'

A logo on a jacket and now a hit from our fingerprint database, both from the Westlands Estates. That's not a coincidence.

'Why do we have his fingerprints?'

'Duncan Hughes was arrested last year for shoplifting. First offence. They let him off with a caution.'

'What does he look like, this Duncan?'

Holt studied the fourteen-month-old photos in the police database. The stab of disappointment was almost physical. What was he expecting? That the image would match the killer in Jyoti Verma's visions? The long, narrow-featured face, pale blue eyes topped with lank, light brown hair and a derisive smile did, by no stretch of the imagination, accord with Jyoti's description of her son's killer.

'Excellent. Get cracking on background info. Find out who Duncan was with that night. This wasn't one person's work. The witness, Walter McCabe, saw four people at that exit.'

'Should we get him in, sir?'

'Not yet. Let's do this right. Duncan is now our main—well, only suspect. He and his accomplices have already had over three days to get their stories right and destroy evidence. If he were a flight risk, he would've gone by now. Dig up everything you can on him, his family and friends.'

An hour later, the team presented Holt with information on Duncan.

Duncan Hughes (eighteen-and-a-half) had dropped out of school at 16, and thereafter, avoided Social Services' attention through token efforts at apprenticeship and employment. He lived in Block C in Westland Estates with his brother Leo (sixteen), his mother and his father, or rather, stepfather, who was currently serving time at HMP Winchester.

Since their father's incarceration, he'd taken his younger brother, Leo, under his wing. Duncan's best friend was a young man named Thomas Wade (nineteen), whom friends called Tommy.

For the past eight months, the three youths and Leo's best friend, Derek Dawson (seventeen), were frequently seen together. They went through a phase of calling themselves the "Xtreem" and even had a logo designed and stencilled on the backs of their jackets.

Holt scrolled through the details and clicked on the images of the younger members of the 'gang' collated from their social media accounts. Leo and his friend Derek appeared together in many of them, the former a quiet, thin, curly-haired lad, while his friend was more extrovert, impish and appeared younger than seventeen.

The next image, that of Duncan's best friend, stopped Holt dead. Thomas—Tommy—Wade's driving licence photo was a perfect match to Jyoti Verma's description of her son's killer.

Short, curly blond hair, deep blue eyes and the face of a Botticelli angel.

His pulse raced. The surge of anticipation coursing through his veins chased off all vestige of fatigue. There was still much to be done, but he could sense closure, taste victory.

'Sir, if Duncan was at the park that night, the PCSO believes the others were likely there as well. Most of the time, they hang out at Tommy Wade's place. We've got eyes on them, and they're in their homes right now. Shall I round up a team of uniforms and go arrest them?' asked Karl.

Yes, Holt wanted to shout, but caution tempered enthusiasm.

'No! If we're right, then these four are killers. They used knives at the park, but what's to say they don't have firearms too? We can't risk it. I'll request an armed response unit. You get the arrest and search warrants. I want full forensics on their homes and cars. With luck, we could still find trace evidence there.'

26

Karl

'The boss wasn't happy, was he?' grinned DI Karl Stringer, manoeuvring his car around parked vehicles.

'No,' laughed DS Rowena Williams. 'He was most put out that he had to stay in to keep the Super and ACC updated. Babysitting them, he called it.'

DCI Holt's request for armed response was granted in record time, as were the arrest and search warrants. The senior brass and even the courts had cooperated, relieved at finally having something to show to the press and the public.

Karl pulled into a parking space two streets away, and the detectives hiked to join the armed response unit assembling on the perimeter of Westlands Estates.

Ten minutes ago, just as the firearms officers were splitting into three groups to raid each of the suspects' homes, they'd received messages from the patrols watching the suspects that all four youths had congregated at Tommy Wade's flat. The officers had reacted quickly to the revised plan and regrouped, but tackling four possibly armed suspects simultaneously had upped the stakes considerably.

Karl and Rowena approached the heavyset, black-garbed sergeant at the centre of a group of a dozen officers in full tactical gear.

'Ah, there you are,' said the officer, turning to the new arrivals. 'Hey Karl,' he pumped the DI's hand, grinning when Karl winced, though he was a lot gentler with Rowena. 'They seem to be holed up inside for now, playing video games from the sounds of it. We're ready to move in. Here, put these on.' He held out Kevlar vests, helmets and gas masks.

A broad shouldered helmeted and masked officer scooped up an enforcer tool stashed between his feet. *It looks well-used*, thought Karl, eyeing the 16-kg item with the red paint long worn off its head and shaft. He hoped it would work the first time, and that the suspect's door, locks and hinges weren't reinforced, needing repeated attempts to smash through. In his last experience in a similar operation, the door had sustained the enforcer's first attempt, and the noise had alerted the gang within. Bullets flew through the door on the second swing of the battering ram, injuring an officer, and leaving only two of the five suspects alive to arrest.

But Karl's doubts turned to relief when he noticed another officer with a backpack containing an electro-hydraulic pump and a door breacher spreader attached to the magnetic clip on his chest.

He tightened the Velcro on the Kevlar vest and nodded 'ready' to the sergeant.

'My guys know what to do. You two stay behind us; enter only when we give the all clear. I don't want to worry about the two of you. OK?' The Sergeant's tone brooked no argument, and the detectives nodded. From Rowena's moue of disappointment, she clearly wanted to be in the middle of the action, whereas Karl was content to take a back seat.

The sergeant had his team check their protective wear and equipment once again and brought his wrist up, his glance dropping to his watch. His officers tensed, their eyes fixed on him, ready to explode into action at his signal.

'Right, let's go,' barked the Sergeant, adjusting his safety glasses and raising his mask over his mouth and nose.

In a synchronised movement, the team split up and dashed off to their assigned positions. Two veered off to cover the rear exit, two positioned themselves on either side of the front entrance while the rest raced silently up the flight of stairs.

On the fourth floor, the officers lined up against the wall on both sides of a grey door that may once have been white, with number 45 in chrome. Muffled sounds—a chaotic mix of rapid gunfire, digital explosions, swearing and laughter—bled through from inside the flat.

A whispered confirmation crackled over the radio—perimeter secured, exits covered. At the sergeant's nod, the man with the backpack knelt before the door, attached the door frame spreader, checked the connecting tube, and stepped back against the wall.

The sergeant raised his hand and dropped it in a sharp motion.

The officer with the backpack pumped up the battery-powered hydraulics while the man carrying the enforcer tool stepped up to the front door.

'Go, go, go!'

The team swung into action. The immense pressure exerted by the door spreader thrust the doorframe apart while the enforcer tool swung back and crashed into the door. Which exploded.

An officer lobbed a smoke grenade inside. A thud and, an instant later, a thick, billowing cloud of grey smoke filled the small flat.

'Police! Armed police! Get down! Don't move!' bellowed the Sergeant, barging into the room.

A swirling haze filled the room before the four young men could react. They coughed and stumbled blindly into the furniture and into each other.

Protected by their gas masks, the police moved with precision through the thick fog. The infrared optics on their helmets cut through the smoke, showing them outlines and movement even in the near-zero visibility.

One suspect scrambled to his feet, but an officer pushed him face-first onto the sofa, knee pressing between his shoulder blades. Another officer forced a second suspect to his knees on the floor and cuffed his hands behind him.

'Hands where we can see them! Do not move!' shouted the sergeant again, kicking aside the coffee table to ensure nothing was within reach of the suspects.

Despite the sergeant's warning, one youth tried to make a dash to the open door but only managed two paces before an officer grabbed his wrist, twisted his arm behind his back and pinned him to a wall.

The fourth suspect coughed and stumbled towards a bedroom, but the sergeant tackled him to the floor while another planted a heavy boot on his back to hold him immobile and cuffed his wrists.

The sergeant checked behind the sofa. Another officer called out, 'Clear!' from the bathroom and yet another repeated the same from the flat's only bedroom. They worked with military efficiency, leaving no space unchecked as the last remnants of smoke thinned and drifted towards the shattered doorway and dissipated into the corridor.

'All clear,' yelled the Sergeant, waving Karl and Rowena into the room.

'You lot better pay for that!' shouted the oldest suspect hoarsely. 'You can't just smash my door in like that!'

'That's your problem, mate, not ours.' Ignoring him, the sergeant asked Karl, 'Are these your suspects?'

The detectives zeroed in on the enraged flat owner gripped in place by armed officers, and grinned. 'Oh, yes! Indeed, they are.'

'Go on, then. Make your arrests.'

'With pleasure,' said Karl. He faced the struggling flat owner. 'Thomas Wade, you're under arrest on suspicion of murder. You do not have to say anything, but it may harm your defence if you do not mention when questioned something you later rely on in court. Anything you do say may be given in evidence.'

Beside him, he heard Rowena recite the arrest caution to the other suspects and their accompanying protests of, 'but we ain't done nuffin.'

'Thank you,' said Karl, bracing himself for the crushing pressure of the sergeant's handshake. 'That was brilliantly done.'

'Anytime. Come on lads, let's get this lot to the nick and safely locked up.'

'Oh, Sergeant, please seal the flat and post one of your men on guard here. It's a crime scene. I'll call the CSI,' said Rowena.

Karl flinched while the sergeant replied in a broad Irish brogue, 'Sure, ma'am. An' do ya not tink te words, grandma, suck and eggs come ta mind, eh?'

Sure enough, when Rowena turned around, an officer was already stringing strips of yellow crime scene tape across the door. She reddened, but rallied and called out, 'Sorry' to the departing sergeant.

He grinned, waved, and the officers marched the suspects out in single file, past the row of neighbours crowding the corridor or gawking from their doorways, and bundled them into the waiting police vans.

The reinforced doors slammed shut and, sirens wailing, the vans sped off to the Station.

27

Holt

'Go fuck yourself,' yelled the suspect, springing to his feet.

'Hey, watch your mouth,' growled the uniformed constable, pushing him back into the chair while DCs Larry Ives and David Plummer leaned back and stared expressionlessly at Duncan Hughes. His counsel made soothing noises and patted the table, which, like the chairs, was screwed to the floor.

A few doors down the corridor, Holt clicked his tongue and huffed at the video broadcast of the twitching young man dressed in navy tracksuit bottoms and sweater issued to him in the custody suite. Forensics had also seized his clothes, shoes and the knives in their kitchen, which Duncan's mum had not at all been happy about.

Too bad they weren't covered in bloodstains. Then we could all go home and get some well-earned sleep.

'Get off me!' The suspect twisted his shoulders. 'I done nuffin.'

'Where were you at 11.30 p.m. last Thursday night, Duncan?' asked Larry.

'At me mate Tommy's.'

'We have CCTV, which puts you at Holburn Park.'

'So what?'

'So obviously, you weren't at Tommy's, as you stated.'

'Maybe I was near the park first before I got to his. So what?'

'Tell us exactly what you did on Thursday evening.'

'Like I told you, my mum was not well, so I got us dinner. My brother Leo washed up an' Mum went to bed. Then we left for Tommy's.'

'What was wrong with your mum? She looks fine in there with your brother.' Larry jerked a thumb over his shoulder.

'She's better now. But she was ill that night. Some woman trouble.'

Holt suppressed a sigh. *Good thing we can hold this lot for thirty-six hours. Looks like we'll need it too!*

He studied the lanky youth. *What's with the tattoos and piercings?* Long, narrow face, close-cropped dark hair, sides bleached white and shaved at the back in a swirl pattern, dyed blue, red and green. His left hand displayed a well-crafted tattoo. It matched the fluorescent logo on the back of the jacket. At first glance, it looked like a pirate skull and crossbones; however, a lightning bolt replaced the left bone, and within the bolt was the word 'treem'. Combined with the X, they formed the gang's mark 'Xtreem'.

Holt wondered whether they even realised the spelling error.

Duncan's arrest a year ago for shoplifting earned him a place in IDENT1, the national fingerprints database. Because it was his first offence, or at least, the first time he'd been caught, he only received a caution.

What did he steal? Holt wondered, flicking through the file. *Ah, here. A Tommy Hilfiger T-shirt retailed at fifty pounds. Hmm, interesting. Was it for himself or as a gift for his friend Tommy?*

The spree of petty thefts and minor vandalism stopped with Duncan's arrest. Sporadic stop and searches following rumours of the boys dealing in drugs found nothing on them, and the PCSOs, who had bigger problems to deal with, left them alone. And while fights between the youth gangs were a part of life on the Westlands estate, they'd never escalated to murder.

'OK, so you went to Tommy's. Did your brother go with you too?'

'Yeah, we both did, and Derek came too. You know, Leo's friend.'

'What time was this, Duncan?'

'Ahem, lemme think, after nine, yeah, just after nine o'clock.'

'So, what time did you go into Holburn Park?'

'Detectives, my client already said he did not go into the Park,' interrupted Duncan's counsel, emphasising the word into.

'OK, what time did you go to Holburn Park, Duncan?'

'Bout ten o'clock?'

'How did you get there?'

'In Tommy's car.'

'And what did you do there? It wasn't a night to be hanging about.'

'It was fine till then, wasn't even cold. Tommy treated us to some burgers and chips, and we hung around.'

'Just hanging around outside the park for two hours on a stormy Thursday night, huh?'

'Well, it wasn't stormy then, was it?' said Duncan. 'That din' start till really late. It was fine when we were there. We sat an' ate our burgers an' just messed around, you know, then when it started raining like, we took off.'

The background information about Duncan Hughes was interesting. His biological father disappeared from the scene when he was two. The story was that Duncan's father, Ronald Kirby, had a penchant for using his girlfriend Crystal as a punching bag, which occasionally extended to their young son. A fortnight after Duncan's second birthday, Kirby beat Crystal senseless for *getting too friendly* with their neighbour, one Daniel Hughes. He had just picked up the crying toddler when Daniel Hughes kicked the front door in, punched Kirby, and broke his jaw.

Witnesses saw Kirby stagger out of the flat cradling his face, followed by Hughes's threat that his neck would be next if Kirby ever came there again.

Six months later, Crystal gave birth to another baby boy, Leo. The mixed-race baby's arrival revealed that she'd been doing more than making eyes at her neighbour.

Daniel Hughes, a car mechanic at a local garage, turned out to be a strict but devoted father to both boys, protecting the reedy, young Duncan through his bumpy childhood and adolescence.

'And where's Tommy's car now?'

Holt thumbed through the briefing notes. Despite extensive searches, the police had not yet located Tommy Wade's car.

'Huh? How should I know? At the back of his building where he always parks it?'

'The jacket you wore that night—the one with your gang logo—where is it?' Holt heard DC Larry Ives ask Duncan.

'We ain't got a gang, man. Us four jus' got same jackets, is all.'

'With the same pattern as your tattoo?' DC David Plummer pointed to Hughes' hand.

'Yeah, so?'

'Who designed the logo? You?'

'Yeah, so?'

'It's very good.'

'Oh!' The suspect frowned and squinted, checking for sarcasm but seeing none, smiled at the compliment.

'So, where's that jacket? You were wearing it on Thursday night.'

'I lost it.'

'You lost it. How? Where?'

'I think I left it in Tommy's car.'

'Is it still there?'

'Dunno, I din' look.'

'What does your stepfather think about what you did that night?'

'My dad? Why should my dad think anything? I already told you, I din' do nothing.'

'We know that's not true, Duncan. You see, we have your fingerprint on one of the victim's phones. Would you care to explain how it got there?'

The youth's face turned blank for a moment, followed by a strange expression, quickly masked by rubbing his eyes. Surprise and indignation covered his face when he faced the detectives and cameras again.

'You lyin' man. That's not possible. I was nowhere near any of them, and I din' touch none of their phones.'

'Well, it certainly was your fingerprint, Duncan. That's how we found you. We matched it to your prints we have on record, from when you stole that T-shirt fourteen months ago.'

Red-faced, Duncan blinked in surprise. *Had he forgotten that incident? Or forgotten they still had his fingerprints on file?*

'No way my fingerprint's on that phone.' He squinted at the detectives. 'You, one of your lot, must've put my print there. I know you can do that now.'

This time, Duncan's counsel pulled at his sleeve, shushing him. They argued while the detectives sat stone-faced, watching.

'Sorry,' muttered Duncan.

'It definitely is your fingerprint on the phone, Duncan mate,' said Larry. 'That, along with the CCTV image, puts you squarely in the frame for a murder charge. We'll take a 30-minute break and let you talk it over with your lawyer.'

Formally suspending the interview, the detectives left the room.

28

Holt

The viewing monitor of the adjoining interview room showed their second suspect leaning back in his chair with his arms crossed and a smile on his face while his counsel whispered urgently in his ear.

The nineteen-year-old looked younger, innocent. Smooth, chiselled face, straight narrow nose, short, deep blond hair springing back from a high forehead. His thick-lashed, deep blue eyes attracted and held attention. Average height, slim build, the lad appeared unconscious of his looks, even played it down.

Tommy Wade. *The boy with very blue eyes and short golden hair. Beautiful, like one of Botticelli's angels...* Jyoti Verma's description of her son's killer in her so-called vision.

While his counsel sat poker-faced and silent beside him, Tommy Wade lifted his head, smiled as DI Karl Stringer and DS Rowena Williams walked in. It brought an instinctive response and lift to the detectives' mouths until their eyes met the startling blue depths of the young man's. Tommy's smile did not extend beyond the mouth; those beautiful eyes were cold, hard, expressionless.

At Karl's nod, the constable standing behind Tommy turned and left the room.

Tommy Wade leaned forward, his eyes fixed on Rowena. His smile widened, then slowly faded at meeting Rowena's narrowed, piercing, and unwavering gaze. A stare she'd perfected over the years. Holt grinned. That man might know a lot about control and intimidation, but he was no match for the detective sergeant.

Not yet anyway, but he's young; he'll learn.

Karl, who was leading the interview, made the formal introductions for the recordings and turned to the suspect.

'Thomas, or do you prefer to be called Tommy?'

'My friends call me Tommy. You can too if you like.'

'Why thank you, Tommy. I'd like to ask you a few questions.'

'Why? I already said I don't know nothing about those park murders.'

'So you said. I'd like to go through them again, please.' Karl's relaxed tone was friendly but firm, a tactic honed and sharpened not only at work with witnesses and suspects, but also daily at home with his teenage children.

'OK.'

'Where were you between 11 p.m. last Thursday night and 2 a.m. Friday morning, Tommy?'

'Like I said, I was out with me mates. Then we went home, slept for a bit and played games.'

'We have CCTV of you near the Holburn Park just before midnight.'

'Yeah, so?'

'What were you doing there?'

'I bought burgers and chips and some Coke from that takeaway near there. Is that a crime now?'

'How'd you get to Holburn Park?'

'In my car.'

'Where'd you park in town?'

'I found a spot on St Mary's Street and dint even have to pay.'

Holt consulted the notes. So far, the youth's answers checked out.

'Where did you go after that?'

'We sat on a bench an' ate our burgers.'

'When did you go into the park?'

'I didn't go inside the park.'

'Did your friends?'

'No, man. No one did. We stayed only on the bench outside.'

'And then?' prompted Karl.

'And then we went home.'

'How did you get back home?'

'Huh? In my car, of course. How else?' Tommy rolled his eyes and clicked his tongue.

Beneath the tabletop, Rowena's fingers curled into fists while Karl's nostrils flared as he drew in a deep, calming breath.

'So, all of you returned home together and nobody went into the park last night?'

'Right, you're clever, man.' He clicked his fingers at Karl.

'Then how do you explain the fingerprints we found at the crime scene?'

The handsome face tightened. 'Fingerprints...' he repeated before pulling himself together. 'What fingerprints? No way. I already told you I wasn't inside the park or where they said the murders happened.'

'That's not true, is it, Tommy? We have witnesses who saw the attackers.'

'Saw me? Inside the park?' His voice was full of incredulity and indignation, eyes darting between Karl and Rowena. 'That's a lie. They're lying, man. I wasn't in the park, and they're lying if they say they saw me and me mates there.'

Holt leaned closer to the screen, staring at the youth, willing him to look into the camera.

'No way, man,' Tommy repeated. 'We ate and hung around for a while outside. We weren't inside the park, and we didn't attack nobody.'

'Where's the jacket you wore last Thursday night?'

'Your lot got it. They took all my clothes and all my knives and things, and gave me this rubbish to wear,' he said tugging at the police issue dark blue sweater.

'I mean your jacket with your gang's logo on it.'

'Oh, that one. I wasn't wearing it that night. I think I wore that two weeks ago – you know, on that one sunny day we had? It was hot, and I took it off and left it in my car. I forgot to take it in, so it's still in the car.'

If he's telling the truth, Duncan Hughes wore the gang jacket that night. Judging by the person's height in the CCTV image, it most likely was Duncan.

'Who else was wearing your gang brand that night?' asked Karl.

'There's no gang, man! And we haven't got no brand. For a while, we thought the name sounded cool.' He frowned. 'That's not a crime, is it?'

'Not unless you use it to intimidate anyone or for illegal purposes.'

Tommy shook his head. 'We don't do neither of those things.'

'I see.'

Unlike Duncan Hughes, Tommy had no record, so no fingerprints on the police database, and no reported anti-social behaviour. Barely two pages of notes lay in the slim folder on the table beside Holt's hands.

Tommy's mother had left her five-year-old son to elope with his father's best friend. She never contacted her son again. For a while, the child's father, Brian Wade, tried to raise the boy by himself, but the man's own problems soon overwhelmed him. Social Services stepped in when a concerned neighbour reported that the father frequently left the five-year-old alone at home while he visited the local pub. A sharp reprimand and the threat to take the boy away resulted in the father doing his drinking at home instead. This had worked out fine for a year until one day neighbours noticed smoke filtering through the gaps in the window frame.

Attending firefighters found the little boy trying to undo the front door latches while his father lay passed out in front of the television. The fire had started in the kitchen, and the investigating officers surmised that the young lad had ignited a tea towel while trying to light the stove. Frightened, he must have thrown the burning cloth on the floor, setting a pile of papers on fire. A paper bin lay empty, likely kicked over as the boy rushed out of the kitchen.

No one challenged the newspaper piled on the kitchen floor. Everyone assumed the father had dropped them there before going into the living room to resume drinking.

This time, the father raised no objections when Social Services took his son away to a foster home. They traced the boy's mother, but she wanted nothing to do with her son. They also deemed her lifestyle unsuitable for the beautiful, well-behaved little boy.

Despite living with the same foster parents until he was 16, Tommy had formed no emotional ties at all with them.

The boy's father, Brian Wade, sobered up enough to keep his job as a cleaner with a public services company. He even had a life insurance policy to pay off the mortgage on the one-bedroom flat, which his son inherited upon his death from lung cancer nine years later. A further sum from the older Wade's death-in-service pension scheme gave his son financial independence, and as soon as he turned sixteen, the youth moved out of his foster home and into his father's vacant flat.

'Right,' said Karl. 'Where's your car?'

Tommy tensed and frowned. 'Huh, what you mean where's my car? Back of the building where I always park it.'

'Well, it isn't there now.'

After a brief consultation with his solicitor, Tommy replied, 'If it ain't there, it must've got stolen.'

'Stolen. I see. When did you last see it?'

'Last Thursday night when we came home from the park.'

'That's four days ago! Four days, Tommy, and you didn't realize your car's missing?'

'Well, I dint need it, did I? I dint think to check. I just took the bus after that. It's cheaper, and parking's a pain in town.'

That's true, thought Holt.

'Did you report it?'

'Report it? Man, I dint even realize it was stolen. Maybe one of me mates might've borrowed it?'

'Who?' Karl and Rowena were alert, their attention fully centred on the suspect, scenting blood.

'Don' know,' said Tommy.

'Are your friends in the habit of borrowing your car?'

'Yeah, sure. It ain't a big deal.'

'They'd have to come to you for the car key, wouldn't they?'

'Oh, yeah. 'Course,' Tommy clicked his finger.

'So, where is it now?'

'It must've got nicked. Some bastards must've nicked my car. Yeah, that's what must've happened. An' now, I'm reporting it stolen.' Another wide smile displayed white, even teeth.

'You don't seem to be overly concerned,' said Karl.

Tommy shrugged. 'Shit happens, man. It was a crappy set of wheels, anyway.'

'What are the make, colour and licence number of your car?'

'It's a dark blue Ford Fiesta, LM52 LTW. You gonna look for it?'

'Of course. Meanwhile, won't it be inconvenient for you to be without a car?'

'Hmm. Yeah, it will.' He brightened up. 'Guess I'll jus' have to get myself new wheels.'

Holt felt a pang of sympathy for Karl. *I bet his fist is dying to wipe the smile off Tommy's face.*

He frowned as a phone buzzed, saw Karl and Rowena glower at the solicitor, who muttered an apology. 'Excuse me, I really need to get this.'

Brows furrowed and glaring at the solicitor, Karl suspended the interview. A knock on the door interrupted them. The custody sergeant poked his head into the room, apologised and beckoned the detectives outside. Holt hastened to join Karl, Rowena and the custody sergeant in the hallway outside the interview room.

'Sir, the duty solicitors representing the four suspects have all received urgent calls from their offices. Apparently, their clients dismissed them all and are replacing them with someone else.'

'Who?'

'They didn't say, sir. But we can't interview any of them until their new solicitor arrives.'

'Damn!'

Stymied, Holt and the two detectives watched Tommy's solicitor return to his client. Two heads bent close together in animated discussion. Three minutes later, the solicitor stepped out of the interview room.

'It seems I'm dismissed and someone else will replace me shortly. Until then, please ensure that you do not question Mr Wade.'

Oddly, the solicitor didn't seem unhappy or put out with the abrupt dismissal.

29

Holt

Rowena poked her head around Holt's office door. 'Sir, one Andrew Metcalf is with the Super asking for his clients,' she said.

Puzzlement replaced the grim lines of anger on his face. 'Did you say Andrew Metcalf, the defence lawyer?'

Rowena nodded. 'Says he's representing Duncan Hughes and all his friends.'

'You sure? Andrew Metcalf representing this lot?'

Metcalf was waiting in the superintendent's office and neither looked pleased when Holt and Rowena arrived.

'I want to see my clients.' He didn't bother to stand or greet the DCI.

'Certainly. DS Williams here will take you to Mr Hughes.'

Holt watched the smartly dressed solicitor huff off behind Rowena. He waited until the door clicked shut.

'We need to detain them for as long as we can, sir.'

'Have you any actual evidence?'

'Only what I already told you. Both the older lads' jackets and Tommy's car are missing. That's suspicious. The evidence could be in the car, and that's why it's missing. We need to ask the magistrate for an extension, sir.'

Simpson drummed his fingers on the desk. 'I doubt you'll get an extension based on the evidence so far.'

Holt threw himself into the visitor's chair. 'I know,' he grouched. 'We may get an extension for Duncan Hughes based on his unexplained fingerprint, but there's nothing on Tommy beyond his missing jacket and car. We could insist that his car is linked to the crime and that we suspect it contains evidence material to a murder investigation and possibly charge Tommy for perverting the course of justice and obstructing the police, but everything we have so far is circumstantial at a stretch. And there's even less on the two younger boys.'

'Well, you have those options available. But for now, you have until 10 p.m—that's seven hours—to work on them. Any longer than that, and they'll accuse us of abusing their human rights. Metcalf's quite pissed off already.'

***

'What the f..., I mean, hell just happened, sir?' Karl loosened his tie and rubbed his forehead. 'I can feel a lump growing right here from hitting that brick wall.'

Holt and his team slumped in their seats in the major incident room, where they had grouped after re-interviewing the four suspects in the presence of their new lawyer.

'Nicely put,' said Larry. 'That lawyer wouldn't let our suspect—Derek Dawson—say anything. The boy kept "no commenting" and grinning throughout. What about yours?'

DC Michelle Bruges shook her curls. 'Salim and I interviewed young Leo Hughes. He gave a prepared statement, then just sat there looking petrified, stuttering 'no comment' when prompted by Metcalf.'

'Same here,' said Rowena. 'David and I questioned Duncan Hughes. Claims he has no clue how his fingerprint got on the phone and insists he was not inside the park. Even accused us of lying and planting his fingerprint. He *thinks* he left his jacket in Tommy's car, which, of course, is missing. Forensics examined their shoes for traces of grass and grit unique to Holburn Park and specific to the SOC but found nothing to put any of them there.'

'The boss and I got nothing either,' said DI Karl Stringer. 'We tried to push him about producing the car, but Metcalf advised him it is up to us to establish relevance and prove that Tommy was even at the crime scene. And for the rest, he kept saying, "My client has already answered the question." He seemed to know you, sir.'

'Yes, I've had the pleasure of meeting Mr Metcalf when I was with the Met. With him on the scene, we must think big. He usually represents companies and their top brass in the gambling sector, so what's he doing representing this lot? He doesn't come cheap; we need to find out who's bankrolling his fees and why?'

'Do you think our victims were targeted, sir? Assassinated?'

'We've got to give it serious consideration, especially with Metcalf involved. But why choose these four youths? If someone can afford Metcalf, they can afford to hire professional hitmen who'd do such a neat job that we wouldn't even suspect it wasn't an accident.'

'Who do you think is paying Metcalf, sir?' asked Rowena.

Karl laughed. 'The boss asked him, and Metcalf said, "*That is none of your business, Detective Chief Inspector.*"'

Holt grinned at Karl's imitation of Metcalf's plummy tones.

'I'll contact former colleagues at the Met. Perhaps they can help.'

'Are we sure it's them, sir?' asked DI Karl Stringer. 'Could it be someone else altogether? Some other students, or even one of the racist or religious groups?'

'If it were a racist or religious attack, there'd be something by now. Some propaganda, someone claiming so-called responsibility, some slogan or at least some chatter on social media, but so far, Ian and Salim had found nothing. Besides, there's some pretty compelling evidence. We have Duncan Hughes' fingerprint on the mobile. That's proof of his involvement, especially when he claims to have no acquaintance with the victims. They don't move in the same circles, so how did Duncan's fingerprint end up on Ravi Verma's mobile? Our witness, Walter McCabe's certain he saw four people run out of the park.'

'And the CCTV footage puts them outside the park,' reminded Rowena.

Holt nodded. 'Yes, but that might not be enough. Forensics searched their homes and turned up absolutely nothing. No sign of blood anywhere – no blood-stained knives, clothes and no blood in the bathrooms, sinks, or washing machines. Whoever killed those lads would have blood on them, so where is it? Anything from the bins and drain searches near their homes?'

'No, sorry, sir,' said Larry. 'We were lucky their bin collection is on Wednesdays, so the Council hadn't yet picked up their rubbish. I've been coordinating with TAC Ops. They've been exceptional. They turned out in force and worked through a week's worth of household waste. You can imagine what that was like. Not pleasant, not pleasant at all. But they found nothing. No weapons or clothes, bloodstained or otherwise.'

'What about Tommy's missing car?'

'Again, nothing, sir. We can confirm the car was in St. Mary's Street, and we checked the ANPR[1] database, but beyond showing it heading towards Tommy's home, there's nothing after that. I've asked for a marker to be put on PNC[2] for stop, occupants arrested, and vehicle secured for a full forensic lift.'

'We've widened the CCTV search around the suspects' homes. Most of the public cameras around the housing estates were vandalised. Businesses and properties in the area have already given us their recordings, and we've started viewing them, but it'll take time,' added Karl. 'Uniforms are carrying out a visual check in the neighbourhood for the vehicle. We should have something by tomorrow morning.'

Holt knuckled his eyes, stretched. 'What we have so far is circumstantial, and I'm sure CPS[3] won't agree to charge. We need more.'

He straightened. 'Rowena, Karl, get people to turn those suspect's life inside out. Check for anything linking them to the victims. If it's this lot, they had some serious help. Larry, dig deeper into the racist angle. Follow up every known group and individual out there. Was this homicide on anyone's agenda? Check whether these suspects have any connections or belong to any of those groups. Get bodies out there to talk to their neighbours, friends, the PCSOs and all community outreach

---

1. Automatic Number Plate Recognition – cameras used to capture images of vehicles, read and record the registration/licence number plates.

2. Police National Computer. The principal police database that stores and shares criminal records and information across the UK.

3. Crown Prosecution Service.

groups again, including churches, mosques, temples – you name it, where our suspects live and hang about. Talk to their teachers. Well, you know the drill.'

'Ian, Salim, continue to find out everything you can about the victims. I know you've done this already, but check again with the University, their friends, teachers, neighbours – anyone who had anything to do with the victims. Did anyone bear a grudge against them? Did they step on any toes? David, Michelle, continue digging into the victims' families' backgrounds. Let's find the threads that connect our suspects and victims. There has to be something, however tenuous.'

He paused, remembering Duncan's father's profession. 'I'll go have a chat with Daniel Hughes in Winchester Prison tomorrow.' He stopped and studied Karl Stringer for a long moment. 'On second thoughts, Karl, I'd like you to do that interview tomorrow. Maybe he can help us with the missing car.'

Karl looked surprised but nodded.

Holt's smile was grim. 'And I'll call Metcalf to give him the news that we are preparing to charge Duncan with murder and his mates as accessories. Let's shake the tree and see what falls out...'

Two hours later, Holt received a phone call from Metcalf to say that his client, Duncan Hughes, would like to make a statement.

30

Holt

'He's lying, sir! He has to be!'

Holt had never known DI Karl Stringer to raise his voice. Red-faced, fists clenched, the man paced the narrow strip of space in the major incident room. Rowena looked like she had walked into a sledgehammer.

'I'd like to throttle the lying bastard.' Karl whirled around to march four steps the other way, then back again.

'Sit down, Karl,' said Holt. 'That carpet's singeing. Let's go over what happened.' He glanced at Rowena's flushed face and tightly clasped hands.

'Rena, get some of that cold water down before you explode.'

The pair had called a break during their interview with Duncan Hughes with his solicitor, Andrew Metcalf, to review the outcome with Holt. Karl sat, flexed his neck and shoulder muscles. 'You were monitoring the interview, sir? You saw and heard what they said.'

'Yes, and so did Ian.'

Two hours ago, Andrew Metcalf said his client, Duncan, wished to make a statement. He asked the detectives to produce the actual mobile phone—the one with his client's fingerprint—for the interview. Not the photo or an image on any screen, but the phone itself. This the detectives did, with the phone still protected in its evidence bag.

Metcalf and Duncan had spent almost an hour in private discussion before Rowena and Karl Stringer walked into the interview room.

'Ian, could you put up the transcript of the interview on screen?' asked Holt.

DI Stringer: 'Duncan, when we asked you in earlier interviews to explain how your fingerprint got on the victim's phone, you categorically said you did not know. You even accused us of putting it there. Are you now saying you can explain?'

D. Hughes: 'Yeah, well. I bin thinking an' thinking, haven't I? And I jus' remembered. One afternoon, I was in High Street, an' I sat next to this man, an' he had a cool phone. I asked to look at it, an' he let me hold it an' showed me some cool apps.'

DS Williams: 'When was this?'

D. Hughes: 'I don' 'member exactly, but I think maybe day they got killed.'

DS Williams: 'Did you know the man who showed you the phone?'

D. Hughes: 'No, I never met him before, but I remember he was Indian or some such. He was nice and friendly-like.'

DI Stringer: 'Was it one of them? Here are photos of the victims again.'

D. Hughes: 'I think maybe this one or this one—'

DS Williams: 'For the record, Mr Hughes is pointing to Ravi Verma and Suraj Verma.'

D. Hughes: '—but I'm not sure. They all look alike.'

DI Stringer: 'Why didn't you tell us this before?'

D. Hughes: 'I dint remember, did I?. It was only for a couple of minutes, an' I dint think it was important.'

DS Williams: 'Not important? Surely it should have registered when we asked you so many times.'

D. Hughes: 'Well, it dint.'

DI Stringer: 'What made you remember now?'

D. Hughes: 'I only saw the phone again this morning, din' I?'

DI Stringer: 'We showed you photo and digital images of it several times.'

D. Hughes: 'Yeah, but it's not the same as seein' the real thing, is it? When I got to hold it again, even though it was inside a bag, I thought what a cool phone it was an' remembered how I had seen it before.'

DI Stringer: 'What happened after that?'

D. Hughes: 'It beeped while I was holdin' it, and the man took it back.'

DI Stringer: 'And then?'

D. Hughes: 'Then, he said, "Oh, bugger, am gonna be late! Sorry, man, I gotta go."'

DI Stringer: 'What happened next?'

D. Hughes: 'He shook me hand then took off real fast.'

DS Williams: 'He shook your hand?'

D. Hughes: 'Yes, he was nice! Not stuck up. I liked him!'

DS Williams: 'So, how come you didn't recognise him in the park that night?'

A. Metcalf: 'Sergeant, my client has already denied going into the park that night.'

DI Stringer: 'Right. I see. OK, we'll take a break and resume in 30-minutes.'

'That's the end, sir,' said Ian.

'What do we do, sir?'

'Ian, do we have anything showing Duncan and Ravi meeting?' asked Holt.

DC Ian Shepherd scrolled through the massive amount of information collected since the murders five days ago. 'Ravi was on the High Street between 12.35 p.m. and 2.15 p.m. He shopped at WH Smiths and Subway, paid by credit card in both places. By 2.50 p.m. he was back on campus and attending a lecture at 3 p.m.'

'What about the suspects' movements?'

'We have CCTV footage showing Duncan and his brother Leo on the High Street between noon and 3 p.m. They spent an hour in the arcade, but we have nothing that places the victims and suspects together.'

'We've already asked the staff in every shop along the High Street, and no one witnessed any meeting between Ravi and Duncan,' said Rowena.

'Which means Duncan could be lying. I knew it.' Karl smashed his fist against his palm.

'Yes, he could,' replied Holt. 'But the onus is on us to prove his guilt, not on him to prove his innocence. It sounds plausible, and a jury would buy it. True or not, it explains his fingerprint on the phone.'

He thought for a moment. 'If we ask him to pinpoint exactly where he allegedly met Ravi, he'll pick one with no camera coverage. Metcalf could find one for him. Which means we have nothing to discredit Duncan's description of the incident.'

'So, now what, sir? It's time to return to the interview,' said Rowena.

'Ask him again when and where exactly that meeting took place. We might as well follow that up.'

'Will we have to release the four suspects, sir?' asked Ian. He mirrored the group's disappointment and dejection.

'We don't have a lot of choice. The CPS won't touch this with a barge pole now.'

'Should we tell Duncan we are letting him go?' asked Karl.

'Not yet. Tell him we may have more questions and hold all four for the full thirty-six hours.' Petty and vindictive though it was, Holt meant to extract every little satisfaction he could. He now had to tell the Super, who'd have to break the news to his superiors, and then all hell would break loose to come right back and bite him on the backside.

Worse, he would also have to tell the victims' parents that justice for their sons had slipped away.

31

Karl

It was hard to miss the grey, cream and brown banded prison turret bifurcating the dull, leaden skyline. The elevated site boosted the Victorian building's gravitas, and the structure screened by thick brick walls still impressed.

DI Karl Stringer drove past the security gates and turned into the visitors' car park at Winchester prison. A large blue and white hoarding at the gate announced in oversized letters: HMP/YOI Winchester. Below that, in smaller letters, it also reassured visitors and passers-by that they believed in 'Encouraging & Supporting Positive Change.'

He remembered coming here as a young constable a quarter century ago. The warden had proudly pointed out its many architectural features and its design of five wings radiating from a central building topped by the turret. The prisoner accommodations, which had been state-of-the-art back in 1849, desperately needed updating to meet modern standards. In recent times, though, with several prison inmate deaths and riots, the prison made the news more often than the governors liked. To add to their woes, here, as elsewhere, severe staff shortages accompanied the chronic overcrowding.

Karl was already itching to get out when a prison officer arrived to escort him to a small room where Daniel Hughes waited.

The man's photos did not do justice to his size. He had filled out. The bunched muscles on his six-foot-two frame evidenced his dedication or addiction to exercising.

Hughes' file also listed two prior cautions for assault, but the victims withdrew their allegations. He was unlucky this time and had already served eighteen months of a three-year stint for involuntary manslaughter, for causing the death of a man who called him a 'black motherfucker'. Hughes claimed he had only thrown a light punch, but the fellow scrambled to his feet, ran backwards, slipped, fell and cracked his skull. Despite Hughes calling for an ambulance and his attempts at administering first aid, the man died.

At the hearing, Hughes told the judge that while he was indeed black and loved his mother, he was not a motherfucker and would not stand for anyone insulting her. This literary approach had surprised and amused the court. That, combined with his efforts to save the victim, explained his relatively lenient custodial sentence.

'What's this about?'

'You had a phone call from your stepson, Duncan, early last Friday morning,' said Karl. 'At 4.10 a.m. to be exact. He told the warden it was an emergency. What was that about?'

'My wife was ill. The boy was worried.'

The red-rimmed, deep brown eyes told of many sleepless nights. Clenched jaws, flared nostrils, rise and fall of his massive chest betrayed his efforts to hide his concern.

The folder beneath Karl's hands also mentioned that Hughes appeared to be a good father and husband, but the family had skidded downhill since his incarceration.

He must be worried sick about them.

Karl's thoughts slid to his own household, and the changes wrought by the new arrival. Surprise, then months of excitement, followed the news of Beth's pregnancy. But after several sleepless nights and the piercing cries of a colicky baby, the novelty had soon worn off. He could feel the fabric of his family wearing thin, fraying around the edges. Even his relationship with Beth was stretching, shredding...

Dragging himself back to the present, he asked, 'Why, what was wrong with her?'

'She gets ill sometimes – woman trouble. Sometimes she's in a lot of pain.'

'What did you ask him to do?'

'Nothing much. I told him it wasn't serious and not to worry; that she would be OK.'

'So, what did he do? Did he stay with her?'

'I don't think so. I told him she'd be fine in an hour. She just needed to rest. Give her a hot water bottle, a couple of paracetamols, make some strong tea and get her to drink it, I said.'

'Why did he call you here in prison instead of calling an ambulance or a doctor?'

'Crystal, his mum, insisted there was no need, but the boy didn't know what to do, so he called me. What's wrong with that?'

'Mr Hughes, you are aware we brought your sons in for questioning relating to the murder of three students last Thursday night?'

'Yeah, I heard. An' my wife called as soon as you lot picked them up. But they wouldn't do that. OK, they're silly sometimes, but they're not bad and wouldn't hurt anyone.'

'So, where were they last Thursday night? Did they stay home with their mum?'

'I don't think so. They were out with friends.'

'Your son's fingerprint was on a victim's mobile phone. How do you explain that?'

'I already told you, I dunno.' Hughes' chest rose and fell faster. Palms flat on his thighs, he took a deep breath. 'Anyway, you lot released them, which means you've nothing on 'em. They're innocent. So why you asking these questions?'

'Mr Hughes, your sons and their friends are released under investigation, which simply means that we don't have enough evidence to charge them at the moment. We are still investigating, so can call them in again for questioning or even arrest them. It doesn't mean that we've eliminated them from our inquiries or that they're no longer suspects. Quite the contrary, in fact. I don't believe the stories your lads have been telling us. I'd advise you to answer our questions if you really want to help your boys. So, I'll ask again, why was your son's fingerprint on the victim's phone?'

'Maybe they and those lads were friends?'

Karl's eyebrows shot up. 'Friends? Really?'

'Why not? You think my boys aren't good enough?'

The guard straightened at the rise in pitch and volume of Hughes' voice.

'I don't believe they were friends.' Karl lowered his voice. 'We checked. I doubt they moved in the same circle or even met. Your sons and their mates said they'd never seen them before.'

'I already said I dunno nothing about this. My two boys wouldn't kill nobody.'

'You've no idea what they've been up to, have you? Since you've been here, they haven't been keeping the best of company. In fact, Duncan's already been in trouble. Now young Leo too is heading that way. You can't be happy with that?'

'No, I'm not happy. Once I get out of here, I'll straighten them out, make sure they go straight.'

'Even with your exemplary behaviour, that won't be anytime soon, will it? Meanwhile, how far will your boys stray? Help us help them, Mr Hughes. Tell us what you know.'

'How many times do I have to say? I don't know nothin' about any fingerprints. I believe my sons.'

The prison officer was alert now, his eyes on Hughes, hands hovering close to his belt.

'Maybe they followed in their old man's footsteps? Only meant to beat those boys up, but things got out of hand.'

Hughes' mouth tightened, and he glared at Karl. 'They wouldn't do that. As soon as my wife called, I thought you lot would try to stitch them up, so I arranged a lawyer for them.'

'So, who's paying for the lawyer? Andrew Metcalf doesn't come cheap.'

'An old friend doing me a favour.'

'Really? Which old friend would that be?'

'I don't have to say.' He sat back and crossed his arms. 'My boys didn't do this. I won't let'em be blamed.'

'What did you do with Tommy Wade's car?'

'Huh? What you talkin' about?'

'You helped get rid of your son's friend Tommy Wade's car.'

'Course not! Why'd I do that?'

'Your son and his friends claim they returned home that night in Tommy's car, and now it's conveniently missing. You have the expertise, and that's the real reason Duncan called you.'

'No, I know nothin' about Tommy's car, an' you won't make me say different, Detective Inspector. Anyhow, I don' mean to be rude or nothin' but I'm done talkin' to you.'

He nodded to the prison officer before turning back to Karl. 'If you want to ask me anythin' more, I want my lawyer here. So, we done for now. OK?'

Karl stared into his eyes, then nodded and stood up. 'OK. Thank you for your time, Mr. Hughes.'

32

Karl

DI Karl Stringer stared at the bulk of the prison reflected in his rearview mirror, confining the damaged and the dangerous within its layers of brick, mortar and metal. To protect the outside, it created a mini dystopia inside. A world of oppressors and oppressed, tormenters and tormented.

Did their father's absence lead Duncan and young Leo to crime? Hughes was no angel, but except where cars were concerned, he appeared to have a certain moral code and, unlike his predecessor, the erstwhile Ronald Kirby, he did not use his family as a punching bag.

Lack of attention, too, is absence, thought Karl. Although his wife and he were physically present, his work, the baby's unrelenting demands and fatigue left them with little time for the two older children. Sinkholes were opening at his feet.

The DCI was disturbingly perceptive sometimes. Intentionally or otherwise, he was forcing Karl to acknowledge a situation he would rather ignore.

He activated the hands-free to call Holt, relegating the difficult elements of his life to the bottom of the pile.

'Boss, am on my way back to the Station. Be there in 40-45 minutes depending on traffic.'

'Good. How'd it go with Hughes?'

'Either he's telling the truth or he's a brilliant actor. He denied knowing anything about anything. Insisted Duncan's call was because his mum was unwell. I think that man's really worried, possibly scared. Why else would he have Metcalf represent them if he didn't know or suspect his boys were involved? He would have used Legal Aid if he thought they were innocent, just as he did last year when Duncan was caught shoplifting. He must've called in a big favour to get Metcalf here so quickly.'

'Karl, that call from Duncan at 4.10 a.m. lasted eight minutes forty-three seconds. Much of that included waiting for Hughes to be brought out of his cell. Which leaves what? Two minutes' actual conversation time? That's barely enough time to inform his father of the murders, much less receive further instructions. Unless they'd already planned every detail beforehand.'

'We can't disprove their story, sir. Worse, it sounds plausible. Calling his stepfather in the dead hours of the morning because he was worried about his mother makes Duncan Hughes seem like a nice kid despite those piercings, tattoos and bad-ass attitude.'

'True...' Holt's voice crackled.

'Sir? You're breaking up. Traffic's picking up too.'

'We'll talk when you get back.' The line went dead.

***

Holt

Matthew Holt placed his mobile phone on the desk and swivelled his chair around to face the window. The overcast sky looked set to fulfil the charming BBC meteorologist's forecast of *unsettled weather, temperatures below normal and more rain.*

Karl was right. Should this reach court, the defence would employ every tactic to sway the jury. He punched DC Ian Shepherd's extension number on the intercom.

'Ian, were there any other calls on Duncan's phone? Received or sent?'

'Nothing of significance, sir. Just to each other and his mum. But Duncan and his father may have a burner phone. No, scratch that. Duncan wouldn't call the prison line if Hughes had a burner phone.'

'Hmm. Good point.' Holt drummed his fingers on the table. 'Check if any calls originated from the prison between midnight and that call at 4.10 a.m. I'm sure they didn't go directly home. They had to dispose of the weapons, clothes and car immediately or soon after, otherwise, we'd have found at least a trace of blood.'

'Sir, wait, sir—' Holt heard the squawk of Ian's voice as he was about to slam the receiver back.

'What?'

'Sorry, sir. Forensics told me they'd already washed the clothes they wore last Thursday.'

'What? All four's?'

'Yes, sir. Derek Dawson's entire outfit was laundered, dried and put away. The others' were still on the washing line.'

'And their shoes?'

'Also all washed, sir.'

'This lot washed their shoes?'

'Yes, sir. Sorry.'

'Not your fault, is it? Argh... I need a coffee.'

'You need some sleep, sir.'

'Yeah, that too. But I'll settle for some coffee right now.'

The receiver crashed satisfyingly into the cradle.

Holt strode towards the galley kitchen at the opposite end of the fifth floor, ignoring Rowena's voice behind him.

'Sir...!'

'Not until I've had my coffee.'

Laptop in hand, Rowena trotted after him. 'You'll like this, sir. Forensics said those clothes were nowhere near the crime scene.'

Holt whirled around, crossed his arms, and glared. 'That's great, Sergeant. Just what I wanted to hear. Grrr...'

He poured the steaming beverage into his mug – a blue and white Secret Santa present from his team printed with the words: 'Me Boss – You Not'.

'Sir, Forensics also said all their clothes and shoes were almost new. Barely worn.'

Holt's hand froze.

'All their clothes?'

'Yes! Down to underpants, socks and shoes. All new, probably worn just once. And recently washed. All four are identical in style – black or navy tracksuit bottoms and tops, hoodies, black socks, underpants and black parka jackets, just in different sizes. Now, isn't that a coincidence?' Rowena grinned.

Holt filled his mug, held out the coffee jug and, at a nod from Rowena, half-filled hers. She added hot water and topped it off with milk.

'A real coincidence. So, all four changed their clothes somewhere. Which means they had these clothes ready and waiting. How did they dispose of the others? Nothing from bin searches?'

Rowena shook her head. 'No, sir.'

'I think their old clothes and weapons are in the car. Double the effort in finding it. Check scrapyards and bodywork shops. If they haven't already crushed it, that car could be any colour now, with who knows what license plate. Ask our suspects how come they were all wearing new, almost identical outfits. When and where did they buy them? They couldn't have driven far otherwise it would be on camera.'

Who's behind this, and why? Who did they call after leaving the park?

Holt leaned back in his chair. *Did Duncan call his father to tell him they'd done the deed and ditched the car? Why would Hughes burden his sons with something so horrific?* From Karl's description, he got the impression that Hughes had a strong sense of family. Did someone threaten his wife? But surely, even from prison, he had recourse to people better suited to the task.

He walked across to Ian and Salim, who were running a complicated computer programme.

'We need to find out who's paying Metcalf. Dig up everything you can on Daniel Hughes. Who his friends are. Look for someone well-off. Someone who can afford the rates Metcalf charges these days.'

'You really think Daniel Hughes organised this from prison, sir?'

'Possibly. But someone a lot cleverer and with more clout is pulling the strings. We need that missing link. Hughes must've signed up to something big to justify this kind of help. And he could've used his contacts to make Tommy's car vanish. After all, he's a professional mechanic.'

In the past, the traffic crimes team had already questioned Hughes about a couple of missing high-end cars, but as yet they had no proof of his link to any stolen vehicles.

'Also, check on all Hughes' known associates. Maybe they helped to disappear Tommy's car. Go through the ANPRs again. Have traffic widen the street search, although I doubt it'll still be out there. Rowena, get more eyes on those CCTV footage. Get Forensics to return to Daniel Hughes's garage. Was it taken apart there? And enlarge the area of searches in bins and dumping grounds. It's possible our suspects dumped their clothes and weapons separately and farther away.'

With his popularity notched several rungs down the ladder, Holt returned to his office and swallowed two more paracetamols.

***

DI Karl Stringer buzzed Holt to let him know he had returned.

'Come in for a moment, will you, Karl? And close the door.'

'Sir?' asked Karl, sitting down opposite him.

'So, what did you make of Hughes? Your gut instinct? Is he involved?'

'My gut says not, at least not in the homicide. But he may have helped them get rid of the evidence. They're his kids, after all. He obviously has some powerful, certainly rich friends. If Hughes wanted any bloodwork done, he could hire a professional. He wouldn't use his sons. They don't give the impression of being Mensa Society material. He's truly worried for them.'

'Hmm. They could be a lot brighter and more callous than we realise.'

Holt cleared his throat, straightened, and looked Karl in the eyes. 'Karl, this isn't work, so tell me to mind my business if you like. How are things with you? Are you and Beth coping? What about Amy and Mike?'

Karl's shoulders slumped. *So, sending me to see Hughes was intentional.*

'It's been difficult. We try to cope, but it's exhausting. Beth and I have no time for Amy and Mike; we're losing touch with them. Teenage is hard enough these days. Right when they need us most, when we must be vigilant to keep them safe and stop them from straying, we're growing apart. I'm hoping Beth's mother's help with the baby will make things better.'

'Go on home. I'll call you if anything urgent turns up. I'm sure your family will be pleased to see you.'

'Thank you, sir. We'll be fine. I'll make sure of that.'

33

Holt

The detectives clustered around the green-sheeted body of Jyoti Verma.

Cummings abandoned his keyboard, rose from his desk in the corner to join them. Dark shadows under his eyes gave them a hollow look, and his skin was chalky white. He took his place by the corpse's head.

'You guys look like how I feel; like you belong on one of my slabs,' he said, voicing Holt's thoughts on the pathologist's appearance.

'What a tragedy.' Cummings stretched his back, and taking a deep breath, leaned over the corpse. 'Let's begin, shall we? Healthy female, ethnicity Indian, in her early fifties, in good physical condition despite having nothing in her stomach. She hadn't eaten for three days before her death. Cause of death: severe blood loss from severed external jugular veins on both sides of her neck using a very sharp blade. A four-inch incision on the left, from left to right. Deep enough to sever the external jugular and slice into the internal jugular. The right-side wound suggests a self-inflicted cut made by the victim twisting her right wrist. Though shallower than the left one, it still sliced through the external jugular. Wounds definitely made by the scalpel found beside the victim. The blood on it is all hers.'

He looked up at Holt. 'Bearing in mind your concerns, Matt, I checked and had my assistant verify my findings. All evidence points to the victim having cut herself. There are no bruises or signs of force or any defence wounds. Her right thumb and forefinger showed two small cuts, probably made by holding the scalpel too near the edge. No other cuts, scrapes or bruises anywhere else on the body. Only her fingerprints are on the scalpel.'

'Could someone kneeling beside her have guided her hand?'

'Hmm... I cannot rule it out, but that doesn't seem likely here. There are no bruises on her wrists or hands. I also think the cuts would've been deeper. Instinct would drive the person to apply more pressure than these cuts indicate, which would sever both internal jugulars. And maybe the carotid artery as well. Or conversely, that person would've applied too little pressure.'

Unless the killer was a surgeon and knew exactly what he was doing. Despite keeping his thoughts contained and his face expressionless, Holt caught the sharpness of Cummings' glance.

'All three men had the victim's blood on their hands,' continued the pathologist, in response to Holt's unvoiced theories, 'more on her husband and brother-in-law than Mr Kapoor. Again, consistent with the two men trying to stem the blood loss. And her bloody fingerprints on their wrists. It fits in with their statements that she held their hands to stop them.'

'Could they have saved her?' asked Karl.

'Hmm, yes. With either of the Vermas there, I'd rate the chances very high. Both are exceptional surgeons, especially Prem Verma, who's a cardiothoracic surgeon. But even they aren't magicians, not if they couldn't reach her in time. I believe they tried. The towel was soaked with her blood, and the imprint of Jyoti's hand on it indicates she pushed it away. Also remember, Jyoti's a surgeon's wife, and if she meant to die, she would know more about means, method and timing than most people. And it appears she was determined. To make two cuts like that! She wanted to be certain. She left little to chance.'

His gaze swept the group before settling on Holt's with a mixture of apology and defiance.

'That's what my report will say. Death was by her own hand. Literally in this case.'

34

Rowena

'You've redecorated; it looks good.'

Rowena swivelled on the bar stool to get a 360 degrees view of the main hall in The Cue Room—a pool and snooker hall on the edge of town.

Her last visit here, an evening out with friends, was almost a year ago. This was her first official call to The Cue Room and her first conversation with its owner, Harvey Endsleigh, whose name had cropped up as an acquaintance of the suspects.

Two rows of six pool tables stood lined up in a guard of honour, with red, yellow and black balls arranged within their confining black triangle frames, all set and ready for punters. A range of cue sticks clipped into holders hung on the walls, with dining tables and chairs at one end of the room near the well-stocked bar. A flight of stairs led to the upper floor with two full-size snooker tables, also racked up with the multi-coloured balls for the more serious players.

'It's OK. Unfortunately, this isn't in the centre of town, but that'll change soon. This isn't public yet, but I'm taking over that building in the city centre and refurbishing it into a Wild West-themed pool hall. It has more floor area than this, and I can double my customers. Anyway, what's this about?' asked Harvey Endsleigh. 'Is Tommy in some kind of trouble?'

'What makes you ask that? Has he been in trouble before?' Rowena had checked the police database and juvenile records, but there was nothing for Tommy Wade. Not even a CPN, a community protection notice designed to stop a person aged 16 from committing antisocial behaviour. But there are other kinds of trouble.

Harvey Endsleigh, a slim, very attractive man with curly dark, almost black hair topping a wide forehead, even features and intense dark eyes, continued polishing glasses at the bar.

The place was empty and eerily quiet without the hum of voices, the background music, the snap, click, clash and clatter of the balls.

'Not as far as I know,' said Endsleigh. 'He and his friends used to come often when they were younger. I try to encourage young people. It keeps them off the streets and, who knows, I might even find the next Ronnie O'Sullivan among them. But they haven't been in recently. Actually, Tommy hasn't visited in three or four months. Maybe longer.'

Which tied in with Tommy's foster mother's statement when Rowena had interviewed her earlier that morning. The woman considered Tommy to be her only failure among the dozen children she had fostered over the years.

Ruth Barnes had sighed and shifted her bulk in the large chenille armchair as she took a sip from her cup of tea, her fingers surprisingly dainty for such a large woman.

'He was only six when he came to us, so beautiful, like an angel. You just wanted to hug and make everything OK for him. But we couldn't get close. He just pushed me away, and his eyes would go all cold and remote. He was never naughty, but I

think he instigated his siblings—we had two others with us then. They'd do things they shouldn't, get into trouble, but they never told on him,' Ruth Barnes told Rowena.

'Tommy left us as soon as he turned sixteen, moved into his father's flat and didn't want our help anymore. We kept most of the other children with us until they were eighteen, and they still visit during the holidays. Our last two are now at uni,' she said proudly.

'I'll need their names and contact details. I'd like to ask them about Tommy.'

'But they aren't in touch with Tommy now that they're at university,' she protested.

'All the same, Mrs Barnes. It'll help us with our inquiries.'

Ruth Barnes reluctantly produced the contact details for Ann-Marie and Graham Saunders, the former a first-year English and History student at Bristol University and the latter in his second year of computer science at Exeter University.

'I'm sorry to say that Tommy was lovely, but not lovable.' The woman looked puzzled and upset.

Is there a link between Anne-Marie or Graham and any of the victims? Unlikely as it seemed, Rowena knew it would have to be checked out.

When asked about his friends, Ruth gave Rowena a list of five names, one of them Duncan Hughes. As for places where Tommy, his siblings and friends hung around, his foster mother mentioned the usual shopping centres, parks, arcades and the pool hall. Intrigued, Rowena had asked Ruth to elaborate.

'When he was about fourteen, Tommy started going to The Cue Room almost daily after school. The owner became a sort of mentor to Tommy, got him to take karate lessons and look after himself. My other two children and a couple of their friends went there, too. I didn't mind, because the owner made them leave by

6, before the evening crowd. It kept them off the street and out of mischief.'

Rowena had decided then that a quick chat with Harvey Endsleigh, the owner of The Cue Room, wouldn't hurt. Especially if, like most publicans, he turned out to be a good judge of character with an in-built radar for troublemakers.

Hence, her visit to the pool hall. *Not exactly a chore,* thought Rowena, gazing at its handsome owner.

'Tommy's foster mother said you were his mentor.'

'I tried to be, and I probably was for a couple of years. Instead of hanging out on the street or even here, I got Tommy and his friends to take karate classes and go to the gym.'

'What happened then?' asked Rowena.

'Nothing really. He continued for a couple of years.'

'Go on. Why'd he stop?'

'Well, he turned 16, didn't he, and knew everything, had all the answers. He had new mates, but that was OK. I understood. He still came in occasionally, and we stayed friends. That is until last Christmas time.'

'What happened? Why did Tommy stop coming?'

Endsleigh looked uncomfortable, re-polished his already gleaming bar.

'Well?'

Tossing the dust cloth over his shoulder, Endsleigh turned to Rowena.

'It was that friend of Tommy's. That Duncan. Have you seen him? Several months ago, he went and got all those piercings and tattoos. And an attitude to go with it. I could see it was putting off some of my customers, especially families.' He sighed. 'I know I shouldn't judge by appearances. He's not a bad kid. He's been coming here with Tommy for years. I felt bad, but I have to think about my business. So, I told Tommy that Duncan couldn't come unless he toned down his look. Y'know, removed some of the piercings, covered up some tattoos. They were furious and said none of them would come again. Only they didn't word it so politely, of course.'

'When was that?'

'Hmm, around last Christmas or just after, I think.'

'And you haven't seen Tommy or any of his friends since?'

'No.' Endsleigh frowned as he polished a glass and placed it on a shelf. Then, palms flat on the counter, he turned to Rowena, whose eyes widened at the missing finger on his left hand.

Catching the direction of her gaze, he removed his hands from the bar.

'An accident with those,' he nodded at the pool tables. 'Don't let anyone tell you that pool and snooker aren't dangerous sports. Boy, can they hurt.' He shrugged. 'Anyway, I heard about their arrest and their release. I don't believe they had anything to do with the Holburn Park murders. Like everyone else, I've been unfair to those lads.'

He paused in thought. 'I'll reach out to Tommy to invite him and his friends back. Even that Duncan. I'll give them free entrance on a couple of days a week. But I'll restrict it to Mondays and Thursdays between 11 a.m. and 5 p.m.' Endsleigh grinned. 'Those are my dead times. And now how about a game, Sergeant? I've never played against a police officer before. I might even let you win.'

Tempting though the challenge was, Rowena laughed and shook her head. 'No thanks, Harvey. Not on duty. This is all work, not pleasure, I'm afraid. Another time, eh?'

Endsleigh grinned and saluted her with a flick of fingers to his temple. His smiling, coal-black gaze followed her out with a flattering and more than cursory interest.

35

Holt

The detectives' determined trawl threw up four possibilities from among Daniel Hughes's contacts. Four people who could afford to pay the gang's defence attorney, Andrew Metcalf's fees. Though their motivation remained unclear, the names were a start.

Holt ran his eyes down the list, stopping in surprise at one name. *I bet it's him*! Pulse quickening, he read the dates and notes against that contact.

'There! Him! Marvin Jackson. He'd be my first choice. Says here, he and Hughes are from Jamaica, and they shared a flat when they first arrived here. Jackson has the clout to mobilize Andrew Metcalf as counsel and can afford the lawyer's exorbitant fees.'

Karl looked sceptical. 'That's rather a big ask, isn't it, sir?'

'Blackmail?' asked Rowena. 'Does Hughes have something on him? I know! Jackson wanted to get rid of the three students and had the boys do it.' But her tone cast doubt on her own suggestion.

'We're not playing three guesses, DS Williams.' Holt's grin took the sting out of the words. 'If Jackson wanted anyone dead, they would have an "accident."' This time, Holt indulged in air quotes. 'No one would even suspect it was deliberate. I'm sure he has people who can make that happen. Or discreetly make people disappear. Whereas this isn't Jackson's style at all, nor the type of publicity he wants.'

He paused. 'Let's not rule it out, though. Start checking up whether Jackson has any links to those three students, either directly or through their families. Gambling debts spring to mind. That's his line of business, after all. Perhaps it's a vendetta or a deterrent.'

Holt straightened. 'It's been a while since I've seen Marvin Jackson. Set up a meeting for us with him in London, will you, Rowena? For tomorrow, if you can. I'd like to ask him why he's funding the defence counsel.'

36

Holt

Marvin Jackson beamed as he stepped around his large desk to greet Holt and Rowena. 'Mr Holt! Good to see you again!'

'Is it?' Despite himself, Holt's mouth widened in a genuine smile as he shook hands with Jackson. It was difficult to dislike the man.

Jackson's laughter bounced around the room. 'Not really! But isn't that what people say? In your case, though, I mean it. You're looking well. Your new job must suit you, and your sergeant's a hell of a lot better looking than your last one!'

His admiring glance rested on Rowena. She smiled back. Jackson's charisma made offense impossible.

The elegant décor in shades of cream and brown trimmed with hints of gold gave the room an aura of luxury. The wall behind Jackson's desk featured an expanse of granite – an illusion of molten lava in chocolate shot with cream and mouldering flames of gold. Backlit alcoves flanking it on both sides contained plants in soft white pots, books, and pieces of art.

Jackson led them to a lounge-style meeting area. A button-back Chesterfield settee in pale tan leather, matching armchairs, surrounded a low, brown glass-topped table on gold legs. Opulent yet chic.

Holt studied the man leaning back in his plush velvet armchair. In his mid-forties, wearing a quiet, conservative but expensive three-piece tailored suit, Jackson could pass off as a polished politician. Rumour was that his ambitions lay in that direction.

Provided he buries all his skeletons really deep.

Five years ago, when he first met and interviewed Jackson, Holt had been the Met's lead detective inspector on a homicide case. The court sentenced the shooter, but Holt remained convinced that Jackson's signature was on that death warrant. The convicted man insisted he had acted on impulse and hadn't been hired to kill. He also denied any acquaintance with Jackson. Which could even be the truth. Maybe the killer didn't know his employer's identity. Despite his best efforts, Holt found no ties, incriminating or otherwise, between them.

Marvin Jackson had obviously prospered since their last meeting, evidenced by his office within a prestigious building in the centre of London. Holt knew the Met police were keeping discreet tabs on the man. Tax inspectors from HMRC had on multiple occasions checked the source of his obvious wealth, but everything appeared to be above board. Jackson may even have become a legitimate businessman. He had the Midas touch. His investments in casinos, properties and, as a venture capitalist, had made him a wealthy man. A bevy of creative, reputable accountants ensured that the HMRC auditors found nothing untoward in his tax returns.

Jackson leaned forward, elbows on his knees, fingers laced under his chin. 'I have an important meeting soon, so I can only spare a few minutes. What can I do for you, Mr Holt?'

'You heard about the triple homicide in Southampton last Thursday night?'

'Yes, of course. It's all over the news. Very tragic!'

'What is your connection to the victims?'

Jackson's wide forehead creased in a frown. 'My connection? Why, none at all! I don't know any of them. Or anything about them. The first I learned of their existence was from the news of their deaths.'

Holt wondered if the man realised the irony of his statement. 'Yet you were quick to provide a defence counsellor for the four youths we arrested.'

Holt held his breath. If Jackson refused to confirm their premise or denied knowledge of it, this interview would be over.

'That's not a crime, is it? Those boys have a right to justice. Innocent until proved guilty, as they say.'

Bingo!

'True, but why would *you* step in? What is your relationship to them?' asked Holt.

'None. But Daniel Hughes is a friend, and he asked me for help.'

'That's a rather big favour, isn't it? Andrew Metcalf and his team's services are far from cheap. This must cost you a lot of money.'

'I can afford it.' No trace of arrogance in Jackson's voice.

'Yes, I see that,' said Holt, nodding at the room designed by expensive interior designers, a stark contrast to his own impersonal space at the Station.

'But why would you care for those four boys? You don't put yourself out to that extent, even for your friends.'

Jackson spun his pen around on the glass tabletop for a few moments before reaching a decision.

'Look, Daniel Hughes isn't just any friend. We've known each other since we were toddlers. We grew up together in Jamaica. When we were 18, we ran with a rough crowd and got into trouble with certain people. Daniel took a bullet meant for me. It would've killed me, but he pushed me away and stepped into its path. By sheer luck, it didn't kill him, but he took months to recover. I owe him my life.'

Seeing Holt's sceptical look, he added, 'I can give you the date and place of Daniel's treatment. You should be able to verify that easily enough.' A gleam of white teeth flashed in the deep brown face. 'Sadly, I cannot recall any more details. It was all so long ago.'

Rowena asked, 'So you're doing this as repayment to Hughes?'

Jackson turned his dark eyes to Rowena. 'A life for a life, as they say. Or in this case, two lives, because I'll be saving both his boys from the noose.' He laughed again. 'I know there's no noose these days, but I'll be protecting his kids from paying the price for someone else's crime.'

'Why pay for all four suspects rather than just the Hughes boys?'

Jackson shrugged. 'Because Daniel asked me to. He knows the police want to close the case fast, that his boys and their friends would be easy pickings. He didn't want any of those lads getting into a muddle, or the police putting words into their mouths to stitch them up because they don't have anyone to advise them.'

The detectives ignored the provocation. They'd heard worse.

'They would get legal representation from the Crown, as is their right,' said Rowena.

'Perhaps so, but not someone like Metcalf.'

Holt leaned forward. 'You think those boys are innocent? They weren't involved in the murders?'

'It doesn't matter what I think, Mr Holt.' His deep voice was low and solemn. 'That's what Hughes tells me, and I shall believe him.'

'I don't believe they're innocent. I think you know that Daniel Hughes doesn't either.'

'Years ago, you thought I was guilty.'

Holt raised an eyebrow. 'Well?'

Jackson smiled, levered himself out of his chair. 'You may believe what you like, Mr Holt, but I prefer my truth, that I had nothing to do with that murder five years ago. And now, I prefer to believe my friend.'

Knuckles rapped on his door, and his glamorous receptionist pushed it ajar. Jackson extended a hand towards the detectives.

'My apologies, Mr Holt, Detective Sergeant Williams. Please don't hesitate to call again if you have any more questions. However, I shall ask my lawyer to be present, especially as you and Metcalf are such good friends.' He laughed.

He shook hands with Rowena and turned to Holt. 'Oh, by the way, guess who I bumped into at a charity function last December? Your ex-wife Alicia and her husband. She looked stunning as ever, and he made a very generous donation. Guess he can afford it, eh? Do you still keep in touch? No? Anyway, I really must leave you now. It's been good seeing you again, Mr Holt.'

Holt mechanically held out his hand and tried to school his frozen facial muscles into a smile. Surprisingly, Jackson's brown eyes held sympathy rather than the malice he'd expected.

37

Holt

Rowena's scrutiny scorched him as he hailed a black cab to take them to London Waterloo station for their train back to Southampton, but to Holt's relief, she refrained from comment or question.

Seated beside her in a busy South Western railway carriage, he said, 'Would you write up the notes on our meeting with Jackson? I'll update the Super and check on progress?'

Rowena sighed and took the hint while Holt opened his laptop, logged in and stared blankly at the screen.

He hadn't thought of Alicia in months, yet here she was again; Jackson's parting comment had unleashed a host of unwelcome memories. In the last two of their six-year marriage, Alicia and he had little to say to each other. After his promotion to Detective Inspector in the Met, they spent even more evenings apart – he at work, she with her friends.

'I'm out this evening with some friends. You don't mind, do you, darling?'

No, he hadn't minded. Just relieved he didn't have to apologise, explain or hear the same old complaint...

Then one evening – 'Matt, we need to talk...'

A romantic dinner together at a French restaurant. Or so he thought. He'd presented Alicia with a bouquet of a dozen red roses.

She'd been kind. Gentle. Held his hand in both of hers, head bowed, her chin-length curtain of glossy black hair swinging along her chiselled jawline. Warm tears from cobalt blue eyes landed on his knuckles.

'I'm so sorry, Matt. I've met someone else, and we want to get married.'

'What! How? When?'

He should've known; he shouldn't have been so stunned. Perhaps he had known and refused to acknowledge it.

'How long has this been going on?'

She'd refused to say, but that hadn't stopped him wondering, imagining...

No! Slam! That door stays shut and barred.

That night, he had returned to their home alone and the following evening to a flat empty of all traces of Alicia.

Seven months after their separation, Alicia gave birth to a baby girl. Tiffany. Holt had toasted the baby by downing an entire bottle of scotch and spent the next two days drooping over the toilet bowl. Alicia asked for nothing when the *decree became absolute*. He wasn't surprised. Her new husband was a multimillionaire. She now had the Paris and New York of her dreams.

With no reason to stay in London, he accepted a position with the Solent Constabulary, returned to his childhood home and, on an impulse, bought a derelict watermill. Although he still missed his colleagues and friends at the Met, he had forged a strong team in his four years here.

Holt sat up and caught Rowena's eye. 'Anything, sir?' she asked.

He shook his head. 'Nothing. And all this meeting with Marwin Jackson did was confirm our suspicion that he's funding the Xtreem gang's defence.'

And rake up painful memories.

'Let's find the real reason for his altruism and his connections to the victims and their families.'

'You still think the gang's responsible for the killings, sir?' asked Rowena. 'Shouldn't we be considering other possibilities?'

'Yes, we should, we are, but so far, they're our best lead. But someone else is behind this. Someone else helped them hide the proof. They're the puppets; we must trace the strings to the puppeteer.'

38

Deepak

'We can't continue like this, Detective Chief Inspector,' said Deepak. 'We've become prisoners in our hotel rooms. We can't even go for a meal in one of the hotel's restaurants without someone taking photos. Going outside is impossible because of the paparazzi. They seem to be everywhere.'

'What would you like to do, Mr Verma? Would it be easier for you to stay either at your brother's place or at Mr Kapoor's? We can arrange a police presence at either location.' Holt tilted his chair back and tapped the speaker icon on his phone, leaving his hands free to make notes.

'I don't think that's a good idea, do you, DCI Holt? Prem and Roopesh's neighbours certainly won't be pleased. They've already had more than their share of media attention and, thankfully, it's lessened in the last few days. Our moving to either place will only kick-start it again.'

'We could move you to a safe house,' said Holt. 'Somewhere rural. It'd still mean isolation, but at least you'd be able to go out for a walk.'

'I have Prem and Roopesh here with me and you're on speakerphone,' said Deepak. 'We've discussed this and decided we'd like to return to India as soon as possible. Roopesh's wife is still in hospital and Prem's wife isn't coping. At least we'd be with them, and we can arrange security to keep the press and the curious away. Is there any reason we cannot leave?'

Caught unawares, Holt hesitated. He'd interviewed the three men on several occasions and gleaned nothing new. No matter how many times he asked or how he phrased his questions, their responses did nothing to progress his investigations into their sons' or Jyoti's deaths. He couldn't legitimately hold them or even ask them not to leave the country. So far, he'd found no evidence to suggest that Jyoti's death was anything other than suicide, so they weren't suspects. Nor was there any sign, however tenuous, of their involvement in their sons' deaths.

He was surprised they hadn't yet 'lawyered up', but if they did, Holt had no doubts their counsel would be sharper and a notch more acerbic than Metcalf.

'It'd be useful to have you here if we have any questions or uncover any new evidence.' Even to Holt's ears, his words sounded lame.

'And do you? Have any new evidence, I mean,' asked Deepak.

'We're pursuing several lines of inquiry and following several leads. But until we can prove them, we can't discuss or disclose them.' Holt rubbed his eyes in despair, glad that the men couldn't see his face or realize how little they had after three weeks of investigation.

'Hello—?' he frowned and queried into the extended silence.

'We're still here,' replied Deepak. 'Look, DCI Holt, if you need us, we'll return immediately, and you can reach us anytime by phone or via a video call. The UK High Commission and the Indian police also know where we live. There, at least we'll be able to comfort our families.'

Holt made his decision.

'I understand, Mr. Verma. Go ahead with your flight bookings and let me know the details. I'll organize your transport from the hotel to the airport. I suggest you book a very early morning flight, so we can get you to the airport while it's still dark.'

He hoped his decision was the right one.

***

Deepak disconnected the call and turned to Prem and Roopesh.

'I'll book our tickets,' said Roopesh. The Verma brothers nodded their thanks. The toll of their voluntary incarceration, albeit in a five-star hotel, was evident in their appearance. Reluctant to engage the services of a barber for fear of unwelcome publicity, they looked shaggy and unkempt.

'Well, you heard the DCI. They have nothing. They had to release their suspects because they had no proof. But we know they did it. Jyoti saw it in her visions, and she described the leader. I'm sure the DCI thinks they did it, even if he won't say so, and I'm sure he'll find the proof.'

He recognised the irony – while Jyoti lived, he'd dismissed her concerns and scoffed at her beliefs, but now, after her death, he and the other parents believed implicitly that she was right. *I should have listened more, believed more.*

'I know you have a lot of faith in DCI Holt, but the police can't do anything,' said Roopesh. 'It's up to us to find our sons' killers. We have to take matters into our own hands to find the evidence.'

'I agree, *bhaiya*[1],' Prem addressed his brother. 'We can't just sit and wait and do nothing. What we don't know is whether our sons were killed in a random, indiscriminate attack or whether they were targeted. In either case, someone helped them after the heinous act. Helped them hide their crime and the proof. We need that damn evidence and that accomplice.'

'And if someone targeted our boys, who is behind it? And why? Who not only instigated the crime but helped those four to carry it out?' added Roopesh.

'But what can we do? We don't have the resources that the police do,' said Deepak.

'We can hire a private investigator,' said Prem. 'Now that the police have released the gang, Xtreem or whatever they call themselves, we can have a private investigator follow and monitor them. They may lead us to the evidence or to whoever is behind this.'

'That's a good idea,' said Deepak. 'Do either of you know a PI?'

'Actually, I do,' said Prem. 'One of my patients was a Detective Inspector in Scotland Yard. Two or three years ago, I did a coronary angioplasty with a couple of stent insertions on him. I heard he retired and started his own private investigation firm. I can ask him.'

'Yes, good.' Deepak slumped back in his armchair with his head cradled in his hands.

Prem and Roopesh exchanged concerned looks over his bent head.

---

1. Brother.

LETHAL JUSTICE

Worried about his health, both mental and physical, they omitted telling Deepak of their intention to provoke the killers into action. They'd eventually have to tell him, but not just yet.

But first, for their plan to work, they needed to enlist the help of Roopesh's uncle – KC and his underworld connections.

Whatever it took, they would get justice.

39

Holt

After the victims' fathers left, the superintendent insisted Holt take a break. 'You've been at it non-stop for four weeks now,' he told Holt. 'You've been making your team get their rest and bring fresh minds to the investigation, but you haven't stopped. When did you last sleep in a bed, not your office chair? I want you to take a break. Go home or, better still, go to the farm. That's an order, by the way. You're no bloody use to anyone like this, especially in that suit, which you've been wearing for three days in a row.'

So, Holt had given in. It wasn't as if he had a choice.

He turned into the drive leading to his family home near Winchester, headlights illuminating trees on one side still bare of leaves and a six-foot, neatly trimmed holly hedge on the other.

He swung the car into his parking bay and stepped out of his four-wheeler. No sooner had he opened the car door than the two Border Collies leapt on him, barking and whining in excitement, their lithe bodies quivering with delight as they shoved their heads into his neck. He backed up against the bonnet, wrapping his arms around their warm, furry necks, trying to dodge their muzzles while they panted, licked, and slobbered all over his face.

He laughed aloud, ruffled their necks, rubbed their backs and warm tummies.

'Good boy, Toby. Hey Tracy, how's my beautiful girl? Come on, calm down now.'

The ache behind his eyes diminished, his shoulders relaxed. God, he had missed this place—his haven, his anchor. A place where conversation revolved around the changing weather, health and antics of the livestock, debates on when to plant, to reap, the best places to buy seed and feed. It kept him grounded, reminded him of the good in the world; that it wasn't entirely populated by thieves, murderers, rapists, kidnappers…

Following a month of sleep deprivation, skipped meals, excessive caffeine, and desperate need for a space to think, he'd come home.

He inhaled the cold, damp air that smelled of fresh earth and wood, tinged with warm animal musk, hay and manure. Farm smells overlaid with the drool-creating aroma of whatever his aunt Susan was cooking. His nostrils flared, and saliva flooded his mouth.

A chink of light glowed along the edges of the heavy curtains in his cottage. *Susan must've turned the light on to make the place look occupied*, he thought, then paused, surprised to find the door unlocked.

With the dogs leaning into him, their muzzles reaching for his hands to extract every pat and stroke they could, he tripped and tottered into his cottage to see both John and Susan waiting in his living room. Anxiety hooked its claws into his stomach, fear clenched his heart until he clocked their smiles and relaxed posture.

He hugged Susan tight and kissed her cheek. He even embraced John, who, after a moment's surprise, hugged him back. Then, typical of their gender, they stepped apart, clapping each other on the shoulder, covering their embarrassment, affection, and pleasure at the reunion. Jumping and barking, the dogs joined the melee.

'So, those two rascals found you,' said John. 'They've been waiting outside for ten minutes. Must have sensed you reach the turnoff.' He clicked his fingers, pointed to a rug by the fireplace. The dogs sloped off to curl up together but watched their every move.

Holt smiled. 'They're lethal, those two. They can drown you in slobber. Tracy's getting fat.'

'She's not fat, she's pregnant! Due in six weeks.'

'Oh, wow!' Holt's grin threatened to split his head in two as he knelt to stroke the proud mum and dad-to-be.

'I didn't expect you two to be here. I'd planned to come straight over after a quick shower. Is everything all right?'

'Everything's fine. How's your case going?' asked John. 'We're so sorry you had to release those suspects. We hoped you could close the case quickly.'

'Yeah, me too. It's been a tough four weeks.'

Every day without progress had been fresh fodder for the media. *'Police get it wrong yet again'* the headlines had screamed after the ignominious release of the Xtreem four. Somehow, the police also ended up being blamed for the three students' deaths, fuelling residents' complaints about the inadequate number of police officers patrolling the streets and parks. The harangued senior officers made their ire known to their immediate subordinates, who then vented on their already stressed staff.

John patted Holt's shoulder while Susan flapped her hands to shush her husband.

'Never mind all that now. Your Lily was here on Thursday, Matt,' she said.

'Who? Who's my Lily? I don't know any—'

***

But his heartbeat picked up pace. *Surely, they don't mean Lily Webster, the lovely buildings inspector? Was it only four weeks since her visit? So much had happened since then; none of it good.*

He recalled her visit – that afternoon before the triple murders. The last good day before his world churned.

He still remembered the feel of her slender fingers as they shook hands and wished he'd taken the time to tidy himself up. She was older than he'd first thought – he placed her age nearer 29 or 30, and her friendliness masked an underlying reserve and aloofness.

'I love buildings when they are at this stage of construction. They remind me of cathedrals,' Lily had said, craning her neck up into the vaulted void of the tarpaulin-sheeted roof.

She'd cupped slim hands around her mouth and called, 'Hello, hello,' into the emptiness above, laughing aloud as her voice echoed and bounced amongst the rafters. Then reddened and apologised on catching his gaze.

Lily Webster wore no wedding ring, but that didn't mean she was single.

She looked around and asked, 'Do you live here on-site?'

'No, I rent an annexe at my uncle's farmhouse just up the path there. It suits me perfectly for now, as I can work on this and help at the farm.'

'And your family? What do they think of this?'

'I moved here from London four years ago after my divorce. We didn't have any children, and as there was nothing to keep me there, I returned here to my childhood home. I bought this on impulse and have been working on it ever since.'

But the woman beside him had stiffened at the revelation of his single status and was once again brisk and professional as she carried out the rest of her inspection, ticking off items on her clipboard and making notes as she checked his work.

Lily had also declined his offer of a hot or cold drink, glanced at her watch and said, 'That's very kind, but I must dash. I need to collect my daughters from school.'

Holt recalled the stab of disappointment he'd felt as he followed her out to her car and stood watching as she turned the vehicle around and drove away.

They'd shared a moment, and real as it was, Holt had no illusion it was anything more. Just a momentary connection, an ephemeral spark.

Like the ships in H. W. Longfellow's poem, he'd thought then. *Ships that pass in the night, and speak to each other in passing...*

***

Apart from receiving approval for his structural modifications, he never expected to hear from her again. Yet, she'd come back.

'Oh, you don't mean Lily Webster, the building's inspector, do you?' Holt said, nonchalantly, he hoped.

'Yes! Oh, Matt, she's absolutely lovely! So pretty and so charming!' Susan bounced on her feet. 'She came by to drop off those papers for you,' pointing to a brown envelope on his side table. 'Said she put together some practical renovation tips and a list of reliable material suppliers.'

'She said she was passing by and dropped it off for you,' said John, nudging him in the ribs.

The farm and watermill were in a *cul-de-sac,* and no one 'passed by', but perhaps she had an inspection nearby.

'Well, that is kind of her.'

'What?' he asked when they still stood grinning at him.

'Are you going to ask her out?'

That was just like Susan, speaking her mind. No holds barred.

He sighed. 'I can't. Not right now. Not for a long time, the way this case is going. It'll be twenty-four-seven until we catch the killers.'

'Oh, Matt!' wailed Susan. 'You can't expect her to wait that long.'

'Leave the boy alone, Susan. He must do what's right for him.'

'You will thank her for the papers, won't you?' his aunt insisted. 'She left her card with her mobile number.'

'Yes, of course I will.'

'And explain how busy you are? She'll understand. Anyone would. Everyone knows about these awful murders and how difficult it's been for you.'

'If by everyone, you mean you two,' said Holt glumly.

No, I won't think about any of that tonight. Not the scathing press, the public's protests, the humiliating setbacks, or the berating from the top brass. Although the Superintendent did his best to shield Holt and his team, rumour had it that the top echelon was looking askance, questioning the Super's ability to see it through. Holt hoped his boss would not become a scapegoat for his failure to deliver results.

'I'll explain to her,' he promised. 'Now, I really need a shower. I'll come over as soon as I'm done.'

True to his word, Holt sent Lily a message. Thanked her for dropping off the papers and explained that he was extremely busy at present. He promised to call or text, but couldn't say when...

And Lily would have understood and sympathised had she known what his actual job was rather than assuming he was a farmer working for his uncle. Or if she followed the media coverage of the murders more closely. She did neither. To her, Holt's message was a brush-off, a slap to the face.

And somewhere, in some heaven, some God or Gods chuckled heartily at the success of their prank...

40

Durgapur, India

Deepak

Two nights after Deepak's conversation with DCI Holt, the police hustled the three fathers through the hotel's rear exit like criminals into an unmarked van and escorted them to the airport where the security staff took over custody. They held the three men in a windowless room in the nadir of London Heathrow Airport until their flight was ready to board.

'It's only for a few hours, and at least we've escaped the attentions of the press,' they'd consoled themselves.

Their reunions with their families broke their hearts afresh. The worst for Deepak had been meeting Roopesh's daughter—Anjali, his son's fiancée—again.

Like him, the poor child had lost two people she loved – her brother Arun and her fiancé, Suraj, and the toll was visible on her once beautiful face, now gaunt and empty. He recalled how

Jyoti and he had rejoiced when Suraj and Anjali got engaged. They'd had such high hopes for their future and dreamt of a house filled with the laughter of grandchildren, of watching them grow. A future where he and Jyoti grew old together.

He hugged the sobbing girl close and cursed the gods. *Those heartless, pitiless beings whom Jyoti worshipped.* The image of the black idol flashed in his mind. That one was the worst of the lot. Revered not only by Jyoti but by generations of his family.

And all for what? What good did any of it do?

41

Durgapur, India

Roopesh

'What! Are you mad?'

Roopesh remained silent, head swivelling to follow his uncle, pacing his study. The wiry seventy-two-year-old was just as liable to clout him round the head now as he did when Roopesh was a boy.

This was part of his and Prem's plan – to enlist Roopesh's uncle to help provoke the killers into action.

Kishore Chopra, known to friends and family as KC, whirled around, his movements those of a much younger man. 'Do you realize what you are asking of me? The sordid world you want me to re-enter?'

'I do.'

'No, you don't,' shouted KC. 'You only think you do. It's ten times worse than you imagine and a hundred times more dangerous. In my younger days, I've done things I shouldn't have. Dreadful things that I deeply regret. But I've turned my life around; left all that behind.'

'I'm truly sorry. I thought of asking someone else, but you're the only one I trust.' Roopesh played his trump card, bracing himself for his uncle's anger. 'If you won't help me, I'll have to go to Uncle Saxena.'

He reared back as KC gripped his shoulders, his uncle's furious face only inches away from his own.

'You will go nowhere near that fat bastard! He's a snake, a deadly, venomous snake. He didn't rise to his position as a minister through his so-called good deeds or the charity work he promises to do. You keep away from him.'

KC released him, stepped back, shoulders sagging wearily.

'Why don't you make it public?' asked Roopesh. 'He's out there week after week, spouting sanctimonious rubbish.'

'I wish I could, but I can't. He knows my secrets too. As you guessed, I haven't always been this straight. But I've closed that chapter of my life. He too has, to a great extent, but not totally. I've kept tabs on him to protect myself.' The room seemed smaller as KC paced some more.

'Look, I fully understand why you want to get to those killers. I, too, loved Arun. We have no children of our own, and he was my future, too. I want justice for him and his friends. Listen to me, please! Let the police do their job!'

Roopesh shook his head. 'It's taking too long, and they're not getting anywhere. Besides, we don't want to see them behind bars. We want them dead.'

Sighing, the older man slumped into the armchair. 'Me too. Let's hire somebody. Just give me the go-ahead and I shall get it done.'

'That'd be too easy. Besides, we want whoever is behind our sons' murders, whoever instigated those monsters or helped them after they killed our boys.'

'OK, then we'll have them kidnapped, taken to a secret place, then beat the truth out of them, and kill them.'

Roopesh guffawed. 'What Bollywood film have you been watching? No, that'd put us at the kidnapper's mercy. What about Anjali and our wives? They'll be at risk. No, we don't want anyone involved. We want to do it ourselves.'

The older man laughed. 'You? And Deepak and Prem? Whose ridiculous idea was it? To dangle a lucrative drug deal before them and then lure them to a convenient location... Ahem, where may I ask?' His tone was caustic.

'One of my warehouses,' muttered Roopesh.

'I see. And then what? They are younger, faster and certainly stronger than Deepak and Prem. They won't stand still while you try to restrain them. And they won't be unarmed!'

'We don't need to capture all four. We'll shoot the younger two as soon as they arrive. That'll only leave the two older ones.'

'I see. You'll shoot the younger two first. With what?' his tone scathing.

Roopesh squirmed. 'Er, with guns, of course.'

'You have guns?'

'Er, no, not yet. But we're hoping you'll get them for us.'

KC's jaw dropped, and he stared at his nephew in stupefaction. 'So, not only do you want me to become a drug dealer, you also want me to get guns for you?'

'Well, *we* don't know how, do we?' muttered Roopesh and flinched when his uncle whirled around.

'So, you want me to get you drugs and guns? Ahem, do you want some bombs, too?'

Roopesh didn't bother to respond.

KC continued to glare at the younger man, who, despite his silence, had a stubborn set to his jaw, his gaze defiant.

These idiots really are going through with this! Worry clenched his heart at the likely outcome of their madcap scheme, especially if they turned to his fat cousin, Saxena the minister, for help.

It could work, he thought. *I could make it work...*

'OK, why drugs? Not all young people use or deal in drugs,' he said eventually.

'This lot will if they aren't already doing so. It's easy money for them. I suspect they'll do it for the hell of it, to show they can get away with it or to thumb their noses at the police.'

'I still think it's a stupid plan!'

'Maybe. But can you think of anything better?'

After a long pause, KC gave in. He still thought it was a stupid plan, but it could work. 'We need someone with close enough ties to them to act as an intermediary. Someone they'll trust. Do you have a list of all their contacts from the private investigator?'

Roopesh smiled at the 'we', got up to scroll through his laptop for the details provided by the private investigator they'd hired. Five minutes later, he handed over two A4 sheets printed on both sides with a tabulated list of contacts.

'Goodness, this is impressive. That PI Nigel Payton does excellent work.'

'So he should. He certainly charges enough.' The PI had not stinted in naming the contacts. The comprehensive list of family, friends, and acquaintances also included those with only the most peripheral connection to the gang.

KC studied the list. 'Hmm, I see five potential. I am certain I can work with three, no, four. Yes, four of them.'

'Who, which ones?' Roopesh peered over his shoulder, but KC twisted away, screening the papers.

'No, you don't need to know. I'll set it up with one of them and prearrange drop-off and pickup points. The dealer will use a codename and an untraceable phone number. I'll handle all the logistics. Your job is to call that person with the dates and codes for the drop-off and collection points, quantities and price, which I'll give to you.'

'Where will you get the drugs from?' Roopesh asked.

KC glanced up from the printed sheets. 'Not your problem.' He held up a hand to stem the younger man's protests. 'Let's try to keep your involvement in this dirty business to an absolute minimum. I'll provide you with a voice-altering gadget, an unregistered phone and several SIM cards. Use those whenever you contact the dealer and choose a code name for yourself. Don't let them find out who you are. And don't waste your time and energy trying to discover who my chap is. If you do, I'll call off this whole deal.'

Roopesh nodded; he didn't doubt that his uncle would make good on his threat. 'Can you trust your contact?'

KC stopped pacing, his brows creased in doubt. While never being a carrier or handler, he'd established safe locations in several towns during his five-year stint as an economics lecturer in London in his younger days. Subsequently, he'd maintained and grown the sites during his regular visits to England. And although he'd been out of the nefarious trade for over a decade, he'd kept a good rapport with his contacts, both distributors and transporters. They'd been trustworthy then. Maybe they still were. Only one way to find out...

'Yes, I hope so,' he said. 'We've worked together before, in my bad old days. It's been a while, though. But I've known him for a long time.'

'He calls himself Tango,' he continued. 'Choose a name for yourself. And you needn't be cute.'

'Codenames, computerised voices. Sounds fun, like a bad Bollywood film. I'll be, um, Charlie. You can call me Charlie.'

'It's not funny, and it's not a game.' KC glared at his nephew. 'These are drug dealers who'll kill without a moment's hesitation. Tell Tango you'll increase the quantity if he proves to be reliable. The quality will be excellent, and he'll pocket a big margin because of the special low price. Better than he can get elsewhere. Soon he'll want to keep in your good books. Once it's working and they're hooked, we can work out how to entice them to your chosen location. We'll decide where later. You'd be stupid to use your own warehouse for the final pickup. It'll lead the police straight to you.'

'Not if they don't find the bodies.'

KC's eyebrows shot up. He found it incredulous that he was sitting here discussing murder with his nephew.

'Give yourselves a chance. And time. Rent a site anonymously. It's easy.' He studied Roopesh. 'And what if all this fails? What if the police find out? Catch you before you get to the puppeteer?'

'Then we're screwed. That's where you come in.'

'Me?'

'Yes you. We are relying on you to finish it for us.'

KC stared at his nephew; then, a smile lit up his face. *Ah, this was more like it!*

42

Durgapur, India

KC

KC parked his car on his cousin's drive. The sprawling white two-storeyed villa with red-trimmed windows and doors lived up to the image which Nagaraj Saxena, his onetime business partner, now a high level politician and a minister in the Indian government, portrayed of being a man of taste.

He turned to the grand entrance porch, lips curling at the sight of the fat politician, who looked like a mummified walrus in a blinding white *Nehru* suit, waddling towards him followed by his entourage.

'My dear Kishore *bhai*,' he exclaimed, using the term brother to address KC. 'What're you doing sitting in the car? Come in, come in, please. This is such a pleasure. An honour.'

Holding back his sidekick, he opened the car door himself to signify his esteem for the visitor and stood back to let him out.

KC wished yet again that he hadn't agreed to his nephew's entreaties. He knew the rumours that the man's immense wealth came not only from the perks of the job but also from his alleged, though unproved, links with organised crime were true. He'd extricated himself from that world, but here he was, entering its clutches again.

The politician led him into a sumptuous marble and brocade-lined private sitting room furnished with velvet settees and original Moghul-style paintings on the walls.

'Come, come, please sit here. This is the most comfortable chair.' He held the back of a plush, heavily padded armchair for his visitor before turning to one of his lackeys. 'Bring fresh tea and sweets for our guest. *Jaldi, jaldi.*' *Hurry, hurry.*

With the preliminaries out of the way and delicate porcelain cups of masala chai in their hands, the minister shooed his entourage away.

'How are Roopesh and his wife holding up? And that poor child, Anjali. I can't believe God would do this to them. As you know, I'd hoped to bring our families closer, that Mohan, my son, and Anjali, Roopesh's daughter, would marry. But that wasn't to be.'

'They're doing as well as can be expected. I'm not here to talk about them. I have a favour to ask.'

'Oh, please. Anything I can do, I'll willingly oblige.'

When KC outlined his request, he spluttered, shot up from his chair. 'How dare you make such accusations! How dare you come to my own home and insult me by—'

'Oh, sit down and shut the fuck up,' said KC. 'You don't have to pretend with me, my dear cousin. I've been keeping tabs; I know exactly what you've been up to.'

KC's cold glance had the fat man licking his lips.

'The secret activities at your lab and the undeclared products your brilliant chemists have been concocting. I hear they are of top quality. Bravo, cousin. I'm impressed. When you do something, you do it well; very well indeed.'

Despite himself, Saxena preened. Praise from KC, his onetime mentor, was rare. It had to be earned.

'Kishore *bhai*, I can loan you money if you need it. You shouldn't do this!'

'Thank you, but no. I don't need your money. I'll buy the stuff from you at a fair price. At the price at which you sell to your dealers. You owe me that much. Other than that, you won't be involved. You'll keep your hands clean.'

The fat politician hesitated, blinking as wheels turned in his head.

KC spoke quietly. 'I won't take no for an answer. And don't even think of betraying me. I can reveal every one of your skeletons.'

He paused, trapped his cousin's furtive gaze. 'Don't think you can have me killed, either. I don't die easily, but you already know that. I taught you everything you know. You won't last twenty-four hours if anything happens to me or my family. You will die. Painfully. You and your family. So, my dear cousin, don't play with fire.'

'How, how could you possibly think that I would...?'

KC interrupted his bluster and got to his feet. He'd had enough. 'Just reminding you, boy. I'll be in touch soon with quantities and schedules. You tell me where to collect and the price. I'll pay in cash or clean money, however, and wherever you like.'

The fat man fidgeted, wringing his hands. Eventually, he nodded.

Then, as custom demanded, he accompanied KC to his car, stood smiling and waving as he drove off.

KC glanced at the shrinking image of his cousin in his rearview mirror and snorted.

43

Holt

'Eight weeks since those murders. How can we have nothing? How can Tommy's car and all their clothes disappear without a trace?'

Heads swivelled as the team followed DCI Matthew Holt's trajectory up and down the incident room.

'Sit down, please. My head's spinning watching you.' Superintendent Simpson clutched his head.

The daily evening briefing had been a depressing one. While reports on background information and transcripts of interviews continued to trickle in, none advanced their case. The only glimmer of sunshine was that during the past two weeks, and for all the wrong reasons, press attention on the case had waned. Other recent tragic incidents diverted media attention—thirteen bodies found in a container at Southampton port and a terrorist attack in London injuring over fifty people.

Now at 7.30 p.m., only the core team of detectives remained to review their findings, or rather, the lack of them, with the superintendent.

Holt lowered his frame to slump into his chair. *If this lot's expressions reflect mine, then I am a glum sod indeed.*

Still no sign of Tommy's car. A shocking number of CCTV and speed cameras had been defective or vandalised when the homicide occurred. It wasn't on the list of abandoned cars, nor was it parked in the area. Searches of garages, workshops, scrapyards yielded nothing. Somehow, between the killings in the park and the following morning, the car had disappeared, and no one was talking.

He sat upright. *They'll hate this, but it's got to be done.*

'Sergeant, I want all those CCTVs rechecked. Get fresh eyes to review those footage.'

'Sir.' There was no mistaking the lack of enthusiasm in Rowena's voice.

'You still think those boys did it?' asked the superintendent.

'They are our only viable suspects. Duncan's explanation for his fingerprint on the victim's phone sounds plausible, but I don't buy it. There are too many coincidences. Everything they wore that Thursday night was new. They claim their outfits were impulse gifts from Tommy Wade, and all agreed to wear them on the same day. Sounds credible enough. Tommy says he bought them at a street market a while back, but he cannot remember when. He paid cash, so there's no receipt or credit card record. Their reason for washing those clothes is equally reasonable – they got wet – yeah, there was a storm that night. Then his car and both his and Duncan's jackets go missing.'

'It's a shame our witness, Walter McCabe, could not pick out any of our suspects from the line-up,' said Karl Stringer. 'If only those dogs had bitten them on the arse, we'd at least have their DNA.'

Karl was right; we'd have DNA, but those dogs would be dead, thought Holt. *Unlike the victims, the dogs would have fought back. Or would they? What if it'd been John's collies?* The notion of anyone hurting them, especially Tracy and her new litter of seven squirming pups, twisted his guts.

'Are you still watching those boys?'

'We can't, sir,' said Holt. 'We've increased uniform patrols and assigned an additional PCSO around the estate. The community workers are keeping tabs too. We're also monitoring their calls, but we can't do a full-fledged surveillance; it's not sustainable. So far, they aren't doing anything suspicious, though I hear they're really cocky. But they know we're watching them, so they're careful. They've been spending a lot of time at The Cue Room, the pool club belonging to Harvey Endsleigh.'

'To be fair, when I interviewed Endsleigh, he said he was going to give them free entrance to the hall on two or three weekdays to show his support,' said Rowena, recalling her interview with the handsome owner. 'He believes they're innocent. Said we're being unfair to them. The Cue Room's a popular hangout for many Southampton students, and our victims too visited the place with friends occasionally. Unless there is a connection we know nothing about, I can't see how Endsleigh's involved. But let's keep him on the board. I felt he was hiding something. It could be nothing to do with our case. Probably dodgy drinks, short measures, undeclared income, gambling without a licence, maybe even small-time dealing.'

'What about Tommy's foster siblings? Anything there?'

'Michelle interviewed Anne-Marie Saunders, and I met her brother Graham,' said DC Larry Ives. 'Nice kids, but they seemed almost afraid of Tommy. Said he was very manipulative. But they loved him too, I think. Michelle got the impression that Anne-Marie used to be in love with him and was heartbroken when he left home. But distance and his absence seem to have given them a better perspective, and they said they haven't been in touch. Tommy simply cut them all out of his life when he moved into his father's flat. He didn't want to know them. Acted like that part of his life didn't happen.'

Holt shook his head. For more than a decade, Ruth Barnes and her husband had looked after Tommy; they'd been kind and caring, even tried to love him. Maybe that was the problem. They had tried but failed to love him. And Tommy knew that...

'Both of them were on their campuses, nowhere near Southampton,' continued Larry. 'We confirmed their alibis. We could find no contact between them and our suspects, and we found nothing to link them to the victims or their families.'

The superintendent turned to Holt. 'Matt, I received a call from the coroner's office about Jyoti Verma. Are you satisfied her death was suicide?'

'Nothing suggests otherwise, sir, and it's not for want of looking. None of them benefit from her death.'

'Well, the coroner's satisfied that it's suicide but was checking before he signed the death certificate. Is there any reason he mustn't release her body?'

Holt hesitated. 'Well, Chris--the chief pathologist--would have taken all the samples they need, as would forensics from Jyoti's clothes and personal items. The hotel room's no longer a crime scene.'

'So, there's no valid reason to keep her body, then,' said the superintendent decisively. 'I'll let the coroner's office know they can release Jyoti Verma's body. What about that statue? I don't want it in our evidence locker if it's no longer required. I don't want us to be responsible for any damage or its loss.'

'They can return that,' said Holt, recalling the three men's frisson on seeing it. 'Again, I'm sure forensics has everything they need.'

'Mrs Verma's death has broken them all, especially Deepak—Mr Verma, for all the calm and composure he presents, sir,' said DC David Plummer, the FLO. 'Deepak told us how they met. He really loved her, and I can't see him hurting her. We went through the families' backgrounds and finances but found nothing suspicious.'

In a separate report to Holt, DC David Plummer had also confirmed that he'd found no evidence of the three fathers showing any untoward interest in cult worship or practices.

Holt re-examined his notion of them organising their sons' murders for religious reasons, but logic told him that ritual sacrifices had to be up close and personal. They wouldn't contract it out. They'd have to do it themselves. And none of them were even in England. That was a verified fact. Besides, he couldn't see them stabbing or cutting anyone.

Then he recalled that two of them were surgeons.

'What about the rumours concerning that Indian minister, Nagaraj Saxena?' asked the superintendent.

'Again, nothing, sir. Our inquiries haven't given us any leads either. Just a lot of grief from our High Commission in New Delhi,' said Holt.

The detectives had a glimmer of hope when their counterparts in India mentioned rumours of one of Kapoor's relatives'—a prominent politician's—connections to the underworld. But it was short-lived. They found no cause to pursue it further, especially when Roopesh Kapoor said that neither he nor his immediate family had been in contact with the politician for several months before the murders. And since then, their only contact had been to thank the minister for his condolences.

'What about Marvin Jackson?' The superintendent glared at Holt. 'Matt, I've had complaints of harassment from his counsel, Metcalf. Unless you got something solid to go on, you need to stop poking that hornet's nest.'

Holt smiled. Hooray! His digging was provoking Jackson. Would it provoke him enough to break cover and expose his part in all this? Because aside from his purported selflessness and desire to aid a friend, they had f-all on him.

Helpful contacts in Jamaica confirmed Jackson's story that he and Hughes were childhood friends. Hospital records dug up from three decades ago confirmed Daniel Hughes' treatment for a bullet wound. The police report stated that neither man saw his attackers nor knew why anyone would attack them.

Rumour from Winchester Prison had it that Marvin Jackson extracted Daniel Hughes' promise to work for him when he got out, as a personal bodyguard, chauffeur, valet or whatever role Hughes wanted.

Jackson had acknowledged the arrangement. 'Mr Holt, I need someone I can trust implicitly. Not as a bodyguard – I can buy that anywhere. A real friend to look out for me, someone with my interests and wellbeing at heart. Which you obviously don't have,' he had added with a laugh.

Repeated interviews and checks disclosed no link between the victims' fathers and Marvin Jackson. His team explored various angles: medical negligence by one of the Verma brothers in treating a member of Jackson's family. Business rivalry between him and Roopesh Kapoor. Perhaps the victims or their fathers owed Jackson money and refused to pay up...

Holt's investigation of Jackson – a proper poke at the hornets' nest, as the superintendent put it, turned up nothing. Nothing apart from annoying his target and infuriating

Metcalf, which Holt considered a good result. But it also provoked the Chief and the ACC's ire.

The superintendent interrupted his musings. 'Thank you, everyone. I know it's disheartening when you don't see results but keep at it. Just be quicker about it.'

'Yes, sir, thank you, sir,' chorused the team as they gathered their papers, laptops and gadgets to return to their desks.

Perhaps I'll give that hornet's nest one more poke and see what happens, thought Holt.

44

Durgapur, India

Deepak

Funeral rites follow innumerable customs and practices but invariably involve offering the remains to one of the four elements. Some are buried six feet deep or more in the earth to become food for worms and insects. Some go to a watery grave, buffeted by the tides, a feast for aquatic creatures. Some are given an air burial, their cadavers picked clean by carrion birds and scavenging beasts. Fire consumes others, their bodies reduced to a pile of ashes.

When the coroner released the bodies, the three fathers had sneaked back into Southampton and returned with four embalmed corpses in zinc-lined coffins.

Today, nine weeks after the murders, was the funeral. The day to dispose of the four carcasses that once housed the spirits of three vibrant young men and a dynamic woman. Young men, who never got to be husbands, fathers or grandfathers.

A woman who'd been a granddaughter, daughter, sister, wife and mother, but never the grandmother she so longed to be.

A narrow band of sunrise glinting on the horizon breached the darkness while gusts of wind rattled the windows, lifted fallen leaves and debris to swirl them around before scattering them farther and wider. Every gust held the promise of a storm. For now, though, it whistled and churned amongst the funeral cortege, sometimes leading the way, other times following, but always keeping close. It heralded the four hearses and the families of mourners making their way to the cremation centre.

Deepak remembered the shock and jolt of seeing his son, Suraj, in the mortuary. But worse was the ritual bathing of his boy's body. Touching the cold, lifeless corpse. Preparing it for cremation. He had almost screamed at the horror of the 'Y' post-mortem scar running from his son's shoulders to his groin.

The wails and sobs of the women performing the rituals and preparing Jyoti for the funeral reverberated in Deepak's head. Twenty-six years ago, he'd met, fallen in love and married her. Today, he would reduce her body to ashes. Her and the son she had borne him.

Prem and Roopesh held him until the shivers that spasmed his body had subsided.

The families of the three young men held a joint funeral. After all, their three sons had spent their lives together. Died together. Their parents drew comfort from knowing that they had not been alone. In their last moments, each had someone they knew and loved with them.

The three fathers tensed as they approached the crematorium. They would need more than strength and willpower to see this through.

Barefoot, Deepak, Prem, Roopesh, and the other pallbearers hefted the traditional wooden-poled, canvas-lined stretchers onto their shoulders and entered the building.

Afterwards, none of them remembered the details or how they got through the ceremony. The choreographed rituals, the litany of prayers, the repetitive, mesmerising chants—the mantras—helped to dull their senses and gave them strength to light the torches. To apply the blazing logs to each of the four pyres and the fortitude to watch the flames take hold. Flames that would scorch and render the bodies of their loved ones to ashes.

Not a sound escaped their throats, but with every flicker, every blaze, every sizzle and every spark, their souls screamed.

***

The Dra watches the humans. Listens to their prayers. No adulation or promises this time. A rare occasion indeed, one where the people gathered aren't thinking of themselves. Making no requests or bargains, at least not for themselves.

Their silent cries are strong. They're in a world of pain. Of despair.

The Dra is tempted to respond, to answer their calls. To spare the man from more anguish. But his fate has already been charted. His future unfolds before the Being. It cannot interfere, but it knows it won't be long now.

The Dra waits.

45

Durgapur, India

Deepak

The sun still had an hour's uphill trek before it brought dawn to Durgapur. The searing heat it promised warmed the earth, creating swirls of mist that dissipated and fled as fast as it appeared.

Dry-mouthed from a night of eszopiclone-induced sleep, Deepak awoke, ending the brief respite from the actuality of his life.

He reached out to the other half of his bed, seeking the sleeping form of his wife. The empty bedside, the emptiness in his soul, the grittiness in his eyes and the tumult of emotions raging in his heart brought harsh reality crashing back to his consciousness.

Head drooping, body lax with fatigue, Deepak sat up. So heavy. Every inch of him seemed to weigh a ton.

He jerked up at the sound of running water and the muffled clatter of utensils. *Jyoti! She was downstairs!* He sprang to his feet, only to collapse a second later.

No, not Jyoti. She had left him; left him alone with the burden of living. Of existing, if one could even call it that.

She was gone. Definitely gone. Didn't he light her funeral pyre himself just thirteen days ago? With these...

He stared at his trembling hands – a surgeon's hands. These hands, meant for healing, lit those pyres. Turned his wife and son's bodies to ashes.

And hadn't he returned to the crematorium the next morning and with these hands collected the two earthen pots, each with a cloth tied around its mouth? Two labelled orange clay pots of ashes. Pots containing all that remained of Jyoti and Suraj.

The Deepak he presented to the world, the one everyone saw, had gone to England, brought home and cremated their bodies. Comforted his extended family, performed all the rituals required of him. Graciously acknowledged the countless messages of condolences that poured in from around the world. And kept in touch with DCI Matthew Holt.

But the real Deepak inside him wanted to scream, to rend his own body to bits, to tear the killers to pieces with his bare hands, to feel the heat of their blood.

The sounds from downstairs increased. He recognised the murmur of his brother Prem's voice. This was once their childhood home. This had once been a happy place.

A faint glow lit the early morning sky as Deepak hauled himself up and shuffled into the ensuite bathroom for a cold shower. Dressed in a simple white cotton collarless *kurta* and pyjama-style trousers, he descended to a sparkling clean downstairs.

Prem and Shanti had prepared the house for this morning's event. The thirteenth-day rituals following the cremation.

His glance landed on the closed door, bolted and locked with an oversized brass padlock. Jyoti's gods' room. A room full of images, statues and paintings of gods and goddesses. A room once replenished daily with flowers and floral garlands and alight with dozens of oil lamps. A room where she began her day with poojas—ritualistic prayers—with supplications to each of the twenty-seven divinities, but always, directing her most ardent petitions to the obsidian statuette of the black goddess occupying the middle of the rosewood shelf.

So many of them, yet none had prevented the destruction of his family.

Oh, how he hated them. Feared them. All those empty eyes watching him, judging him and finding him wanting.

On his return from Southampton, he had replaced the little obsidian statue in the centre of the shelf. Jyoti's dried blood still marred its glassy sheen.

He shuddered, remembering the heat and feel of it in his palm, the arms pulling him away from the edge of that precipice.

He had gone straight out, bought the brass padlock, and no one had stepped into that room since.

Until last night.

46

Durgapur, India

Eyes watch him, follow his every move. They are everywhere, every direction he turns. Eyes watch him from immobile faces, some beautiful, some not, a few downright demonic.

He grabs a heavy glass-lidded wooden display box from the carved rosewood shelf and flees. Far enough out of sight of those probing eyes, or so he hopes, he flings himself down on the edge of a bed, forces himself to relax, to calm his palpitating heart. A waft of fresh air chills his damp scalp; bare feet flex on the cold polished stone floor.

His nostrils flare to draw in a deep lungful of the subtle scent of the sandalwood case inlaid with slivers of exotic woods in contrasting colours. Fingers trace the Sanskrit word ▫ (Om) embossed in gold.

A small brass hook latch holds the lid shut. Deep red felt, the colour of drying blood, lines the insides, and hidden in a cavity behind the back panel is a silver-framed ink painting wrapped in a wad of black silk to protect the image from light and sight.

The painting itself is small, smaller than his hand. Set within a silver frame, its colours are still bright and vivid from being secreted in the dark during the six centuries of its existence.

Painted on cotton canvas, the scene features the four-armed goddess in deep blue-black, with outsized, red-rimmed eyes, long tongue protruding from a wide open mouth.

Heavy gold bangles clasp her wrists, upper arms and ankles; several necklaces adorn her neck. Thick, long, frizzy black hair flows to her generous hips. She holds a khadga—a crescent-shaped sword—in one hand, a trident in the other. Her third hand grasps aloft a severed head by its topknot, and in the fourth, she cups a bowl to catch the blood gushing from her victim's head.

Displaying large, round, heavy breasts, a skirt of human arms wraps her broad hips and a garland of demon heads around her neck, she appears to levitate. Cushioned by soft white clouds, she gazes at the two men kneeling on the earth below.

They stare up at her, arms extended in supplication. A third man lies between them, his face contorted in agony. Bright red splashes encircle the gaping black hole in his chest. More covers his torso and stains the surrounding earth. Red bloody vines stretch from the victim's body to his heart, held in the bloodstained hands of the kneeling men.

A gruesome and detailed depiction of a human sacrifice to the black goddess Kali.

He studies the painting – the naivety of its rendering, the horror of its content. With a shudder, he re-wraps and returns it to its dark home.

He picks up a black felt-tipped pen from his desk, removes his white cotton kurta and turns to a full-length mirror on the wardrobe door. Draws an X to mark the exact location of his heart. Pen held like a scalpel, he sketches a line down his sternum, continuing it along and just below the curve of the lowest left rib, all the way to his side. Chin down, he admires the smooth unbroken black line on his torso.

Yes, a cut along here to expose the ribs. Then, saw through the sternum, separate it to access the heart, and—

No! This is madness. Insanity.

But this is what it takes to face another day...

47

Durgapur, India

Deepak

Deepak got through the day performing everything expected of him, following the rituals and rites, appeasing the many gods to tide his wife and son's journey to heaven.

Night falls fast in Durgapur. By 7 p.m., the fading daylight emptied the house of families, friends and strangers who had turned up to pay their respects. He was physically and mentally exhausted, his mouth parched from a day of thanking people for coming, for their sympathies.

Now, only his brother Prem and their friend Roopesh remained. The three men huddled in Deepak's study.

'Last evening, I arranged for the second drop,' said Roopesh. 'It seems to be working smoothly.'

Deepak's reaction to learning of his brother and Roopesh's plan had surprised the two friends. Instead of the anticipated admonitions, Deepak absentmindedly tugged his beard, shrugged, and said, 'If you think it'll work...'

Things had progressed in the four weeks since Roopesh had spoken to his uncle, KC. Roopesh had contacted the dealer, whose real name KC still stubbornly refused to reveal, and had already made two deliveries. Not personally, of course.

At his uncle's insistence, Roopesh did not handle the narcotics or the money. Those involved knew him only as "Charlie," a digitally altered voice, albeit one with the wherewithal to transact the deals. KC provided the drugs, arranged the drop-offs at locations convenient to the dealer and collected the cash.

Roopesh's role was simply to convey messages between KC and the dealer, someone he only knew as Tango. A man – he assumed it was a man – who also used a computer-altered voice.

'Good,' said Prem. 'But it's too slow. Can you persuade KC to speed up the process?'

'I tried,' said Roopesh, 'but he won't budge. Says we need to be extra cautious in the beginning, act as if we're not sure whether to trust Tango. With the profits he's making, he'll want more. He'll try to prove that he's reliable. But it'll take time.'

Listening to the exchange, Deepak slumped. *Time. Time's my enemy. How will I find the strength to see this through when every second without Jyoti and Suraj is agony?* He had no confidence in their plan, but he'd never say so or give Prem and Roopesh the slightest sign of his doubts. They needed this. It was something for them to cling to. A reason to go on living. To see justice done.

'Have you heard from the Chief Inspector?' Roopesh asked.

Deepak shook his head. 'I haven't called him today, but I will tomorrow. He had nothing new when we spoke last Thursday, and I doubt he'll have anything new tomorrow. He is a good man, but he won't find our sons' killers. Or whoever orchestrated it. And he cannot give us the justice we want.'

He sighed. 'Maybe your plan will succeed where his cannot.'

48

Durgapur, India

He can barely control it now. That oppressing darkness, ever present on the fringes, growing, threatening to swallow his mind.

He opens a drawer, brings out the ancient painting and studies the image. There should be three people. All three aware and the donor willing. The sacrifice must be of a living, beating human heart.

But three out of four isn't bad.

Out comes the black pen, and with his eyes shut, he traces the now familiar line in one smooth, fast swoop. A smile lights up his face at the steady black line. Perfect.

Practice is good. Especially as it has to be done quickly.

But pain – excruciating pain at that, and shock would be the fiercest enemies. The donor needs to remain alive. And conscious. And his heart beating.

His hands reach behind him, fingers unerringly find the spot between the L3 and L4 vertebrae on his spine, the site for an epidural.

'Should I combine it with thoracic epidural anaesthesia and chest wall blocks? Hmm. This needs more research,' he decides. 'But meanwhile, I can work on my shopping list.'

He puts on his kurta and begins:
- *Plastic sheets, Towels, kitchen rolls*
- *Bleach*
- *Scalpels*
- *Suture needles, thread, scissors*
- *Oscillating saw...*

49

Durgapur, India

Anjali

May is one of the hottest months in Durgapur, with temperatures climbing into the mid-forties Celsius without straining a muscle. The scorching heat penetrated the darkest corners, sparing no one, giving no respite. The blinding brightness should have livened up the streets, but the intense blaze sucked the energy out of everything it touched.

In her air-conditioned bedroom, Anjali picked up a rubber band and twisted her long hair into a high ponytail. Was that her in the mirror? That stranger with the gaunt face, sallow skin, enormous lifeless hazel eyes and cracked lips? She stretched her mouth in a parody of a smile. The stranger mimicked her, even teeth revealed in a grimace, bright white against the red of the blood oozing from the split crusts. She reached out with a tissue to dab the stranger's mouth, snapping back into reality when her hand collided against the cold, smooth glass. With a shudder, she wiped her mouth, turned and walked out.

Twelve weeks since the murders and she was still here in India, with no energy to return to London or to her studies at Imperial College. Recently though, recollections of her past carefree life, her friends, the challenges of coursework, had crept into her mind like a dusting of snow, softening and reshaping the jagged edges of those memories. Guilt and shame soon followed. It was too soon. She needed the pain. She must continue to mourn them, as her parents did.

It was her birthday today, and all she wanted was to be left alone. Instead, she had comforted her parents when they knocked on her door with a birthday card.

Last year, a lifetime ago, they had celebrated her birthday with such joy and laughter.

Her brother, Arun, had hugged her. Their friend, the effervescent Ravi, had picked her up and whirled her around, and Suraj had held out his hand.

'What, a handshake?' Ravi said, 'Give her a kiss, man!'

'Go on, she won't bite.' Arun pushed Suraj towards his sister.

Suraj's arm on her shoulder brought a flush to her face as his lips burnt a light kiss on her forehead. When they sprang apart, Anjali's face was bright red.

Her watching parents raised their eyebrows and exchanged knowing smiles.

No celebrations today, though. She thanked family and friends for their cards and wishes, remaining stoic and shedding no tears until that call from her dead fiancé, Suraj's, father. The man she called Uncle Deepak from the moment she could speak. Her heart broke anew listening to his deep, sombre voice wishing her a happy birthday, telling her to please look after herself.

She checked the watch hanging loose on her bony wrist; it needed resizing, two or more links removed to fit. Time to leave for her rendezvous with friends at a cafe in town.

Anjali paused by the living room. Her mother sat in her usual spot on the settee, staring at nothing, the smell of the aromatic spices drifting from an untouched cup of *masala chai* on the centre table. She took a step towards her mum, stopped, retreated, and headed out of the door.

We are broken, all of us, she thought. *Uncle Deepak most of all. He has no one left.*

The worst part was waiting for news from DCI Matthew Holt. For a call telling them the murderers were in custody. But each week brought nothing. The police were no further forward, no nearer to catching the culprits.

Anjali recalled her video interview with the DCI over two months ago. He had seemed nice, he and Sergeant Rowena.

She wondered again why she had not mentioned Mohan when DCI Holt asked about boyfriends or spurned lovers. But then, Mohan was neither. A few passionate kisses and urgent fumbling did not count, especially since he soon found compensation elsewhere after she had stayed his hands and rushed away.

She had told no one. Was it guilt at her own betrayal of Suraj that held her tongue? Mohan attracted and repulsed her in equal measure; she sensed his underlying ruthlessness and knew full well that there was no love in her own feelings for him.

Then there was his father. The fat, loathsome man, the corrupt politician with his lustful eyes and disgusting hands that 'accidentally' touched or brushed against her. Rumours circulated that father and son shared women, but that couldn't be true. No, Mohan wouldn't do that. She shuddered.

Anjali had panicked when she overheard an aunt mention that Mohan's father intended to approach her parents with a marriage proposal between her and Mohan. The craving that underscored her desire for Mohan, despite knowing his true nature, had terrified her.

That evening, she talked Suraj and her parents into announcing their engagement.

Mohan's disappointment, if he felt any at all, had not lasted long. Two months later, he married a mega-rich industrialist's daughter, and pictures of the happy couple appeared frequently on social media. The most recent ones showed him with his heavily pregnant wife.

But all that had nothing to do with Suraj, Arun, or Ravi's deaths. No reason to mention Mohan or even his loathsome father to DCI Matthew Holt. So, she hadn't.

Closing the front door softly behind her, she hurried into her car, turned up the air conditioning to full blast, and set off to meet her friends.

Twenty minutes later, Anjali pulled into a parking space in Durgapur town centre. Reluctantly, she stepped out of the luxurious cool of her car into the sweltering heat. Within seconds, a fine sheen of perspiration covered her. By the time she crossed the main road to the cafe, she'd be soaked in sweat.

The branches of the many trees planted and maintained by the municipality drooped as the relentless heat leached moisture from the leaves, turning them dull and dusty, more brown than green. How could those trees survive the constant exposure to petrol and diesel fumes and dust from countless construction projects? The stark and angular steel frames of dozens of construction cranes loomed in the surrounding skyline, some static while others swung their long booms over multi-storied concrete buildings.

Once a village, then a small comfortable suburb, Durgapur was now a mishmash of hastily constructed high-rise blocks, with developers vying for every square foot of space with little or no regard to the infrastructure required to support and sustain the influx of residents and businesses.

During peak hours, vehicles of all kinds jammed this road, hooting, causing a complete bottleneck as they attempted to slip past one another. Pedestrians jaywalked, blithely ignoring drivers who stuck their heads out, swearing and shaking their fists. Occasionally, there would be traffic policemen on duty, their shrill whistles piercing the ocean of noise but making little discernible difference to the congestion. But at this time of day, few people ventured outside.

Anjali hurried to the pedestrian crossing and waited for the light to turn green. Just as she stepped out onto the main road, the mobile phone in her handbag rang. Head swivelling in both directions, she walked along the zebra crossing, listening to an automated female voice say, 'You have a pre-recorded greeting from...'

A brief pause, then a voice she knew so well said, 'Suraj Verma.'

Anjali stopped dead in the middle of the road, her eyes and mouth open wide in a furore of emotions – shock, horror, pain followed by overwhelming happiness.

He was alive! Suraj was alive! They all were! They weren't dead! Why did she think they were? She had imagined it all. This was proof! Suraj had phoned her, left her a message! It had all been a ghastly dream. A nightmare.

With a surge of happiness, she listened to her fiancé's voice.

'Anjali, happy birthday to you, my love. I didn't know if I'd be able to call you, so I pre-recorded this to reach you at the exact hour you were born. I love you so much. Hope you have a great day, and I'll speak to you soon.'

The automated voice resumed, '*End of pre-recorded message. To listen to the greeting again, press 1; to save it, press 2; to delete, press 3.*'

She pressed 1 and listened again, one hand pressing the phone to her ear, the other clenched in a fist, pushed hard against her chest, her eyes shining and a smile of incredible happiness on her face.

Anjali never heard the horrified shouts from the pavements, nor did she feel the impact of the bus as it hit her. The screams of horror from her fellow pedestrians and cries of distress from the bus driver reached her through a dense haze. She wondered why they were all making so much noise.

Slipping into merciful unconsciousness, she did not sense hands lifting her off the road and into the ambulance.

50

Durgapur, India

Deepak

Roopesh Kapoor stared at the figure on the bed. The caricature of Anjali. His daughter.

Uncertain if they could save her, the doctors did their best to repair the internal damage. Steel pins and plates held broken bones together. A plaster cast encased her lower half.

He struggled to reconcile the still form on the stark white bed with the vivacious girl in his memories. She lay in a deep, induced coma, her thin form covered with the white hospital bedsheet, skin stretched across bones above sunken cheeks. The once-glossy dark hair on the stark white pillow was coarse and dull. A tube inserted into her mouth twisted her lips into a grimace. Another entered a vein on the back of her thin hand, and a third, hidden beneath the sheet, disappeared into her abdomen.

Hope and dread rode on each of Roopesh's shoulder. Equally strong, their whips propelled his vacillating mind, sending him lurching between optimism and despair.

Wounds will heal. Bones will mend... hope whispered.

She'll never wake up... scoffed despair.

The beep, beep of the machines reminded him they were the ones keeping her alive. There was little brain activity, but as long as even the smallest hint of brain function existed, he would make sure those damn machines kept working. For the rest of her life, if necessary.

The door clicked open, and his friend Prem entered, accompanied by another man who seemed familiar. Roopesh gasped when he recognised the bald and clean-shaven man as Deepak. Without his hair and bushy white beard and moustache, he looked old, frail. The recent tragedies and trauma marked them all, but it had extracted a special toll on him.

Deepak joined Roopesh to study the comatose figure, walked around the bed, trained eyes checking the tubes. Picking up the folder at the foot of the bed, he scanned the report and passed it to his brother Prem. The cardio-surgeon scrutinised the notes.

'She's in good hands here,' he said.

Deepak stared at the sorry form on the bed. *My son, my Suraj, loved this girl. They were our future. Those bastards stole everything from me!*

The knot of anger in his stomach was like a steel ball, so large that it threatened to engulf him. THEY stole his son, his nephew, and their childhood friend. THEY murdered the three young men whom he had known from the day they were born. THEY killed his wife just as surely as if they'd slit her throat.

This innocent girl, too, was their fault...

A growl escaped his throat, startling Roopesh and Prem. Deepak's eyes blazed with anger. He could barely speak for the rage consuming him. Rage so intense that killing the killers was no longer enough. He needed to decimate the world that birthed them.

Through clenched teeth he said, 'Come see me at home this evening,' and strode out of the hospital into the blazing sun.

51

Durgapur, India

Deepak

The two men climbed the wide steps to the sheltered porch, lifted the heavy brass ring and tapped it on the ornate front door. No answer.

Prem glanced behind him. He'd expected the *chowkidar*[1] to challenge him, but both the night watchman and his dog were absent. Something wasn't right. Puzzled and a little worried, both men glanced at their wristwatches – 12.15 a.m. Spot on time, just as the note instructed. Prem then remembered that the note had also asked him to use his key to enter the house.

From habit and custom, they removed their sandals and placed them on the purpose-built shelf in the corner of the large, white-ceilinged hallway. The white note on the floor was

---

1. Security guard.

hard to miss, as were the two parcels beneath. Prem unfolded it while Roopesh peered over his shoulder.

Dear Prem and Roopesh,

Thank you for coming.
I know you are wondering why I asked you to come at this hour, and you will soon know why. I have given the chowkidar the night off, and the cleaner will not be in until 8.30 a.m. We shall be alone until then.

But first, I need you both to follow these instructions exactly. Please do not question me – just do as I ask. It is very important.

Please:

1. *Lock the front door and draw the security chain.*

2. *Remove your shoes and all your clothes*

3. *Put on the items in the parcels*

4. *Then, and only then, come to Jyoti's gods' room*

I'll see you soon.

Yours,
Deepak

The friends hesitated, but a lifetime habit of looking up to Deepak, following his lead, and doing as he asked on the rare occasions he did, was hard to break. Shrugging their shoulders but with increasing disquiet, they obeyed the bizarre instructions. The sinister implications dawned on them only when they saw each other clad in identical white disposable coveralls and booties.

A roar from one end of the house tore the silence apart. They turned, dashed to the end of the hallway, and shoved the door open.

The heady smell of incense stung their noses, the scented smoke a shimmering haze from floor to ceiling. Dozens of ornate *diyas*—oil wick lamps—lit up the room Jyoti had dedicated to the gods. Polished metal, wood and glass gleamed in the soft glow, and in the flickering flames, the multi-headed, multi-armed idols seemed to be alive, and watching the men—

—whose eyes were riveted on the figure crouched in the centre of the red rug. Naked. Covered in red paint. Holding a red glistening object in his hands.

'No!' screamed Prem, rushing to his brother. 'What have you done?'

Roopesh's horrified howl melded with Prem's as he followed and sank to the floor beside him.

Prem grabbed clamps from the assortment of surgical instruments on a tray and tried to straighten Deepak.

'Roop, help me. I need you!' he yelled, but his friend remained frozen, unable to drag his gaze away from the scene. Prem shook him by the shoulders and dug his elbow into his midriff. With a grunt of *ooff* Roopesh snapped alert.

'Help me straighten him. I need to clamp his blood vessels.'

But Deepak stopped them. 'No. Don't,' he gasped. 'I have to do this. I... I beg you. I give my heart to *Kali-Ma*. She... will help you.'

Breath bursting in short, loud gasps from his wide-open mouth, Deepak held out his hands. There, cradled between his trembling palms, was his pulsating heart, with dripping tubes leading to the gaping hole in his chest. He laid the throbbing organ at the feet of the little obsidian statue of the Goddess Kali on the floor before him.

The little figurine shimmered in the surrounding glow of lamps. Its silhouette stretched from its tiny feet up to the ceiling. On the wall behind, four giant shadowy arms waved in the iridescent light. From the ceiling, the dark outline of its fearsome head watched the tableau below.

'Deep, stop. I can still save you,' Prem reached out desperately, despite knowing it was already too late.

He must be in agony, he thought, then noticed the fine epidural catheter in his brother's spine and the empty syringes on the floor. Deepak, a neurosurgeon, knew all about pain and how to thwart it.

'No!' Deepak's voice was strong, fierce.

Where was he getting the strength from?

'No!' Deepak repeated, his gaze full of pity. 'Don't have – time. Clean up. Don't, don't let anyone know how I died—' His words stuttered, and his voice dropped as fatigue and unconsciousness threatened to overwhelm him.

He forced himself awake. 'Promise me you'll see this through.'

The two men, their voices choking with tears, murmured their oaths.

'Pray with me,' he whispered. He forced his throat to invoke the many gods of his upbringing. Logic and reason now abandoned, replaced by the only thing left. Blind and desperate faith.

The two men joined their voices in his guttural cry, '*Kali Ma...*'

The three men's prayers were no longer pleas, supplications or implorations; they were commands issued to forces that existed beyond the realms of reason; demands that dared the gods to ignore at their peril.

The black idol stared at the bloody, throbbing mass at its feet. Its eyes glowed red and bright, and its serene smile widened.

52

The clamouring summons, the imperious calls to this day of reckoning, jolt the entity. Awareness fills it with renewed vibrancy and eagerness.

It absorbs the force, the ferocity of intense belief flowing from the mortals. The goddess to whom they pray is old, but the Dra is older still. It recognises the demands they presume upon it. It recognises the shape and form into which their faith moulds it.

But form and shape are immaterial to the Dra. It can and has assumed many other shapes. The humans kneeling on the blood-soaked rug will recognise this one. This one will do for the task ahead.

Yes! It is time to walk again.

53

Durgapur, India

Deepak

Tired, he was so very tired. His arms felt like lead, legs no longer able to support him. He still had no feeling, no sensation or pain, but he was weakening fast. He knew he had little time left.

I'd like to sleep now, he thought. Or did he say that aloud?

Supported by his companion's arms, Deepak gazed at the throbbing, bloody organ lying before the little idol.

'*Kali-ma*. Avenge us, I beg... hear me, you must...'

He reached for the black figurine, but his strength fled as unconsciousness overwhelmed him. He crumpled into the arms of his companions, drew one last rasping breath.

Flames of every lamp flared, swaying in the hot waft of air swirling around the room. The shadows on the walls deepened and danced in the dazzling light. The shadowy black goddess seemed to extend its ethereal arms to embrace them. Eyes, mouth and nose took shape in the enormous head silhouetted on the ceiling above the crouched trio. Fiery eyes stared at the men below. Hot breath rustled through their hair.

Prem held his brother close and threw his head back. A howl tore from his throat, desperate and forlorn. Roopesh was unaware of his own long, thin, wailing cry.

And on the red rug, the glistening red organ clenched and relaxed, its rhythmic pulses growing weaker, slowing with each passing moment.

At last, it stopped.

Silence and the smell of blood intermingled with incense filled the room.

54

Now the Dra is alert.

Time has changed this universe. The sky and the stars are different.

Despite the billions of twinkling lights and tall, impressive structures, the world is worn and weary, grey and bleak. A barren place, stripped of faith, denied hope. These humans – how they have multiplied, stripping the world of its humanity.

The Dra scans the creatures inhabiting Earth in their billions, scurrying like mice trapped in a maze. It probes the psyches of those still asleep and those awake. Watches their thoughts and emotions scuttle back and forth like ants, their purposes mislaid, nests forgotten.

Sighing, it focuses on a time and place – three young men dying in a park under a dark stormy sky.

No, that was in the past. The Dra readjusts its vision, follows the threads to the present, searching for a mind and body to serve it.

It follows the threads connecting the dead to the living. Pauses on the man called Matthew Holt. Those dead young men and the woman, Jyoti, are foremost in his mind, haunting his restless sleep. He seeks justice for them. He'd make a good host.

But the entity hesitates. Experience has taught it caution. No, this man has far too much self-belief. Of course, the Dra could impose its will, but the man's mind would shatter.

In the act of turning away, it pauses as another image floats into the man's mind. A softer, more pleasing vision. A woman named Lily Webster.

It finds her. A mind writhing in anxiety yet filled with love. The Dra tracks the bright strands leading from Lily's mind.

Hmm, this is interesting...

It studies the two pools of unconsciousness. Curious, it probes deeper, fascinated by the young creatures who attract and hold its attention. Perfect.

Grimly, it nods.

Yes, one of them will do.

***

Lily Webster's twin daughters lie on the big double bed in their room, their heads close together, their arms entwined, guarding and protecting each other. They have no qualms or worries. And they do not dream.

The children bolt upright. They sense something searching behind their eyes, seeking a pathway into one of the two minds.

The girls cling together. Each reaches out an arm in supplication, in deference, in defence and defiance. Their combined will is surprising in strength and intensity.

They rage, 'Both of us or none!'

***

Startled, the Dra stops. This is unexpected, intriguing even. It considers the options and the enticing opportunities this presents.

Hmm... fascinating!

The Dra sighs. It splits in two and, attuning its strength to the fragility of its chosen hosts, eases into the subconscious of the frail mortals.

***

Their demands met, the two small heads fall back onto their pillows, slipping into unconsciousness as the entity merges with their bodies and minds.

55

Durgapur, India

Roopesh

Roopesh wiped the sweat off his brow and mounted the wide grey granite steps up to Deepak's front door. Drooping with fatigue, he leaned against the frame, the ordeal of the previous night etched in the grey pallor of his haggard face.

In just four hours last night, Prem and he had washed the corpse and the tools, cleaned the room, and bagged all evidence of the macabre act. Deepak had prepared well, anticipating their needs. He'd left another longer note for them, and stacked bin liners, paper towels, bucket, mop and bleach in a corner of the room.

He'd even prepared the disposal site for the debris – the evidence. In the back garden, a large, deep hole gaped open, with a shovel sticking out of the mound of earth piled to one side. Beside it stood a large potted jasmine bush, the tiny white flowers filling the night air with its glorious fragrance.

The hardest task had fallen to poor Prem, to suture his brother's chest and to wash his corpse. Deepak had made the task easier by shaving his head and facial hair.

They'd then carried the lifeless form up to his bedroom, dressed him in fresh white *pyjamas* and *kurta,* laid the cold, stiffening body on the bed and covered him to his neck with the crisp white top-sheet.

Roopesh smothered the sob clutching his throat. Deepak's face had been so serene, with a gentle smile on his lips. His friend was at peace, but their own miserable, torturous journey had only just begun.

He squinted against the bright sunlight and peered at his watch. 9.30 a.m. Even England's hottest and sunniest day was never so bright. He pressed his ear to the door, listened to the faint sounds of the maid working inside, then, drawing a deep breath, he rang the doorbell.

When she opened the door, he said, 'Is Deepak *saab* home? I left my pocket diary behind last night.'

'*Saab*'s still asleep.' The thin, harried maid scurried aside to let him in.

'Asleep? At this time of the day? Is he ill?' Roopesh hoped he looked surprised.

'I don't know, *saab*. He's still in bed.'

'Deepak *saab* was tired but sounded fine when I spoke to him on his mobile phone after I got home last night. I hope he's OK. You didn't check?'

She shook her head.

Roopesh sniffed, his nose twitching at the smell of putrefaction tainting the air.

'I think the drain's blocked again, *saab*,' said the maid, clamping her nose with her fingers. 'I've called the plumber.'

With a sigh of irritation, he marched up the stairs with the woman trailing several feet behind him.

The smell grew stronger.

'Deepak,' Roopesh called out as he neared the bedroom door. He turned the brass knob, flung it open and reeled at the stench. He now understood the reason for one of Deepak's instructions – *turn off the bedroom air conditioner and make sure the windows are shut.*

'Deepak, why're you still in bed?' He leaned over the recumbent form, pretended to shake him by the shoulder. 'Deepak, wake up. What's wrong? What's the matter with you?'

Conscious of the maid watching from the doorway, he laid his fingers on Deepak's forehead, then pretended to feel for a pulse beneath his jaw.

'I think he is dead!' His voice quivered. 'Oh God, he must have had a heart attack. I need to call the doctor.'

The woman wailed, fled from the room. With a quick look at her disappearing back, Roopesh reached into his own pocket, drew out Deepak's mobile phone, pressed the dead man's fingers over it several times from different angles, dropped it on the silk bedside rug, and nudged it under the bed with the edge of his foot. Pulling out his own mobile phone, he made a call.

Unbidden, tears flowed unchecked down his cheeks as he descended the stairs.

'I've called his brother, Prem *saab*. He's a doctor; he'll know what to do,' he told the weeping woman.

He left the maid crouched on the floor in a corner of the kitchen, went into Deepak's study and buried his head in his hands.

Ten minutes later, the doorbell rang.

'That must be Prem *saab*,' he called out. He paused for a moment in the kitchen doorway. 'I'll take him upstairs. You make yourself a cup of tea with lots of sugar; it's good for shock.'

Prem stood at the front door. Pale, with the scores of fatigue and grief etched deeply on a face already ravaged by many sleepless nights, he had his medical bag in one hand and a stethoscope around his neck.

The two men stared wordlessly at each other. Then Prem walked in to play his part in the charade.

56

Lily

The alarm jerked Lily Webster out of a deep sleep. She shut it off. The warm early-summer morning sun filtering through her window blinds had her trying to nestle back under her light duvet and return to the fantasies of her dreams.

Sometimes, loneliness led her to seek companionship, but the face behind her closed eyes was never of the man entwining her. The face she imagined belonged to a stranger. The twins' father. David. The man who stole her heart at first sight whilst on a six-month language course at a university in the south of France. One brief encounter six years ago on a summer evening with a fellow student. The young man with a head of dark brown hair streaked gold by the sun's caress, eyes of molten amber, brown sinewy arms holding her tight, long muscular thighs pressed against hers. Voice husky with passion, murmuring endearments in Italian in her ear, *'cara mia...'*

For the past few months, however, a pair of steel-grey eyes and a dust-covered face had slipped into her dreams. Her visit to the watermill seemed a distant memory now, but Lily still remembered the intensity of his gaze. And that flash of unguarded emotion when she stopped in the middle of the cavernous hallway, head tilted up to the vaulted ceiling, spread her arms and twirled. That moment of tenderness and longing on his face, as her laughter echoed and bounced around the exposed rafters.

The persistent, intrusive ringing of the alarm clock jarred her awake. She sat up, swinging bare feet down to the carpeted floor, and bashed the off button.

Shame and anger flooded her as she remembered his polite thank-you text message, his rejection of her clumsy approach. *What on earth had possessed her?*

Lily pulled her long, curly blond hair up in a high ponytail, twisted it into a knot and headed into the bathroom for a shower.

Dressed for work, she walked into her daughters' bedroom, pulled the cord to open the blinds and smiled at the two heads on one pillow, the small chests rising and falling.

'Come on, sleepyheads, wake up!'

Their faces were flushed. Worried, she felt their foreheads, sighing in relief to find them cool. The girls sat up, rubbing their eyes. They looked dazed, squeezing their eyes shut in the bright sunlight. Lily hastened to the large window, pulled the underlayer of sheer curtains closed, dimming the over-bright room.

She returned to the beds and put her arms around them. 'I love you both so much!'

57

Lightly spoken words, but the depth of love in that simple sentence is indescribable. It washes over the Dra in a tidal wave of unfamiliar warmth. Suffuses it with a glow of tenderness.

It has, of course, experienced the devotion of countless worshippers, but their adulation always carried an element of bargain. This is new. Never has it known such unconditional love. Without expectations, making no requests, no pacts or deals.

The reciprocal feelings bubbling inside the twins for their mother take the Dra by surprise. Its presence within these fragile creatures seems to have unlocked a floodgate of sensations.

Screened behind the girls' consciousness, the Dra watches through their eyes. It will be amusing to bide its time, sit back and enjoy the interesting possibilities. Bask in this newfound rhapsody of human emotions.

The bargain it has so recently struck can wait for a little while longer.

But the call to respond to this intense affection is overpowering. A tiny indulgence won't hurt...

58

Lily

'We love you too, Mummy,' the girls smiled up at their mother. Their voices were strange, harsh and guttural from disuse, rasping like a metal file over sharp iron edges. Unfamiliar with speech, the words tripped over each other.

Stunned, Lily's legs gave way.

'What – what did you say?'

The girls scrambled out of bed and dashed into the bathroom.

Unable to believe her ears, she sat on the edge of the bed, her eyes wide with shock as her body trembled. Eventually, her heart pounding and giddy with happiness, she followed in their wake.

The girls were brushing their teeth, leaning against the washbasin streaked with toothpaste. She knelt between them, her arms around their waists, tears drenching her cheeks.

'Oh, my God! Oh! Thank you, God!'

Her blue eyes met the two pairs of deep gold in the mirror. She gasped, her heart clenching in fear as she reeled back. Instead of the normally limpid irises of amber, Lily was staring into the heart of a volcano and, from within its depths, something or someone else looked back.

Examined her; studied her with curiosity and was amused.

Straightening up, she gripped the girls' shoulders. Fierce protectiveness overriding her dread, she stared into their eyes.

'Who are you? What are you?' Her voice barely audible above the pounding of her heart.

'It's OK, Mummy,' they said.

The two raspy voices blended perfectly in pitch and tone, impossible to tell apart. Two soft hands reached out, touched her face. Lily gasped at the heat, held the little palms to her cheeks, staring into each pair of eyes.

Whatever she had seen in them an instant before had retreated. The pools of liquid gold were now serene.

'We're hungry!' they announced.

The twins took Lily's hands and marched downstairs, tugging their bemused and terrified mother behind them.

59

The Watcher

The watcher moved closer to the large-screen TV, assessing the frozen image. A masked man, his body twisted to allow the camera to zoom in on the centre of action. On the slim female form.

My beautiful Sarah, Sarah Mitchell.

He was the artist responsible for bringing such creativity to the work. He was also the critic, reviewing and refining his handiwork. And the actor playing one of the two key roles.

His clients expected quality, high standards – they were paying him enough.

There're too many shadows around the waist and hip. More light, right there, next time...

He sighed, turned away. The stimulus wasn't working. He needed more. He returned to the laptop by the bed, logged in, clicked on a folder, and set the video clip to 'play.'

She was thinner, her bones more defined, eyes enormous in the gaunt face, and her lips moved in soundless entreaty. The lens tracked the masked man's hand creeping up the pale body.

Up the shoulder, to the neck. Fingers softly caressed the throat, stopped and began squeezing.

Desperate hands pushed against the man's chest, thin legs kicked, heels drumming out a staccato. The listless eyes shot open, fearful and aware as her mouth opened wide in a wordless scream, trying to gulp in air through the constricted throat.

The already ashen face gradually lost its last vestige of colour, the pale blue eyes bulged, lost focus. All animation fled from the pallid face. Arms lay lifeless on the bed, palms turned upwards in surrender.

The man clicked the remote, powering off the television.

Brilliant though it was, this clip too was time-limited. It would not satisfy for very much longer. It lacked the smell and feel of the real thing. The silky skin beneath his hands, the heat, the velvety softness. The sense of power and control. But most of all, it lacked the palpable fear of the victim.

Patience! There was still so much to do. After months of searching, he had finally found the perfect place. Somewhere remote with no callers, no curious neighbours. Soon he would be ready. Just as he'd been for Sarah and the ones before her.

Sarah's replacement too was ready and waiting.

60

Durgapur, India

Deepak

Deepak Verma was pronounced dead.

The local doctor accepted the cause as 'natural'. The unmistakable stench, a glance at the pallor, a quick check for a pulse on the cold, limp wrist already showings signs of putrefaction were all he needed to issue the death certificate. Which listed cardiac arrest in the early hours of that morning as the cause of death.

'He died so peacefully in his sleep; that's a blessing,' they said.

The maid tearfully recounted her version of the events to anyone and everyone who would listen. 'Poor Deepak *saab*. I thought he was still asleep upstairs. But he was already dead. He'd been lying there dead all night! I didn't even know I was in the same house as a corpse! If Roopesh *saab* hadn't arrived, the poor man would still be upstairs. Rotting!'

LETHAL JUSTICE

In line with Hindu religious traditions and customs, the funeral took place within twenty-four hours, early the following morning.

Only a distraught brother, his childhood friend, and an ancient, near-blind priest attended the '*abhisegam*,' the traditional washing of the body. Prem and Roopesh washed and dressed the corpse in fresh, simple white clothes, shrouding it to the chin before allowing anyone else to see it.

Despite the short notice and hasty arrangements, family members within a 50-mile radius, friends, colleagues, and many of the residents of Durgapur gathered for the wake and the cremation.

A fortnight later, as soon as custom allowed after the funeral rites, both Prem and Roopesh left for England. With Anjali still in hospital in a coma, their wives stayed behind in India.

61

Lily

Lily parked her car near the Bluebell Grove Primary School and turned to the twins. As usual, they sat as close as their car seats allowed, their hands clasping each other's. She looked at them with trepidation.

'You remember what we talked about?' As their eyes met, Lily felt the force of a penetrating glance, but an instant later, it retreated into familiar disinterest.

She had taken a full week off work, keeping her daughters away from school, saying they were sick. In that time, she learnt their sudden change was capricious, switching between probing intelligence and the all too familiar avoidance of eye contact. The twins too seemed to learn fast – that curiosity and interaction caused their mother to worry, whereas retreating, shuttering behind placid detachment and indifference calmed her racing heart.

'Please, please be careful!' Worry and fear filled her pleading. The girls nodded.

Lily got out and opened the back door. They scrambled out, stood before her, still holding hands. She helped them with the backpacks and held out a hand. Two small hands reached out and clasped hers. A week ago, she would have had to take their hands to lead them indoors. Tearfully, she knelt on the gravel, put her arms around them, and hugged them close.

The teacher, Jo Latimer, hurried across to them. 'Good morning Cara, good morning, Mia. Morning, Lily, how are they now? What was wrong?'

'They had colds and were feverish, so I thought I'd keep them at home. They're fine now.'

'That's good! Welcome back, my dears. It's good to have you back.'

Lily stopped her as she guided them into the classroom.

'Jo, they've started speaking and react a lot more to what I say. They've even started doing small things for themselves!'

'Really? That's wonderful,' but doubt soon replaced Jo's surprise. The girls were staring at the floor as usual, ignoring everything and everyone.

She called to her assistant, 'Savannah, come over here, please.'

The young woman hurried over, a wide smile lighting up her face. Her black hair, braided in dozens of cornrows, adorned with multi-coloured beads, was an endless source of fascination for the children. She wore colourful, soft, flowing clothes, brightening the room like a vibrant swirl of dancing rainbows. The children loved her for her bubbly personality, quick laughter, and endless patience.

'Miss Webster says that the twins have been trying to talk.'

A broad smile lit up the young woman's face. 'That's great!' she kneeled to hug them.

Lily stopped breathing, her heart racing in panic. But the children stood stock-still, heads bent. Savannah exchanged glances with Jo.

'Don't worry.' Jo patted Lily's arm. 'We've often seen it happen. Sometimes there's a little breakthrough. We'll watch them, do everything we can to encourage them and let you know how they are doing.' The class was getting restless, so the teacher moved away.

Lily nodded and reluctantly left the room as Savannah led the girls to their seats.

***

True to their word, the two women monitored the twins, but they seemed to be their normal, placid selves, ignoring the other children around them. By noon, the women decided it must have been a fluke, or more probably, wishful thinking on poor Lily's part.

They turned their attention to six-year-old Johnny, who was especially agitated that day. He stood in front of the girls, shouting incomprehensible words, waving his arms in wild gestures. They ignored him, gazing at their colouring book.

'That's a giraffe. Try to colour it in. Yellow and brown would be nice,' said Savannah, guiding the little boy away.

Replete with lunch, the children were quieter in the early afternoon. Even Johnny was calmer, although still fidgety and restless.

Satisfied the adults were too far away to stop him, Johnny picked up a plastic building block and threw it hard at the twins.

Without glancing up, Cara's hand shot out, caught the red cube, and set it on the floor beside her. Frustrated, Johnny grabbed and threw another block. Again, Cara plucked it out of the air, set it atop the first one. Screaming in anger, Johnny ran at them, fists clenched, arms whirling like windmills.

Hearing the ruckus, Jo rushed to the three children, but by then, Johnny was already on the floor, with Mia pinning his shoulders, and Cara sitting on his legs.

Jo was stunned. Though Johnny often threw tantrums and lashed out at the girls, their response was unprecedented. Previously, they'd stoically accepted the taunts, even the occasional punches from Johnny, only crying when he hurt them.

As Jo reached them, they got off Johnny and stood looking down at him. The boy lay there, his face crimson with anger, while Jo tried to soothe him, her puzzled gaze on the twins.

Ignoring their teacher, they stared at young Johnny.

'No more,' they said to him in unison.

Jo's mouth dropped open in amazement at the deep husky tones. She felt the tension ease away from Johnny's shoulders, his body relax.

Savannah finished dressing a little girl who'd had an 'accident', settled her down, and joined the little group. 'Did they speak? I thought I heard them say something.'

Jo nodded and beamed. 'You can talk! Say something again, please.'

The children looked up at her, and the smile froze on her lips. Her mouth went dry. She reeled as two pairs of probing, knowing looks bored into her mind, gripping and holding her immobile for an instant, like prey trapped in the arms of an octopus. A moment later, they turned away from the flustered teacher and returned to their crayons.

Disconcerted, Jo shook her head. 'Let's leave them alone for a bit. I'm sure they'll speak when they want to.' But as she walked away with the now calm Johnny, Savannah stayed her with a hand on her arm, pointing to the girls' colouring book.

Filled in shades of yellow, brown and black, the animal looked almost alive, alert, wary, poised to flee from an unseen threat. The two women stared as the girls continued their colouring, working in complete harmony to put the final touches on their picture. They sat back in their chairs, tilted their heads, and studied their handiwork with small smiles on their faces.

Then, with a quick, dismissive glance at the two adults, the twins lapsed into their usual behaviour – fingers laced in each other's, staring into nothingness.

62

Roopesh

Frothy seawater swirled at his feet. Roopesh Kapoor threw another empty shell back into the choppy sea. Despite its being late June and officially summer, the grey, drizzly and windy weather kept people indoors. The few passers-by greeted the tall, handsome, well-dressed man baring his soul to the sea, but after a glimpse of the tight, tormented face, their pleasant greetings died mid-sentence, and they hurried away.

Salty sea spray mingled with his tears as Roopesh tried to conjure up the image of his son Arun. To his shame and horror, he only saw the little boy who ran up shouting *'papa, papa,'* throwing himself into his father's arms.

He had lost that delightful boy a long time ago when Arun grew up to become a reticent young man. One with a tight rein on his emotions, discouraging displays of affection. Slowly drawing apart.

As if he had a secret to hide, thought Roopesh. *What couldn't he tell us?* But they knew, though neither he nor his wife acknowledged the truth.

I would have understood, he thought. But that was his own guilt talking. Worse, he knew Arun would have lived a lie rather than cause them pain.

And then there was his little girl. Anjali. Lying in that sterile hospital room. A broken doll. It was easier to think of her as dead. He could not bear to hope that she would live. Did not deserve to; not after what he had done.

'Call me when she is dead.' Those had been his last words to his tearful, heartbroken wife.

His whole being was one enormous ball of hatred, hungering for revenge. He felt no grief, and it was too late for regrets. Whatever the consequences, there was no return.

His and Prem's paths pointed only in one direction. Self-destruction. But it got them both up each morning and, with each dawn, brought them one step closer to justice.

The deals with Tango were now routine. They, or rather, the two computer-generated voices, greeted each other like old friends. Roopesh chuckled wryly. But it was working.

Cautious at first, the transactions had grown in size and frequency. And now, three months into the collaboration, Tango and he had a good rapport bordering on trust.

Roopesh's next move was to play on their greed. Use Tango to draw the Xtreem gang in.

Until now, Roopesh had not realised just how easy it was to buy fake identities and valid credit cards. All you needed was money and someone who knew someone. And he had both. He'd also taken KC's advice. *'Using your warehouse is plain idiotic. Give yourselves a chance. Lease or buy someplace else anonymously. An industrial site or a farm rather than residential.'*

So, a month ago, an offshore company calling itself CT Enterprises Ltd – C for Charlie, T for Tango – leased a disused brownfield site twenty miles outside Southampton, ostensibly for conversion to warehousing and self-storage units.

Location—now sorted. Timetable—open. All they now needed was the bait. A plausible reason to bring all four members of the Xtreem gang to the site.

He had the bare bones of a plan:

I'll tell Tango I know when and where my rival supplier will meet his two major dealers. I'll offer him a ludicrous amount to eliminate them and ask him to bring the four Xtreem gang members with him. Hmm, 'why them?' he might ask. Er, because they worked well together and knew how to stay schtum. Prem and I'll wait for them at that old factory. We need to capture Tommy and Duncan alive but incapacitate them first. Make them give us the name of their accomplice. Too bad Tango will be collateral damage. An unfortunate casualty.

The plan still needed polishing, and the details filled in. But the outline was there.

The chilly wind biting through to the marrow of his bones finally got Roopesh's attention.

Shivering, he returned to his car, lifted his coat from the passenger seat to reveal the long, slim object beneath.

With an instinct born of practice, he reached out, wrapped his fingers around the metal grip, his thumb caressing the cold, smooth golden topaz set in the centre.

Mohini, his *talwar.*

63

Durgapur, India

Roopesh

The young boy stared with wide-eyed wonder at the object on the low table. He shifted from foot to foot, lips mouthing, 'Come on, come on!' as the man unwrapped the soft cream and gold embroidered silk swathing.

Finally, after what felt like an eternity, only one fine layer remained. He made out its slim shape, three feet long, only four inches at its widest across the width of its cross-guard, tapering to a sharp point at the bottom.

The long brown fingers holding the last layer paused.

The boy sighed in exasperation. 'Come on, Papa! You are taking forever just to unwrap it.'

He turned to the old man leaning on a stick beside his father. 'Dada, tell Papa to hurry, please,' he pleaded.

Laughing, his father lifted the last layer to reveal a magnificent talwar inside a bronze scabbard. The one-edged, curved sword's bronze hilt, inlaid with an intricate pattern of copper, gold and silver, glinted in the sunlight. Eye-like patterns adorned each side of the grip. And set in the middle of each eye was a large yellow topaz.

The boy reared back from the glowing orange-yellow eyes. The sword was watching him, like a tiger watching its prey.

His father bowed before hefting the talwar. Laying it across his open palms, he held it out. The boy reached out a tentative hand and touched the scabbard. It was cold.

'Here, hold it,' said his father. The boy held out both arms, elbows tucked into his waist, palms facing upwards. The man placed the sheathed sword in his son's hands and stepped back.

'It's heavy,' said the lad, although his father had held it with ease. Hand grasping the grip, he looked up at his grandfather.

The old man nodded, his eyes crinkling with a smile and a glimpse of white teeth from amongst his bushy silver beard. His father held the scabbard while the boy drew out the weapon. With a soft swish, it slid out of the leather and sheepskin-lined scabbard. He stepped back, gripping it with both hands. Lighter without the sheath, it still required all his strength to hold it steady at arm's length. With its flared tip resting on the marble floor, the top of the talwar's hilt reached the boy's chest.

The father reached out and showed the boy the correct way to grasp the handle, with one finger wrapped around the cross-guard. But the eleven-year-old could not lift it one-handed. His father placed the boy's left hand around the grip.

'Yes!' The boy triumphantly hoisted the talwar.

He pranced into various positions while the two men laughed. The lad danced his way down the granite steps, posed on the dusty earth outside. He held the sword high above his head and brought it sweeping down towards the stone, just as both men shouted, 'No!'

Startled, the boy's head jerked up and then dropped in horror as the blade clanged against the smooth, dark slab. The impact shuddered through his body, knocking the weapon out of his hands.

The trio stared at the broken sword; only eight inches of blade remained still attached to the hilt; the rest lay in two pieces on the steps. A deep fracture cracked the solid granite, running from the point of impact to its base.

'Now look what you've done,' shouted his father.

The old man laid a calming hand on his son's shoulder. The boy looked into his grandfather's sad eyes and burst into tears. His grandmother rushed out, gasped in shock at the broken heirloom at her grandson's feet. She scolded the men. As they shuffled their feet in embarrassment, she noticed the cracked stone, which added fuel to her grievance.

While the father collected the precious pieces, the old man laid a hand on his weeping grandson's shoulder. The three returned indoors, leaving the old woman grumbling about the granite block.

'I am sorry, Dada,' sobbed the lad. Ignoring his painful knees, his grandfather knelt and drew him into a hug.

'Never mind, child,' he said. 'That talwar has been broken at least twice before,' he glanced at the boy's father, who reddened and fidgeted, 'and sadly, the repairs don't seem to hold too well.'

The younger man wrapped the broken pieces in the silk once again. The three of them walked together into the old man's bedroom, where the boy's father put it away into a cupboard, locked it, and gave the key to his father.

'It looked very old,' said the boy, as they walked into the living room.

The old man nodded. 'Indeed, it is. It was already ancient when my great-great-grandfather inherited it. This talwar has been in our family for many centuries, passed down through generations from father to the oldest son. It has a long history behind it. Would you like to hear its story?'

'Yes,' said the boy and his father together. *Although he had heard the tale many times over the years, the parent was just as eager as his eleven-year-old.*

With a grin, the old man settled on the diwan and leaned back against the bolsters. Cross-legged, the boy squatted on the floor while his father pulled up a chair, turned it around, and sat with his hands and chin resting on its high back.

His voice magnificently mysterious, the old man told his tale.

'A very long time ago, a prince rewarded his warrior with a beautiful talwar for his bravery. It was a treasure beyond price. The proud warrior...'

'What was his name?' *interrupted the boy.*

'His name? We don't know. His name is lost in the mists of time. But we shall call him Balveer, because besides being brave, he was also very strong. He brought the talwar home and showed it to his wife.'

'What was her name?'

His father frowned. 'Shhh, let Dada tell the story.'

'It's alright,' *said the grandfather, waving a hand.* 'Again, her name is no longer remembered. But let's call her Kalyani, because she was beautiful, and the love of the warrior's life.'

'That's my grandmother's name too,' *said the boy. The two men exchanged a smiling glance. They could still hear her fussing about outside.*

'Yes, I know.' *The old voice had a smile in it. He cleared his throat and continued.*

'Kalyani gasped at its beauty. She was so proud of her husband. "You must give it a name. What will you call it?"

'The warrior smiled and said to his wife, "You can name it." *She thought for a moment.* "I would like to call it Mohini," *she said finally.*

'"But that's a girl's name," protested her husband. "This is a weapon; it must have a strong, manly name."

'The warrior's wife ran her fingers over the sword, tracing the intricate design on the hilt, and stroking the golden stone set into the eye on both sides. "But it is so beautiful! It looks delicate, like a woman, but it will be strong, quick, and invincible in battle. Just like the daughter we will soon have."

'Balveer was delighted that they were having a second child but still wasn't sure whether to give his beautiful talwar a girl's name. "I'll think about it for a few days."

'Two days later, he came home late in the evening to find his front door ajar, and his house ransacked. He searched frantically for his wife and their two-year-old son, but they were nowhere to be found. He ran outside, saw his neighbour stagger towards him. Blood poured from the wounds in the man's head and leg.

'"A gang of Thuggees attacked our village," he said through broken lips. "They took your wife and son. I tried to stop them, but they were too many. We are gathering the men together. We will go out and fight them."

'But anxious and enraged, Balveer would not wait. He jumped back on his horse and rode away alone in search of the Thuggees. He rode for hours through the night, heading for the hills and forests beyond, looking for the kidnappers.

'It was hard going in the dark. Several times, his horse tripped and almost fell, but he kept going. Finally, just as the first rays of dawn touched the sky, he spotted their campsite. He tied his horse to a tree and crept closer.

'In the light of the dying campfire, several men lay snoring. He also spotted his wife, curled up on her side in a tight ball. She was deathly still. His son was nowhere to be seen.

'Crazed with anger, he rushed into the camp. Drew his sword, and with a piercing cry, thrust the blade mercilessly into the *sleeping Thuggees. But the commotion woke up the others, and in an instant, fierce, armed fighters surrounded him.*

'*He pirouetted, swinging the talwar around, slashing and thrusting the sharp metal into anyone who ventured within its reach.*

'*Suddenly, the Thuggees surrounding him changed shape, turned into demons, snarling ferociously.*'

The boy frowned. The story had taken a bizarre turn. '*Demons, Dada?*' he asked sceptically.

'*You don't believe in demons?*' His grandfather raised an eyebrow in amused query.

'*Well,*' said the lad. '*Demons are in stories, in mythology. But the talwar is real.*'

'*Ah! Yes, I see. Well, this is one version of the story. Would you like to hear it, anyway?*'

'*Oh, yes, please.*' The boy nodded, bouncing up and down in excitement.

The old man continued. '*So, the Thuggees transformed into demons of all shapes and sizes, into all kinds of frightening monsters, attacking him from all sides.*

'*But Balveer was strong and fast as lightning. The sword cut through the monsters, chopping a venomous snakehead here, a wild boar there, hacking off arms, tentacles, and limbs faster than the eye could see. He danced among the demons like a whirlwind. He was so fast that every time they slashed at him, he was already somewhere else, and they ended up hitting and killing each other.*'

The boy's gaze focussed on his grandfather's face, mesmerised by the deep voice narrating an ancient tale. He imagined the scene playing out in front of him. His body quivered with the depth of his involvement in the unfolding story.

'*I too shall learn to fight like that! One day, I shall be as good as Balveer,*' he told his grandfather.

The old man turned to the boy's father. 'Teach him, as I taught you. It is a good time to start.' The younger man nodded, studying his son with a critical eye.

'And then what happened?' asked the youngster impatiently.

'Balveer fought and fought, ignoring his aching arms, his bloodied feet, his tiring muscles, and the hundreds of cuts and bruises where some demons had reached him. Finally, there were no demons left alive. Nearly a hundred monsters lay dead or dying around the camp.

'Blood dripping from his talwar, Balveer ran to his wife. She was covered in blood; her face bruised, her clothes torn. With a cry of fear and worry, Balveer shook her, begging her to be alive, to talk to him. Her eyes opened, and she took one last deep breath. "Save our son," she said, sinking into his arms.

'Balveer had no time to mourn his loss. He turned at the loud crash from the forest. Through his anguished tears and sorrow, he saw a figure step out of the woods, carrying a bundle in its arms.

'It was a huge demon, a Rakshasa, with three heads and eight arms. It held several weapons – a sword in one hand, a trident in another, an axe in a third, a club in a fourth, and many more besides. Its many eyes were enormous and red with rage. The mouth in each head opened wide in anger, showing sharp fangs and blood red tongues.

'The Rakshasa, the Thuggees' leader, was furious at the slaughter of his gang.

'Balveer got to his feet, gripped his talwar, and stepped forward to meet the monster. The Rakshasa carelessly tossed the bundle into the bushes nearby.

'"No!" Balveer screamed in anguish as a child's cry rang out in the early morning mist. But the demon's savage roar and the warrior's battle cry drowned its voice as they ran full tilt at each other.

'The sounds of fierce battle filled the frosty morning air, of the demon trying to slash, punch, claw, pierce, and club the puny human. But Balveer danced and whirled around it, always just out of reach of its long arms and weapons.

'The warrior was tiring. He had already fought a hard battle. He knew he would not last much longer, but the thought of his son spurred him on.

'With a burst of energy, he clasped the bejewelled sword in both hands and swung it in a wide arc at the devil's stomach. The talwar opened a huge gash, spilling blood, guts, and gore. With a loud cry of pain echoing from all three heads, the Rakshasa bent over to clutch his stomach.

'Balveer jumped back, and leaping high, he brought his talwar down on the bowed neck, decapitating all three monstrous heads in one stroke. Thus, Balveer slew the demon and all his minions.

'But he did not feel any joy at his victory. Tears pouring down his face, and with fear in his heart, he ran towards his son. Luckily, the soft leaves and grass had cushioned the boy's fall; he was unhurt. The warrior gathered his son up to his chest and went back to his dead wife. With a heavy heart, he carried her over one shoulder and returned home.

'In honour of his wife, and the daughter lost before she even arrived, the warrior named the talwar Mohini.

'He lived on to fight many battles and raised his son to be equally valiant. His talwar Mohini accompanied him on all his battles, passed on to his son and oldest grandson after him. And so, Mohini reached us today.'

The old man fell silent. His son handed him a tumbler of chilled water. With his eyes on his grandson, the old man sipped the refreshing drink. The youngster frowned, a thoughtful look on his face.

'What's the other version, Dada?'

The old man took his time with the water. When he emptied the glass, he smiled and, with a dismissive wave, said, 'Oh, it's not as exciting as fighting so many demons. In the other version, Balveer found the camp with half a dozen sleeping men. He fought and killed them all and cut off the chieftain's head with his talwar. He rescued his son, brought his dead wife home and named the talwar "Mohini" as his wife wished. It carries that name to this day.'

He squinted at his grandson. 'Now, which version do you prefer?'

Under the scrutiny of his elders, the boy hesitated, worried about choosing the wrong version and disappointing them. Finally, he replied, 'The one with the Rakshasas is more exciting, but the second version sounds as real as the talwar.'

A fierce look of decision crossed his childish face. 'I enjoyed the first version, but I believe the second one is probably truer. Besides, fighting and killing seven baddies is still very brave.'

The men laughed. 'Ah, we have a scientist here rather than a poet,' said his grandfather. 'That is also good.' The boy's father reached down and ruffled his hair.

Delighted, the boy promised his grandfather, 'I too will become a strong and brave warrior like Balveer. And one day, I will forge a new blade for Mohini; one that will never ever break and will last forever!'

With a smile, the old man murmured, 'And so may it be, my boy... and so may it be.'

64

Holt

Fingers digging into his spine, Matthew Holt groaned and stretched. Everything hurt. He removed the plate of supper that his aunt Susan had left warming in the oven. Delicious though it was, he picked at it half-heartedly, too tired to eat. His week's enforced leave was proving to be painful, but not as much as his conversation with Superintendent Simpson last Friday.

'Fifteen weeks since those poor lads' murder, millions down the drain, and we have sweet FA to show for it.' The superintendent stopped pacing and whirled around. *'We're just going round in circles. You need to find another angle. I'm already under pressure to stand you down and bring in someone else.'*

He'd flung himself into a chair that creaked and groaned in protest. *'I'm missing something, sir. It's right there, within reach, but retreats and slips away the harder I try.'*

'Very poetic, lad, but unhelpful. If we're brutally honest, we should have had this conversation weeks ago. Luckily for you, the dreadful terrorist attack at Westminster, the terrible

Manchester arena bombing, and the discovery of those poor souls in that container last month diverted the media's attention.'

That, plus the victims' parents' loyalty and faith in Holt. But that grace period was in its death throes. The news of Deepak's death had shocked and grieved him. When the two remaining fathers, Prem and Roopesh, returned to England, Holt continued to keep in touch with them. But week after week, he hated having nothing new to tell them. During every worthless call, they stoically accepted his explanation, his empty promises, and courteously thanked him.

When Holt offered only glum silence, the superintendent had sighed and knuckled the bags under his eyes. 'Here's what I want you to do, Matt. I'll temporarily reassign another DCI to oversee the whole caboodle, and you, my lad, are going to take a week's leave starting today. You have until this evening to clear your desk.'

'Am I being taken off the case, sir?'

'No, not yet. What the Chief decides to do about us, I haven't the faintest. I might be on traffic issuing parking fines when you get back. No, I need you to step back and gain some perspective.'

'But, sir...'

'Bloody hell! Did that sound like a request? It was a fucking order! So, get going. I don't want you here for a week. I meant what I said. Get some distance, get a helicopter view or whatever the hell it's called. Use the time to think. When you return, you'll have two weeks. After that, I suspect we'll both be off the case. They can bring in so-called consultants or specialists...'

As always, he had come home to the farm to lick his wounds, but neither John nor Susan allowed him to wallow in self-pity.

'You needed the break, dear,' said Susan. 'You're looking very peaky.'

'Good,' said John, 'you can get your watermill's roof finished before you go back.'

'You mean *if* I go back?'

'Of course you will. Once they get their heads out of their arses.'

He did as John suggested – hired a roofer and worked on the watermill, blanking his mind to the case and his ignominious departure. For the past five days, he had focussed on the task, labouring for the professional roofer. It was hard and demanding for someone unaccustomed to this level of strenuous physical activity. His leg muscles cramped and spasmed from climbing up and down the ladder, arms and shoulders screamed in pain from carrying roofing material all day long. But it felt good; stopped him from thinking, from allowing the bitter bile of resentment and anger to eat into him.

The watermill's structure was now watertight. Another day's slog to install the fascia and gutters and the roof work would be complete.

He glanced at his phone as it buzzed, skittered and vibrated on the table. DI Karl Stringer. He ignored it, just as he had been doing all week with calls from his core team, and sighed in relief when it eventually fell silent. Two minutes later, it began vibrating again. After the fourth time, Holt picked it up. Karl was a persistent bugger.

'Karl, I thought I'd made it very clear—'

'I know, sir. But this could be important.'

Despite himself, his interest piqued. 'What is it?' *Talk about curiosities and cats—*

'Sir, the PCSO at Westlands Estate called me. She said they noticed surveillance of our four suspects. When she confronted the guy, turns out he's a PI acting for a client he refused to name. He asked us to contact his boss at

Nigel Payton Associates. It's a detective agency in London. Which I did. Payton said he knows you and if we wanted any information, you are to call him.'

'Did you say Nigel Payton?'

'Yes, sir. Do you know him?'

'I'll say. He's a retired DI from the Met. A good man.'

'He won't talk to me, or at least, won't give me anything useful. Could you call him, sir?'

It'd be churlish and childish to refuse. Besides, he was curious and still the SIO even if all that changed next week.

'Do you have his number? Thanks. I'll call him now.'

Despite the late hour, Nigel Payton was still at work and delighted to hear from Holt. He admitted to being hired to compile detailed profiles on several people, including the four youths, especially Tommy Wade. Although Payton refused to divulge his client's name, he did not deny it when Holt suggested the victims' fathers.

'Has your man been following those four all these months?'

'No, just Wade, on and off. He and his chums have been up to something, but I don't know what. Now that my man's been made, I'll have to swap him out.'

Holt laughed at Payton's grump. 'I assume he had nothing interesting to report?'

'Not with your lot cramping everyone's style. But my guy's good. He's been on your patch for over three months, and no one noticed,' laughed Payton. 'My client also asked me to investigate seven others, all business owners, in Southampton. Why would he do that, Matt?'

'Who are these people?'

Patton hesitated, then recited several names. Holt frowned as he jotted them down. 'Hmm. Sorry, Nigel, I can't see any connection. I need to think on it. I'll get back to you if there's anything for you.'

Holt leaned back and rocked in his armchair. None of Payton's information about the gang was new; the police already knew a lot about them. Given Jyoti's 'vision' of the killer and the uncanny match to Tommy Wade, Holt could well understand the fathers' interest in the four suspects, but their interest in the other seven names on Payton's list was puzzling.

The excitement of the chase quickened his pulse. With aches, pains and fatigue forgotten, he picked up a notebook and doodled.

Holt recognised the company names. His team had already interviewed people from each of those businesses while investigating the victims or when they arrested the four youths, but nothing more than the obvious customer-supplier or employee-employer had surfaced. But something had attracted the fathers' interest. What did they have in common?

The next morning, Holt had his answer.

65

Holt

The hollow echo of a long silence filtered down the phone line.

Maybe I should have waited until he'd had his breakfast. He'd have been in a better mood then, thought Holt, with a wry grin. But the next question tied a knot in his chest. *Will he go out on a limb for me again?*

Few bosses would. The Super was already in enough trouble with his superiors. Anyone else would be more concerned about his or her own career, especially if the SIO stubbornly clung to his pet theories, despite months of no results. *Will he trust me once more, or is that well bone dry?*

After an eternity, the superintendent sighed. 'OK, lad. I hope you are right. For both our sakes. This really is shit or bust. See you later.'

His team greeted Holt with gratifying and heartwarming enthusiasm.

'Did the PI say who his client was?' asked Karl.

'No, but I suspect it's the victims' fathers.'

'I don't blame them. So far, we have nothing. With all the tragedy they've suffered, they want answers,' said Rowena.

'Yes, it must be difficult for them to sit back and do nothing, hoping we'll catch the killers.' Holt pointed to the names on the evidence board. 'Besides our four suspects, these are the seven others Payton gave me. First one's the owner of our victims' favourite Indian takeaway and catering business. I see your initials against it, Larry.'

'Yes, sir, I interviewed him. Atul Gill, the owner. He confirmed that the victims had been regular customers. But that's all they were. Customers. However, the Xtreem boys preferred a place closer and cheaper to their homes. So, the triangle between Gill, the victims and suspects, doesn't really work.' DC Larry Ives paused in thought. 'Unless there was a connection between the owner and one of the fathers. Most likely, Roopesh Kapoor. Business rivalry? Seems odd, though. I can't see a catering company taking over a surgical instruments business.'

'Hmm. Yes. The second name's Harvey Endsleigh, owner of The Cue Room, the pool club, whom you interviewed, Rowena.'

'The victims only went there as part of a group for birthdays or Christmas. Whereas the suspects had frequented there for years. Until that argument last Christmas and they stopped visiting The Cue Room for nearly four months. Since my interview with Endsleigh, though, they've once again started spending time there. Not surprising since Endsleigh's allowing them free entry on Mondays and Thursdays.'

'So that triangle doesn't compute either,' said Larry. 'Can't think why Endsleigh or any of the other companies would want Roopesh's business, even if it is to asset strip or some form of money laundering.'

'So maybe it's another family. Revenge for a medical cock-up, perhaps?' But Rowena looked sceptical.

Holt turned back to the board. 'The third and fourth are a husband and wife owners of a furniture removal company.'

'I interviewed them, sir,' said DC Michele Bruges. 'They moved the three victims into their student house four years ago, and they hire Duncan Hughes whenever they are a man short. Mr Hales said Duncan's not the best of workers. He's lazy but does fine if he's supervised.'

'Right, the last trio comprised two brothers and a sister, who are in business together at a self-drive car and van rental company where Tommy Wade works, cleaning the vehicles. Who interviewed them?'

'That was also me, sir,' said DC Larry Ives. 'I spoke to the managing partner, Nirman Patel. Apparently, Tommy does a good job, but they only use him when their regular cleaner's away or they have a fast turnover. Recently, they've started using him to pick up and deliver cars and vans. Apparently, Tommy's an excellent driver. He seems to enjoy the work and gets to drive some nice cars.'

'That's the link to our suspects, but what is their connection to either the victims or their families?' asked Holt.

'Roopesh's company uses them to hire cars for business visitors and occasionally gets them to make deliveries to his buyers, too,' said Larry.

Holt waited while the detectives tried to work it out. Why any of them would kill those poor students, and how they got away with it.

'I guess we'll have to re-interview them and ask what they did that night; dig deeper to find the connection.' Karl was already jotting a task list.

'Does it concern the families, sir? And does this mean that our prime suspects are off the hook?' asked Rowena.

'I think it concerns the families. I don't know exactly what. And no, our suspects aren't off the hook. If anything, I'm more certain they're guilty.'

From their sceptical looks, Holt guessed most were wondering whether his insistence on the gang's guilt had jeopardised their investigation.

'What's the connection, sir? Do you know?' asked Karl.

'No, I don't. At least, not yet. But the fathers are interested in these seven people, or rather, these four businesses, for a different reason. It took me a while, but I finally figured out what they have in common. Why they're on Payton's list.'

He looked at their intent faces. Several asked the inevitable, 'Why, sir?'

Holt told them.

And now they questioned both his judgement and his sanity.

***

'They all own big vans or lorries,' said Holt.

Furrowed brows and an exchange of puzzled glances greeted his statement.

'What are you thinking, sir?' asked Rowena. 'Why this interest in a van?'

'I was wrong about Tommy's missing car. While we were searching everywhere for it, it was right there, under our noses. Inside a van or lorry. It was used to hide and then to transport Tommy's car.'

DC Khan looked sceptical. 'Would it fit inside a van, though, sir?'

Holt repeated the words of the conversation with his very practical-minded uncle John. 'Oh yes, provided you don't care what it looks like afterwards.'

Silence and several sidelong glances in his direction, but Holt also noted a couple checking the dimensions of Tommy Wade's car and calculating the smallest size van needed to fit it.

Karl nodded. 'You are right, sir. It was only a small hatchback. It could fit into a few models of vans and several lorries if no one intended driving it around afterwards.'

Ian projected a small list of vans capable of accommodating the car. 'It'd fit into those vans and bigger lorries, of course.'

'Whose lorry?' asked Rowena.

'I don't know, but it must be one of them. Someone with a close bond to the suspects and a strong reason to commit murder, although I can't imagine what that would be.'

'If it is a close bond, then that rules out Atul Gill, the Indian takeaway owner who has none with the suspects, and Harvey Endsleigh of The Cue Room who has none with the victims,' said Rowena.

'You may be right, but let's investigate them, anyway.'

'Shall we get search warrants, sir?'

'Goodness no, not at this stage. We're walking a tightrope as it is. Check CCTVs and ANPRs. Locate those vehicles' whereabouts after the killings. I know it was three months ago, but we may get lucky. Narrow it down, identify the most likely ones before we make a move.'

66

Holt

'We tracked the movements of those vans and lorries, sir.' Ian beamed a spreadsheet to a large monitor with the make, model, colour, licence numbers of every LGV and HGV registered to the four businesses and the seven individuals. Each journey included a detective's verification tick and initials; otherwise, a cross indicated pending confirmation. Most were ticked.

'This is great. Thanks, Ian. I see three Xs. I guess they're not yet verified?'

'No, sir, but we're on it. The first one's Harvey Endsleigh. He sold his old Luton in May, two months after the murders. According to the reg, it's only an LGV with a three-and-a-half tonnes gross weight. Doubt it would support a car. Anyway, we checked the paperwork. It was a valid sale. Apparently, he wanted a newer and bigger van to refurbish his new site and didn't want to waste money on his old one. He uses it mainly to transport building materials.'

'OK, next?'

'The second's the car and van hire company – the Patels. They gave us details of all their van hires, but one doesn't match the ANPR data. Although their records indicate the van wasn't rented, our logs show it was out at night. Two days after the murders and again ten days later, both near Portsmouth. The managing partner, Nirmal Patel, told Larry that a staff member had borrowed it, which they occasionally do, and they don't keep a record of every internal use.'

'That sounds dodgy,' said Rowena. 'We'll dig deeper and find out more from the Portsmouth team.'

'The third is Atul Gill's catering van. There's a marker on PNC from Customs and Excise. It sounds like Mr. Gill's been involved in some illegal cross-channel trading, but they haven't managed to pin anything on him yet.'

'That's the connection, sir!' Salim almost bounced off his chair in excitement. 'The victims found out, threatened to expose him, so he got rid of them.' The curly-haired twenty-nine-year-old appeared younger than his age. His vibrant, cheerful personality was a perfect foil to the nerdy Ian Shepherd, and the pair were best friends, although this was far from apparent from their constant bickering.

'What? Using the Xtreem gang?' scoffed Ian.

'No, not them. Someone else altogether. If he's involved in smuggling, he must know people he can hire. And – oh!' Salim flushed with embarrassment as his voice tailed off. He realised he'd refuted his boss's pet suspects.

And there it is, thought Holt. Even his team didn't believe in him or his presumption of the gang's guilt. And there was his suspicion of Marvin Jackson's involvement, which had spearheaded their key lines of inquiry. Suspicion which had involved his team in weeks of investigation that had led nowhere. Wasted time and effort. How much did Jyoti Verma's vision influence his conviction of Xtreem's guilt? How much did his animosity towards Jackson affect his judgment?

'Sorry, sir,' muttered Salim.

'Nothing to be sorry about, Salim. You wouldn't be much of a detective if you didn't question everything; follow your instincts and consider all possibilities. That's an excellent point you've raised about Gill's van and his link to the victims. Inquire with customs officials. Tell me if you want me to talk to anyone. It could have happened exactly as you said. What was Gill into? How big is his operation? He must have a lot at stake to resort to murder.'

It also meant that he'd made a big mistake with the four youths and that they simply were in the wrong place at the wrong time.

***

Holt leaned back in his chair, rubbed his tired eyes. Almost 11 p.m. He was alone reviewing reports, looking for the tiniest glint leading to the vein of gold. Trying not to dwell on his meeting with the Super earlier that morning.

'Sorry, Matt. The Chiefs are bringing in an external SIO. Someone with experience in dealing with multiple homicides. You probably know him, Detective Superintendent Samuel Bradley from the Met. He and your friend DI Trevor Radcliff start on Monday. You'll hand over to them and temporarily handle cold case reviews.'

This time next week, he would be down two floors, in a windowless office amongst dusty files, picking at threads that led nowhere.

Not so different from this case, then. This isn't going anywhere either.

He considered his options. While he couldn't envisage a life outside the force, could he endure the disgrace? Stand to see familiar faces avoid his gaze, their embarrassment for him? Put in those stark terms, he had but one option. Not a bad one either. Work full-time on the farm. John and Susan would be delighted. They'd always hoped he'd take over one day. It was Holt's long-term plan, too. Just not yet, and not as a failure.

Decision time. He'd resign tomorrow morning, hand over to the new SIO on Monday, and walk out. Change the course of his life.

***

Four hours later, Holt was at his desk, gripping the edges of the nebulous thought that had brought him out of a restless sleep and back to the Station.

A comment made earlier that day nagged at his mind. He recalled wondering *why* in passing but did not voice the question. Instead, he'd allowed it to slip away as he moved the discussion on to more concrete possibilities. But the itch had remained, refusing to be ignored.

Back in March, he remembered a similar query flickering on the outer edge of his visual field, but it had not seemed relevant or germane to the investigation, and he'd let it pass. Just as he had this afternoon when Rowena, Ian, Salim and he talked about vans and lorries.

He pulled up Ian's spreadsheet, stared at it for a long time before realisation bloomed.

Holt glanced at his watch. 6 a.m. Five full days remaining until Monday, to his embarrassing departure and the humiliating end to his career.

He knew the how and the likely who, but could he prove it before Monday?

Of course, he could be totally wrong, but either way, he had to know.

He needed help. Who could he ask? With young Salim declaring a viable suspect, he had to reassign resources to investigating Atul Gill and his nefarious activities. The Portsmouth van also raised questions, although he suspected that was most likely a cash-in-hand, under-the-table deal. So, the bulk of his team's efforts had to refocus on those leads rather than chasing Holt's shadows.

I'll ask Karl and Rowena, he decided. *Lay it all out for them. Point out the potential setback to their career and the guilt by association that could stigmatize their prospects.*

As it turned out, the imminent appointment of the new SIO, and his decision to leave, surprised neither of them. And both readily agreed to help.

'I'm not worried, sir,' said Rowena with a grin. 'I'll simply say you insisted, and I had no choice.'

'And this is a good opportunity to tell you I've decided to quit, sir,' said Karl. 'I've been thinking about our conversation and, much as I love this job, I need to put my family first. Excel Security offered me a position a few days ago, and seeing you're leaving, I shall accept it. It's a nine-to-five desk job. It'll probably be boring as hell, but it pays well, and I'll be there for the kids. So definitely count me in. I've got nothing to lose.'

'You could be next in line for promotion to DCI, Karl. There'll be competition, but your chances are excellent,' protested Holt. Although he understood the DI's decision, Karl was too good a detective and police officer to lose.

'Now I'm even more convinced it's the right thing,' laughed Karl. 'I've seen the hours you put in, the mountain of paperwork, the HR nightmare, the crap that's slung at you and not just by the media, either. I couldn't do it, especially now. Not with the baby and all. But come on, let's solve this before I go.'

Heads bent, they charted a growing list of inquiries, actions, tactics and best approaches involving the least number of staff.

67

Lily

Junk, and more junk! Lily Webster frowned and shuffled the handful of mail, set aside one envelope and dropped the rest into a bin, already a third full of recyclables.

The kettle fell silent following its imitation of a steam engine, and Lily poured the boiling water into her tea mug. Sitting at her worn oak dining table, she slit open the envelope and winced at the amount on her monthly credit card statement.

The past weeks had been a mix of her worst nightmares and most precious dreams come true, of happiness and fear. Sheer joy of hearing her daughters talk, their animation, the feel of their arms around her after years of hugging two warm but unresponsive bodies. Fear followed this euphoria. Anxiety that someone might decide their change in behaviour warranted closer scrutiny.

So far, she'd got away with it. The twins too seemed to pick up on her thoughts and modulate their behaviour. But they were capricious, responding and participating only when they wanted. One thing, however, had not changed. Nobody could separate the girls. No amount of cajoling, coaxing, or bribes could part them. Force was out of the question; any attempt to split them up resulted in heart-wrenching screams.

Rain tapped on paving stones as the weak afternoon sun pushing through grey clouds shone on the peeling kitchen paint. Yet another chore to add to the list. Lily's shoulders slumped, drained by the roller coaster ride that had been her life since her daughters spoke for the first time. Every moment apart filled her with panic, wondering what they had done, hoping they had not attracted someone's attention or curiosity. The strain was enormous. Her strength and mental resources stretched to a breaking point. Worst was her incomprehension of what was happening to them.

And she had no one to talk to, no one to confide in. Not even her mum and dad…

Why did they have to go to Italy? And why were they driving down those treacherous mountain roads so late in the evening? What was the exciting news they said they had for me?

She never got to find out. The following day, the Italian police found her parents' hired car at the bottom of a ravine, and three weeks later, a heavily pregnant Lily had flown to Italy and brought their broken, battered bodies home.

Lily dragged her mind back to the present, squared her shoulders, and glanced up at the kitchen wall clock. Almost 4.30 p.m. Time to go collect the twins. She checked her handbag for her mobile phone, house and car keys, and stepped into the narrow hallway to use the tiny cloakroom.

Drying her hands, she checked the mirror and headed out of the front door. She did not hear the swish of the truncheon. Nor did she register the sharp, blinding pain of the black cosh crashing into her head.

Lily collapsed. Blood bloomed, turning the blond curls crimson, and she lay still.

The intruder leaned forward, hit the fallen woman twice more, but the narrowness of the hallway tempered the force of the swing. The attacker smiled, satisfied by the volume of blood seeping into the carpet and the victim's immobility.

The trespasser stepped over Lily, checked his clothes for blood.

Nothing! Good. Right. What do I need? Handbag. Ah, there it is! Keys. Coat. Mmm, this is nice!

He lifted Lily's knee-length, deep red coat off the banister and squirmed into its tight confines. *Damn, I can't button it up.* He turned up the collar and left it unfastened.

He paused before the hallway mirror to readjust the blonde curly wig, styled like Lily's, and, despite the cloudy day, donned a pair of large-framed sunglasses.

With a quick backward glance at the motionless woman, Lily's attacker grabbed the umbrella from its stand, stepped outside, and pulled the door shut.

It was drizzling. *Perfect!*

Umbrella up, head down, he hurried across the street to Lily's car and drove off to her daughters' school.

68

Jo Latimer

The twins' teacher glanced at her wristwatch yet again. 5.15 p.m., and Lily was late. The other children had already left, fetched by their parents or guardians, or aboard the school bus. Lily, too, should have collected the twins no later than 5 p.m. That was the rule.

Today had been especially hard on Jo Latimer and her assistant, with several children playing up, demanding more attention than usual. She needed to be home soon to prepare. Tonight, she and her husband would have that long overdue talk and she wanted to look her best, make a real impression; to make sure he realised what he would be missing.

This is unacceptable, thought Jo. She fished out her mobile phone, scrolled for Lily's number and dialled. The phone at the other end rang and rang before diverting to voicemail. She tried again and again, while her indignation and concern rose in equal measure. A large worm of worry wriggled and squirmed. She could not recall Lily ever being late. *This is not like her; she always arrives early. I wonder if something's wrong.*

But the prospect of the daunting evening ahead overrode her concern.

She should call if there's a problem. After all, she has my number.

Alongside her, the twins waited with their backpacks at their feet, staring into the distance.

'Come on, girls, let's go check if Mummy's outside.'

Jo drew the hoods of the children's coats over their heads and led them out of the school's black metal gates. Her head swivelled up and down the street but saw no sign of Lily's car.

She shivered in the cold, annoying drizzle. They would have to return indoors for her forgotten jacket if Lily didn't show up soon. She laid a hand on each of the girl's shoulder. Their tension was palpable. Jo forced herself to relax so that the girls did not sense her anxiety and anger.

About to pivot and head indoors, Jo heaved an enormous sigh of relief when a green Peugeot pulled into a gap about 20-feet away and parked facing away from them.

'There's your mum.'

Through the window, she saw Lily in her red coat lean over and open the back door. She beckoned to the kids.

That's right; sit in the warm and dry while I get soaked! Jo fumed.

Before she could stop them, the twins ran ahead, clambered into the child seats and belted themselves in. Jo hurried after them. She'd just reached the tail end when the car engine revved, eased out into the street. The children turned and waved, and she saw Lily lift a gloved hand in farewell before speeding off, going faster than she should on a school road with a ten-mile speed limit.

Jo stood frozen in place, her mouth open in an O of surprise, unable to believe what had just happened. Seething, she marched back into the building.

That was dangerous! She should know better! I'll give her a piece of my mind when I see her next time!

She finished tidying up, thankful to Savannah, her assistant, who had cleared up as usual before leaving.

69

The Watcher

The five-year-olds sat upright in the car, staring at the back of the curly blond head.

'You are not our mummy,' said Cara.

'Your hair is just like Mummy's, but you aren't pretty,' said Mia.

'That's Mummy's coat.' A forefinger pointed. 'Why're you dressed up like Mummy?'

Forehead creased, his eyes swivelled between the girls reflected in the rearview mirror.

I thought they couldn't speak!

'Your mummy asked me to pick you up. She had to work late today. I'm taking you to meet her.'

'You hurt Mummy,' said Cara.

He shot a panicked look in the mirror. *How did she know?*

'But she will be OK.' The child appeared to be reassuring herself.

'She needs to rest,' said Mia. 'We won't wake her up just yet.'

How strange! I'd better humour them. More than a little confused, he nodded at their reflection. 'That's good. She'll wake up and join us later.'

The pair fell silent and leaned back to gaze out of the windows. Hands clasping each other's, they watched the unfamiliar scenery flash past. In the gathering dusk, the car sped out of town, heading for the countryside.

The man cast puzzled glances at them. *I hope they behave, do as they're told otherwise I'll have to gag them and put them into the boot.*

'What are your names?'

'We are Cara Mia,' they said, their low, husky, raspy tones blending so well that it sounded like one voice.

He smiled. 'Do you know that means *'my beloved'* in Italian?'

'Yes.' Two pairs of deep golden eyes held his in the mirror. The hairs on his nape rose, goose bumps prickled his arms, and heart raced as a band tightened around his chest, leaving him breathless. A second later, he shuddered as they turned their gaze upon the growing darkness outside.

Soon their eyelids drooped, heads lolled on the padded seatbacks. He exhaled, tense shoulders sagging in relief.

70

The Dra stirs within the minds of its young hosts. Was it a mistake allowing them to see their mother lying hurt and bleeding? Their anxiety about the woman is crushing.

The Dra reassures them, 'Nothing that cannot be fixed.'

The children relax.

It feels their fury as they glare at the driver. It wants to crush the man; erase the plans and designs brewing inside the skull beneath the soft pale curls.

But it resists.

It has conceived another plan, one that brings a faint smile to the twins' lips.

The Dra senses both fathers' growing desperation to fulfil their vow to their dead brother and friend. Their thirst for revenge – although they call it justice. They and their extinct companion responsible for its presence here and now.

The time for reckoning has come; time to tip the balance.

Behind the children's slumbering consciousness, the Dra reaches out to Prem and Roopesh.

71

Prem

Prem Verma unlocked the door to his home on the edge of Winchester Golf Course, tossed his keys into the tarnished silver bowl on the ornate sideboard, its decorative inlays invisible under the thickening coat of dust.

Shanti would have a fit if she saw this, he thought. This house, once immaculate, screamed of neglect. Without his wife's vibrant presence, the place was just a shell. Walls within walls under a slate roof. Somewhere to shelter from the cold and the rain. No longer a haven, it offered no peace.

With Anjali still in hospital, he had insisted Shanti stay behind to support Roopesh's wife. Besides, he did not want her here, an unwitting party to their plans and actions.

As for his son, Ravi... The emptiness inside him had turned the world grey, the void unfillable. The house rang hollow in his absence, as though it too had lost its soul.

He walked through to his son's room. This had become part of his routine – his penance. Decorated with posters of heavy metal bands, it remained untouched since Ravi's last visit home, just a few days before that fateful night in March.

An open magazine on the desk, his jacket draped over a chair, a CD still lodged in the player.

Through sheer willpower, Prem held on to his son's presence. He inhaled and swore he caught a whiff of Dior aftershave. Eyes shut, he heard his son sing, loudly and badly. Saw that wide, cheerful grin, deaf to his father's scolding and his mother's nagging.

His legs gave way, sat him down on the empty bed. He mended hearts for a living, but the organ in his own chest was irreparable. He had cut out his brother's heart, detached it from its trailing tubes, and buried it with the obsidian idol beneath the jasmine bush.

The aroma of incense and the tang of melted ghee—the clarified butter used in the oil lamps—filled his nostrils again. So real, he could taste it. Always present wherever he went. He smelled the blood and sweat in the gods' room in his brother's house. Deepak's shuddering, rasping breaths. Roopesh keening and the howl from deep within his own soul. That too was a constant echo in his skull. And those shadows...

Prem rose, walked out of Ravi's bedroom and into his ensuite bathroom. He lost track of how long he stood under the powerful shower, but a blast of cold water snapped him out of his reverie. He had drained the boiler tank. Shivering, he dressed and went into the kitchen.

The refrigerator yawned empty. Damn! He had forgotten to buy food yet again. The cupboards yielded a half-box of cereal, but there was no milk to go with it.

Oh, well, a whisky will help wash it down.

Prem shook the cereal box, stuffed a fistful of the crunchy flakes into his mouth. The message light on his phone blinked red. Another voicemail from his wife. He glanced at his watch. 6.10 p.m. here meant 11.40 p.m. in Durgapur.

Too late to call her now. I'll phone tomorrow.

He booted up the laptop in his study, hoping the private detectives, Nigel Payton and Associates, engaged to track his son's murderers, had some new information. He knew those four so well now. Their families too. Where they lived, who they saw, how much money they had and what they did with it, what they wore, ate, drank, sniffed, and injected.

Hope Roopesh is doing better than I am. It's a stupid plan, anyway, luring the gang to that new site. But after these agonising months, they had to try something. *Who knows, it might even work.*

'Just wait for my call. I'll try to give you as much notice as I can, but be ready to move the instant you hear from me. Until then, just sit tight,' Roopesh had told him.

Easy for him to say, but hard to do.

As the days turned to weeks, then months, Prem vented his frustration. *Not long now,* Roopesh had promised yesterday.

He chewed another handful of cereal, savouring the sugar rush which did nothing to assuage his hunger.

Prem lifted the tumbler of whisky to his lips and froze. The warm, smoky, musky, malt scent filled his nose, and saliva flooded his mouth in anticipation, but his hand would not move. He grasped the glistening crystal glass and held it against his lower lip.

His eyes unfocused as an unrecognised voice, deep and low like thunder on mountains, inundated his skull. He replaced the glass on the table, and the box of cereal clattered to the floor as his fingers released their hold. Like a remote-controlled robot, his body pushed the chair back and rose, imbued with urgency.

He was being summoned.

Where? Who?

His legs propelled him towards the door. He tried to regain control, to comprehend the situation, but a wave of overwhelming, compelling sense of danger drowned his thoughts and rationale.

Fingertips digging into his temples, he sought to suppress the voice inside, but it only grew louder, more clamorous, and unrelentingly peremptory in its demands. It was futile. He could no more resist it than he could stay an impending storm. The urgency to respond crushed his fear and quashed his instinct for self-preservation. He had no choice but to heed the summons.

Hurry!

Prem delved under his desk and grabbed the gun, delivered courtesy of Roopesh's uncle, KC. He wrenched it from its sellotaped moorings, jammed it into his jacket pocket, snatched his keys and medical kit and rushed to his car.

Within seconds, he was speeding out of his driveway, following the images and directions flashing through his skull, heading to an unknown destination.

72

Roopesh

Out of the wind, the car's heater warmed cold bones, and the smoky aroma of leather replaced the salty tang of sea breeze. Roopesh Kapoor clipped the voice-altering gadget to the old phone with no internet or GPS to track him and dialled the only number programmed into it.

'Afternoon, Tango,' he said.

Despite their best efforts, neither he nor Prem could identify who the dealer was, and KC refused to say.

'Hey Charlie. Just a moment.'

Unlike his own generic robotic voice and much to his annoyance, 'Tango' had chosen Homer Jay Simpson's as his alter ego.

Half a minute later, Tango was back.

'Sorry about that, Charlie. All OK?'

'Sure, why wouldn't it be? You did well in getting rid of that package so quickly. You know where to drop off the money. Now, I'm willing to give you a bigger pack. Twice as big as the last lot. You ready for that?'

'Course I am! But I'll need a bit more time.'

'Alright. Two more weeks.'

A pause while Tango mulled it over. 'OK, that should work fine.'

'Good. I have another proposition for you if you are up for it.'

'Go on.'

'I want the four Xtreem lads involved in this. Tommy Wade, Duncan and Leo Hughes and Derek Dawson. No one else. I know they can do it, and I trust them. Tell them they'll be protected, just like last time.'

Would it work? Had he got the whole thing wrong? If Tango wasn't one of the seven on their list from the private investigator, their entire plan was doomed. Oh, he and Prem would still fulfil their promise to Deepak, but getting all four was improbable. They might have to settle for just two. Tommy Wade and Duncan Hughes.

Roopesh placed a hand over the mouthpiece to mute the sound of his harsh wheezing. He was hyperventilating. His racing heartbeat was all he could hear. He felt lightheaded. The walls of books in his study swayed. He shuffled to his chair and lowered himself into it.

After an eternity, the phone crackled.

'OK. I'll get them. What's in it for me and them?'

Giddy with relief, Roopesh almost laughed aloud. He choked, turning it into a cough as tears sprang to his eyes.

It worked! It had actually worked! He could now direct the four killers to the new brownfield site he'd leased. Then, Prem and he could deal with them. Too bad Tango would be a casualty.

'Forty grand for you, ten for each of them, plus double your cut from the next package.'

He jerked away from the long, low whistle down the phone.

'What's the proposition?'

That's when it happened. When it all changed. Roopesh no longer had control of his thoughts or his words. The voice he sometimes heard in his worst nightmares used his throat and took over the conversation.

'I need an obstacle removed. And it has to be done tonight.'

'Tonight? Oh, wow! I don't know, man. What is it?'

'Not what... who.'

Dead silence as Tango grappled with the implications.

'Well?' Roopesh sensed his own impatience.

'Phew. I was not expecting that, man. Who is it?'

'No one you know. Are you in?'

Another long silence before Tango's response. 'OK, I'll do it for sixty plus the sixty per cent on the package.'

Typical, thought Roopesh. 'You aren't in a position to bargain.' His tone was icy. 'You've done exceptionally well out of my deals so far, and I haven't let you down. If you're too scared, I can easily find someone else. Fifty grand for you, ten for each of them and half the takings from the pack – that's my final offer.'

A much faster response this time. 'Deal! But why tonight, man? I like to make my own arrangements.'

He laughed. 'You wouldn't get within a mile of the man. He is way out of your league,' he told Tango. 'It's a one-time shot – I know where he'll be tonight. I want you and those four there at 7.45 p.m. sharp. Don't arrive any sooner, or you'll spook him, and he might leave. Don't be late either; he usually leaves soon after.'

'What if he doesn't show up?'

'Well, in that case, all you'll have lost is petrol money. I'll pay you five grand for your trouble, and another five grand on top of your usual cut on the package. And,' he added before Tango could haggle, 'this is not negotiable.'

'Will you be there?'

'Don't be silly. I'm a businessman. I pay experts like you for these jobs.'

'Sure, I understand.' Tango sounded flattered. 'How many will there be?'

'Oh, he'll be alone, believe me. He doesn't take witnesses with him on these outings. He has some peculiar – um – let's call it tastes. And he doesn't like anyone around when he indulges in his peccadilloes. He's been careful and protected his secrets until now. I'm certain he'll be alone this time, too.'

'What weird stuff is he into, man?'

'You'll find out.'

'Sounds fun.'

'Not quite how I'd put it,' said Roopesh.

'OK, where is it?'

He repeated the address and directions, which the voice enunciated in his head.

Where the hell's that? he wondered, absolutely certain he'd never heard of the place before, let alone been there. Ever.

'Hey man, that's miles away! I need time to get my men and stuff together!'

'Unfortunately, it's difficult to obtain advance notice of our friend's activities and even more so to get him alone. This is a unique opportunity, and I don't know if there'll be another. I intend to grab it. Say so now if you can't do it!' Roopesh's voice was urgent, insistent. 'Or I can call someone else.'

'No, no. That's fine, man. I got it. We'll be there by 7.45 p.m. If we're early, we'll wait until then.' Tango sounded cool, confident, the excitement clear in his Homer Simpson voice.

'This place is well-camouflaged with trees and woods. It's off the main roads, up a dirt track. Difficult to find. Be quiet and approach slowly. Keep your lights low and park your car at the top of the drive. Walk the rest of the way. Take flashlights with you. There are no streetlights around. Our friend will be inside, busy and occupied. Wear gloves and don't touch anything if you can help it. I'll leave the rest up to you. I'll know whether you've succeeded and call you tomorrow to arrange your payment.'

'OK, thanks, and—' said Tango, but Charlie had already disconnected.

73

Roopesh

What just happened? What the hell did I just say? How did everything get so weird?

Roopesh stared at the burner phone in confusion. His plan was for Tango, whoever the hell he was, to bring the gang to the derelict site, where Prem and he would be waiting. But he'd lost all power over his senses. *Something else had taken over.* The words had rolled off his tongue of their own accord.

What was the place I just described? What was all that about eliminating someone? Eliminate whom? Who was the man I talked about? Why did I say all that?

Although they weren't his words, Roopesh remembered every sentence he had uttered. The directions he gave were nowhere near the disused factory, his original destination. He didn't recognise the place to which he had directed Tango. And he was dead certain he'd never heard of, let alone met, the person he'd described.

After a moment's thought, he shrugged. *The destination might be different, but the purpose remains. Nothing will stop me.*

The killer's image was seared into his soul. Tommy Wade. *Botticelli's angel.*

Soon he would strike. Avenge his son, retaliate for his comatose daughter, and numb the pain of his friend's death. He might even wash away some of the ever-present, gut-wrenching guilt for his part in Deepak's sacrifice.

The gods' room, the flickering lights, the smell, the shadows, the blood... oh God! That pulsating heart... And Deepak...

No! Stop! Not now. There's a lot to do.

The imperative to go to that place heaved at his senses, the pull irresistible. He'd been summoned. Roopesh shivered as fear and excitement gripped him in equal measure.

He programmed the address into his sat-nav. Sixty miles to his destination. He wanted to reach there first, to be in position before they arrived.

Prem should be home by now unless he has an emergency at the hospital.

He pressed the hotkey on his normal phone to call Prem, shrugged when it went straight to voicemail. *I'll try again on my way there.*

He pulled out of the car park and sped to the address he'd given Tango.

74

The Watcher

Deep in the countryside, Lily's car turned off-road before pulling into a clearing outside a small wooden chalet. Surrounded by trees and dense undergrowth, shadows cloaked the place. It was ideal. Tucked out of sight, no traffic noises disturbed the still night. No visitors ever called. Nothing collected or delivered, not even the rubbish or post.

To his relief, the roads had been clear, the drive uneventful. The children had remained silent throughout, asleep for most of the journey. They did not seem to worry that they were in their mother's car with a total stranger. Their acceptance of him and their situation astonished him, especially since kids today learn to distrust even familiar people, let alone strangers.

He switched off the engine, swivelled around, disconcerted to find them awake and alert, those deep yellow eyes fixed on him.

'We're here now. You must be hungry. I'll get you something to eat. Do you like chicken and mash?'

They nodded.

'Then you can have a nice warm bath before bed.' His voice hoarse with anticipation.

Another simultaneous nod.

They are so exquisite!

Up close, they were more beautiful, their skin so soft, their features so perfect. Their eyes glowing amber in the dim light of the vehicle, held no fear, worry or anxiety, or even curiosity.

If only I'd known, maybe I could've done this sooner.

He picked up Lily's handbag and a sturdy backpack from the passenger seat, got out, opened the rear door, and waited while they scooted across the seat to jump out. Side by side, they considered the brooding shape of the wooden building, its simple outline barely distinguishable from the deeper, darker surrounding shadows.

The man tapped a code into his mobile phone to disengage the house alarms and unlocked the door. A PIR-operated motion sensor light clicked on in the small hallway.

He ushered the girls in, reactivated the alarms, and shot the heavy deadbolts.

They are now safe inside with me.

He smiled at the irony and flicked a wall switch. The bright ceiling lights illuminated a large, minimally furnished space set out as an open-plan living room and kitchen. A narrow dining table with four chairs served as the dining area.

No rugs or carpet cluttered the smooth pine floorboards. A cheap three-seater settee, upholstered in printed material, sat beneath a large boarded-up picture window with a small table in front.

The L-shaped kitchenette was practical. A single sink fitted with a long-spouted mixer tap and drain board set into the laminate worktop under a sealed window.

Nobody could see in or out.

The children gazed around as they removed their jackets, still damp from waiting for their mother outside the school, and handed them to him to hang up.

His breath hitched in his throat as he stared at the pair, dressed in their white polo shirts, topped with deep purple V-necked sweatshirts with the bright yellow and green school logo on the left pocket, and the grey and black chequered pleated skirts.

'We are hungry.' The strange, harsh tones snapped his attention back.

'OK, I'll get your dinner right away. Sit down.'

While they clambered into the chairs, he set out plastic picnic cutlery, plates, and tumblers, and popped two trays of ready meals into the microwave.

'It'll be ready in five minutes,' he said, turning around. His smile froze. An icy shiver crawled up his spine. Fear, like nothing he had ever known, choked him. An instant later, it vanished.

He glowered at them, but their gazes rested on the whirling trays inside the microwave. Given that they had special needs, he expected their perceptions and responses to be different, but so far, they had been more than easy to manage. They didn't cry or keep calling for their mummy. *Not like Sarah. Little Sarah Mitchell.*

But the uncomfortable feeling remained.

I won't keep them too long, he decided. A week? Or less. That'd be a real shame. But they seem docile, obedient. Will they participate without force? Although that was a whole different game.

Nine months ago, a chance pit-stop at a fast food café in Southampton had changed his plans and given him a new purpose. The beginning of an obsession.

The little family sat at a corner table, their mother holding a one-sided conversation with them while her daughters tucked into their tall cups of ice-cream. He had seen nothing more beautiful or extraordinary. They were so alike and so different. He had waited in his car and followed them home.

Until now, he had taken only one at a time. Five so far, spread far and wide. But the idea of 'working' with the twins had gripped him. Besides, the money he would make out of them was beyond ridiculous. Not that he needed money – he already had over ten million pounds out of HMRC's reach.

It had taken him a while to set up. First step – find a suitable job – easy with his IT skills, and the job provided an excellent cover, a reason for his presence in their area. Finding this chalet had been harder, a real challenge, requiring him to invest a lot of time and money to acquire it.

The microwave pinged. He removed the heated trays, pulled off the covering film. Saliva flooded his mouth, and his stomach growled at the aroma of chicken breasts in gravy, mashed potatoes, and the mix of diced carrots and peas. For a moment, he was tempted to heat a meal for himself, but it was far too early. Besides, he had other things to do. He placed the dishes in front of them. They eyed it, sat waiting.

Am I supposed to dish it out too? He spooned out the contents onto their plates, filled their glasses with cold water from the tap and smiled as they tucked hungrily into the food. *Like little puppies.*

'I'll fill the bath up while you eat.' They nodded.

He hurried into the bedroom, which showcased a king-size bed made up with black satin sheets and matching pillows. Its window, too, was boarded up. A computer workstation occupied one corner, and an enormous TV screen dominated the wall opposite the bed.

The man picked up a remote control and clicked it to switch on the four cameras. The TV screen sprang to life with images of the room from four angles.

He shrugged out of Lily's red coat and draped it over the back of a chair, stopped before a full-length mirror, assessed himself.

The black turtleneck sweater and slinky trousers look good on me. Makes me seem taller and slimmer.

He wiped his face clean of makeup, took off the blond wig and replaced it with a headband mounted with two tiny but powerful video cameras. A quick check showed the children still absorbed in their meal. *Good.*

From the bottom of the wardrobe, he removed a box containing professional video recording equipment and a tripod and carried them through to a roomy bathroom. He affixed the camera to the tripod, adjusted its focus to encompass the bath opposite.

He poured a hefty dose of baby bath bubbles under the warm running water. Shimmering foam and glistening bubbles grew to cover the surface, filling the bathroom with steam and a soft baby powder fragrance.

When he returned to the kitchen, the children's plates were empty, and they leaned back in their chairs, hands wrapped around the plastic tumblers, sipping water.

'Good, you've finished.'

He turned on his head cameras and strolled towards them.

75

Tommy

The man who called himself Tango phoned Tommy Wade.

Tommy reluctantly hit pause on the game controller and answered the call.

'Yeah?'

'Hey Tommy.'

Tommy shushed Duncan Hughes sitting hunched beside him, clutching an identical video game controller, and wearing an irate expression. Duncan, who had been winning, resented the interruption. He picked at the remnants of the pizza and swigged the remaining half of his beer while Tommy jumped off the tatty sofa and listened to Tango outline the deal.

'Are you up for it, Tommy? I'll let you use my new toys.'

Oh, wow! thought Tommy. *I'd do it for nothing if I could handle those motherfuckers. That plus forty thousand to split any way I choose, and another ten when we sell the stuff. What's not to like?* He'd quite fancied himself as a hitman, like in the movies, but the work required to get himself to that level of fitness had not been so appealing. Now, without him even asking for it, he was turning into one.

'Oh, yeah!' Tommy laughed

'The target will be alone tonight. Charlie wants all four of you. Said he trusts you, that you work well together. I think I'll come along for the ride. Are they with you?'

'No, just Duncan.'

'OK, go get the others. Dress to kill.' Tango laughed. 'By that I mean dark clothes, shoes, hoodies. We'll take my car. I'll bring the toys, disposable coveralls and gloves.'

Tommy checked out Duncan and his outfits. All set. Just need the hoodies.

'Oh, Tommy, what are you doing about Leo?' asked Tango.

'Huh? What do you mean?'

'He's been acting strangely; twitchy. Sort him out real soon, or else he could put you all in danger.'

So, Tango too had noticed!

Duncan's younger brother, Leo, was becoming a worry. He'd become quieter, nervy, and clung to Duncan and his best friend Derek Dawson. Tommy worried another police interview would break the boy and take them all down with him.

'I'll sort it out,' said Tommy.

'Good. See you at Duncan's in fifteen.'

Tommy turned to Duncan, who paused the game. The large TV screen showed a frozen image of destruction. Walls and towers exploded in a shower of stone, brick, and dust, the cobbled streets strewn with dismembered bodies. Pools and blotches of realistic-looking blood added bright splashes of colour to the gory scene.

'Come on, time to go.'

'Go? Go where?'

'It's a shit of a package, and there's a fucking bonus too!'

Duncan frowned. 'To do what?'

Tommy's cold blue eyes locked on Duncan's. 'A contract, to wipe out that motherfucker who's trying to step into our territory!'

'Wha'? Wha' you mean, wipe out? Like kill someone, you mean?'

'Sure, what else? You have a problem with that? And we'll be protected so the police can't touch us.' Tommy's narrowed gaze probed for any sign of weakness.

'Tango's going to let us use his new toys,' he added. That should sway Duncan.

His friend's grin was answer enough. 'Really! Oh, man! No problem, yeah, no problem at all.'

'Right! We need to leave now. Let's go get Leo and Derek. We'll need 'em to watch our backs. I'll call Derek. You tell Leo. Tango's meeting us at yours.'

'Erm, do we need Leo?' asked Duncan. 'He hasn't been very well.'

Tommy froze. 'Why? What's wrong with him? He looked fine when I saw him before we came here.'

'He was feverish. Coughing, an' sputtering something awful. Might be comin' down with some'fing. Best not to bring him. He might give us away if he gets an attack.'

Tommy stared at his friend for several moments. *Something's very wrong with Leo. I need to take care of it.*

'Hmm. OK, he needn't come then, but I want to see him before we go.' Tommy's voice brooked no further argument or discussion.

***

LETHAL JUSTICE

Tommy and Derek Dawson were waiting outside Duncan's block of flats when Tango arrived in a car they hadn't seen before. After exchanging a complicated, synchronised series of handshakes, Tango studied the second youngest member of Xtreem.

Derek was something else altogether. At just 16, he exhibited an unnerving lack of empathy, of cold-bloodedness. A sharp contrast to his impish features and comical demeanour. He appeared to hero-worship Tommy Wade, but Tango suspected it would not be too long before Dawson challenged his leader.

'Where are the Hughes brothers?'

'Duncan's upstairs sorting his mum out but seems Leo ain't well an' won't be coming,' said Derek.

Tango's expression tightened, but he held his tongue.

'Tango, you still got those uncut samples you showed us?' asked Tommy.

'Yeah, why?'

'Let me have a couple, will ya?'

After a moment's hesitation, Tango's hand slid into his jacket pocket and surreptitiously slipped two packets to Tommy.

'Careful with those. Just one of these babies and it's bye-bye forever. Won't feel a thing.'

76

Tommy

In their flat upstairs, Duncan scowled at his younger brother. 'Tommy's coming up to see you. I tol' him you're ill. You better cough and splutter like hell, or that's where he'll send you.'

At the worry on his brother's frightened face, Duncan added, 'It shouldn't be hard, you look like hell already!'

For months now, Duncan had been covering up for Leo, hoping nobody else realised how nervous he'd become. The boy struggled to sleep, and when he did, he often woke up from nightmares.

Things had got so bad that their mother also noticed. She now talked about taking Leo to a doctor. The situation was getting dangerous. Duncan also suspected Leo had taken to using hard drugs, injecting himself, although he vehemently denied this.

With worry gnawing inside him, Duncan joined the rest of the gang and Tango downstairs. All were dressed for action, in dark clothes, hoodies. Not a logo in sight. They'd learnt their lesson.

Tommy scanned Duncan's expression. 'Stay here. I'm goin' up to see Leo.'

Even Duncan's piercings could not disguise his concern.

'I'll come too,' said Derek Dawson.

When Tommy nodded in agreement, Duncan sighed in relief. Derek was his brother's best friend. *It'll be OK,* he thought.

***

In his room upstairs, Leo sat up in bed trying to hide his jitters when Tommy marched in with Dawson in tow. Seeing his best friend helped to calm him down and remember his brother's advice. He coughed with exaggerated gusto until his throat was hoarse, clutching at his chest in pain.

'You look like shit, Leo.' It was hard to tell from Tommy's expression whether he was convinced by the act.

'Yeah, real bad,' Derek added.

'Sorry, man,' Leo said, his voice genuinely hoarse. 'I seem to have caught some'ing. I'll be OK soon.'

After another long stare, Tommy said, 'I'll see you tomorrow.' He turned and left the room.

Leo suppressed a gasp of relief.

Derek sidled up to his friend, slipped a packet into his palm. 'Go on, shoot up,' he whispered. 'It'll put you to sleep.' With a grin and a quick thumbs up, he scooted off behind Tommy.

Leo tucked the little pack deep under his pillow. His mum was shuffling about in the kitchen. He heard Tommy call out, 'Hello, Mrs Hughes.'

Through his open bedroom door, he watched his mother step out into their living room. She was in her dressing gown, her hair lank, hanging in stringy trails about her pale face.

Despite her haggard and tired appearance, Leo thought his mum still looked pretty. He was glad of Derek's presence, that she wasn't alone with Tommy.

He smiled when Derek went up to her and extended an arm. 'How are you, Mrs Hughes?'

'I'm fine, thank you, Derek.' She shook his hand, her smile widening into a grin.

'Be seein' you both.' Derek waved cheerfully and trotted off to join Tommy, waiting impatiently by the open front door.

Hands in her pockets, his mum returned to the kitchen. When the latch clicked shut behind Tommy and Derek, Leo squeezed his eyes shut and released the breath he'd been holding.

***

Footfalls thudded down the stairs as Tommy and Derek arrived at a run, leaping off the last five steps.

'You're right. Leo looks like shit,' said Tommy. 'Don't wan' him givin' us all the bugs.'

Duncan grinned at the respite.

'Your mum's up too,' said Derek, 'and she don't look too bright either.'

'Oh, shit. I'll quickly check on her and tell her we'll be gone for a while.'

Before anyone could stop him, Duncan raced off into the building.

'Five minutes!' Tommy growled after him.

'You OK, Mum?'

Crystal had a glass of water in one hand, and the other tucked deep inside her dressing gown pocket. But Duncan knew the water was heavily diluted with cheap gin. His mother nodded and raised over-bright eyes to his.

Oh, shit. 'Come on. Don't drink anymore, Mum,' he said, taking the glass from her. Unresisting, she allowed him to lead her to her bedroom. He hoped she'd sleep it off.

Both Duncan and Leo knew she couldn't help herself. Ever since their dad got sent to prison, their mum had fallen to pieces.

We just have to hold on until Dad returns. Then he'll sort everything out.

Duncan entered Leo's room. 'How'd it go?'

Leo coughed, clutched his chest dramatically, earning himself a clout to the head. 'I'm off now. Get Mum some'fing to eat, yeah? An' make sure she eats it! We'll sort you out when I return.'

It was both a promise and a threat.

'Have fun,' said Leo, as his brother hurried out of the flat.

Leo did not know their plans. He hadn't asked and didn't want to know. He was simply glad that he wasn't a part of it.

77

The Watcher

'Good girls, I see you've eaten all your dinner. Did you enjoy that?'

Two pairs of expressionless eyes swept over him before resting unblinkingly on his face. They didn't bother to respond.

Oh well, at least I'll enjoy the next bit, he thought.

'OK, it's time for your bath now. Come on.'

They ambled across the room.

'In here,' he said, pointing to the bedroom, unable to believe his luck when they went in without hesitation.

'Take off your clothes and put them on the bed.'

Eyes fixed on them, he stood motionless, not daring to breathe or blink while they took off their shoes and socks. As they pulled their sweaters over their heads, a series of loud beeps from the living room distracted him. Damn! The temptation to ignore the incoming message was overwhelming, but it was too important. With a grunt of frustration, he left the bedroom.

He returned a few minutes later to an empty room, their clothes piled neatly at the foot of the bed. Heart racing in panic, he spun, stumbled, and then sighed in relief at the soft splashing noises from the bathroom.

Only their heads were visible above the mountain of froth and iridescent bubbles. He switched on the video cameras and watched their innocent play.

Then, unable to contain himself, he walked across and knelt before the bath.

78

Holt

Matthew Holt, Rowena, Karl and two uniformed police waited at the gate a safe distance away, watching the four bomb disposal experts go into yet another huddle before the team leader approached them.

'All clear, Matt,' he said with a grim smile. 'There was only one. We've defused it and checked the inside. All safe, nothing else is rigged.'

'Thanks, Tom.' Holt shook his burly friend's hand. 'Glad it wasn't a wasted trip.'

'Far from it. It wasn't a large or sophisticated device, but whoever tried to open those doors would have lost a limb and a few other bits.' He held up the bagged remnants of the defused IED—improvised explosive device. 'And it would've messed up your evidence. I'll send you a report as soon as I can.'

Within the fenced, overgrown scrap of land, the detectives had found no shed or outbuildings. Instead, a big old forty-foot and a pair of smaller steel shipping containers nestled amongst overgrown grass and weeds.

Holt's uncle stored machinery and equipment in similar containers on the farm. Sturdy, waterproof and, apart from rustproofing and painting them once every three or four years, they were virtually maintenance free and lasted a lifetime.

The detectives and police officers eyed Holt with new respect. Even his staunchest supporters had considered the DCI's request for a bomb squad excessive. An overkill.

They watched the Explosive Ordnance Disposal team leave, sobered by what could have happened.

The forty-foot container's double doors stood wide open, and crouching within its dark, cavernous depth was the hulking shape of a car.

Despite the bomb squad's 'all clear,' they hesitated. *Was it really safe? What if—?*

Dressed head to toe in white disposable crime scene protective clothing, Holt stepped forward, strode to the container, aimed his torch at the car huddled inside like a giant hibernating metal bear. He expelled his breath in a loud wheeze and edged into the container. With no room alongside, he peered in through the rear windscreen. Piles of clothes lay on the seats. He backed out, turned and gave a thumbs-up.

They had finally found Tommy Wade's missing dark blue Ford Fiesta.

The next hour and a half involved a lot more aimless waiting – waiting for CSIs to arrive, waiting for the vehicle to be winched out to access its interior, waiting for the investigators to bag the evidence.

Finally, after what seemed an eternity, the forensics team waved the detectives forward, holding up large evidence bags of bloodied clothing right down to socks, underwear, gloves and boots. Separate evidence bags held four blood-stained knives and another, a mobile phone. Best of all were the individual pouches containing black hoodies with fluorescent logos that glinted in the light.

Rowena instructed the uniformed officers to secure the property and to arrest anyone attempting to enter the site.

It would be hours before forensics finished, and then there was the car to process.

'I don't get it, sir,' said Rowena. 'Why would they hang on to all that? The car, the phones, the weapons, their clothes? Why didn't they just dump it at sea or torch it?'

'Actually, it was simpler to keep it. It's more difficult to dump stuff at sea or to burn or bury it. Or perhaps their accomplice kept it as leverage for his own security. As long as he was OK, unharmed, and they did his bidding, the evidence stayed hidden. He certainly had a chokehold over them.'

'That's true. And now, we need to wait until the fingerprint and DNA results are in. What about Tommy Wade's claim that his car was stolen?'

'Well, he'll still have to explain the blood on those outfits. I wonder what he and Metcalf will cook up. I bet they'll say they were trying to help the victims, and that's how they got bloody. Bet they'll also claim the knives were put there by whoever stole the car,' said Holt.

Rowena's jaw dropped.

Holt grinned. 'But the blood spatter pattern should refute that. Karl, please organise the arrest and search warrants and let's round up the lot of them before they get wind of our discovery.'

That still left the question of motive. Why?

Holt updated the superintendent, smiled at the enormous sigh of relief whooshing down the phone. This could have gone so wrong, yet his boss had supported him. Many in his boss's position would put their own careers first, especially when their SIO had little more than instinct and faith in his team to offer. It had been a close call, though – just one day before his replacement arrived to take over, and he walked out of the job forever.

'Thank you, sir.'

'What for? You did all the work.'

'For believing in me. It was a big ask, and...'

'Never had a moment's doubt, my boy.' The Superintendent laughed. 'You cut it really fine, though and had me shitting bricks. But well done, lad. I'm glad it worked out, for both our sakes. I'll see you later. Now I can't wait to go rub the Chief and ACC's noses in it.'

79

Holt

As the Super said, it was indeed a close call, thought Holt grinning and pocketing the phone. Besides the undeniable satisfaction of being right in his suspicions and line of inquiry, his biggest relief was that he'd justified the Super's faith in him. Although the superintendent had only hinted at it, and in jest at that, the threat to his boss's career had been very real indeed.

If only I'd paid more attention to the details and asked the questions: Where was Endsleigh getting the money for the new site? Why would he buy a new van to move building material? We'd have solved this much sooner. Holt berated himself. *I should have dug deeper into the relationship between Endsleigh and Tommy—*

Eventually he had. First, he had Karl confirm his suspicion about Endsleigh's van, then Holt had Rowena check out with the Land Registry for every property owned by the man, which had revealed this vacant site. When he'd spotted the shipping containers on the property during a quiet drive-by in an unmarked car with Karl, he knew they'd come up trumps.

But they were still missing the connection between Endsleigh and Tommy Wade. Yes, the pair had known each other for years, and Tommy used to hang out at The Cue Room in his youth. Still did occasionally, but then, so did other teenagers.

Questioning either of them would be a waste of time. Not only would it alert them, but the pair would continue to maintain their original assertion that they were nothing more than casual friends. And the police had nothing to prove otherwise. So, Holt had his team dig up records of Endsleigh's previous employees, going back five years to when Tommy first appeared on the scene at the pool club.

The list of ex-employees turned up a gold nugget. Well worth Holt's trek to London two days ago to meet Vince Cameron, who worked as a bouncer at 'Unleashed', a nightclub in Soho.

***

Two Days Ago

'Thank you for meeting with me,' said Holt to the giant seated opposite.

The man's big enough to block a doorway all by himself. I can't see many people getting past him, he thought, *and if he bounced anyone, they'd stay bounced.*

Unlike its nighttime persona—glitz, glitter, flashing lights, and laughter—*The Unleashed* by day was dim, unremarkable, almost indifferent to its own identity. From the whine of a vacuum cleaner and the clatter of glassware behind the scenes,

Holt figured the evening's illusions were already being rebuilt. The tea towel slung over Vince's shoulder suggested his role extended beyond just guarding the door.

'What's this about?' asked Vince Cameron, his deep voice rumbling like one of Rowena's bass drum rolls.

'Five years ago, you worked at The Cue Room for Harvey Endsleigh. Were you there when he met Tommy Wade? He'd have been just a boy then, about fourteen-years-old?'

'Yea, I was.'

'Can you tell me about it? I'd like to know what the nature of their relationship was.'

Vince straightened and seemed to grow larger. 'Why? Is Tommy saying Mr Endsleigh was – was improper with him? If he is, it's not true. Why, the boss was the one who saved him from those creeps.'

'What creeps?'

'One night, me an' the boss went out back to put some rubbish out, an' we saw these two guys had got the boy bent over with his trousers down. We chased 'em away and took the lad inside. He was real frightened and upset, and we calmed him down. The boss was so mad, he even shouted at him. Said he shuda been more careful. Shuda known 'bout that kinda people and how to protect himself. The boss then kinda became interested in the boy—'

'You mean he was sexually abusing him?'

Vince shot upright and glared at Holt. 'No, Mr Holt. 'Course not. Now why'd you say something so awful?'

'My apologies, Vince. In my work, I see more of the worst human traits than the good.'

Vince nodded wisely. 'That's OK. I understand. No, the boss kinda looked out for the boy. Became his mental, y'know.'

Holt's mouth twitched, but he waved for Vince to carry on.

'He, I mean the boss, later tol' me he knew those two an' wanted to teach 'em a lesson, 'an asked if I would help. I don' enjoy violence, Mr Holt, but I was that mad I was up for anything. Two nights later, the three of us snuck into their bedrooms, me and the boss held 'em down, an' the boy took a knife to their balls. Tommy woulda cut 'em off too if the boss hadn't stopped him. They got away with jus' a nick, an' we said we'd take the whole works off next time if they came anywhere near the lad or our place ever again.'

'Didn't they complain?'

'Oh no, Mr Holt, not them. The lad was only fourteen, and they know what happens to paedos.'

Holt nodded. Given Tommy's looks, he could believe how he would be a target for predators.

'What happened to those two men?'

'Somehow it got out how they rape young boys, and they had to leave Southampton in a real hurry,' said Vince with a grin.

'So, Tommy and Endsleigh became friends?'

'Yea. And me too. I taught him a bit of boxing, and Mr Endsleigh made him go to the gym and take karate lessons.' Vince paused and shook his head. 'But Tommy wasn't very good. He was happy enough hurting someone but couldn't take any pain. Still, he learned a bit. Better than nothing, I suppose.'

'I see from the records that you left Southampton six months later. Any particular reason?'

'My wife – she was my girlfriend then – wanted to move to London, so I found this job. It's good, and the boss is fair. He includes me when he shares out the tips.'

Holt stood up. 'Well thanks, Vince. You've been really helpful.'

'Mr Endsleigh is a good man. If Tommy is allegg—, um, saying different, he's lying.'

'I'll bear that in mind,' said Holt, extending his hand and bracing himself for the crushing force of Vince's handshake. But to his surprise, or perhaps unsurprisingly, Vince released his hand after exerting the gentlest of pressure.

A man who doesn't have to prove his strength, thought Holt.

And now he had an answer to why Tommy would do Endsleigh's bidding.

80

Lily

Lily's eyes fluttered open. Her shoulders hurt, her head was a mass of agony. She tentatively touched the back of her skull and cried out at the wave of intense pain.

Where am I? Fingers touched and patted the surface beneath. The texture was rough, hard, strange, yet familiar. Not her bed. The slit between her eyelids showed nothing but darkness. Was it night?

She reached out, encountered a wall, recognised the space. Why was she on the floor? Had she tripped? Fallen and hurt herself?

Stand up! Urgency drove Lily to lift her head, but another wave of dizziness engulfed her in a black swamp.

An hour later, Lily awakened. Holding her neck steady, she tried once again to orient herself and reached out an arm to touch a wall.

I am face down. On the hallway floor. It's dark. Is it night? Where're the girls?

She tried to call out, but all she managed was a weak croak. Lily tried moving but stopped as vertigo threatened her consciousness. She lay immobile until it passed, then tried again, inch by inch, until she rose to her knees.

Lily sensed the emptiness in the house. The children weren't home! Something was very wrong.

Help! I need help.

On hands and knees, Lily crawled towards the front door, a shuffle at a time, pausing between movements to steady the spinning hallway. Finally, she was there. Panting, she stretched out a hand sticky with congealed blood, gripped the door handle and pulled herself up.

After several tries, she opened it and stumbled outside. The security light above the small porch lit up, illuminating the narrow garden path. The chilly air helped to clear some of the fog in her brain.

Swaying and staggering like a drunk, Lily grabbed at the rose bushes beside the pathway to keep her balance. She ignored the pain of twigs and sharp thorns tearing her palms, concentrated on keeping herself upright. Step by tottering step, she lurched to the hip-high gate, pushed it open, reeled into her neighbour's garden, mounted the wide steps, and slammed a palm on their doorbell.

Lily leaned against the door for support and fell over when her irate neighbour wrenched it open.

Robert Fisher grabbed her by the arms and shouted for his wife. Horrified at the blood matting her hair, shoulders and hands, the couple half-carried Lily to their kitchen and sat her on a chair.

'My girls,' she whispered, 'please, find my girls.'

Cathy Fisher raised a panic-stricken gaze to her husband, who was already calling for an ambulance and the police.

The ambulance arrived first. Worried, the paramedics insisted Lily go with them to the hospital.

'No, no, I'm fine. Please, just take me back home. My children—'

'I'm sure they'll be fine,' said a paramedic, looking around but unconcerned when he didn't see any. They're in bed, he assumed.

'No, oww,' yelped Lily, holding her head in two hands and swaying with dizziness. 'No, you don't understand. My daughters are missing...'

When they finally understood her gasping statement about the missing children, they carried her next door, accompanied by her neighbours. One paramedic phoned for a doctor. From his side of the conversation, it seemed he had to argue his case and insist before a GP[1] agreed to visit Lily's home.

The painkiller injection soon worked its magic, helping Lily to think and respond more lucidly. She did not know who had attacked her. Or why. She had no memory of collecting her daughters from school.

Worse, no one had brought them home.

•

---

1. General Practitioner, a community doctor.

81

Holt

The Station fizzled with the excitement of finding the missing car and evidence, and everyone cheered when Matthew Holt and Rowena entered the homicide squad's office on the fifth floor. While many questions were still unanswered and the culprits remained unapprehended, after the months of frustration and despondency, everyone from the most senior to the lowliest rank felt vindicated.

'How'd you know it was Harvey Endsleigh, sir? What put you on to him?' asked DC Larry Ives.

Rowena, who along with Karl had colluded with Holt in pursuing his condemned strategy, looked smug.

'I should've cottoned on to him much sooner, way back in March when Rowena first interviewed him. I remember wondering then where he was getting the money to purchase the site for his new cowboy western themed club, but when we learnt that he'd had no contact with our suspects since last Christmas, I didn't ask.'

Holt paused, considering the cold-bloodedness of it all, the planning, the lies. They'd kept it simple, believable.

'Go on, sir.'

'It was premeditated. Planned far ahead. When we started looking at vans and lorries, it struck me as odd that Endsleigh would get rid of his old van and buy a new one. To move building material to refurbish his new site, he claimed. It'd make more sense to use his old van, or if he needed something bigger, to hire or even buy a tatty second-hand lorry for the job. I should know – I wear my oldest clothes and use John's oldest pickup to transport materials when I'm working on the watermill. Then we couldn't find any information about his backers. It's an offshore company registered in the Cayman Islands, with a lawyer and accountants as nominee directors.'

'That's so tenuous, sir.'

'Well, I was getting desperate, clutching at straws, wasn't I?' grinned Holt. 'I asked Karl and Raoul, our master mechanic, to check out the old van, if only to rule Endsleigh out. That's where they struck gold.'

'When Karl and Raoul approached the new owner about the van,' said Rowena, 'Raoul spotted that someone had strengthened the chassis, a fact Endsleigh omitted mentioning in the sale. Guess he couldn't remove the struts before selling it, not with us looking for anything odd in garages and workshops. But best of all was his attempt to repair the deep scratches and scrapes inside the van. Forensics found dark blue car paint, consistent with that used by the manufacturers on Ford Fiesta 2012 models. They also found bits of glass from broken headlights and wing mirrors embedded deep in the corners inside, which we matched up to Tommy's car.'

Holt picked up the thread. 'Once we had that, Rowena and Karl compiled a list of all of Endsleigh's properties. When we found that site listing him as the owner, Karl and I checked it out. As soon as we saw the shipping containers, I suspected that's where Tommy's car was stashed.'

'Why would they do this? It can't be something as stupid and mindless as because they could, or a mugging gone wrong!'

'No, this was meticulously planned ages ago. I mean, imagine the logistics involved. It was bold, brazen, and they almost got away with it.'

Rowena nodded. 'With no connection between the killers and those poor students, we still can't establish a motive. Once planned, all they had to do was stay away from each other and not have any contact that might imply a relationship, other than as ordinary regulars at Endsleigh's club. I believed him! Oh, to think I was taken in by his story!'

'Almost taken in,' reminded Holt. 'I recall you suspected him of something.'

'Yes, dodgy drinks, cash transactions, even drugs, but not murder!'

'If Endsleigh instigated this, how could he be so sure the gang would go for it?'

'Actually, he only needed to be sure of Tommy Wade,' said Holt. 'And we now know why Tommy would do his bidding. Maybe he feels he owes Endsleigh for saving him from those paedophiles when he was fourteen. The other three, especially Duncan, seem in thrall to Tommy. That plus money, I guess.'

'That Tommy is more than capable and cold-bloodedly so. You saw what he was like, sir. And that lad, Derek Dawson. He looks so innocent, likable even, but he's seriously weird. I don't understand the Hughes brothers' involvement, though. It seems out of character.'

'Well, the psychiatrists will enjoy analysing that lot. I feel sorry for their father, Daniel Hughes. He believed his sons were innocent,' Holt said, remembering Karl's visit to Winchester Prison.

'Why would Endsleigh want those students dead? It must be connected to their families and his new club.'

Holt sighed. 'I don't know. Yet. And I've no idea how the victims' fathers worked out about the van before we did. They asked the PI, Nigel Payton, to investigate seven businesspeople with large vans and lorries. I wonder if they also know what the motive was for their sons' deaths. Now that we have so much evidence against them, Endsleigh and the gang may talk. Let's just find them, eh? They can't all have disappeared. Have you put out the alerts?'

'Yes, sir. Traffic and all ports, sea and air. They won't get far,' assured Larry.

DC Ian Shepherd rushed into Holt's office, his eyes bright with excitement. 'We have the prints, sir. They match! We even found fingerprints on a knife. Looks like young Leo took off his gloves. The lab's analysing the blood on the clothes, weapons, and in the car. None other than our four. They'll send over a preliminary DNA report within twenty-four hours, but the detailed analysis will take at least another week.'

Holt straightened. 'Great! But where the hell are our suspects? What's Karl playing at?' He fumbled for his phone and pressed the hot key, while Ian returned to his desk.

'Karl, what's going on? Why isn't that lot in the custody suite already?'

'Sir, we've only just picked up the warrants! I'm heading to Tommy's. Rowena's going to pick up Endsleigh, Larry's tackling the Hughes brothers, and Michelle's going to pick up Derek.'

The reproach in Karl's voice tempered Holt's impatience. Haranguing his DI would not get the task done any faster. They can't have gone far, he thought, and four men don't just vanish into thin air.

'Sorry, Karl. I know you're on it. But I want them in custody ASAP. We can't risk their fleeing, especially as Daniel Hughes seems to have the clout to call in favours. Who knows, this time he may arrange for them to vanish. I want them here, in sight, especially now that we have enough to charge them.'

'Yes, sir.'

'Oh, and don't let the media catch a whiff. We do everything by the book; I won't let them wriggle away again.'

'I know, sir. Don't worry, we'll have them in soon.'

'Thanks, Karl.' Slipping the phone back into his pocket, he said, 'I need a coffee,' knowing full-well that was the last thing he needed in his heightened state.

***

En route to the kitchenette, Holt paused, his attention caught by the commotion in the Mispers unit where two officers grabbed their jackets and rushed away, and others made frantic phone calls or pounded their keyboards while the unit's screens pinged frenzied alerts.

Must be a missing child, he guessed. Holt's next thought shamed him. *Damn it! Now they'll divert everyone to search for the kid, and our culprits will escape if they haven't already.*

He stepped into the missing persons unit's area and peered at their information board.

High-Risk Missing Persons Report – Webster Twins
Missing Children: Twins – Cara (5), Mia (5)
Mother: Lily Webster
Reported: 20:20
Last seen: 17:15 at Bluebell Grove Special Needs Primary School.

Holt jerked in surprise as his gaze locked onto the mother's name. Lily Webster. *Could it be the same Lily Webster*? His heart lurched when he recalled her mentioning her daughters.

His expression must have given him away, for the admin officer updating the board asked, 'Do you know her, sir?'

Holt shrugged. 'Well, I met a Lily Webster way back in March. This might be someone else entirely.' He hesitated, but his need to know urged him on. 'What do you know about Lily Webster so far?'

'Not much, sir. She works as Buildings Inspector at the Council, and it appears she was attacked in her home.'

Holt's heart clenched, and blood drained down to his boots.

'Who's the SIO?'

'DI Carmen D'Souza, and she's on her way to Webster's house. The Super has diverted a dozen PCs there, and they've started searching for the kids, and although Carmen is trying to coordinate it all, she's still half an hour away, and it's getting a bit chaotic. The mother's hurt, but she's refusing to go to the hospital. Those kids are only five, and she's frantic.'

It's not my case; I'm neck-deep in my own problems, and I'll be stepping on God knows how many people's toes. Besides, I met the woman only once! I've no connection to her...

Yet his instincts would not let him turn around and walk away. *Don't get involved,* reason warned him, even as his brain computed exactly how he could.

My reports to the Super can wait. I can't do much until Endsleigh and the others are in custody. Even then, processing them will take 2-3 hours, and we can't question them until Metcalf arrives—

'Sir?' prompted the admin officer.

'I can spare a couple of hours, so I'll go to that address and coordinate operations until DI D'Souza arrives. Give me all the details you have so far. I'll notify the Super on my way there.'

Oh shit, Holt thought. *The Super's going to be so pissed off.*

82

Holt

As it turned out, Superintendent Simpson was more surprised than pissed off when Holt told him where he was headed.

'Huh? How'd you know?'

'Know what, sir?'

'That I was coming to see you to ask you to release Karl to this case? I've diverted PCs there, but we're short on senior officers in mispers today. DI Carmen D'Souza's on her way, but she's nearly thirty minutes away. Plus, she's new and at the moment everyone's all over the place like blue-arsed flies.' The Super paused, then added. 'Actually, it makes more sense for you to pick this up than for Karl to change tack at this stage. Matt, this could be a child abduction, and we may need to issue a CRA. I'll start the paperwork, so it's ready to go as soon as you say so. Right. Keep me posted on both cases.'

Should I have mentioned I know Lily? Ah, well, it's too late now. I'll burn that bridge when I get to it. Holt's next calls were to Rowena and Karl to let them know where he was. 'The

Super was going to pull Karl into this,' he explained, 'but as he said, it makes more sense for me to step in temporarily.'

All true, with the only omission being his emotional involvement.

***

Holt looked for a space to park, but found none in front of Lily's house, already crowded with police cars and an ambulance. He parked on a double yellow and trotted up to the house. The residential area, with a row of terraced and semi-detached houses set close together, had well-tended gardens and litter-free pavements.

A police constable at the door checked and, undaunted by the DCI's rank or impatience, logged Holt's identification.

'They're in the kitchen, sir.' He pointed to the open door at the end of the hallway.

Holt entered a warm, uncluttered kitchen to find a white-coated doctor checking the blood pressure of a hunched figure seated at a small dining table. Beside them were a female PC and a man in plainclothes, whom he recognised as Detective Constable Bill Adams. A middle-aged woman fussed around, pouring out teas and coffees and passing them to a man in his fifties, whom he assumed was the woman's husband.

With muttered greetings, the officers stepped aside, revealing the view of a woman's head swathed in bandages, the curly blond hair matted with blood. Holt's heart thumped several beats faster.

Sensing Holt's presence, the woman looked up.

Holt struggled to keep his composure. *It was definitely her!* His pulse quickened as recognition replaced the puzzled look. She remembered him too!

'Hello Lily,' he said, holding out his hand.

Confused, she grasped it with both of hers. 'Matt? What're you doing here?'

Holt's heart lifted at the easy familiarity with which she uttered his name.

DC Adams cleared his throat and interrupted, 'Er, do you and Miss Webster know each other, sir?'

'We met once briefly several months ago.' Holt turned to Lily. 'I'm a police officer, Lily, a Detective Chief Inspector. I am here to help.'

'Oh, Matt. Please, please find my girls.' She clung to his hand.

'We'll do our best.' He slid into a chair beside her. Despite knowing how unprofessional it looked, he left his hand in hers. It would have been rude and heartless to shake hers off, he justified. Besides, it felt good. Reluctantly, he let go and placed a mug of tea in her hands.

'Drink it up and tell me what happened.'

He tried to make sense of the conflicting narrations from Lily, her neighbours, and the officers.

Lily didn't think she had left the house at all, whereas her neighbour, Cathy Fisher, said she saw Lily leave a little after 4.30 p.m., but hadn't seen her return.

'My daughters have special needs. They have problems relating to other people. They simply would not go off with anyone else, and their teachers certainly would not have allowed it,' insisted Lily.

The school's name showed it was a special needs school. Like others of its kind, it had limited places available and nowhere near the capacity needed within the community.

Children were carefully assessed before admission to the Bluebell Grove Special Needs Primary School, as were the teachers, who were thoroughly vetted and specially trained, and who would not have released the twins to a stranger's care.

The photographs of the twins – one a dusky brown, a stark contrast to her sister's rosy-white pallor. However, their features, hair, and eyes were identical, and despite their unsmiling countenances, they were beautiful. The same person in two shades. But their expressionless gaze was disconcerting, like a pair of porcelain dolls – beautiful but slightly creepy.

Lily was distraught. 'I don't remember driving to the school this afternoon or picking them up. The last thing I recall is using the loo downstairs around 4.30 p.m. I am positive my children were not with me then, and I'm sure I didn't leave home after that.'

'Their teacher told DC Adams that you were late getting there, and you'd collected the children around 5.15 p.m. this afternoon,' Holt told Lily.

The teacher had also griped to DC Adams that Lily not only arrived late but had also not apologised for her tardiness.

'No, no. I didn't go to the school. I—' Lily shook her head, almost passing out.

The doctor grabbed and steadied her. 'Please try to stay calm, Miss Webster. You should go to the hospital to get X-rayed. Those wounds look bad. You might have hairline fractures, or internal bleeding.'

'No! Not until my daughters are home.'

'What about their father, Lily? Could he have taken them?'

'David?'

Of course, there's a David in her life. There are two kids to prove it, for God's sake! Regardless, Holt was surprised at the stab of pain.

'No, he doesn't even know about them.'

At Holt's shocked expression, she added, 'He was someone I met and fell for. I... I don't know his last name. There was an enormous group of us, Erasmus students. We met just once, in France, six years ago. The next morning, we all went our separate ways. I came home, and then a couple of months later, realised I was pregnant.'

'Could he have found out? And taken his children?'

'No, he wasn't like that. If he had known, he could have just knocked on the door and asked to see them. I wouldn't have minded. It would have been good for Cara and Mia, too.'

'OK, what about your husband, boyfriend, partner?'

'No, there's no one. I'm single.'

'Sir,' interrupted DC Adams. With an 'excuse-me' to Lily, Holt stepped out of the room.

'We can't find Miss Webster's car, her handbag or her red overcoat. There's worse. It looks like someone's jimmied the back door lock.'

DC Adams had already put out an alert and a search for Lily's car. If someone picked up the children at 5.15 p.m. as the teacher claimed, they should have reached home by 5.40 p.m. at the latest.

Three hours since Lily was attacked, hours lost before the police were notified. This was now a possible abduction.

But it could have been worse! Lily could have been killed, and not a soul would have known. Days could have passed before anyone came to check on them.

The officers dialled Lily's mobile phone repeatedly, but it appeared to be switched off with no signal to help locate the phone or the children.

The neighbours had heard nothing. Although it was too dark to see clearly, there were signs suggesting an intruder had crouched in the rear garden shrubs. DC Adams surmised the intruder was waiting when Lily and her daughters returned home, attacked the mother and grabbed the children.

She looked up at Holt. 'They'd never go with anyone else, especially if I was hurt. They'd scream the place down!'

Holt learnt the girls didn't have any friends. They didn't mix well with other children, rarely got invited to birthday parties, and had never been on a sleepover. In fact, the twins went nowhere without their mother.

None of the children's things – school bags, shoes, or jackets – were in the house. No evidence of meals or snacks. Their toys remained tidied away, and there was nothing to show that they had actually returned home.

The other possibility was too gruesome to contemplate, but contemplate he must, however much he hated doing so.

Was all this an elaborate charade? Did Lily kidnap and dispose of her daughters?

Holt asked the doctor and DC Adams to follow him to the hallway, out of earshot.

'Could Miss Webster's wounds be self-inflicted?'

'I already asked that, sir,' said DC Adams.

'And as I already told DC Adams, not unless she can rotate her arm one-eighty degrees and bash herself at least three times on her head. Even then, I doubt she could hit herself so hard or at that angle,' said the doctor. 'I'm really concerned about her wounds. It needs to be X-rayed, but I can't force her to go. Look, I must leave. I can do no more here. Try to get her to A&E, will you?'

The detectives watched him hurry out in a swish of white coat.

'OK, not self-inflicted. An accomplice?'

'Those are pretty nasty injuries, sir. Would an accomplice strike her that hard? Head wounds are unpredictable; it could've killed her. Be easier to tie her up, lock her upstairs, from where she eventually escapes and calls 999. I'm quoting from a textbook scene in a staged kidnapping,' he added hastily at Holt's frown.

'Unless her accomplice changed the plan,' said Holt grimly.

His stomach knotted as he examined the hallway carpet, at the trail staining it from the cloakroom to the front door. The intermittent palm prints and stains on the wall showed where Lily had leaned for support. Someone had assaulted her in the corridor. She had fallen face down, which meant her assailant had hit her from behind.

The neighbour, Robert Fisher, joined Holt. 'Those poor girls,' he said. 'They've only just started to speak. It's been so hard on Lily. She's very good with them and totally devoted to them! How can we help?'

'Can you persuade her to go to the hospital? She needs to be checked out.'

Fisher shook his head. 'My wife, Cathy, and I have both tried, but she won't go; she wants to be here in case her daughters return, or someone brings them home.'

Holt nodded; if they were kidnapped for ransom, it was best the children's mother remained here should the kidnappers call. But he doubted it'd be for ransom. There were far more lucrative targets out there. Lily's mobile phone was in the missing handbag, so to reach her, they'd have to call her landline. But her injuries worried him. 'Would you and your wife stay with Miss Webster? She seems to trust you both.'

Fisher nodded and hurried to speak to his wife.

Holt asked DC Adams for the teacher's number.

Jo Latimer sounded awake and alert; the previous phone call and questions troubled her. Although she had crossly insisted to DC Adams that Lily had picked up the girls, doubts and misgivings now plagued her as she pictured the scene.

'It was dull and cloudy this afternoon, yet I recall clearly that Lily wore sunglasses. Big, round, dark sunglasses. No, I didn't actually speak to her or see her face. She stayed put in her car. The car moved the instant the twins got in, without waiting for them to fasten their seatbelts. Now I think about it, that isn't like Lily at all. The children turned around and waved to me, but not Lily. She simply raised her hand, a gloved hand,' Jo said, remembering the dark of the gloves, 'and drove off. Just shot off too fast. I was too cold and annoyed, but I should have realised that something wasn't right,' confessed the teacher. 'I thought nothing of it then because the twins didn't seem worried or scared even after getting into the car.'

That last statement concerned Holt. *Was it someone they knew?*

He returned to the kitchen and addressed Lily's neighbour. 'Mrs Fisher, you said you saw Lily leave around 4.30 p.m. Did you actually see her face or speak to her?'

'No. I was in my front room and just glimpsed her walking fast to her car, as she was later than usual. She was wearing her lovely red coat and sunglasses, which I thought was odd. I didn't notice her coming back, but I might have missed it as I was doing laundry.'

Holt and DC Adams exchanged glances. *So, despite her assertion, Cathy Fisher could not confirm it was Lily she saw leaving the house.*

He suspected that someone else had gone to the school in Lily's stead. Could be a man or a woman, but someone in a wig. Her hairstyle would be easy enough to copy – a mass of long blond curls reaching well below her shoulders. In an identical wig, wearing Lily's distinctive red coat, and driving her car, the kidnapper could pass off as the girls' mother, especially from the back.

It was an enormous risk, yet simpler than taking two unwilling children from their home.

But the kids would soon realize it wasn't their mother.

Unless someone hurt them, too, to keep them quiet.

83

Leo

I should've gone with them, thought Leo Hughes. *It'd have been better than staying here with Mum. Wonder how Duncan and the others are getting on.*

He shuddered when he remembered that the 'others' included Tommy.

Earlier, he had made her some toast and eggs, sat with her while she nibbled at it, coaxing her to eat a mouthful, then another. It had been so different when Dad was home. Now he barely recognised the gaunt, lethargic woman with her overbright eyes. They had flicked through the TV channels, settling on a music competition, but she fell asleep halfway through.

Poor Mum, she's so lost without Dad. He'll be so pissed off at her. At all of us!

By 7.00 p.m., an exhausted Leo called it a night, shook his mother awake, helped her up, waited while she used the bathroom and got ready for bed, kissed her goodnight and watched her shuffle off to her bedroom. He wished he could help her; wished he could help himself, but he was on a runaway train, a deadly crash the only inevitable outcome.

He'd coped until that night at the vigil, until that speech by the victim's father. He'd attempted to remain as nonchalant as the others, to swagger and strut, but the blackness of the fathers' despair seeped into him.

I've done nothing wrong. I only pretended to stab those men, only nicked that tall young man leaning over his fallen friend. But he knew that by being a part of it, he was as guilty as the other three. Maybe guiltier.

But the maggots of worry and guilt gnawed at every inch of his consciousness. Terrible nightmares jerked him awake whenever he dozed off. Each night, the victims' fathers trapped him, laughed as they stabbed him. In his waking hours, they followed him, hiding in the shadows, waiting for him. His paranoia cost him his sleep and his peace.

Leo heard his mother shuffling about, the rustle and clink as she searched for her kit, followed a few minutes later by the whisper of an ecstatic sigh.

Leo realised Derek must have slipped his mother a little packet, too, earlier that evening. He shuddered at the memory of his brief meeting with Tommy, of that beautiful face, those soulless eyes. But Derek was great. A real mate!

He got out of bed and dropped onto all fours. His groping fingers found the small plastic toiletries travel pouch hidden between the coiled springs. *I shouldn't again so soon, but this pack's so tiny, the dose less than half the last. Besides, I'm all tensed up after seeing Tommy, and as Derek said, it'll help me sleep,* he reasoned.

He mixed the white powder with a few drops of sterile water and drew the mixture into a syringe. He lay back, his eyelids dropped as the warm liquid seeped into his veins, drawing him into its comforting embrace.

No nightmares, he thought, drifting into the soft swirling mists, sinking into fluffy clouds of sensuous softness.

His body jerked and thrashed, pulse racing, straining and testing the capacity of his circulatory system to its limits. Leo didn't feel the warmth of the blood oozing out of his ears and nose or smell the astringent scent as his bladder emptied.

But he knew the nightmares wouldn't get him anymore.

84

Prem

Prem rolled his car into the drive and braked to a halt beside a dark green Peugeot Estate.

Not Roopesh's. For some reason, he expected to find his friend here.

He squinted at the simple lines of the chalet encircled by its army of trees.

This was it! He was meant to be here, although he still didn't know why. What was he meant to do? He had tried to fight, to resist, but the urgent summons had overruled rational thought. The voice inside his skull gave him no option but to do its bidding.

His car's headlights illuminated the closed solid-wood door. The sense of danger lurking behind it set his pulses racing. He had no choice. He had to get inside.

Prem patted the gun in his jacket pocket, grabbed his medic case, ran up to the front door, and tried to push it open. It was locked.

He banged with his fists. No response. Slammed his shoulder against it, but it remained shut. A hard kick yielded no result. He stepped back several paces, ran at the door, throwing all his weight against it, but apart from causing him to grunt in pain, it did not budge. He clawed at it with a growing sense of urgency.

Prem looked for something to use as a battering ram. His glance landed on his car. Perfect.

He got in, jammed his foot on the accelerator and drove straight into the door. The 1.6 tonne BMW demolished the entrance, destroying its frame and parts of the surrounding walls. Apart from the dent in its fender, the car was unscathed.

Prem surveyed the damage and smiled.

That's how you do it!

85

Holt

Although he had handed over to DI Carmen D'Souza from missing persons, Lily had become so distraught when Matthew Holt prepared to leave that he had agreed to stay on. *I can pace the floor here just as easily as at the Station*, he reasoned. Both the newly promoted DI D'Souza and DC Adams appeared relieved to have him there, especially as the situation was going pear-shaped.

With all evidence pointing to the children's abduction, Holt had already alerted his superiors, mobilised an impressive number of police officers and issued a county-wide CRA. This Child Rescue Alert, based on the American concept of 'AMBER Alert,' would assist the police in alerting the public through all media channels and seeking their help to search for the children and for Lily's car.

Three hours had passed before the police even learned the twins were missing. Holt and his colleagues were nerve-rackingly conscious that the delay had devoured half of the 'golden hours' – the first six hours since the twins were last seen.

The police looking for the green Peugeot Estate had posted alerts and were doing everything possible to locate the children but to add to their problems, a glitch with traffic cameras in Southampton and all along the A36 and A31 had them floundering without the means to track Lily's car after it left the school. Engineers were working to fix the issues, but Holt knew that every minute's delay edged the five-year-olds closer to danger and tipped the scales against them.

86

The Watcher

Face flushed, his chest heaving, the man rolled up his sleeves, reached into the bath. Tiny fizzes of the bubbles tickled his bare arm.

He stilled as the twins arose, covered in thick, gleaming foam, bubbles right up to their small chins, splotches of froth on their cheeks and noses.

He beamed, tilting his chin up, aiming his camera to capture the delightful picture they made.

His grin faded. *What the—*

They blurred and flickered, became more shadowy, or rather, their shadows stretched and grew, inching upwards.

He recoiled on his heels, gasping aloud, his jaw agape in disbelief.

No! This isn't real! I am hallucinating. But how? I've taken nothing.

He blinked and knuckled his eyes hard, but the nightmare persisted. His head tipped further back, gaze locked on the spectral shapes, now twice as big as he was. The eerie forms solidified and materialized, became more real, while the children blurred, until they were indistinguishable from the shadows. The apparitions' amber gazes glinted.

Beeps from the mobile phone in his pocket jerked his attention. He recognised the sound. Someone had breached the chalet's perimeter. But he stayed frozen, unable to move or shift his stare from the unfolding hallucination.

A thudding impact, followed by a deafening crash, shook the entire building. The movement and noise pierced the deadly silence, kick-started his sense of self-preservation. He scooted backwards on his haunches.

The girls – no, the creatures – one dark, one pale, stepped out of the bath, dripping water, lathered in soapy froth.

Without warning, an arm covered in a million iridescent soap bubbles reached out, grabbed the man's hair, and lifted him to his feet. The second figure seized his throat, cutting short his wild scream of shock and pain. He hung like a rag doll. Sharp claws dug into his neck, almost severing his windpipe. He felt a warm trickle down his chest.

The beeps grew louder, more urgent, but the agony and terror absorbed his full attention.

It's a nightmare! I'm asleep, and this is a terrible dream! Wake up! Come on, wake up!

He tried to focus on the beeping, to cling to something concrete, normal.

Hurry! Wake up! The alarm's gone off. Get up. This isn't real.

But the pale and dark forms towering above him were as real as he was. Above all, the pain consuming him was very real indeed.

The hands gripping his hair and throat loosened; he crashed to the tiled floor. He scooted further away, hissing air, guttural sounds escaping his torn windpipe. But there was nowhere to go.

Worse, the gigantic creatures filling his vision kept pace.

The pale figure held up a crimson-streaked hand and examined it curiously. It extended a scarlet tongue and licked the blood off a scarlet-coated finger.

The man on the tiles shivered, unable to take his terrified gaze off them. He didn't know what to call them anymore. They were too beautiful to be monsters or demons; too frightening to be angels. Perfectly proportioned, glorious in their beauty, terrifying in their intent.

His brain screamed at him, urging him to run away, but he remained rooted to the spot as the other figure sauntered over to him.

The dark, unearthly form stooped, grabbed his hair once again, dragged him into a sitting position. An arm reached out towards his chest.

He was beyond terror. Shock destroyed his fight-or-flight instincts. He watched as long slim fingers rested on his rib cage.

No, no, please no! Oh God no!! Please! His lips mouthed the words, but the air escaping from his torn throat made them indecipherable.

Time froze wrapped in pain and horror. The figures looked down on him, their visages blocking out the spotlights set into the ceiling. His gaze darted from one to the other, his brain churned, unable to comprehend or believe what he was seeing. A light touch on his chest calmed his racing heart.

Images of his past victims and his heinous acts whirled through his mind. Every single detail, even those he had forgotten. He relived them all in full colour, with all the feelings and the sensations. But not as the perpetrator. He replayed each moment of his preys' time with him – felt their terror, their anguish, suffered their pain, and their loss. But worst of all, he experienced their hope – hope that somehow their nightmare would end, they would go home to loving arms, comforting them, keeping them safe...

A voice he recognised as his own pleaded, *'Please, please don't hurt me. I'm so sorry. Oh God, please help me!'*

The words resonated within him, blending with the voices from his past. The tones that should have melted the stoniest of hearts had instead provided him and his many audiences with hours of pleasure.

Two pairs of inscrutable eyes stared into his. Their awful retribution allowed no absolution, mercy, forgiveness, or escape. That realisation hit with the force of a freight train.

Two voices spoke in unison, melding together like thunder and pouring rain. 'No more!'

The fingers resting on his chest lifted.

He sagged with relief. *A reprieve! They would spare him.*

Promises of the most extravagant kind hissed from his throat and mouth, oaths on things most precious to him, vows of restitution he could never deliver.

They listened, nodded. And repeated in the same thunderous, metallic tones, 'No more!'

Then, the fingers hooked, dug into his chest, shattering his ribs. His body arched in excruciating agony. He screamed, his painful howl turning into a loud, wet whistle through his torn larynx.

He continued to whistle-howl as the probing digits found his heart and wrenched the beating organ out of his chest.

87

Prem

Automatic gear switched to reverse, Prem squeezed the accelerator down and immediately stomped on the brake. The car shot back a few feet and screeched to a halt. He grabbed his medical bag and barged through the wrecked doorway.

From somewhere inside the urgent *beep, beep, beep* of an alarm sounded. Gun in one hand, his black case in the other, he stopped to listen. Other noises reached him from deeper within the chalet.

He followed the unintelligible but unmistakable sounds of someone in agony. Pain was something he understood; something he could deal with; something he spent a big part of his life easing, bringing relief to the sufferers.

He burst into the bathroom and slammed to a dead stop. The gun and medical case fell from numb fingers while his brain registered the man splayed out, his torso covered in blood. Already beyond Prem's help, the glaze of death settled in the vacant open orbs staring into nothingness.

These gigantic creatures can't be real. I'm hallucinating, he decided, rationale and logic rejecting the evidence before him.

It took him a few moments to recognise the human forms in the shadowy figures.

A keening moan escaped him as they turned to him. His knees buckled, and he fell on all fours. One creature held an object dripping blood and trailing tubes. Despite his terror, Prem recognised the horrifying object. It clutched a heart. The dead man's heart.

'No more,' they said.

It was the voice that summoned him here.

Frozen in fear, Prem watched as it crushed the organ and dropped it onto the lifeless man's chest.

No! How is this even possible? He'd seen these terrible silhouettes in Durgapur with his dying brother. Did Deepak do this? How—

The fearsome figures took a step towards him.

The words '*Devi, Devi Ma*[1]' spilled from his parched throat as he sought refuge in blind faith. Logic and rational thinking had no part in this.

His mind blank, he stared. His mesmerised gaze drowned in the bottomless pools of gold.

He saw himself – a miniscule, inconsequential object, with his whole life open and bare; every guilty thought and action exposed. Their inescapable gazes penetrated his very essence, judging him. All his good swept up into a pathetic pile, laid on the implacable balance of justice and weighed against the sins besmirching his soul. He'd always considered himself to be a decent human being. He'd never set out to hurt anyone. *Until this thirst to avenge his son's murder, and the unbearable guilt of his part in his brother's death.*

---

1. Divine Mother/Goddess Mother

Overcome, he bowed low until his forehead touched the cold tiles, acknowledging and accepting his failings, ready for whatever may befall him. The prayers and chants he had learnt as a child and spent many hours memorising forgotten, he repeated '*Devi Ma*' over and over with no hope of absolution.

Prem sensed the approaching figures stop in front of him, waiting for him to look up. He raised his head. Beautiful and serene, they were no longer the terrifying creatures of an instant before. His jaw dropped as they morphed into two small girls, who ambled away from him and climbed into the bath.

Incredulous about what he had just witnessed, he sat stunned and bemused while the children splashed in the tub, ignoring both him and the grisly corpse.

88

Roopesh

The headlights illuminated a narrow, unkempt path leading off the main road into the woods, just wide enough for a car. Roopesh drove in ignoring the twigs and branches scraping against the Porsche's sleek, glossy body.

The voice in his head ordered him to stop. He slammed the brake. The trees and bushes hid the vehicle from sight, its black hulk blending into the dark shadows cast by trees and bushes. He got out, shivered and pulled on his overcoat. Reaching in, he removed the sword, the *talwar Mohini,* from the car. With the ease of long practice, he strapped it to his waist.

Roopesh didn't know where he was, so he followed his feet. They seemed to know where to go.

Five minutes of ducking under overhanging branches, shielding his face from thorny blackberry brambles, pushing reeds and weeds aside, brought Roopesh out of the woods to the edge of a tarmacked B-road. Opposite, a gravel drive led to a clearing.

Hemmed in by mature trees in full foliage and a dense canopy of vegetation, the outline of a low building disrupted nature's abandon, announcing its man-made presence with its sharp geometrical silhouette.

7.30 p.m. They'll be here soon!

His heartbeat climbed several notches when he spotted the two cars parked side by side in front of the cabin.

Oh, no! They're already here!

He crept to the nearest and peered inside. The Peugeot Estate was empty. He tried the door. Locked. Crouching low, he sidled to the second vehicle. Even in the dim light, he recognised it. He'd seen it a million times before, the same model as Prem's. He shone his phone torch at the licence plate and gasped.

No! Impossible! It cannot be! How can Prem be here? I couldn't reach him. It's someone else. Someone has stolen Prem's car. He remembered a recent news item. *Someone has cloned Prem's licence plate. Yes, that's more likely!*

No, not with that scratched side, which he said he'd fix, but never did.

What if... He recalled how he'd reached here. Maybe that voice also brought Prem. Was he the gang's hostage?

For all his excellent traits—charming, funny, popular, great company—his friend was useless at defending himself. He wouldn't, couldn't, hurt a fly. Why, he couldn't even run.

They had once been a trio. Deepak - the brains, the wisdom, the sage. Prem, the clown. He brought fun, joy, and laughter into their lives. And he, Roopesh, was the might, the muscle. The soldier and defender. They had already lost the head. Now, the heart and soul were in danger. If anything happened to Prem, only useless muscles would remain.

Desperate, he straightened and drew the sword, *Mohini*, from its scabbard. He flexed his wrist, gripped the handle, wrapped his fingers around the cross guard and nestled the weapon in his palm.

89

Prem

Terrified of attracting the children's attention, Prem remained crouched on the tiles. But eventually, with his knees seizing up and shooting painful cramps up to his waist, he rose stealthily to his feet, pausing with every movement to check on the girls. He froze whenever they glanced at him and released his breath when they returned to playing with the bubbles.

Ignoring the sprawled corpse, Prem threaded his way to the tripod, removed the video camera and crept out without looking behind. Goosebumps crawled up and down his spine, expecting the apparitions to descend on him with each step.

He entered the bedroom.

What the—? He gasped, startled to see his face on the large-screen television.

Prem scanned the room, taking in the setup. Bed with satin sheets, children's clothes folded at one end, the blond wig, ladies' jacket and handbag on the table. The man in the bathroom. The camera. His mouth stretched into a snarl as realisation dawned.

How do I turn these damn cameras off? Where the hell are the buttons? No, never mind. Just find the controller. It should be close by, within easy reach of the bed.

Prem found it under a pillow. Larger and more complicated than any he'd seen, it took him several attempts to switch off the cameras and television.

He studied the video recorder from the bathroom. *If it happened, it should be on this video.*

He pressed the replay button, amazed at the quality of the pictures. This was a far more professional camera than the gadget his wife used to record family events.

The sequence of images rolled on the camera's screen. He trembled as the girls transformed, extended, and expanded into their own ethereal versions. Insubstantial, yet so real. He watched the man's unavailing pleas, the merciless ending, his own entry, his prayers and entreaties and the reconversion of the entities into the children.

It was all true! It happened! I'm not crazy!

He was relieved he was not going mad.

He worried he was not insane.

Much easier if I were insane, and this a psychotic episode.

He removed the SD card from the recorder and slipped it into his pocket.

Now what? Should I call the police?

He'd have a tough time explaining what he was doing here, but the recording would exonerate him. His instincts rebelled. If those images were released, they'd lock those kids up. Forever. He shuddered at what could happen to them in captivity. Or to anyone who tried to incarcerate them!

I've been brought here for a purpose, he thought. *To protect the children. I need to return them home and wipe all traces of their involvement with that monster.* He scoffed. *How ironic! People would treat the twins as monsters rather than that pervert.*

He returned to the steamy bathroom on unsteady feet. The girls were still in the bathtub. They had topped up the hot water and added more bath foam.

He took a deep breath. 'I'm going to remove that—,' he pointed to the corpse. 'And clean up. OK?' His tone squeaky with nervousness. He saw them nod.

In the kitchen, Prem rooted through the cupboards and drawers, found several rolls of black plastic sacks and large bottles of strong bleach under the sink. And beside them, stacked in their original packaging, were four body bags.

Why would there be... Oh! Rage dissipated much of his fear.

He gathered up the materials and wobbled as the enormity of the task struck him.

I've done this before, for my brother. I can do it for that... that animal!

Prem returned to the bedroom, stripped the black satin sheet off the bed. Back in the bathroom, he picked up the pistol, tucked it into his coat pocket, and hung the garment on the double hook screwed into the door. He removed a pair of surgical gloves from his medical case and pulled them on.

He detached the cameras from the man's headband and smashed them to pieces with the heel of his shoe. With a moue of disgust, he rolled the corpse into the bedsheet, wrapped it around several times, shrouding it from top to toe. The material absorbed the blood and wiped the tiles clean. In went the black-wrapped mummy into a body bag.

And all the while, he kept his gaze averted from the twins watching his every move.

90

Roopesh

Sword in hand, Roopesh edged closer to the chalet, seeking the deepest shadows, tiptoeing, disturbing nothing.

I hope Prem's brought his gun.

Then, remembering his friend's clumsiness, Roopesh hoped he had not. *He'll probably shoot himself, or his captors will take it off him. No, guns aren't for me. I'll put my faith in this.* He hefted the *talwar*.

As his grandfather had recounted over four decades ago, the ancient sword *Mohini* had continued its journey through the generations. Three summers after that bright, sunny afternoon, the gentle old giant slipped peacefully away. When his father succumbed to cancer fifteen years later, Roopesh inherited the *talwar*. Although mended again, he knew the blade wouldn't survive another strike.

He worked for months to fulfil the promise to his grandfather. With his knowledge as an expert metallurgist, the skills gained during his working life, and the sophisticated facilities in his factories, Roopesh crafted a new blade for *Mohini*. He combined the remnants of the ancient blade with other elements to create an alloy lighter, stronger, sharper, more flexible and resilient than anything he had encountered. It withstood innumerable tests – brushed off tension, laughed at pressure, sliced through most things and bowed to nobody.

He engaged the finest sword-maker he could find to craft the blade and fuse it to the ancient hilt. *Mohini* was whole once again. She gleamed with a blue sheen that reflected the world. She was magnificent, and he believed she would last an eternity.

Hard though he tried, Roopesh could not replicate the alloy. It would have made him incredibly wealthy, but the results of his experiments always fell short of the blade's perfection.

His grandfather would have said it was the *Rakshasas' blood* – the demon spirits trapped within the ancient blade – which made the difference.

His father, too, had honoured his promise to the old man on that sun-drenched day. He taught Roopesh everything he knew. When his son's skills and prowess exceeded his own, his dad arranged for experts to tutor him.

And he'd tried to pass those skills and knowledge on to his own son, Arun. But although the lad tried, his heart was not in it. He did not possess the fire. In the end, both father and son gave up.

Should I have persevered? Insisted he continue? Would Arun be alive if I had? For the millionth time, he wondered what he should or could have done differently? Could he have thwarted fate?

But I also taught Anjali. A wry smile twisted his lips. His daughter had insisted on learning alongside her older brother. She was good – better than good. Far better than Arun ever was. And to his wife's horror, the girl loved it and practiced hard.

Even today, she can give her old man a run for his money. Then he remembered. *No, she can't. Not lying motionless in a hospital bed, inching closer to death every day.*

But this wasn't the time for regrets or recriminations.

Roopesh shifted his stance, accommodated the weight of the unsheathed sword by his side, positioned for fight and crept nearer to the building.

Someone or something had smashed the door in. Someone was inside, but except for the beep, beep of an alarm of some sort, the building was silent.

Roopesh turned at the soft crunch of tires at the top of the lane. Undecided, he stood immobile for an instant, then slipped into the darkness of the tall rambling bushes nearest the wrecked frontage as the silhouette of a car rolled in and ground to a halt.

Motionless, he willed his heartbeat to slow down, breath to quieten, and waited.

Doors clicked open, and four hooded figures got out. He frowned. There should be five.

If this lot is Tango and the Xtreem, then who the hell's inside with Prem? What's going on?

The new arrivals used their mobile phones' flashlights to find their way to the cars. As nonplussed as he was, they grouped into a huddle, whispered urgently before splitting into two groups, peering into the vehicles. One silhouette slunk off towards the rear of the chalet.

Damn. I should've checked for a back entrance. Too late now. Besides, I mightn't have seen this lot arrive, Roopesh thought.

'Fuck!' exclaimed the three remaining new arrivals on seeing the smashed frontage.

Roopesh gasped. Two of them held guns.

91

Tommy

Tango, Derek Dawson and Tommy Wade gaped at the smashed front door.

'What the f—,' whispered Tango.

'Shush,' breathed Tommy as they crowded in behind him.

The trio bunched together, straining to catch any sound from beyond the closed inner door, but apart from the whispering leaves and creaking branches, they heard nothing. Tommy half turned at the tickle of Tango's raspy breath against his ear as the older man peered over his shoulder.

He grinned. *Tango's nervous.* He sensed Derek close, trying to get in ahead. With a soundless snarl, he grabbed and held him in place, digging his fingers painfully into the boy's flesh. Derek yelped and received a clout from both men.

The boy worried Tommy. *Boy?* Derek was sixteen, almost seventeen, but looked fourteen. The childlike, gawky, impish exterior hid a scary ruthlessness. Recently, he had begun to undermine Tommy's authority, albeit subtly. He made a mental note to think a lot more about Derek.

As promised, Tango had brought his toys along. One each for Tommy, Duncan and himself. Derek had begged and sulked, but no way would they give him a gun.

He lifted the pistol, adjusting his wrist for the unfamiliar weight. Amazing what a difference it made. Made him feel twice as big, ten times stronger. The power it fed him was incredible.

Tommy entered the hallway and beckoned to the others. Pressed back against the wall, gloved hand gripping the doorknob, he waited for Tango and Derek to take their positions. They had seen it done a gazillion times in movies, on telly, and in their games, so of course they knew how it should go.

With a sharp nod and a rush of adrenaline, he flung open the door.

They sprang inside.

And stopped. Gasped at the scene before them.

The startled man in the middle of the room froze in the act of dragging a large black bag along the pine floorboards.

Three pairs of bulging stares riveted on the bag. Its shape left no doubt of its content.

The man dropped his cargo, straightened and raised his arms, his eyes wide with shock, jaws and mouth slack with surprise. The trio winced at the thud of the body bag hitting the floor.

Tommy relaxed at the man's dishevelled appearance and shocked expression. No weapon in sight.

A sharp glance at Tango showed him equally puzzled. With growing disdain, the trio took in the mess of curly greying hair surrounding a balding head, the untrimmed goatee, the glasses perched on the top of a brown forehead glistening with sweat. The deep brown eyes with dark shadows and bags beneath, however, showed no fear.

Tommy glanced at the man's arms, and his heart lurched on realising what the red stains on the gloved hands were.

Beside him, Tango drew in a deep hiss of air, reached out to clutch his sleeve.

The man's unwavering gaze held Tommy, his face calm, accepting their presence as though they were guests.

'I know you. I wasn't expecting you, but I'm glad you're here. You killed my son. You killed him, and my nephew, and their friend.' His deep voice was flat and emotionless.

Tommy gaped. Derek and Tango frowned.

'By the way, I am Prem Verma.' His tone was polite, as if he were introducing himself at a cocktail party. 'I've waited so long to meet you.'

'Did you do that?' Tommy pointed to the body bag.

'Yes.'

Tommy turned to Tango. 'Did you know he'd be here? Who's the target? Him or whoever's in the bag?'

But Tango looked confused, angry. Clearly, he hadn't been expecting this.

Prem interrupted their exchange. 'Where are the others? The other two who were with you when you murdered our sons?'

Noises outside disrupted the silence. Muffled swearing, a sharp cry cut short, followed by a dull thud and the rustling of bushes.

They stiffened. With guns trained on Prem, they half turned, listened intently, but hearing naught, they returned their full attention to him.

'Must be that idiot Duncan blundering about in the dark,' muttered Tango to Tommy. Derek rolled his eyes.

'So, the others are outside, are they? That's good.' Prem smiled, the perfect host.

Though baffled, the three did not drop their guard. Their target looked inoffensive, was apparently unarmed, but then he also claimed responsibility for whatever had happened to whoever lay inside that bag.

'Why did you kill them?' Prem's focus remained on Tommy.

The trio stayed silent.

'Look, I am unarmed. You have guns, and I know you'll kill me, too. But at least answer my question before you do.'

Tommy considered. 'Because we were asked to. And paid. We were supposed to only get Suraj, but they were always together, like the three musketeers.' He scoffed. 'So, we never got the chance before. Besides, it wasn't easy to tell the two of 'em apart. Y'know, all of you guys look alike, but them two looked like brothers.'

Gun aimed unwaveringly at his target, Tommy stared at Prem while his thoughts veered to that night in March.

'We were larking about outside the park, jus' getting ready to go home when we saw this man come around the bend looking at his phone. It was dark, but his mobile torch was on. We thought we could have some fun, y'know, scare him a bit, but not hurt him or anything. Derek here wanted his phone—,' Tommy cuffed him around his head. 'Idjit doesn't know phones can be traced.' He turned to Derek again, but the boy had prudently slid out of his reach.

'Hey, imagine my surprise when I saw it was one of them! I jus' couldn't believe it. I wasn't sure which of the two it was, so I stepped in front of him an' said, "*Suraj? Are you Suraj?*" He looked up and smiled confused like he should know me an' said "*yes.*"' Tommy shook his head, 'can you believe it?' he asked Prem, who narrowed his eyes to slits but otherwise remained impassive.

'I knew we wouldn't have 'nother chance like this. Not finding him alone, and no one 'bout. I din' even realize it, but suddenly, my knife was in my hand, and I—' Tommy's gaze glazed, and he made a thrusting movement with his left hand. Twice.

Prem's stomach churned in pain and rage, his fingers curled into fists, but he held himself still.

With a jerk, Tommy refocused. 'He, like, grabbed his stomach an' shouted, an' fell down. That's when I realised I'd stabbed him. I knelt down, thinking what to do, and then the other two appeared around the bend. We dint even realize they were there! I jumped up, and they asked, 'What happened? What did you do?' and we, we jus' stood looking at them. They knelt down an' the tall one took off his jacket an' pressed it to, um, Suraj's stomach. They kept saying something, but I couldn't hear 'cause of the thunder. Then the other man, y'know, the one who looked like his brother, got up and started dialling on his phone.'

Tommy stopped and shook his head. 'I thought he's calling the police an' I told the others, *"They've seen us, they'll identify us,"* and Duncan said, *"I can't go to jail!"* Tommy paused again. 'That's 'cause his dad's in prison, you know, and there'll be no one to look after his mum,' he told Prem as if that was a justification.

'Duncan was jus' behind him, an' I saw he too had his knife in his hand. He sort of grabbed the man's hair an' swore like mad, and then, like, he drew a line on his neck. Then he kicked at the man's legs and pushed him down. He made a cracking sound, must've hit his head on a rock or something. Y'know, the guy dint say a word or cry or shout. He held his throat and jus' lay there.'

Prem clenched his teeth to prevent the howl seeking escape while tears rolled unchecked down his cheeks as he lived through the last moments of his son's life.

'And Arun?' he asked and, at Tommy's quizzical expression, clarified, 'The tall one.'

'Oh, yeah. He was still bent over Suraj but turned when the other bloke fell down and looked straight at us. We couldn't leave him, so I had to do it again. Stab him, I mean. Then I said, *"You too,"* to Derek and Leo so we were all like, um, tied together, so they too did it.' Tommy's tone had almost no inflection. He didn't appear or sound remorseful, but then neither did he seem to derive any pleasure from his deeds. He recounted the event, as if was something that had to be done.

'And then?' asked Prem.

'Then we heard some dogs barking, an' it was thundering too. I knew we had to leave quickly, so we all ran off real fast.'

Tommy tilted his head and met Prem's eyes. 'Was Suraj your son, or the other one?'

'The other one. His name was Ravi.' He choked down words desperate to erupt like impounded water from a burst dam. Words to extol his son, to applaud him not just for his achievements but also for the person he was. Words he should have spoken to Ravi but never did and now, never could.

'Um, yeah. Sorry, man. Like I said, we were supposed to only get Suraj, but the others, they saw us, and we had no choice.'

'I see.' Prem turned to Tango. 'You. You should leave now. You weren't involved in their killing.'

Derek giggled. 'Actually, he asked us to. We'd never have done it if he hadn't asked,' he snickered, 'or got away without his help.' He reached out and punched Tango in the arm.

Tango bellowed. 'You little shit! I'll wring your fucking neck!'

Face crimson with rage, he cuffed Derek hard.

Tommy glared at the two of them. 'Shut the fuck up!'

'Ah, I see,' said Prem. 'Who are you?'

Emboldened that the man before him would not live to tell the tale, Tango replied, 'My friends call me Tango.'

Tango. Isn't that the name of Roopesh's mysterious contact? What the hell is he doing here?

Schooling his expression to show none of the confusion raging within, Prem said, 'Tango. I see. Then I'm pleased you're here too. Tell me, who asked you to kill Suraj?'

'Go on,' urged Prem when Tango hesitated. 'You've all the advantage,' Prem nodded at the weapon in Tango's fist, 'and nothing to lose.'

Tango straightened, smiled. 'My business partner, Saxena. He wanted to get rid of Suraj. Family business, he said. He wasn't too happy about the others, but then paid us a bonus, anyway.'

'Your business partner. I understand,' said Prem thoughtfully.

So, the rumours are true. The fat politician is obsessed with Anjali. His son Mohan's marriage to her would put her within his reach. Or is this to do with money? Knowing that bastard, probably both. Anjali and her wealth.

A thought struck Tommy. He turned to Tango. 'Wait, is this your contact? Did he set this up?' His tone was tight with anger and confusion.

Tango had never met his contact. Although the voice on the phone had always been electronically altered, he doubted this was his contact. He didn't think this was Charlie.

He shook his head. 'No, I don't think so.'

'No, he isn't. But I am. I am Charlie,' said a voice from outside the doorway.

92

Roopesh

'I am Charlie,' said the voice from the open doorway.

Four heads spun to face the new threat.

Prem smiled, lowered his arms, flicked a glance at the three men squinting into the darkness beyond.

Something hit the floor with a loud wet plop, rolled and bounced like a rugby ball towards them.

Derek squealed and jumped up onto the settee. Tango and Tommy trained their revolvers on the ball. Shots shattered the silence, louder than expected, the deafening cracks echoing in the boarded-up room.

With guns still aimed, they stared at the object.

The object stared back.

Duncan Hughes' glazed eyes looked at them. His mouth was wide open, white teeth gleaming in a soundless scream. The pale face with its tattoos and piercings lay like a comet, oozing a trail of blood.

None of the shots had touched the neatly severed head.

Tango gagged. He turned towards the wall, doubled over, his forearm clutching his stomach, dry heaving.

'Not Deadly Duncan, just dead.' Derek laughed hysterically.

'Shut the fuck up!' screamed Tommy, his tone high and squeaky. With a shudder, he averted his gaze from Duncan's head, got himself under control. He snarled, whirled, weapon pointed at Prem.

Footsteps clacked on the wooden floor in the dark entrance hallway. Tommy aimed his pistol at whatever was approaching.

'Get a grip, man! Tango, get your gun up. Derek, get the fuck off that settee.'

Tommy's commands, delivered in loud, sharp tones, snapped his companions' attention to the advancing danger.

Tango straightened, pointed a trembling pistol towards the entrance. Derek crouched beside Tommy, a knife in each hand.

A dark silhouette filled the doorway.

The four gasped in horror as a headless form—the rest of Duncan Hughes—walked through, or rather, floated through the doorway.

His feet were a foot off the ground, toes of his Dr. Martens shoes pointing down, body slack, arms flopping at his sides, and with blood dripping down his jacket and jeans, the decapitated Duncan glided forward.

The youths and their accomplice shrieked and backpedalled.

'You took your time,' said Prem.

His voice refocused their attention. Tommy concentrated on the tall figure behind Duncan. He moved to one side, keeping his old and new quarries in sight, weapon trained on the newcomer. Derek, knives ready, remained poised for attack.

The tall man stepped forward. His arm draped around Duncan's waist, holding him up as a shield. His right hand gripped a curved sword, the inky blue sheen of its blade marred by bloodstains. Red droplets gathered along its groove and dripped from its tip.

He studied each of them, his gaze resting on Tommy for a protracted moment before sliding toward Derek. A puzzled frown creased his forehead when his scrutiny landed on Tango.

'Where is the other boy? The youngest, thin with curly hair?' he asked.

No answer.

'My name is Roopesh Kapoor, but you may call me Charlie.' A tight smile flashed across the handsome face.

'So, you're Tango. I know you. I did not expect **you** to be Tango, to be my contact, but now it makes sense. You know, I find your choice of Homer Simpson's voice most annoying?'

'He's more than just your contact,' said Prem. 'He's their accomplice; he set it all up on instructions from—'

'I heard.'

***

Roopesh squinted at Tango. 'I know you. You are Harvey Endsleigh. You own The Cue Room. I've been to your club a few times. A couple of those occasions were with our sons.'

'Ah, I thought I recognised him!' Prem slapped a palm on his forehead.

Without taking his gaze off Harvey Endsleigh, aka Tango, Roopesh nodded. 'I think I understand why Saxena would want Suraj dead, but why would you do his bidding? What was in it for you? What was big enough for you to commit murder?' His mild tone belied the intensity of his stare.

With a hiss of indrawn breath, Tango calmed himself. After all, he was the one with a gun.

'You wouldn't understand.'

'Try me.'

'I owed money to the wrong people, and they said they'd hurt me. Not kill me, you see, but put me in a wheelchair so I could still work and pay off my debt. And they would too. You don't know them. They did this.' Tango paled at the memory and held up his left hand with only a knob in place of the little finger. 'My only solution was to sell the club, and when I told my partner, he said he'd pay off my debt plus give me the money for the new site if I, er, if I did what he wanted.'

'I see. It's going to be an old western saloon-themed pool and snooker hall, I believe?'

'Yes, it is.' A vision of his salon filled Tango's mind. The batwing doors, the bare rough-hewn floorboards, the aroma of polish on the wood-panelled walls, the stretch of dark oak bar...

'And I assume the drug deals gave you the money to fit out your new club.'

Tango shrugged. 'Not something I wanted to return to, but an old friend persuaded me. Besides, it's easy money, easier than squeezing blood out of banks. Quicker too. I couldn't afford to keep paying for two sites while the banks umm'd and ahh'd. The drugs plugged a gap.' He stopped. He was never this garrulous. Must be nerves, he thought.

'That's enough talk for now,' he growled, raising his gun.

The floorboard behind them creaked.

93

Roopesh

The five people in the room whirled, eyes widening in stunned surprise.

The dull thud of Duncan's headless body slipping from Roopesh's arm and sliding to the floor barely registered as their brains struggled to adapt to the new walk-ons to the stage.

Someone had changed the diegesis of the play.

The wooden floorboards glistened where their small feet left damp prints. Wrapped in oversized towels, shivering, their hair lank and dripping wet, two little girls walked into the stunned silence.

For the first time, Prem showed fear. He rushed to them, arms outstretched, shielding them with his body.

'No! Please go inside.'

The twins took no notice. They stepped around him, stood in front, absorbing the gruesome sight—the decapitated head, the suspended body—before scrutinizing each person. They smiled when their amber gazes rested on Roopesh.

Four pairs of eyes scuttled between the girls, Prem, and the black body bag. Four brains ran through endless conjectures.

Prem glanced up at his friend, rooted in place, skin ashen, bloodless mouth open, attention glued on the children. In disbelief and distress, Roopesh had dropped his guard, his sword arm limp at his side.

The twins looked up at Prem. 'We'd like some milk, please.'

Both their mouths moved, but their gravelly voices, with its metallic undertone like tolling church bells, melded into one. 'Warm milk,' they added.

Roopesh gasped. It was the voice that had brought him here!

Tango narrowed his eyes. *Didn't Charlie, er, Roopesh – no, it's easier to think of him as Charlie. Didn't Charlie mention a target? Who is it? Whoever's in that bag or that baldy Prem? Why would Charlie want to kill his friend? Who are these children? What're they doing here? Are they his kids? Or...*

The significance was not lost on Tango. Charlie had mentioned that the target had secret predilections. *Are these girls...?* His mouth tightened.

Beside him, Tommy squinted. 'My, my, what have we here?'

Derek continued to stare at Duncan's head, his mouth twisted in a grimace.

Tango reached a decision. 'Grab the kids,' he shouted to Tommy, grasping Mia's shoulder, and pulling her to his side.

Tommy responded fast, grabbed Cara by the hair, and dragged her across to him. The pair held their guns to the girls' temples, triumphant eyes flitting from Prem to Roopesh.

They scowled, their triumph turning to perplexity when, instead of attempting to rescue them, Prem scuttled away from them, his face warped in fear.

The puzzled men realised the kids weren't struggling or trying to break free. The fragile shoulders, damp and cold beneath their hands, were still.

Prem buried his face in his hands, muttering, 'Oh no!'

The twins opened their mouths and shrieked, the strident sound reverberating within the confines of the cabin. All five covered their ears, fingers digging in to deaden the penetrating screech. But the noise breached through, rendering thought impossible.

Tango and Tommy removed a hand from their ears and clasped it tight against the children's mouths, stifling the sound.

Blessed silence.

A heartbeat later, they were holding nothing.

The twins were together once again, standing close, facing them, just out of arm's reach.

The five grown-ups watched them shift nearer to each other until they seemed to meld into one. They flickered, their shadows coalesced, enveloped them, and swelled, multiplying in size, becoming vivid and tangible. Becoming more real, drawing on the girls' essence.

Mouths hanging open in horror, the men edged away from the huge shadowy form. Bemused, they stared at the gigantic, four-armed creature.

Am I hallucinating? wondered Tango. *No, this is a nightmare. I must be asleep, dreaming...*

What the fuck is this? What's happening? wondered Tommy, edging towards the front door.

Roopesh pressed himself against the wall, unable to move or take his eyes off the scene.

He had seen this, this *thing*, before. In Deepak's house. On that awful night in Jyoti's gods' room.

He tightened his grip on the sword, his feet assuming the stance, poised to spring.

He didn't know yet whether he was facing a friend or a foe, but in either case, he was ready.

94

Holt

Operation Storm's core team of detectives gathered in the major incident room for a videoconference with DCI Matthew Holt, who was still at Lily Webster's.

'Any news about the children, sir?' asked Rowena.

Holt cast a quick glance behind him to the living room at Lily, sitting upright in an armchair, her eyes and face filled with hope. When he shook his head and stepped away, she slumped back and returned to cradling her head in her hands while her neighbours and police officers milled around her, wanting but unable to help.

'Nothing as yet, but we've widened the alert, so we should hear something soon.' He kept his voice low and infused it with a note of positivity he did not feel. They were running out of places to look. The kids' appearances were so distinctive that he suspected they'd been kept hidden, maybe even separated. Their father being Italian, he worried that someone might have already transported them abroad.

'What's going on with the suspects? What have you all checked out so far?' he asked.

'I went to Derek Dawson's home,' said DC Michelle Bruges. 'His mother was in and wouldn't let us enter until I showed her the warrant. She said that Duncan Hughes phoned Derek around half-five, and he left soon after. He didn't say where they were going or when he'd return. I've never seen a cleaner or tidier home, sir. It was spotless, even the boy's bedroom. His mum said Derek doesn't like her going into his room and cleans it himself. The forensic guys are in there now, sir, but I don't think they'll find anything.'

'What about Harvey Endsleigh? Who handled that?' asked Holt.

'Me, sir. I wanted to be the one arresting him,' said Rowena, her voice tight with anger and disappointment. 'I should've known or suspected when I interviewed him in March. I wanted to see his face when I arrested him. When we got there, The Cue Room was busy, but he wasn't there. His assistant was running it, but I shut it down. As you can imagine, neither he nor the punters were happy. We had all the usual crap about police brutality and how they were going to sue us.'

Holt didn't blame her for the satisfaction in her tone. A small victory, but it counted.

'His assistant said that Endsleigh had left earlier in the evening, saying he expected to return by midnight,' continued Rowena. 'But he didn't say where he was going. We entered Endsleigh's flat upstairs, found his stash of drugs and cash, but nothing else. No sign of him. His car and van are still here, though.'

'And I went to Tommy Wade's flat,' said Karl. 'There was no answer, so we forced the door. How anyone can live like that is beyond me. It was a mess – food crumbs, empty pizza boxes, beer cans and dirty laundry everywhere. The place reeked. He's probably never made the bed, so it's impossible to tell when it was last slept in. The ale in the cans was at room temperature, and Tommy's new car's parked outside. Its engine's cold. The neighbours, as usual, saw and heard zilch. We have search warrants for all their homes, but so far, we found nothing of interest.'

'What about ANPRs? Can we trace the vehicle?'

'We don't know which vehicle they're in. It looks like they have access to another car,' said Karl, 'but we're checking with the DVLA and also trying to identify and trace every vehicle that was in the area when they were last seen. As you know, sir, there's a glitch with traffic cameras in Southampton and all along the A36 and A31, so we're stuck until they sort that out. Plus, we're not getting anything on any of their mobile phones.'

Hearing Holt's sigh of frustration, Karl added, 'There's a bit of a silver lining, sir. It doesn't seem like they planned on being away for long, though. None of them took clothes or toiletries or anything that hinted at even a night away. Endsleigh's the only one with a passport, and it's still at home. It seems they all intended to return tonight. What do you want us to do, sir?'

Holt huffed and clutched his hair. After all these months, they'd located the evidence, but now their suspects were missing. *If only we'd found the evidence sooner,* thought Holt. *If only I had had them arrested the moment we found the car, we wouldn't be chasing our tails all over the place now.* He sighed. There wasn't much point in *if onlys*.

'Extend the alert for them. Find out what vehicles each has access to. Did they rent a garage nearby? Check the DVLA records again for any vehicles previously owned by them but are now off the road. Did they borrow someone's car? Someone must know. Check with traffic patrols, PCSOs and traffic wardens for vehicles leaving Westlands Estate. I want that lot found and in custody. And what about the Hughes brothers?'

'One of Duncan Hughes' neighbours said that she saw him go off with Tommy. She thinks Derek Dawson was with them and another man, but she didn't recognise him,' said Karl. 'We showed her Endsleigh's photo, but she said she wasn't sure, and whoever it was, he stayed downstairs. Larry's gone to their place, so we should hear from him anytime now.'

95

Prem & Roopesh

At the chalet, the monstrous yet beautiful thing spun and swirled like a lazy whirlwind.

Young Derek reacted first. He drew back his arm, aimed and threw the knife with all the force he could muster straight at the centre of the ethereal form. The weapon passed through the swirling mass and skidded under the dining table.

The creature twirled. Two spectral arms of dark mist reached out to pull Derek in. Fiery talons gripped him in a close embrace.

Derek screamed, flayed his limbs and thrashed from side to side to break free, but the wraith's arms held him in a vice.

A look of annoyance crossed the creature's visage at the youth's struggles. Its second pair of hands grasped his flailing arms by the upper biceps and yanked. With a howl of agony, the youth passed out and hung, dangling like a rag doll in his captor's embrace.

The creature lifted Derek and shook him. Puzzled at the lack of response, it dropped the boy and studied him. With a shrug, it stooped and laid a hand on his chest.

'No, don't,' shouted Prem, taking a step forward, his instinct overriding his sense of self-preservation. He'd seen what the apparition had done to the man in the bathroom, the one now in the body bag. He'd seen more hearts ripped and torn from their chests than he could bear. Yes, he wanted the boy dead, but not like this.

With a surprised expression on its beautiful face, the creature glanced at Prem, smiled and nodded. When it straightened, Derek lay limp and lifeless. An easier death than he deserved, but a death, nonetheless.

Ignoring Prem, the creature spun, its pirouette ending in a predatory stillness as it locked eyes on Tango. One arm stretched out, fingers curled inward in a silent command. *Come.*

But Tango darted sideways out of its reach, gun snapping up. His sight fixed—not on the creature—but on Prem.

Prem's eyes widened, and his lips parted, but no sound emerged.

'No!' Roopesh's roar shattered the silence. Sword in hand, he lunged, straining every muscle, legs driving him forward. But he knew he couldn't make it. He couldn't outrun the bullet. And Tango was still several lengths out of reach of his blade.

Smoke coiled upward as the gun thundered.

Roopesh's arm wrenched backward and hurled the *talwar* with every ounce of his strength. The blade spun through the air in a silver arc.

But still slower than the bullet's trajectory.

A shriek ripped through the room.

Roopesh crashed to the floor. 'No, no,' he whimpered through a burning throat, scrambling on all fours towards Prem, bracing himself for the sight of his friend, broken, bleeding—

But Prem still stood frozen in shock, untouched.

Roopesh sprang to his feet, and both men turned to the apparition.

It raised a translucent hand. Caught between its fingers, as if holding a butterfly, the bullet gleamed. It opened its hand, and the bullet tumbled to the floor.

Not Prem, then who?

Tango stumbled forward, his spine arched, curving around the *talwar* buried deep in his back, its tip projecting a full six inches through his stomach. With a thud, he landed face down, squirming and screaming in agony.

Prem scooted away as the shadowy form strolled towards the fallen man and plucked him up. A sharp twist of his neck silenced Tango—Endsleigh's—wails and relieved his pain.

It then turned to Tommy.

For a long moment, the glowing amber irises studied the perfect countenance. It smiled.

The young man broke the spell. With a growl, he raised his pistol. A second later, he yelped and flung it away.

'Fuck, fuck!' he gasped, shaking his hand violently and blowing on it to cool the red scorch marks on his palm and fingers. The pistol hit the floor with a dull clatter, smoke curling from its grip. Heat shimmered off it, the stench of burned oil sharp in the air.

Clutching his blistered palm to his chest and keeping clear of the weapon, Tommy twisted lightning-fast, shoved hard at Roopesh, who yelled and crashed to the ground.

Tommy stumbled from the shove but regained his balance and plunged into the night.

96

DC Larry Ives

The armed response van rolled to a halt outside a building block in Westland Estate. Doors slid open, and boots landed lightly on the cracked tarmac. The team sergeant led the way up the four flights of stairs to the Hughes' flat at a run, with DC Larry Ives bringing up the rear.

The four armed officers lined up on either side of the door and waited for Larry to catch up. The sergeant's lips twitched as the DC steadied himself against the handrail and wheezed.

They listened, but there was no sound from within, and no light showed in the gap beneath the door. At a nod from the sergeant, Larry raised a fist and pounded on the door.

'Police! Open up!'

No response.

'Again.'

A harder bang. The door shuddered, but still nothing. Not even a shuffle inside. Larry's gut churned. This was not good. Their intel was unsure whether Leo, the younger brother, was home, but his mum should certainly be in there.

'Take it,' ordered the Sergeant.

The ram hit the lock, splintering the door inwards, and the team surged through, their lights cutting across the gloom, bouncing off the mishmash of furniture, peeling wallpaper and stained carpet. The air reeked of stale fish and chips, beer and urine.

'Front room clear!'

'Kitchen clear!'

Carbine at the ready, the sergeant kicked open the door to a room nearest the living room. A bedroom.

'Check for weapons,' he growled.

Two officers fanned out, scanned the corners before lowering their barrels.

Clear.

The sergeant trained his weapon on the motionless figure sprawled across rumpled bedsheets.

'Jesus—'

Larry barged past him, crouched beside the boy. Leo Hughes. He pressed two fingers to his throat. Nothing. Then—. The faintest flutter, like a moth's wing.

'He's alive,' he yelled. 'Get medics now.'

The sergeant barked orders into his radio.

Boots thudded outside the bedroom door. 'Sarge, there's a woman in the other bedroom. She's barely got a pulse.'

The officer, having delivered his message, rushed off back to the other room to assist his colleague with CPR.

'Two casualties. Both critical. Ready transport to Southampton General,' shouted the sergeant into his radio.

Within minutes, paramedics stormed the hallway with kit bags, barking orders of their own. Frantic hands deployed defibrillators, oxygen masks, checked for pulse...

Sweat prickling his forehead, Larry stood back and watched the team work. Leo's lips were still blue; his mother's head lolled to the side.

'Looks like an overdose,' a medic muttered, not looking up. 'It's touch-and-go. Too early to say if they'll make it.'

Larry clenched his jaw. He noted the time and brief details in his notebook and then called DCI Holt.

'No sign of Duncan Hughes, sir, but we found Leo and his mum. Both were in their beds. Leo was lying so still I thought I was looking at a corpse. Grey skin, blue lips, the lot. One of the AFO[1]s found the mum. She too was barely breathing and had just a flicker of pulse. Luckily, we had medics downstairs, and they're working on them now. They suspect a drug overdose.'

He listened for a moment and responded, 'We don't know, sir. The medics say it's too early to tell if they'll pull through, but they'll be rushing them off to Southampton General in the next few minutes. We'll know more in the morning. I'll get forensics here and then head back to the station.'

Larry pocketed his phone. Morning would bring the verdict. Life—or death.

---

1. Authorised Firearms Officer.

97

Prem & Roopesh

Tommy's flight caught them by surprise.

Prem whirled around. 'Oh, no, you don't,' he snarled and started after Tommy but tripped over Endsleigh's body.

The man lay flat, arms splayed, neck twisted at an odd angle, the *talwar* sticking out of his back. Prem, grabbing the sword with one hand, tried to yank it out, but it would not budge. He gripped it with both hands and tugged hard, but other than bounce the body on the floor, it remained embedded in muscle and bone. Prem pinned Tango down with a foot on his spine and hauled at it with all his strength.

Like a knife sliding out of melting butter, the *talwar* slipped out, unbalancing Prem. He landed on his back, legs up in the air, holding the sword aloft. He rolled over to ease the weapon's weight before he stabbed himself.

A scratchy, gurgling sound startled him. It took him a moment to recognise it as laughter. The apparition had morphed into a pair of bedraggled kids. They pointed at him and giggled.

Prem scrambled to his feet and ran outside with the *talwar* in hand. Roopesh, too, had recovered and, snatching up the gun, he sprinted after the fleeing figure, his strides eating the distance. His long reach yanked Tommy's hood, and the young killer crashed, sprawling face down.

Tommy rolled over, attempting to sit up as Prem strode towards him.

'The fuck was that?!' gasped Tommy. 'Those girls, that... that monster! What the fuck?!'

Prem thrust the figure down with his foot.

The youth's attention remained transfixed on the chalet, more afraid of what lay within than of the man pinioning him or of his lethal weapon. Tommy shoved at the shoe, tried to roll away, but Prem pushed down harder, holding him immobile.

'Get off me. Let me up! Who the fuck are you?'

'I already told you. You killed our sons and got away with it once. But not now.' Prem stomped on the youth pinned beneath his shoe. 'Not again,' he growled, lifting the *talwar*. It was heavy. He clasped the sword in both hands and, with the blade pointing downwards, raised both arms above his head.

The weight on his chest finally alerted Tommy to the reality of his situation. He looked up at the figure looming above him, the features indistinguishable from the shadows above.

Staring at the angelic face frozen in a rictus of terror, Prem brought *Mohini,* the *talwar,* down. Plunged the lethal blade unerringly between the ribs.

Tommy scrunched his neck and shoulders, curling forward to stare at the sword in surprise and disbelief. He grasped the blade and tried to pull it out, but the unrelenting weapon nailed him to the bare earth.

Prem and Roopesh watched all expression fade from the handsome face and the bewitching eyes glaze.

LETHAL JUSTICE

***

Prem sank to his knees beside Tommy's body, his gaze glued to the serene visage. *Botticelli's angel,* Jyoti, had called him.

How can he appear so peaceful when he must surely be burning in hell? Why am I still in torment? Where's my peace now that we've avenged their deaths?

Then he remembered – it wasn't finished yet.

A hand fell on his shoulder, and fingers unlocked his grip from the sword's hilt.

'This isn't over,' said Prem. 'Leo, the youngest of the gang. We must deal with him before the police catch up with us. And then there's the prime instigator. The man who wrecked our lives and caused all these deaths. Maybe then we'll find peace.'

98

Prem & Roopesh

Roopesh pulled his sword out of the body, wiped the blade clean on Tommy's clothes, returned it to its scabbard, and helped Prem up. They inched towards the chalet, unsure of what awaited them.

Past the bodies littering the floor, the soft sound of sobbing reached them. Prem pushed himself upright, and treading over to the children, pulled them away from the mess.

'Shhh, it'll be alright,' he murmured. 'Roop, we must take them home. No one must know they were here.'

But Roopesh stood frozen, his gaze locked on the carnage strewn across the pine floor.

'Roop,' Prem snapped, 'I need your help. We've got to clear up this mess and take these kids home.'

But his friend was drowning, trembling as he relived the events. Prem stepped up to Roopesh, swung back his arm, and slapped his face hard.

'Get hold of yourself! There's work to do, and I've something to show you.'

The shock treatment worked. Roopesh snapped to the present, rubbed his cheek, and glared at Prem.

'Come on, let's bring that body indoors.'

They hauled Tommy into the chalet and stacked the corpses in the centre of the room.

'How on earth will we clean all this up?'

'Burn it all down? It's a wooden chalet and should burn easily enough. This place is isolated. It'll be a long time before anyone notices, or the fire services arrive.'

Prem nodded. 'Yes, we could drain petrol from their car. That should set it alight. But first, let's get the kids cleaned up and home to their mother.'

For the first time since he had met them, the twins smiled. They headed off to the bathroom. Prem pulled at his friend's sleeve, dragging him along behind them. He pulled the plug to empty the bath, turned on the shower and left the children huddled under the warm water.

He led Roopesh to the bedroom, ignored his friend's gasp of horror at the setting. 'I didn't have time to search for the cameras. We must destroy the recordings.'

They were in luck; they found the four video cameras mounted in each corner. Prem removed all the micro-SD cards and nuked them in the microwave oven, ignoring the sizzles, crackles and noxious fumes filling the kitchen.

'And now watch this. I got it from the recorder in the bathroom.' Prem inserted the SD card from his pocket into a video camera. 'This'll prove we weren't dreaming, that this isn't all a nightmare. I'll fetch the kids and see if I can find them some milk.'

Interpreting Roopesh's dubious look correctly, he added, 'Whatever else they are, and whatever power is within them, they're still kids. Their parents must be frantic.'

While Roopesh fiddled with the camera, he gathered up their clothes and went to the bathroom.

Roopesh was still watching the unearthly scene, the unbelievable tableau unfolding on the small screen, when Prem returned with the girls in tow dressed in their school uniforms.

'Now, can we have our milk?' asked Cara.

'Put on your socks and shoes; we'll see if there's any in the kitchen.'

He'd learnt their names were Cara and Mia, but couldn't fathom who was who, as they both responded to either or both names, and more often than not, their strange, raspy voices merged.

They're one soul in two bodies, each lost and incomplete without the other, he thought.

He also learnt that their mummy was waiting for them at home.

'Mummy is frightened and worried. She's hurt. The bad man hit her on the head,' they told him. 'But we'll kiss it better. The bad man dressed up to look like Mummy, but he wasn't pretty like her. He brought us here in Mummy's car.'

That must be the green Peugeot Estate parked outside, thought Prem

While the kids sipped their warm milk in the kitchen, he went back to the bedroom, took out the small SD-card from the video recorder in Roopesh's hand, and tucked it into his wallet.

'Roop, let's sort this,' he said, removing two pairs of clean surgical gloves from his medical bag. He put one on and passed the other to his friend. He picked up the dead man's backpack, unzipped it to reveal a sophisticated and expensive laptop.

'We need to eliminate all traces of this place and what happened here.' He switched the power button on and stopped, stumped at the cursor flashing in the 'enter password' box.

'Big L, small t, l, o, i, m, big X, 7, 0, 5, small y, 3, star, star, smiley face, ladder,' said a raspy voice. The girls were watching them from the bedroom doorway, their upper lips sporting identical milk moustaches.

'What?' Prem stared at them perplexed until he realised they were reciting the password to the computer. He grabbed a sheet of paper from the desk and asked them to repeat it.

'Smiley face? Ladder?'

A finger pointed to the '@' symbol, then the '#' key.

'Ah, right, smiley face, ladder,' smiled Prem.

He jotted down the password, then entered it into the computer.

The screen lit up and demanded another password. The twins rattled off a series of passwords to folders, sub-folders, images and other content. All of which Prem noted down.

The men sorted the folders by date and scanned through the contents, their expressions tightening when they recognised the photographs and video clips of the twins along with an attractive blond-haired woman in various locations – in front of a house, in the street, shopping and in a playground. One picture showed the three of them in a green car identical to the one parked outside.

'Mummy.' The children reached out and touched the screen. Their voices trembled.

'Come, let's take you home.'

Prem shut the laptop and began slipping it into the backpack. But the kids stayed his arm. With a strange expression, they enunciated a string of words, numbers, symbols, and special characters. He recognised it as a website address, but nothing else. They also listed the name of a browser he'd never heard of. Prem wrote it all down, along with further sets of complicated passwords. Tempted as he was to reboot the laptop to check that website, a quick glance at his watch dissuaded him. He slipped the paper into the laptop, returned it to the backpack, and zipped it shut.

Roopesh picked up the blond wig and the red coat. 'Prem, wear these and take the children in their mother's car. It'll help disguise you. There's a service stop with a fast-food restaurant at Ringwood, about forty miles from here. You can drop them off there. I'll follow in your car. We can then return and torch this place.'

Reluctantly, Prem took off his jacket, tried on the long red coat, but it was too small. He draped it across his shoulders, pulled the wig on, arranged the blond curls around his shoulder and picked up Lily's handbag. He glared at his friend, daring him to laugh or say anything.

Both men swivelled, startled at a strange gurgling sound. The five-year-olds were clinging to each other, pointing at Prem, giggling.

But soon their laughter died when the display of the evening's violent events in the front room brought them to an abrupt halt.

'Let's go.' Prem held out his hands, but the twins were stock-still, their gaze riveted on the body bag.

'Bad man.'

'Yes. But he won't hurt you or anyone else again.'

They stepped up to the bag, knelt and unzipped it to expose their predator.

'Please don't,' pleaded Prem. 'He can't hurt you anymore.'

He might as well not have spoken. The girls pushed the thick plastic material aside and grasped the corpse's head. The dead body grew redder and redder as though heated from within. It became lumpy and turned waxy. The cadaver steamed, then crisped and blackened. Heat permeated the room.

Frozen in place, the men watched the predator burn without flames. His features blackened and shrivelled within the twins' volcanic embrace. The black crust fractured, revealing crimson veins of fire glowing through the cracks, like molten lava pulsing beneath the hardened shell. Thin wisps of steam curled into the air, and the stench of burning flesh combined with its plastic sheath filled the chalet.

They gasped as blackened bits of the corpse crumbled to the wooden floorboards until all that remained of the abductor was a pile of ash.

The girls rose to their feet and, with a last glance at their handiwork, they returned to Prem's side.

'Now we can go.' They took his hand.

It required every ounce of his willpower to kill his instinct to jerk his fingers out of their grasp. Suppressing a shudder, he led them out of the front door.

Out in the cool night, they breathed in the fresh air and serene silence. Prem unlocked the boot of Lily's green Peugeot and tossed in the backpack and handed the keys to his BMW to Roopesh.

'We won't get away with this, you know. There must be several CCTV cameras along the way,' said Roopesh.

Prem shrugged and shut the boot. 'There's nothing we can do about it. What will be, will be. We must complete what we started and deny any knowledge of these little ones.'

With the girls settled in their car seats, Prem got in, waited until Roopesh had reversed the BMW. Moments later, both cars left the chalet.

99

Prem

Lily's green Peugeot crawled into the fast-food restaurant's car park, seeking the most isolated spot. Apart from the two vehicles in the area marked 'Staff Only', the place was deserted.

The children had been silent throughout the journey. He'd never heard them speak to each other, yet their minds and actions were perfectly synchronized. Unlike other children, they did not chatter or play. They relaxed in their seats, staring out of the windows, although there was nothing to see in the darkness except the shadows flashing past. He wondered if they were as unaffected by their ordeal as they appeared to be.

He picked up their mother's handbag, rummaged for the mobile phone and switched it on. But it remained locked, waiting for a passcode. He pivoted in his seat.

'Do you know how to unlock this?'

They nodded and drew a pattern along the dots. The screen flashed with a stream of missed calls and text messages.

'Good. Now phone home and talk to your mummy. Tell her you're at Stop N Eat at Ringwood Service Station on the A31. Say you're alone and you'll wait for her in the restaurant.'

One of the girls, he was almost sure it was Mia, pressed a hot dial key. A woman answered with a tremulous 'hello.'

'Mummy,' said Mia. 'We're at the Stop N Eat at Ringwood on the A31. Please come and get us now.' She paused, listened to the hysterical, excited voice on the phone and nodded. 'We're OK.' She listened for a few seconds longer before interrupting, 'Can we have ice cream when you come?'

Beside her, Cara grinned.

In the background, the crackle of voices talking, asking questions. Mia frowned.

Moments later, another woman's voice reached Prem – pitched low, calmly asking questions. Police, he guessed.

Mia sighed, shook her head, and repeated, 'We want Mummy to come to us now. And we want ice cream.'

The woman spoke more urgently, but the girls rolled their eyes, and Mia disconnected the call. It rang again, but she switched it off and handed it to Prem.

'The police will be here shortly. As soon as we hear the sirens, go inside, and wait for Mummy. Don't go with anyone else and don't say anything to anyone about what happened today. Not even to your mother. Tell no one where you were, or who you saw, or who brought you here. Nobody can know what occurred in that place.' Prem's voice filled with panic.

What if someone finds out, realises what these kids did, what they were capable of, what they could become?

Cara gently touched his arm. They seemed to understand. Little did he realize how familiar they were with his sense of foreboding. It was the same feeling their mother lived with every moment of her life.

Soon, the distant wail of sirens reached them.

'They're nearly here. Go on inside. Remember, only go with your mummy. I must leave now. Call us anytime if you need us. I am sure we will meet again.'

Prem let them out and walked them close to the entrance. The children smiled up at him, then holding hands, they ran into the brightly lit, glass-fronted restaurant.

He watched them walk up to an empty table, clamber into chairs side by side. Except for two staff members at the serving counters, the place was empty. A young woman in the distinctive purple, green, and white uniform approached and leaned over their table.

Prem watched the silent mime inside the bright, cheerful place – the woman mouthing questions, the twins pointing towards the car park in reply. She peered at Prem's silhouette, still wearing the wig and coat, and pretending to fiddle with his phone. Satisfied, she nodded, smiled, and returned to her position behind the counter.

The sirens and blue flashing lights were almost at the edge of the car park. Prem dared not wait any longer. Keeping in the shadows, he slunk past hedges and trees to Roopesh waiting on the other side of the road, and the pair headed back to torch the chalet. To wipe it from existence.

100

Holt

They arrived with sirens blaring and screeched to a halt.

A dozen police officers spilled from cars and vans, surrounded the restaurant while several more surged indoors with Lily, Holt, DI D'Souza and DC Adams leading the way. The young waitress and the man in a chef's hat were pale and shaky from the sudden onslaught of uniformed and armed police at their workplace.

The twins jumped off their seats and ran to their mother when Holt ushered Lily into the restaurant. *This could've gone so wrong,* he thought, watching Lily muffle her sobs in the girls' hair while they patted their mother's shoulders as though *they* were comforting *her*, each murmuring, 'Poor mummy; kiss better,' then pressing their lips to her bandaged head and hands. Soon, they struggled to free themselves from her embrace and demanded their ice cream.

Lily became hysterical when she realised her daughters were clean and bathed, with the scent of baby shampoo in their hair. But the paramedics kneeling beside the little girls, who were trying to spoon ice cream into their mouths while having their blood pressure checked, calmed her down.

'They'll need to be checked at the hospital, but they seem OK. No signs of any wounds, not even the slightest scratch on either of them,' they reassured her.

But they knew the twins would need to be examined more thoroughly, swabs and samples taken, their clothes, hair, and bodies checked to see if their kidnapper, or kidnappers, had harmed them or left any trace evidence.

'Plus, their behaviour doesn't indicate any trauma or stress,' added the medic.

In fact, apart from extreme annoyance at the barrage of questions and the police officers surrounding them, the children appeared calm and composed.

When asked, they looked puzzled. 'No, we aren't hurt. No one hurt us.'

A frustrated Holt and DI D'Souza tried to draw information from the five-year-olds, but their responses were less than helpful. Most of the time, they simply stared back and ignored their questions. Other officers, male and female, had even less success getting anything from them. Lily tried as well; the details they put together were very sketchy.

'We got into Mummy's car, but it was the bad man. His hair was like yours, Mummy, and he had your red coat on, but he wasn't pretty like you,' they told their mother.

'So, a man dressed to look like Mummy picked you up from school?' asked Holt. The twins nodded.

'Where did he take you?'

No reply. He kept his queries short and simple, but after responding to some, they turned away and asked their mum for more ice cream.

'Darlings,' Lily said, taking their chins in her hands. 'The police need your help; otherwise, the bad man may take other children.'

'No, he won't,' declared Cara.

'I know he brought you both back, but he may not return others to their mummies and daddies. He may hurt them.'

'No, he can't,' said Mia, then added with a smile, 'the nice man brought us back; he was funny.'

Holt got the impression they were talking about two different people. 'Was there more than one man?'

They nodded. The detectives exchanged dismayed glances. *Oh God, there's more than one kidnapper!* However, when he tried to probe further, the children yawned, their eyelids heavy with sleep.

'Can't,' he thought. *She said 'can't,' not 'won't'. Does a five-year-old know the difference between can't and won't? And they talked about a 'bad man' and a 'nice man' who was funny.*

He wanted to shake the answers out of them while protecting them from the answers. He met Lily's pleading eyes and didn't know how to help her.

Soon, the family left in the ambulance, followed by a relieved DI D'Souza.

'Sir, you should see this,' said DC Adams.

The police had Lily's car doors unlocked, the boot open. Her handbag lay on the passenger seat, keys on the floor. Holt aimed his torch at a backpack in the trunk, pulled on a pair of gloves, inserted the tip of his pen into the small gap in the bag's zipper, and slid it open to reveal the laptop inside.

Lily had not mentioned a laptop, and this backpack, though sturdy, was utilitarian. Her handbag was stylish, and although not exorbitantly expensive, was of good quality. If she used a laptop bag, it would be chic, not like this one. Therefore, the chances were high that this belonged to the kidnapper.

A flash of white caught his eye. He inched it out by its edge. His eyes widened at the rows of writing on the sheet of paper, a website address at the bottom, a jumble of alphabets, numbers, and symbols. *Passwords?*

Holt slipped the paper into an evidence bag, handed it to DS Adams. 'If these are the passwords to that laptop, I don't want anyone else trying to access it. Get this, that bag and laptop to the lab immediately. I want them checked for prints and other traces and I want the results on my desk within two hours. Then have DC Shepherd clone it and help him find out what's on it.'

He phoned DC Ian Shepherd, their IT wiz. 'Ian, I'd like you to stay on, please. We have a laptop from the Webster twins kidnapping that I need you to check. DS Adams will be joining us. I'm heading back to the Station, but I'll stop at the hospital first to check for any developments.'

Almost midnight. Now where the hell are Endsleigh and the gang?

101

Roopesh

KC—Roopesh's uncle—listened in incredulous silence to his nephew's edited version of the previous evening's events.

The two friends had agreed to keep everything about the twins and the '*bad man*' out of the story. Who'd believe them anyway? Not that they didn't trust KC – quite the contrary, but it just felt wrong to talk about it. It'd also have meant disclosing the truth about Deepak's death and their part in it.

'So, that fat cousin of mine was behind all this,' fumed KC when Roopesh's narration ended. 'How could I not have guessed? If he'd found out you and Prem were involved in our scheme, you both would've been in such danger!' His voice quivered, contemplating what could have happened.

'But he didn't,' assured Roopesh. 'All the precautions you took paid off, and I followed your instructions to the letter, so neither Fatty nor his associates knew who I was. But why did he want to kill Suraj, Ravi and my—my boy?'

'I wasn't aware before, but now that probate of your maternal grandfather's will has been granted, you and your children stand to inherit land between Delhi and Agra. You should hear from the lawyers soon, but I think my cousin Saxena must have known about it last year. If anything happens to either Arun or Anjali, their share will go to Saxena and his family.'

'What? All that for a piece of land?'

'It's around 600 acres. Most of it is agricultural and cannot be converted, but there's 100 acres of prime development land near New Delhi. That's worth serious money.'

'I thought that corrupt politician was rich enough. Why does he need this so much that he's prepared to kill for it?'

'I heard rumours he gambled heavily in the stock markets and got scorched. Which is why I suspect he was more than willing to let me into his drug chain.'

Roopesh mulled it over, struggling to understand how greed could push someone so far. 'But how did he convince Tango, I mean, Harvey Endsleigh, to carry it out for him? I didn't realize they even knew each other—'

'Neither did I, but I remember now,' interrupted KC. 'I need to check something. I'll get back to you.'

Two hours later, Roopesh received a WhatsApp message from KC, with a scanned photograph of an old press cutting. KC's message read:

This article and picture should explain it all. I didn't suspect the fat bastard had been playing such a long game. But he won't for long. I'll take care of it. KC.

102

Lily

Lily clutched her daughters' hands as they huddled close together asleep in the hospital bed, their eyes shut, chests rising and falling.

The children were stoic and unperturbed while Lily flinched at the intrusive nature of the check-up and collection of samples. She vacillated between fury and fear, fury at what the monster had done and fear of just how much worse it could have been.

With a puzzled frown creasing her brow, the doctor said, 'Nothing. They've not been interfered with. There's no sign of any assault, sexual or otherwise, no bruises, scratches, or cuts. They've been well fed and are squeaky clean. They've even brushed their teeth. There's nothing under their fingernails, in their hair, or feet.'

Tears streaming down her cheeks, Lily hiccupped, covered her face and compressed her lips to suppress the wails seeking release.

The soft-spoken, middle-aged doctor glanced at the sleeping girls, dimmed the lights and stepped closer. 'Now, let's look at your head.'

Lily jumped up with a sharp 'No!' and an arm held out to ward her off, sending the startled woman stumbling back.

'No,' she repeated more softly, 'it's fine. Really. It doesn't hurt anymore.'

That was true; it didn't hurt. Not since her daughters kissed her head in the restaurant. Warmth had flooded her, wiping out the pain, easing the tight pressure inside her skull, relieving the waves of nausea and dizziness. Lily knew what would be beneath the bandages. Wounds that appeared days old rather than inflicted only a few hours ago. The injuries scabbed over, almost healed. The cuts and bruises on her palms had already disappeared, and the dirt and dried blood on her unwashed hands masked the mended skin.

'Well, OK. Take some painkillers. Go to A&E immediately if you are nauseous or dizzy.'

'I will,' she promised. 'May I take them home now?'

The dozen reasons she'd prepared for why the children would be better off at home remained unsaid when the doctor agreed.

They looked up at a knock, and Holt stood framed in the doorway.

With a cry, Lily flung herself at his chest, felt his arms encircle her sob-racked body, holding her close. The doctor raised her eyebrows, then with a knowing smile and a murmured *'excuse me,'* she edged out of the room.

Lily's sobs slowed, then died, but she stayed, allowing herself to luxuriate within the warm confines of his arms. She felt the steady beat of his heart against her cheek, and the rise and fall of his chest.

Eventually, heart thudding, she raised her head to look into his eyes. They showed concern, tenderness, and a longing that made her pulse race. She reached up and caressed his cheek, feeling the roughness of his stubble.

He leaned down and hesitated with his mouth just inches from hers. Instinctively, her arms crept up to his neck, and she reached up to brush her lips to his. With a sharp indrawn breath, he drew her closer, deepening the kiss. Her body melted into his.

The door swung open, smacking into Holt's back and jerking them apart.

'Oh, I'm so sorry,' said a startled nurse. 'I didn't realize anyone was here. I thought the room was empty.'

'I'm just leaving,' Holt told her, then to Lily. 'Would you like a lift?'

Red-faced, heart racing, she nodded and hurried across to the twins and shook them awake before anyone changed their minds or started more tests.

As soon as Holt belted the children into the borrowed car seats, they slumped into sleep, their heads cushioned against the curved backrests, while Lily sat beside him in the front, her thoughts in a confused jumble.

Months had passed since their initial encounter at the watermill, yet he had lingered in her thoughts. She recalled how hurt she had been by the implied rejection in his message. Now, realising his actual profession, in particular, the case he was investigating, Lily realised she had misunderstood. She recalled his reaction when he'd walked into her kitchen, and his kiss left no doubt he felt the same about her.

But she reminded herself, *he's a policeman.*

Aware of the looks he shot her, she kept her eyes lowered, focussed on her hands clasped in her lap.

'Did you find my car?' She made a Herculean effort to keep her voice from wobbling.

With a sigh, Holt turned the ignition key.

'Yes, we found your car and handbag, but not your red coat. We also found a backpack and laptop in the boot. Are they yours?' He scrolled through his phone and showed her the images.

'No, my laptop's at work, and I have a desktop at home. That's not mine.'

As he drove out of the hospital carpark, she nodded resignedly when he told her they would need to keep her handbag, mobile phone, and her car for a few days, possibly two or three weeks. She was even less enthusiastic about the girls' interviews with psychologists and other specialists.

'We need their help to piece together what happened. This was a serious crime, and they're eyewitnesses.' Glancing at the twins' reflection in the rearview mirror, he added, 'They were lucky to have escaped without harm. But he's still out there, and other children may not be as lucky.'

'I understand, but they don't react like other children. They may not be of help at all. We'll do everything we can. Of course, we will.'

But Lily realised the girls had already said as much as they were going to; further questions would only elicit mute blank stares in response. She suspected it had not gone well for their kidnapper and was immeasurably grateful to whoever brought them back. But she also accepted there was no escaping the official processes, or the prolonged, in-depth questioning.

They were nearing her home. Lily stole a glance at Holt's profile, her fingers longing to soothe those lines of fatigue, to wipe the shadows beneath his eyes. She could still sense the comfort of his arms, the warmth of his lips on hers, and she ached with a longing she hadn't felt in a long time.

But it made no difference.

No matter how much she liked him, how attracted she was to him, the man beside her was a police officer. A detective. He could not be allowed to get close. To unveil the secrets she suspected lay hidden in her daughters.

***

Holt

What the hell just happened? What did I do?

Holt stared at the expanse of wood painted a deep glossy blue that was Lily's front door. A closed front door.

With arms wrapped protectively around her daughters, Lily had turned to him with a bright, impersonal smile. She shook his hand, thanked him formally, shepherded the twins indoors, and slammed the door.

He had sensed her withdrawal as they neared her house, pulling away, shutting him out of her life. He knew the attraction was mutual; knew he hadn't been mistaken. The embrace might simply have expressed her relief at having her daughters returned unharmed – a grateful mother seeking comfort from someone she knew. But that kiss was far more.

Or was he reading too much into it? Assuming it meant as much to her as it did to him?

This unequivocal rejection was a physical slap. He raised a hand to knock, to tell her how he felt...

How do I feel? What can I say? What can I do? The timing was so wrong. Yet again.

Lily's immediate future held gruelling days of questioning, probing and grilling, the invasion of privacy and dealing with the media. For now, both Lily and he had more pressing matters to worry about. His feelings would have to wait.

But maybe when this is all over...

Holt's arm dropped to his side. Head down, he strode to his car.

103

Holt

Back at the station, Holt headed to the major incident room. 'Still no sign of them?'

'No, sir. With the CCTVs offline for most of yesterday evening, we're having to track them the old-fashioned way, and it's taking time. Plus, we don't know which vehicle they used.'

'Meanwhile, they could have skipped the country.' *And guess who'll be blamed for that?*

'Don't think so, sir,' said Karl. 'We put out all ports alerts the moment we realised they were missing and no one matching their description boarded any flights, ferries or cross-channel trains. None of them have passports with them, so unless they all have fake passports, which seems unlikely, they can't have gone far. Besides, if they intended to disappear, why wait until now? Anyway, four of them would be hard to miss, especially Duncan with all his tattoos. Tommy too, with his looks.'

'They could've split up and gone in different directions.' Holt huffed in frustration.

'We'll find them.'

But Holt wasn't so sure.

'Sir,' called a voice from the doorway. Holt swivelled in his chair to find DS Bill Adams, visage white with shock.

'What is it?'

'It's—it's bad, sir. Really bad! Please come with me.'

Holt followed him to the station's tech room to find DC Ian Shepherd inside, staring into space. DS Bill Adams closed the door behind them.

The laptop found in Lily's vehicle sat on a separate trolley, quarantined from other equipment, its contents already cloned to a police computer to preserve the original.

Holt followed the unbelievable horror unfolding on the screen. They recognised her instantly. Sarah Mitchell, 9 years old, missing for over fifteen months.

He stopped the video and slammed the police computer shut. Saw his own horror reflected on Adam's face while Ian, arms wrapped around himself, shivered.

'Get the laptop locked up in special security. I'll call in the experts; they'll know what to do. Not a word to anyone. This, this is pure evil!'

'Ian.' He knelt before the young DC. 'I'm so sorry you saw that.'

Tears streamed down Ian's cheeks. 'I— I'll be OK, sir. We need to catch that bastard. That monster—'

The sheet of paper with the handwritten rows of text, numbers, and special characters was indeed passwords and web addresses. Without it, they could never have accessed the contents. Perhaps they might have triggered a self-destruct code protecting it from unauthorised access. They would not have known the website existed, let alone what it contained. More frightening was the fact that it had thousands of subscribers across the globe, all paying sizeable amounts of money to view those distressing scenes.

Worse was the title of the clip they had just watched: 'S5, E7 – Seventh Heaven.' Holt's heart constricted at what that might mean. Series Five, Episode Seven. There had been four other children before Sarah Mitchell. Lily's girls had been lucky. So, so lucky.

How did the twins get away? Why were they released unharmed? What did—?

Endless questions that needed answering, but this wasn't his case.

He phoned the team working on Sarah Mitchell's disappearance. Things sped up after that. Two detectives and an officer from the national Missing Persons Unit arrived surprisingly fast, debriefed Holt and his detectives and took the laptop with them.

After a brief session with the laptop's contents, the pale and grim-faced officers said, 'We can't thank you enough, sir. First thing tomorrow morning, we'll visit Lily Webster to interview her daughters.'

Hmm, yeah. Good luck with that, thought Holt.

104

Holt

Rowena spun around in her chair to Holt working at a nearby desk.

'Sir, sir, they found Endsleigh's car.' She pointed to her laptop. 'An unlicensed old Renault Megane registered to him and supposed to be off the road. It's petrol's been drained, and it's parked in front of a burnt-out house or cabin in Bishops Down in Dorset. That's about fifty-eight miles from here. They checked it for prints and matched them to Endsleigh, Tommy, Duncan, and Derek.'

'Whoa, come on, let's go.' DI Karl Stringer sprang up, grabbed his phone and jacket, surprised to see their boss sitting stock-still, watching Rowena's face pale as she read the rest of the bulletin.

'Go on,' said Holt quietly.

'Oh! Oh no! The fire officers found charred human remains among the debris. At least four, they believe.'

Eyes wide in disbelief, she continued. 'Earlier this morning in Bishops Down, a neighbouring farmer noticed thick smoke and called the fire services. But by then, little remained of the chalet. They found charred human remains among the debris at the burnt-out building.'

Holt's shoulders slumped.

'The fire engines and emergency vehicles attending the site will do their best to preserve any evidence,' read Rowena from the report.

Holt rose to his feet. 'Rowena, come on. Let's check this place out. Karl, please mind the shop and update the Super for me, will you?'

It must be them. At least they didn't go far. And it seems they didn't get away.

***

The acrid smell assailed their nostrils when Holt pulled onto the verge behind the row of emergency vehicles and opened the car door. Beneath the scent of smoke and ash was the unmistakable odour of burnt meat.

Rowena and he crunched their way along the gravelled path to the clearing where the Dorset Fire and Rescue Services officers circled the blackened husk of the building. They stared at the skeletal frame with its charred beams jutting out at odd angles, the jagged timbers pointing to the sky like broken ribs. Rusted nails jutted from splintered planks, and the roof had collapsed askew. Empty soot-streaked holes stood in the spaces occupied by windows and, at the chalet's rear, a solitary door, blackened and burnt, clung defiantly to its hinges.

It was an obscene sight amid the beautiful countryside. The gravelled clearing around the ruins had contained the fire, and aside from some burned bushes and a few singed birch trees, their trunks licked by flames, the surrounding woods were untouched, and the flames hadn't spread to the neighbouring farms.

Since the last report, the Dorset fire service had revised its body count to five and mobilised FIOs—fire investigation officers to the scene. A small bone fragment within a separate pile of ashes led to this conclusion, although the fire officers could not explain how or what generated the heat required to incinerate a body to that degree.

'When we got here, most of the flames had died down, so water damage to the building is minimal,' the Chief Fire Officer told Holt. 'We extinguished whatever was smouldering and doused the edges and the clearing, so there's no risk of it spreading, but we'll be keeping a watch on it overnight. The FIOs and forensics should be able to go in tomorrow.'

The FIO—fire investigation officer—who'd been circling and photographing the scene, joined them. 'I'm told you believe the bodies in there are your suspects, sir?'

'Well, the car belongs to our prime suspect. We've been looking for him and his three associates since yesterday. Perhaps four of the corpses are theirs, but we don't know why they were here in this isolated place. Nor do we know who the fifth person is. How bad is it? What are the chances of identifying them?'

'From what I've seen, the four bodies, though severely burnt, still have sufficient bone structure and remnants of tissue for DNA analysis. The fifth could be a problem, but our forensic team will do their best, even if all they have are just bone fragments,' assured the FIO. 'Whoever they are, they came armed. We found two knives. We may find more weapons when we sift through that lot.'

Holt sighed. If the DNA results identified their suspects, he could close the case on the murder of the three students. Not the result he wanted, but it would at least give their families closure.

But this scene also meant that his suspects were now victims themselves, and he'd soon be involved with the Dorset Constabulary investigating who killed the Xtreem gang. Who started the blaze? Who was the fifth victim? And that was just the start of many questions.

'I know you need time to sift through the debris and determine the cause of the fire, but I'd like the DNA analysis prioritised. Our lab can help with that. I'll call your SIO when I get back and work something out.'

Holt and Rowena exchanged names and contact details with the Dorset team and left the scene.

105

Holt

Wallet in hand, Roopesh Kapoor answered the doorbell, startled to find himself staring into a pair of steel-grey eyes.

'Good evening, Mr Kapoor. May I come in?' asked DCI Matthew Holt.

'Yes, yes, of course,' stammered Roopesh, stepping aside to allow the DCI into the luxurious hallway of his apartment. 'I was expecting the boy delivering the takeaway we'd ordered.'

Holt's eyebrow rose in a silent question.

'My friend Prem Verma's here. Prem, we have a surprise visitor. Detective Chief Inspector Holt,' he announced loudly leading the way into a beautifully appointed, high-ceilinged living room.

Prem set his whisky down on the little table beside his velvet upholstered armchair, turned off the television and stood up to shake Holt's hand.

Their visitor looked around with genuine admiration. 'What a beautiful room!'

Roopesh waved a dismissive hand at the compliment and gestured for Holt to take an armchair.

Holt studied the two men. They looked gaunter, their cheeks hollower than a week ago when he'd met them at the station to inform them about Harvey Endsleigh's involvement and finding the proof in the shipping container. But he hadn't mentioned the chalet or the burnt bodies. There'd been nothing to tell until the DNA results were in.

'Do you have any news for us, DCI Holt?' asked Prem. 'Have you apprehended our sons' killers yet?'

'Yes, and no. Did you see or read the news about the fire in Bishops Down? It's a small town in Dorset. They found five charred bodies. We've now received DNA results on four of the bodies confirming they're three of the Xtreem gang and their accomplice or instigator, Harvey Endsleigh.'

The two friends looked shocked. 'What were they doing there?'

'There's strong evidence that Endsleigh was dealing drugs. Speculation is that he and the Xtreem members went there to meet their dealer, and their discussions turned to dispute, or they were there to confront a rival gang. But there's no doubt it was arson, deliberately started to destroy evidence of what occurred there.'

Holt's gaze sharpened as the men exchanged glances. *Did they look relieved?*

'We're glad they're dead. That's the truth, and that, DCI Holt, is true justice,' said Roopesh.

'We couldn't face reliving our sons' deaths. To sit in a court and listen to every detail of what they suffered. And worse, to have hanging over us Damocles' sword, that they might get away with it somehow.'

Holt started to protest but reconsidered when he recalled the many cases dismissed on technicalities, cases the court deemed lacking sufficient evidence, or cases where the jury remained unconvinced.

'You know it happens,' Prem pressed home his point.

Holt changed the subject. 'I told you of Endsleigh's involvement when we last met. Do you know why he killed your sons?'

He'd almost given up hope of a response when Prem replied. 'We've recently learnt that someone wanted Arun—Roopesh's son and my nephew, Suraj, killed. We can think of only one person who would want this. And my son was what they call collateral damage.'

Holt sat up. 'Who was it? We can arrest him for this.'

Prem grimaced a smile. 'That person is outside your jurisdiction, DCI Holt. Even with the bilateral agreements between the police here and in India, he is untouchable unless you have solid, irrefutable evidence. Which I suspect you don't. Do you?'

Cornered, the DCI clenched his jaw and shook his head.

'I thought not. So, neither you nor the Indian police can prove anything, especially with Endsleigh dead.'

'But why? Why would anyone do this?'

Roopesh replied, 'Because of greed, pride and arrogance. There's an inheritance worth a lot of money involved. With my son's death, his share will transfer to that man. And he needed that money to fund his lifestyle. One way for him to have achieved that would have been for his son to marry my daughter, but we rejected their proposal. He didn't take kindly to that. My wife told me she suspected his intentions towards our daughter, towards my little girl, who... who...' He stopped, jaws and fists clenched, unable to continue.

'We suspect that his obsession with Anjali played a significant part in our boys' deaths,' explained Prem.

'Tell me who it is. Is it the minister, Nagaraj Saxena? Even he's not above the law. We'll work with the Indian authorities to convict him.'

'As Prem said, DCI Holt, you need proof for that. Do you have any? I thought not. Anyway, please don't worry about it. It's already taken care of.'

Prem smiled.

'But you cannot—'

Roopesh interrupted, 'Too late. It is done. Even as we speak.'

'But—' Holt paused as his hosts sipped their drinks and waited. *They're right*, he thought. *I couldn't touch him. I've nothing to prove he's involved*. He nodded.

'What I don't understand is the relationship between Harvey Endsleigh and Saxena. Why would Endsleigh undertake such a horrendous crime for him?'

'We can help you there,' said Roopesh. 'Please give me a moment.' He returned half a minute later, handed a sheet of A4 paper to the DCI.

Holt stared at the printout of an old black and white newspaper clipping in Hindi, of which he could read not a word.

'Look at the picture, DCI Holt,' said Prem.

Holt studied the cutting. It took him several moments to realize that the faded image was of a young Harvey Endsleigh holding a snooker cue, standing next to a large, older man and accompanied by a dozen young boys. In the background were blurry images of three more men, presumably locals.

'Is that Harvey Endsleigh? When and where was this taken? What does this say?'

'It was taken fourteen years ago, when Harvey Endsleigh was 21. He toured India during a gap year. It says that he visited a local pool club near Delhi, gave the kids there a demo and two days' free lessons on how to play the game correctly. The man in the photo was only a local politician then. He's now a minister, a VIP in Indian politics, and that boy on his left is his son, Mohan. They had had no obvious contact since that event, but we've recently learnt that they remained close. That politician is a major investor in Endsleigh's club through an anonymous offshore company. We think the club's being used for the politician's money laundering and drug dealing, although the latter's more of a sideline, an easy cash generator for him. We believe the incentive offered to Endsleigh for Suraj's death was money for his new club and a chance to realize his dream of a Western-themed pool room. An incentive estimated to be worth over a million pounds.'

With a whoosh of surprise, Holt sat back as another piece of the jigsaw slotted into place.

Prem's account omitted a crucial detail—one of the three men in the image's background was KC, Roopesh's uncle.

'DCI Holt, we now have a question for you. Those boys, the Xtreem gang members – why would they commit murder on Endsleigh's say-so? What hold did he have on them?' asked Roopesh.

'Endsleigh and Tommy Wade have known each other for years, and when Tommy was fourteen, Endsleigh rescued him from a sexual assault. I guess that strengthened the bond between them and warranted Tommy's loyalty. We also know that Duncan Hughes hero-worshipped Tommy and that Leo would do whatever his brother asked. The fourth boy, Derek Dawson, is odd. His profile shows psychopathic tendencies. Or perhaps he just wanted to fit in, but I rather suspect he gave in to his inclinations.'

'What about the boy and his mother? The one who overdosed? Will they make it?'

Holt took a moment to re-orient himself. 'Well, it was touch and go, but I'm told they'll live, although both mother and son will probably have lifelong health problems. The boy's still not well enough to be questioned, but I'll probably get to make at least one arrest even if it's the least guilty of that gang. We found Leo's clothes and knife along with the rest, but unlike theirs, there was no blood on them.' Holt looked from one to the other. 'He was with them, but I don't think he hurt anyone that night.'

'But he was just as culpable!' Anger gritted Roopesh's voice.

'Yes, he was,' agreed Holt, 'but not his mother, who almost died that night. Had we arrived minutes later, neither would have survived.' Expressionless, he watched the men.

'The newspapers claim they were addicts; they injected themselves with a lethal, almost pure mix of drugs.'

'Yes, it's something new. We don't see that mix on the street. We doubt the mother or son realised what they were using, but someone gave it to them, fully aware of what it could do if used undiluted. It could have been Endsleigh or Wade, especially if they suspected Leo was weakening, or thought he was becoming a danger to them. Or was that person unaware of the drug's potency and wasn't planning to kill them?'

Silence.

'Anyway, I wanted to tell you before you heard it in the media regarding the identity of the bodies. The evidence in the container was compelling and would've convicted them. Your sons would've got justice; their killers would have been sentenced. But I suppose what happened to them was a different, a far more lethal justice; one with no pity or clemency. I wonder if it was also without remorse.'

They neither moved nor spoke.

'There'll be further investigations into the gang's death, and their suspected drug links, investigations about where they were getting their stuff from, who was supplying them... But another division will deal with that, and they won't give up easily. Whoever was involved will look over their shoulders for years.'

In the heavy silence, Holt studied their slumped shoulders, pain-racked expressions and empty eyes. He reached a decision.

'As far as I'm concerned, though, my case is closed.'

106

Durgapur, India

KC

His silhouette a deeper black in the night's gloom, Roopesh's uncle, KC, crept alongside the wall, keeping to the shadows, hugging the darkness, stooping to accommodate the weight of the bulky backpack slung across his back. His footfalls muffled by the leaves, he timed his movements to the wind rustling through the trees and bushes.

Despite the night's coolness, his black cotton *kurta* was damp with perspiration running down his spine. He swiped his sleeve across his forehead to clear the sweat dripping into his eyes and sidled towards the rear of the house, staying out of the range of security sensors.

I'm too bloody old for this shit.

KC weaved his way past the waste bins in the backyard, and after a few seconds of fiddling with the locks, unlatched the back door. He readjusted the load on his shoulders, slipped into the empty kitchen and into the hallway to get his bearings.

Suppressed giggles, followed by a man's rhythmic gasps and grunts, reached him from a room nearby.

Well, the watchman's having a good time.

Except for this couple, the villa, used by the politician to entertain friends and contacts he did not want to advertise to the world, was empty. Occasionally, such as tonight, he employed it for his own entertainment.

KC tiptoed to the far side of the house and into a large bedroom. Loud snores echoed in the room, and the faint glow of a night lamp bounced off the twin hillocks of chest and stomach rising and falling on the white silk-sheeted mattress.

He crept closer, gazed down at the obese man lying naked, spread-eagled on the huge, ornate, antique brass-framed bed. KC set his burden at his feet with an inaudible sigh of relief. Two empty crystal glasses stood on the bedside, alongside a half-empty bottle of expensive Scotch. A rich, woody aroma filled the room as wisps of smoke rose to the ceiling from a Cuban cigar stub resting in an ashtray.

KC glanced in disgust at the man's flaccid penis drooping like a fat slug against his massive thighs. The girl had spent the early part of the night entertaining this corpulent, rich client before taking a well-deserved break with the younger and more virile security guard.

He attached lengths of silk cord to the two metal posts at the foot of the bed, tied a noose into each of the free ends, glided them over the lax ankles, and pulled them taut. The sleeper did not stir. Moving to the top end, KC clipped a handcuff to the solid brass uprights at each end, lifted the chubby wrists and slipped them into the rings, clicked the ratchets to lock. Except for a snort and a grunt, the politician slept on.

For a moment, he considered finishing the task and leaving, all without waking the man, but that would be far too easy.

Despite the black gloves sheathing his hands, a grimace of disgust twisted KC's face as he grabbed Saxena by his doughy shoulders and shook him hard.

'Wakey, wakey.'

No response.

He longed to slap him, but knew it'd leave marks on those podgy cheeks. He leaned forward, clamped a hand over the sleeper's mouth, and pinched his nostrils shut with the other. Within seconds, Saxena jerked awake, gasping for breath, struggling to sit up.

KC removed his hand, dragged a scarf from his pocket and stuffed it into the gaping hole of a mouth. When the politician rolled his bulging eyes towards him, KC released his nose, listened to the wheezes and watched him gulp in a lungful of air.

While his cousin jerked his arms and legs to free them, KC leaned against the wall with his arms crossed and waited until he gave up. Ignoring the torrent of muffled, incomprehensible curses and questions, KC unzipped the side pocket of his backpack, removed a large syringe, and fitted it with a needle. Next, he pulled out a vacuum flask, upended it into his cupped hand to trap an injection bottle full of yellowish fluid. He plunged the needle into the bottle's cap, drew the liquid into the syringe, swapped the straight needle for a curved one, and laid it on the bedside table.

'Don't make a sound unless you want to suffocate again.'

Chest heaving, the man's gaze followed KC's movements as he opened the bag and drew out a long, writhing creature. It was as thick as his forearm, and he needed both hands to restrain it.

A live adult king cobra.

Furious at its incarceration and the jostling, uncomfortable journey, the squirming reptile coiled itself about his wrist, snaked its thirteen-foot body up to his shoulder and encircled his waist. KC braced himself as it spasmed its powerful muscles, numbing its captor's arm and compressing its weight, all twenty-two pounds of it, to squeeze him.

Thank goodness this isn't a python or a boa-constrictor, he thought, grunting in pain.

The serpent twisted and writhed but could not extricate itself from the hold gripping it around its neck with both hands. It spread its magnificent hood, its fangs exposed, as its forked tongue darted in and out, tasting the air, assessing its enemy.

KC turned to face Saxena. 'So, you are Endsleigh's mysterious business partner. I didn't realize you had kept in such close contact with each other. But I see why. It's a good way to wash your dirty money. And you promised him the new site for his club in return for killing Arun and his friends? Why? Because we rejected the proposal for your son to marry Anjali?'

A blink of puzzlement, then a flicker of recognition flashed in the politician's eyes, and he shook his head vehemently in denial.

'Did you think that with Suraj gone, my grandniece would wed your son? Is he as obsessed with Anjali as you are? Or is it because our grandparents chose her as their heir instead of your son? Did you kill them just to get your hands on our ancestral properties?'

Understanding replaced the incomprehension in his quarry's eyes. The politician blinked and struggled to speak, but with the scarf wedged in his mouth, could only shake his head furiously.

KC moved closer. 'Did you think we'd never find out?'

More thrashing of the head, as the politician cried fat tears.

Pity I can't take the scarf out. He'd only scream. Wonder what his excuses would be. Would he even apologise? People of his nature don't feel guilty. Oh well, too late for that now. He knows too much.

Suddenly, the king cobra growled, the loud, ferocious sound vibrating all the way down its writhing body. Startled, KC almost dropped the magnificent creature. He remembered reading that king cobras growled rather than hissed. But it was frigging scary all the same.

With a firmer grip on the serpent, KC directed it towards the thickest part of Saxena's flabby inner thigh. The angry reptile reared its hooded head as the grip around its neck relaxed, its powerful muscles contracted, and the king cobra struck, sinking its fangs deep into the soft, quivering flesh.

His eyes rolled back and the fat man collapsed in a dead faint.

The cobra relaxed as it recoiled from its strike, and KC returned the squirming creature to his bag.

He shook his arm and flexed his fingers to ease the numbness.

Back in April after his meeting at the minister's house, KC had decided the fat politician had to die. Days later, he visited a private snake farm and licenced venom laboratory in Bengaluru, a city located hundreds of miles from his home where he had watched the handlers demonstrate how they 'milked' the snakes for their venom.

The lab technicians had been kind to the elderly, doddery man, who had '*accidentally*' knocked over a tray of lethal vials. Seemingly shaken by the experience and apologising profusely, he offered to pay for the loss, an offer which the lab manager waved away. KC had left soon after, richer by two vials of cobra venom.

He sank the hooked needle into the point of entry of one of the fangs and pumped half its contents into the man's thigh. He repeated the process and emptied the syringe into the second bleeding spot. The huge dose of the king cobra toxin surged through the politician's body.

At the snake farm, he had learnt that a cobra's venom contained postsynaptic neurotoxins which spread rapidly in its victim's bloodstream. Experts say that paralysis begins when the central nervous system is attacked, followed by cardiovascular collapse, coma, respiratory failure, and eventually death. All this within thirty minutes if left untreated.

The lethal double dose of toxin coursing through Saxena would kill him within fifteen minutes, or quicker aided by his racing heart. KC hoped it would be agonisingly painful.

He stared at his dying cousin, the politician Mr Nagaraj Saxena, whose first name, Nagaraj, meant 'king cobra' in Hindi.

Now that's what I call poetic justice.

KC had considered releasing the snake into the wild, but with its venom sacs removed, the poor creature would not survive its freedom for long. It must go back to the snake charmer, who was unaware that his pet had been 'borrowed' for the night.

He removed the scarf from Saxena's mouth, aware that he'd be too busy struggling for breath to call for help. He also released him from his restraints. Paralysis already rendered the man immobile.

As for the marks on his wrists and ankles, tomorrow there would be rumours that Mr Nagaraj Saxena enjoyed the occasional bondage session in his extramarital activities. The woman on the other side of the villa would shyly confess her client had asked for the handcuffs and ankle ropes. The ropes, though strong, were of soft silk, and the handcuffs were fur-lined.

Without a backward glance at the politician, he made his way to the kitchen. Reassured that the security guard still snored alongside the buxom figure, KC sauntered out of the side gate and into the cool night.

He adjusted the weight across his back.

Cousin Nagaraj had been giving king cobras a very bad name.

107

Roopesh

The persistent trilling pierced Roopesh's uneasy rest. He groped for the phone, his brain recognising the ringtone even as his wife's voice drove away the remnants of sleep.

Her call this late in the night, her heart-wrenching weeping, could only mean one thing. She was calling about their daughter, Anjali.

He clutched the phone to his ear. He'd been right. Among her incoherent words, he recognised a name. Anjali.

Roopesh's heart plummeted. So, the inevitable had finally happened. His daughter had left this empty world to join her betrothed and her brother. She was dead.

Amazing how little pain he felt. No loss, no sorrow, just a calm acceptance.

He heard the murmur of voices, then a male voice replaced his wife's.

'Roop?' It was his uncle, KC.

'Yes,' said Roopesh, his voice calm.

Steel in his heart, ice in his veins, and a lead coffin where feelings dwelt.

'Someone here wants to speak to you,' said KC.

He heard a brief cracking, then a soft, tremulous voice, weak, and hesitant – a voice he never thought he would hear again.

'Papa? Where are you, Papa? Please come home.'

108

Holt

The phone in Holt's jacket pocket buzzed. The accompanying ping alerted him it was an incoming text message.

Now what? he grumped. Although tempted to ignore it, he drew it out and frowned.

A second later his eyes widened at the sender's name even as an enormous grin split his face.

Hi Matt, this is Lily Webster. I'm so sorry for my rudeness when we last met, especially after your kindness. Just wanted to say sorry and thank you.

Best wishes,
Lily

Epilogue

*B*ehind the eyelids of the sleeping twins, the Dra sighs in contentment.

Its job is done; its promise fulfilled. It could now return to its abode beyond human cognisance.

The idea is tempting. To ignore time blissfully once again.

But the past few months – or was it days, or just a few moments ago? The Dra's concept of time encapsulated within eternity is hazy.

Whether moments, days or months, its stay here has been interesting.

Amusing even.

The Dra hesitates.

Go? Stay?

The Dra smiles...

Glossary

- **Beta** – Son

- **Beti** – Daughter

- **Bhabhi** – Elder brother's wife.

- **Bhai** – Brother

- **Chowkidar** – Watchman, security guard.

- **Dada** – Grandfather

- **Diya** – Oil lamps

- **Kurta** – A long, loose, collarless shirt

- **Laxmi, Saraswati, and Parvati** – Hindu goddesses representing wealth/prosperity, knowledge/wisdom and strength, respectively

- **Mama** – Maternal uncle – mother's brother.

- **Mantras** – Chants, repeated words, sounds or phrases to help concentration and meditation

- **Masala chai** – Black tea leaves boiled with a blend of aromatic spices, traditionally peppercorns, ginger, cardamom pods, cinnamon sticks and cloves.

- **Memsaab** – Equivalent of ma'am, madam

- **Nagaraj** – King of cobras, king of snakes

- **Nehru suit** – Named after the outfit made popular by Jawaharlal Nehru (the first Prime Minister of India from 1947 to 1964). It features a hip-length jacket with a mandarin collar, and buttons down the front.

- **Pallu** – The decorated end of the sari draped over the shoulder

- **Pooja** – Rituals of prayers and worship performed by Hindus – followers of Hinduism

- **Saab** – Equivalent of sir, boss or master.

- **Saree/Sari** – A garment worn by women in India and parts of SE Asia.

- **Talwar** – An Indian one-edged, curved sword or sabre.

Abbreviations used:

- **A&E** – Accident and Emergency

- **ACC** – Assistant Chief Constable

- AFO – Authorised Firearms Officer

- **ANPR** – Automatic Number Plate Recognition. Cameras used capture images of vehicles, read the plate number, and instantly check it against databases of vehicles of interest to law enforcement or for private use in managing car parks and security.

- **CPN** – Community Protection Notice issued by the Court as punishment for persistent antisocial behaviour.

- **CPS** – Crown Prosecution Service

- **CSI** – Crime Scene Investigator

- **D2D** – Door-to-door inquiries

- **FIO** – Fire Investigation Officer

- **FLO** – Family Liaison Officers are specially trained to work with bereaved families and provide liaison between the police and families of victims of crime

- **HGV** – Heavy Goods Vehicle.

- **HMRC** – Her/His Majesty's Revenue and Customs, the UK government's department responsible for assessing and collecting taxes

- **HR** – Human Resources
- **IDENT1** – The national automated fingerprint system used by police forces and law enforcement agencies in the UK.
- **IT** – Information Technology
- **LGV** – Light Goods Vehicle
- **ME** – Medical Examiner/pathologist
- **Mispers** – Missing persons
- **NHS** – UK's National Health Service
- **PCSO** – Police Community Support Officers
- **PI** – Private Investigator
- **PIR** – Passive infrared detector used to operate motion sensor lights.
- **PNC** – Police National Computer. The principal police database that stores and shares criminal records and information across the UK.
- **Public Schools** – Public schools in the UK are prestigious, private (independent) fee-paying schools.
- **SIO** – Senior Investigating Officer
- **SOC** – Scene of Crime
- **SOCO** – Scene of Crime Officers

Thank you for reading Lethal Justice.

If you enjoyed this book, please tell your family and friends about it and

please help by leaving a review today.

Reviews and recommendations are crucial for independent authors like me. Even a short, one sentence review can make a big difference.

Simply locate this book on your Amazon site, scroll down to the Customer Reviews section and click on 'Write a Customer Review' to let people know what you thought of it.

With my thanks and best wishes,
Jay

Acknowledgements

I wrote the first draft of this book over a decade ago, but for years, it lay buried in my computer's innards afraid of daylight.

In 2022, I dredged out the manuscript, reworked it and even entered it in a few competitions. To my delight, Lethal Justice won 'The Greene Door Project' by Literary Agents Greene & Heaton. The same year, it was also longlisted in The Yeovil Literary Prize, the Page Turner Awards (Crime genre) and shortlisted by Headline Publishing Group in their Modern Stories Initiative. And in 2024, it was longlisted by Page Turner Awards in the Supernatural genre.

Even though I still worry about its reception, I hope that eclectic readers who appreciate books of different genres will enjoy this cross-genre thriller.

I owe thanks to many people for their help in getting Lethal Justice to this stage:

Rajan: I can never thank you enough for the countless hours you so generously continue to give me or for suffering through my numerous rewrites. Without your patience, your honest and helpful feedback, this book would still be buried in my computer.

Gavin: What would I do without your enduring support, insight and advice? I knew you'd love the supernatural elements but your feedback on the crime and investigation parts helped me correct several faux pas.

Aviv: Thank you for painstakingly line-editing my very first draft. Looking back, that version really was atrocious. I'll always treasure your patience and kindness, and the hours of work you put in to help turn my writing into an intriguing narrative.

Pascale and Deryl Hart: I truly appreciate you taking the time to read the early version of my manuscript and for your valuable feedback. It gave me the courage to consider publishing it.

Rebecca Benson: Thank you for sharing your experience as a murder squad Detective Sergeant and your vital feedback which corrected many of my errors and ignorance of police procedures. I am also grateful for your sensitivity reading and advice in helping me deal sensitively with autism and neurodiversity in the story.

Paddy Johnson: Thank you for your sensitivity reading and advice. I'm relieved you weren't put off by the more gruesome descriptions.

A huge thanks goes to my cats Maggie and Sooty who kept me company through my long journey with this novel. I miss you both so much.

John Hart: I would like to give special thanks to John Hart (multi award-winner and author of six New York Times Bestsellers—The Last Child, Redemption Road, The Unwilling...). I am so grateful for your generosity, the gift of your time and your invaluable feedback. Your insight helped me to pull this book into a much better shape than it would otherwise be.

Alan Nicholls: Thanks to my fellow creative writing group member, whose dislike of adjectives, adverbs and lengthy descriptions helped to refine my manuscript, while reducing it by half. Well, it would have if I hadn't sneaked some of it back in.

I give my heartfelt gratitude to each and every one of you. I couldn't have done it without your help.

Although two characters in this book— Lily Webster and Kalyani—are named after people I loved, they and all other characters in this book are imaginary and any resemblance to actual places or people are purely coincidental.

To keep the narrative flowing, I have taken liberties with the timelines for several police procedures (e.g., autopsies, forensic results, interviews, etc.). Also, to avoid confusion of too many characters and names, I've reduced the number of named police officers involved in the investigation. For this, I apologise to Rebecca Benson, who explained how much longer it all actually takes in real cases and how many more detectives and experts would be involved in an active investigation.

While the city of Southampton located in Hampshire, England is a real place, many of the street names and sites in Lethal Justice, such as the Holburn Park, Westlands estates, St John's Hospital, the Solent Constabulary, the Southampton City Police, their headquarters, are fictional.

Durgapur, too, is a fictional town, which I have placed near New Delhi in India. And thankfully, the 'thirteen bodies found in a container at Southampton port' mentioned in the book is also a fictitious event.

A very special thanks goes to my very first reader and critique—my husband, George—for his unstinting support, encouragement, love and patience.

And finally, a huge thank you to all my readers. I hope you enjoyed this book as much as I did writing it.

ABOUT THE AUTHOR

Winner of the 2022 Page Turner Crime Genre Award, Jay Jones has always been an avid reader. As a teenager, she filled cheap notebooks with stories, essays and poems.

But with a background in accounting, finance and law, spreadsheets rather than words dominated her working career. It wasn't until she took up creative writing again a few years ago, that Jay realised how much she missed it.

Her award-winning debut crime thriller, **I, Said The Fly** was published in 2024.

Lethal Justice is a cross genre thriller combining Jay's love of crime/police procedurals and the supernatural.

Jay lives in Worcester, England, with her husband. When not writing or reading, Jay enjoys painting, cooking and slow walks – slow because of the numerous stops made to rescue suicidal earthworms and snails along the way.

www.jayjonesbooks.com

Want to know when my next book is released?

Sign up to my website and you'll be among the first to know!

www.jayjonesbooks.com

It is spam-free, and I promise not to share your email address with anyone else and I will only contact you about my books.

And if you enjoyed this book, please tell your family and friends about it.

Thank you,

Jay

A GRIPPING CRIME THRILLER

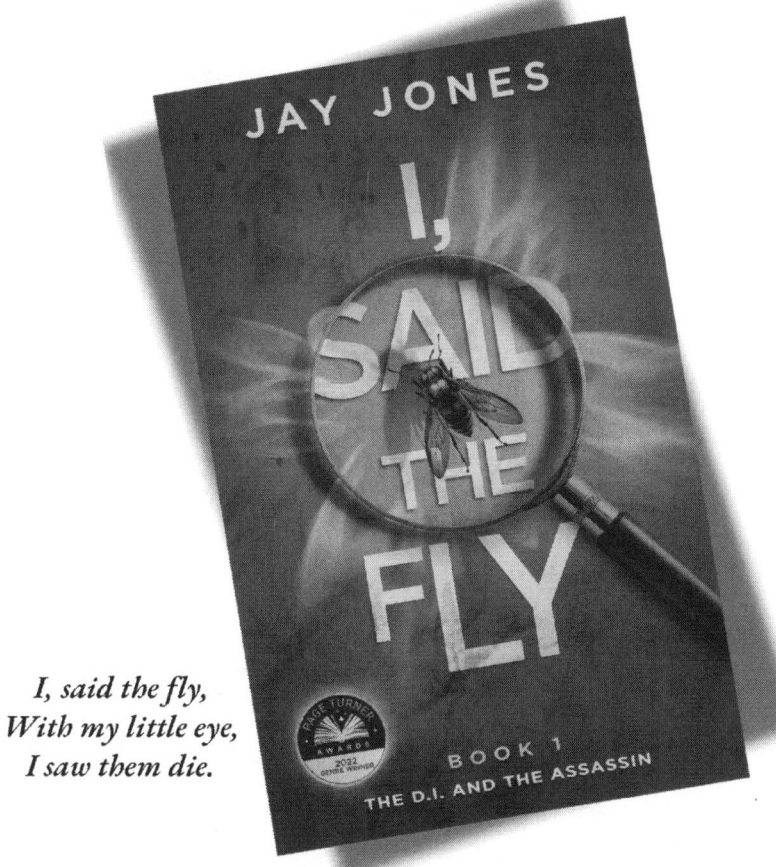

*I, said the fly,
With my little eye,
I saw them die.*

Why were the Dwyer twins tortured and killed?
Something they saw? Heard?
The only witness—a homeless veteran, swears he saw a ghost that night. When Stanley turns up dead, D.I. Cathy Collins suspects the "ghost" may be real.
And what part does her lover, the secretive ex-SAS Captain Mick O'Neal, play?
As bodies pile up, Cathy's pursuit may cost her life.
How far ahead is the killer—and can she ever catch up?

Available on Amazon

Printed in Dunstable, United Kingdom